CUT FROM STONE

BOOK ONE OF

CRAFTING HUMANITY

First Edition

ISBN: 979-8-9861289-0-0

For Alexa.

PART I

CHAPTER 1

James held his throbbing head, thinking he might be sick. His room was dark, but faint trails of light streamed inside around the corners of the heavy canvas covering his windows. He reached over to check his nightstand for his wallet. Still there, as were his HOLO and keys. Thank God, he thought, letting himself breathe.

James brushed the blue arrow glowing on his HOLO. He waved his finger and a transparent screen popped up, casting a soft light across his face. He crossed his fingers and scrolled for drunk messages he might have sent the night before.

His stomach unclenched when he saw nothing on his screen. He pushed his hand on the top of the HOLO, letting it fold into itself. James swung out of bed, his joints creaking. His body ached, and his head felt like a tiny man was in his forehead banging on his brain with a wrench. He sat back on the bed to deal with the sudden onset of vertigo.

I feel so old, he thought, cracking his neck. When he felt more stable, he pushed his body from the bed and propelled himself toward the door.

Poking his head out, James checked for signs of life. The last interaction he wanted was a run-in with a member of his family this hungover, his mind oatmeal, his tongue sandpaper, and his thoughts swimming above the fumes suffocating his brain. The hallway was all clear, and James darted for the bathroom.

Why don't we have blinds in here? he thought grumpily, steadying himself on the windowsill. The sun pouring in only added to his pain. He battled his vampiric instincts and looked out the window at the late morning activities of the neighborhood as he enjoyed his morning relief.

Ms. Culver was walking her dog, searching for signs of life in the neighborhood to talk with her. Two middle school boys sped by on bikes while a younger boy rode behind them, struggling to keep pace, determination on his sweaty, red face.

James stared into the distance, last night was a blur.

He remembered his friends picking him up from school and stopping by his house to drop off his bag. James found a note on the kitchen counter. His mom was out with Michael picking up Caitlin and Mar from school. He was free, he thought, rushing up the stairs. He would have no problem leaving without questions, but he would have to act fast. He ran to his room, throwing his bag on the bed and tearing off his shirt. He grabbed a stick of deodorant from the top of his dresser and applied it quickly while looking for a clean shirt to wear.

Pulling the t-shirt over his head, he jumped the staircase in two hops and ran back through the kitchen, pulling a box of leftover Chinese food from the fridge.

James ate the sticky General Tso's chicken with his fingers in the car while Ed drove them to the nearest energy station. They bought two thirties of cheap beer and headed to Joe's house to celebrate James's birthday.

The night started out the same as most. Jennifer and Carrie showed up with their wine coolers while James and his friends drank crappy beer, stopping occasionally for a swig of whiskey.

The night progressed rapidly as dozens more people arrived with cases of beer and bottles of booze. James's eyes lost focus, his voice grew louder, and warmth spread throughout his extremities. Finally, they were too loud for the closely packed houses and the party migrated to the park nearby where James found himself walking with Kaylie.

He had no idea how he arrived in this situation and was thrown off by his confidence. Kaylie was a gorgeous, long-haired brunette with dark brown eyes. She was a midfielder on the soccer team and used to be a gymnast. They were friendly during James's soccer season when she helped his coach manage the team, but she intimidated James. Now, while they walked together James glanced over, absorbing the full extent of her beauty from the corner of his eye.

She had high cheekbones with dimpled lips, a straight nose, and delicate features. Her eyes were deep pools, permanently set in a half-drowsy slit, uninterested in the rest of the world but undeniably intelligent. She came off as distant and edgy, but never standoffish. James caught his eyes trailing down to look at her chest before snapping out of it. Knock it off, he thought, looking at his feet.

"You having a good time?" he said, immediately regretting it. Stupid question, he thought.

Kaylie looked at him, smiling. "I am, actually! My friends and I don't do this much, so it's a nice change of pace."

"Really? I thought you and your friends were always out," James replied.

"Well, we're not normally outside like this. It's usually a party at someone's parents or a college guy's house, but this is a lot of fun." She sounded sincere, and James's confidence grew.

"Happy to have you along," he said and raised his beer, tapping her drink as they walked.

She grinned and James's stomach did a flip. "Cheers."

When they arrived at the park, it was pitch-black, the only light coming from HOLOs popping up randomly in the darkness. James turned to Kaylie, "Do you want another drink?"

She shook the beer in her hand and drained the last sip. "I would love one," she said. "Meet me by my friends. They're over there."

She pointed out her friends under the treetops talking with each other, their HOLOs illuminating their faces.

"Will do," said James, nodding as he walked away.

3

James was ecstatic. The best looking girl there was talking with him *and* seemed interested in him. Fuck, yeah, he thought, doing an internal fist pump.

A second later, two sets of arms grabbed him and yanked him aside. Ed and Conor pulled him into a circle of their friends. They were standing with a bottle of whiskey, passing it around and taking pulls.

"Drink up, boys!" crowed Ed, taking a deep gulp from the bottle and passing it off to James.

James tipped the bottle back in a swig. He wiped his mouth and turned to go meet Kaylie again, but Conor pulled him back.

"Not until we're done," Conor grinned, pointing at the bottle making its way back to them, while a second bottle started at the other side of the circle.

I'll finish this quick and head back over to Kaylie, James thought. The bottle came around again, again, again, and on and on. The last moment James remembered was an upside down label blocking his eyes.

James finished his stream and looked down. He flushed, grimacing at the acrid smell of the gold fluid rushing down the toilet. Gross, he thought turning on the sink and looking in the mirror.

His usually bright green eyes were cloaked in a red haze, his chestnut hair plastered to the side of his face. He was not wearing a shirt and the prickly hairs on his chest were pushed flat, while lines from the folds in his bed sheets tattooed across his rib cage.

He pushed the longer strands of hair away from his face. "Crap," he mumbled. There was a gash on his forehead, and dried blood stained his skin all the way to the neckline of his shirt. He turned the water back on and cleaned off the blood, soaking the scab with a wet towel.

4

James tried to recall a single memory of how this happened but had nothing. One memory is all I need, and I can get out of this alive, he pled with his alcohol-soaked recall.

Just gonna wing it, he thought, giving up, his head hurting from the brief effort.

He peeked out the door again. No one there. He sprinted to his room reaching the doorframe, thinking he was free when he heard a yell behind him.

"JAMES, SO NICE TO SEE YOU!" yelled James's dad, grinning at the top of the stairs. He shook his head at James. "Fun birthday?"

James's father was about his height with an athletic frame and strong jawline. His easy-going manner and endless energy combined to create a man with a charming, confident personality James strived to imitate.

James froze. "Yeah. Got some pizza, hung out with the boys. You know," he said uneasily, playing it cool. His father was a tough guy to read, and his eyes had a mischievous glint. James remembered too many times interacting with his father, messing up the signals, and getting in trouble.

His dad walked closer, putting on a mock face of questioning. "Huh, you know, that's funny. Did you take a brewery tour? Because the entire upstairs of the house smells like it."

James looked down, knowing he was caught.

His dad was standing closer to him now. "Hop in the shower but get some Febreze first and try to get some of your new cologne out of the air. I'll turn on the vents. Maybe we can get this stank through the filters. Hopefully, get it all done before your mom gets back home, and—*Jesus*, what the hell happened to your head?!" he said, taking a step back, noticing James's gash.

"Oh, I... it... it's nothing," James said, looking away, his relief vanishing instantly as he pretended to go open his windows.

Please, let it go, he thought.

"Well, whatever it is I hope you come up with a way to explain it to your mom otherwise I can't do anything for you," his dad warned, walking away. "And happy birthday!"

"Thanks," James said in a wilting voice.

James spent his shower reviewing a series of questions he thought his mom might ask. Where were you, who were you with, what'd you eat, where did these people come from earlier in the night, adding on layers of complexity asking names, people's parents, siblings, and so on and so forth. It was a simple game they played, but James had yet to win.

The garage door opened and his mom yelled, "Now get inside. I'll make you lunch. An entire diet consisting of McDonald's would taste good, but it will kill you one day."

He heard the groans of his siblings as they were shepherded through the door.

James walked downstairs carefully, not wanting the steps to sound like someone with a pounding hangover.

His sister Mar ran up the stairs. Mar was a year younger than him, and they ran into each other frequently at parties, an occurrence they both despised. She sported hazel eyes like his mother and curly hair she kept behind her head with a ribbon. Recently, she changed her look trying different styles throughout the year. Their faces indicated a clear familial relation, Mar keeping all the softer female characteristics of his mother's looks mixed with the physical traits, sharp cheekbones, and smile of his father.

"Hey, we won our game!" she said, smiling. "Score was three to zero. They had the crappiest offense I've ever seen." Her normally bouncy hair was matted with sweat.

"Awesome." He gave her a thumbs-up, moving past her.

"James?" his mother called from the kitchen. "Is that you?"

"Yeah, Ma, it's me." James gave Mar a nervous look and she grinned, shrugging knowingly.

6

I hate her, James thought.

He finished the last few steps and entered the kitchen seamlessly. Nice, he thought, congratulating himself. Easy entry—way to go.

"Well, come in. How was your night? And happy birthday!" his mom said, turning around to hug him. His mother was a short woman with shoulder-length hair influenced by the seasons, dark in the winter and light in the summer. Her face had soft edges and high cheekbones accompanied by strong hazel eyes with the potential for a lethal glare.

James noticed her eyes break for a split second as she glanced at the gash on his head, but she erased any indication of interest. James pretended not to see.

"Soooo, how was last night?" his mom asked as she cooked a grilled cheese for his younger brother, Michael.

"Fun."

"Who was there?"

"The usual. You know, the guys."

"And what'd you do?"

"Got some pizza, hung out at Joe's," James said vaguely. They had gotten pizza and hung out. There happened to be several cases of beer and a couple of bottles of whiskey present as well.

"Anything else?"

"Watched a movie." Partial truth, a movie played on in his friend's next-door neighbor's house, and they watched it, trying to figure out what movie it was.

"Which one?"

"*Gangs of New York.*"

"Was it good?"

"Yeah, not bad." He acted nonchalant as he bent over in the fridge, letting the cool air relieve his headache for a split second. "Really long."

"Huh, I should watch it." His mom paused as she finished the grilled cheese and delivered it to his younger brother who was oblivious to the conversation.

"Any girls show up?"

"Yeah, a couple." James's mind flashed back to ditching Kaylie and guilt panged in his stomach.

"Oh, which ones?"

"The guys' girlfriends and their friends."

James's mom lost interest in the conversation and was distracted getting Michael to stop eating his sandwich with no hands.

James's dad ambled into the room. His attempt to eavesdrop was obvious.

Jerk, thought James. He can't even set up a distraction?

James grabbed a Fresca and walked tentatively over to the couch, mindful of his mom's presence. He sat carefully, leaned back, cracked open the Fresca, and took a sip. He picked up the remote and began flipping through the channels. He was in the clear.

"James?"

"Yeah, Ma?"

"What happened to your head?" His mother was standing over him. He had not noticed her approach.

"Um… I… uhh…" James stumbled, thinking of an excuse. "Tripped this morning getting out of bed. Hit my head. But don't worry, I'm fine. Cleaned it with rubbing alcohol." He gave her a thumbs-up, hoping she would walk away.

"Are you okay?" his mother said, bending for a closer inspection.

"Yeah, I'll be fine. It looks a lot worse than it is."

"What about your leg? Did you hit that, too?" She was speaking more sternly now.

"My leg?" He had no idea about his leg. His mom's eyes were focused directly on his. No more excuses. He was done for.

8

"Uh... I don't know," he said feebly. "Didn't feel it happen but may be from something else."

"I heard a loud crash down the stairs at three in the morning. I know it wasn't you because you were safe in bed, considering it was four hours after your curfew. I woke up because I was worried about intruders, and you know what I found?" Her voice rose sharply, and her face became an angry mask James knew well. "I found my newly seventeen-year-old son sprawled out at the bottom of my staircase, bleeding from his head and leg, LOOKING LIKE A TRAUMA PATIENT IN THE ER."

Damn it, James thought.

"Why don't you go upstairs? Because we all know what actually happened last night."

He had lost.

His dad came into view behind his mom with a look as if to say, "What the hell, man?"

James got up meekly from the couch and headed to the stairs.

In his room, he flopped on his bed. Great birthday, he thought pulling the blinds closed. He took off his pants to check his leg and there it was. A long cut stretching from the length of his calf. One deft slice with a slight turn in the end when he must have rolled off whatever cut him at the bottom of the stairs.

"Well," James said, resting his cheek on his hand, "happy seventeenth, I guess." He pulled up the screen on his HOLO when a message from a tag he didn't recognize appeared. The profile picture was Kaylie's face.

He opened the message with a pit in his stomach. God, what had he done, and how had he done it? he thought, prepared for the worst.

He steeled himself and opened the message.

Happy birthday! I thought you ditched me last night but heard you got pulled away by your friends. We should hang out again soon. I had fun.

9

James closed the HOLO, stunned.

He lay back on his pillow and grinned at the ceiling, closing his eyes despite the sound of his impending punishment, storming up the stairs.

CHAPTER 2

James's parents had not gone too hard on him—a lot less than what he would have thought. The first time he was caught drinking he was a sophomore in high school. His parents had shut his life down for a whole semester to teach him a lesson. Didn't work out as they planned though, he thought, drifting to the party he attended the first weekend he was allowed out again.

This time he was grounded for a month and sentenced to yard work on the weekends. He was halfway through his punishment in the front yard laying mulch around the mountain laurel next to the house. James grabbed one of the heavy, plastic bags stacked in the driveway, still wet from the rain earlier in the week. The plastic dripped icy water onto his shirtfront, numbing his skin. He lugged the sack onto his shoulder and walked to the side of the garden, dropping it near his next deposit. He tore open the bag, the tips of his fingers raw from the cold plastic, and dumped the clumpy mulch into piles throughout the garden.

On his hands and knees, he broke apart fistfuls of plant debris, spreading it across the garden, stacking extra into moats around the bottom of each shrub. He still remembered a time when he hated doing work outside, but he grew to enjoy it, calmly concentrating on the task at hand, feeling the dirt under his nails and the soil staining his palms. He liked the feeling of getting beyond tired, the lucid state where he pushed the boundary of his stamina.

He used the time to play through his thoughts coming up with different stories. The plots involved him and his friends going to wild parties, traveling, or simply what it would be like when they left for college.

Today, his mind turned to Kaylie. The Monday after the party she approached him in school, teasing him about how he ditched her to black out and make an Irish exit with his friends. At first, James was unsure if she was angry or annoyed, but the wry smile at the corner of her lips gave her away and he played it off, suavely explaining it was required of him to stand in a circle full of kids acting like men drinking whiskey. Birthright, he postulated solemnly while they walked to class together. She was not put off by the heavy sarcasm because they had hung out in school ever since.

James shook his head to clear his thoughts. This was his last chore of the day. Afterward, he could relax and watch TV. The only other thing on his mind was the President's address to the country at five o'clock.

A week ago, the President announced he would make a speech addressing concerns in the Federation over the constant unknown of the BlankZone. At least it was the message the talking heads kept buzzing about on their respective stations.

There were the usual rumors: military buildup, nuclear disaster sites, alien raid, or nothing was left because the world split in two. All the theories fascinated James, but he had no clue what to believe. It was probably because no one knew what actually happened. It was not every day—or any day for that matter—an entire half of the world went completely dark. James knew there were attempts to reestablish contact. When the split happened, thousands of people were lost in attempts to enter the BlankZone through Eastern Europe and Southeast Asia. All missions failed with only a note of static radio silence.

That was over forty years ago—way before he was born. His only memories were the surface worries of a kid. His father came home at night wiped from work, carrying the family's only meal of the day in a bag at his side. Life was harder. From food to medicine to clean water, nothing was certain, and each day carried a new burden. James remembered the day the United States

12

became the Federation of the Americas, the two continents joined under one flag. James was six at the time and still saw the lights from the fireworks flashing against the night sky along with the smell of sulfur in the warm air, blowing across his face. People were happy and relieved. They went through so much with so little. Finally, they could rebuild.

Dirt embedded itself further under his nails as James worked in the garden, he recalled watching the first President of the Federation come on and speak those many years ago. It was past midnight when his father came in to wake him up.

"Come on, buddy," his father said, gently pushing him. "Want to watch with us?"

James jumped at the opportunity. He took a seat on the floor of the family room watching the President announce the official end of the Melt in the West and the formation of the Federation.

The President and his wife were escorted to the podium by their security detail. He was an older man with ruddy cheeks and a face ravaged by the tumult of national poverty. His wife held his arm supportively and gazed out on the crowd with empathetic eyes.

The balconies and rooftops of the surrounding buildings were packed with people and millions stood in a dense crowd, eagerly awaiting his announcement. The entire scene was dead silent, and James only remembered the sound of rustling grass through their open window.

The President's words were fresh, delivered by a strong voice, a paradox to the frailty portrayed by his body. "In this great moment in human history, I have the honor of calling an end to our strife. As a country and a global community, we have endured hardships not felt since the time of the Great Depression nearly one hundred years ago. Our purpose and will as a people have led us in defining a new sense of resiliency among our people, our government, and our world community. It is with great pleasure

13

and promise on this first day in May of the year 2023, I am honored to present a joining of South and North America to create our new great nation, the Federation of the Americas!"

The President dramatically turned around, stretching out his hand to point to a flag unfurling behind him with an imposing white star surrounded by a sea of blue and red lines. The scene on the television erupted, and James's father lifted him in the air, hugging his mother. They had tears in their eyes and the celebration reverberated down the street. It was the moment their lives changed.

Someone flipped a switch, and the entire world was thrown into a different gear. James's father got a union job. They ate three meals a day. And his mother smiled again. Technology revived and people were finally where they were before the Melt, before the world crashed and the East stopped responding.

Now the newly elected President Braxton was to address the looming question: what happened beyond the BlankZone?

There was one bag of mulch left. James glanced at his HOLO laying on the grass next to him and checked the time. Still an hour until the speech. Enough time to finish his work and shower.

He grunted hoisting the last bag of mulch over his shoulder. He started walking to the last bare spot in the garden when there was a screech of tires. Ed's silver coupe barreled around the corner. James dropped the bag and wiped his face on his sweat-stained sleeve, leaving a smudge of dirt on his forehead. Ed pulled up and gave James the finger. James laughed as he walked to the passenger side door and propped his hands on the window.

"What's up, man?" Ed asked, leaning over Chris in the passenger seat.

"Nothing. About finished here. What've you gents been up to?"

"Literally nothing all day. I woke up at two, called Chris to get food, and now we're here," Ed replied.

"Yeah, there hasn't been much going on," Chris said, taking a bite of his BLT. "It's been boring as hell."

"Makes me feel a lot better," James said. "Are you guys gonna watch the President's thing?"

"Yeah, my mom asked me to come home," Ed said. "I think it's gonna be stupid, but whatever." He shrugged. "There's nothing else to do."

"James?" James heard his mom calling from the backyard.

"I'm out front, Ma," he yelled back. He heard the back door close, and his mom appeared walking across the front yard moments later.

"Hi, Mrs. Coffey," Ed said, and Chris waved, his mouth full.

"Hi, boys. How are you?" said James's mom, smiling. Without waiting for a response, she turned to James. "Are you done yet?"

"Almost," he replied.

"Finish up and shower. We're going to eat after the speech. Bye, boys. Tell your families I say hello," his mom said with a wave and went back inside.

"We should get going," said Ed, putting his car in gear. "See you later, man."

Chris gave him a nod, wiping the grease from his sandwich with the back of one hand and waving with the other as they drove away.

When James finished his work, he took the empty bags stained with the mulch's refuse and threw them in the trash. He went into the garage and took off his work shoes, shaking off the leftover mulch while he clapped the soles together, breaking off the claylike muck from the grooves.

He trudged upstairs, his legs jelly, his arms sore, and his knees indented with pieces of grass. He turned the shower on extra hot, letting the water steam. His legs were filthy from the kneecaps down, where his shorts stopped. There was a clear line where his arms were protected by his sleeves, and grime coated his skin to his elbows. He looked like a chimney sweep from one of the old movies his parents watched with him as a kid.

His legs cramped when he stepped over the ledge of the bathtub into the shower. He faced the wall with the spigot overhead, rivers running down his chest carrying the mulch, dirt, and plant debris from his torso into the drain. The silt from his skin piled up in small banks around the white ceramic and his legs turned back to their natural color. The loamy scent from the garden infused with the steam, and James took a deep breath, letting his lungs absorb the dense humidity.

"James, hurry up!" his dad yelled from downstairs. "You still have to set the grill!" James was knocked out of his semi-lucid state and slipped in the shower, grabbing the ceramic soap ledge to regain his balance.

"Be down in a sec!" he called back, hurriedly squeezing a bottle of shampoo in his hand and rubbing it into his scalp.

James finished his shower, set the grill, and sat on the couch next to Mar. Michael and their mom came into the room, followed by Caitlin close behind, and finally their dad. He had a serious look on his face, clearly deep in thought.

"Dad," said Michael inquisitively, "why do we need to listen to the President's speech?"

"Because it's going to be important."

"But how do you know it's important?"

"Because it's the President and there's a lot of stuff going on in the world. We're guessing this is going to address some serious issues." James sensed his dad's patience was being tested.

"But why?" Michael pressed.

"Because I said so. Now keep quiet unless you have a real question," his dad said, shooting Michael a sharp look. "You can ask me any questions you want *after* the speech. Otherwise, I know as much as you do, all right?"

The screen turned to an attractive news reporter with bleached blond hair and overdone eyeliner standing in a throng of people telling the audience the President was walking to the podium and would be delivering his speech momentarily.

The camera panned to the President making his way from the back with his security detail intact.

James admired the grace and stature of President Braxton. He was a tall, broad-shouldered man with black hair and the stance of a person built for leading other people. His entire demeanor surged with a fierce sense of competitiveness. The crowd was silent as he took the podium. Déjà vu washed over James as the grass rustled outside the open windows.

"Friends, countrymen, fellow citizens of the Federation, for more than a decade we have lived in a world unencumbered by national violence, harsh poverty, and civil unrest. We have taken great strides in our business ventures, building and innovating to regain our once lost sense of future. Our joined nations created the most impressive feat in human history—one of unity, community, respect, and peace. Unfortunately, the other side of the world has undergone a different set of drastic changes.

"I am here with you today to talk about the growing unrest the world has endured over the past decade. The BlankZone has changed. And it is time for the Federation to realize its dire threat to our society.

James's stomach tightened and he gripped his knees unconsciously.

"From civil war to revolution, the world is becoming more dangerous and provides ever changing threats for us to manage. The formerly sovereign countries to the east have now come under the rule of a single governing party. The Forgotten World is what they call themselves, and they have expanded to encompass all of Russia, East Asia, the Middle East, the South Pacific, and India.

Now, they wish to come to our shores." The President paused, letting his words sink in, calmly examining the faces of those around him.

"That is why the leaders of our great nation and I have decided to reinstate an old tradition in the military. We will begin a draft for those over the age of eighteen."

James glanced at his father who kept the same stoic look, his eyes unflinching, his jaw steady. James turned back to the TV, confused.

"I understand the feelings many of you may have, but with the rumors of violence in the BlankZone and information we have gathered regarding the Melt, we cannot be too careful." The President looked at his notes and continued, "In addition, the Federation of the Americas will begin a process of recruitment for those eligible under the age of eighteen. We must produce the most viable source of protection for our nation. We believe this is the only way.

"The world is changing. The Federation is no longer alone in the world and the BlankZone's aggression will become more prevalent in the years to come. We must prepare in the present or we will have no future. We are doing all in our power to maintain friendly relations with the rest of the open world, and we will succeed with the support of our citizens. The embodiment of strength and perseverance has forever been the backbone of this country. We will triumph as a people, a country, and a driving force for the rest of the world to take notice. They will learn we are the strongest nation in the world, and we will not fail."

The TV turned off, and James turned around to see his mother holding the remote, staring shakily at the screen while his dad looked out the window at nothing.

CHAPTER 3

James's mom recovered quickly. "Steve, what time will dinner be ready?" she asked.

James glanced over at his dad still sitting in his armchair, watching the sky outside.

"Stephen!" his mom yelled. "What time will dinner be ready?"

His dad turned away from the window coming back to the real world. "Sorry, I've got to put the steak on. So, eat in ten?"

"Michael, would you please set the table for dinner?"

"But—"

"Now," his mom said, glaring.

"Yeah, I'll do it," he said, grumbling under his breath, already stomping to the dining room.

Caitlin walked toward the remote still sitting on the counter. She turned the TV back on.

"NO!" his mom yelled. "No more TV tonight. You can sit quietly, or you can talk with one another. There're only ten minutes until dinner and I think you can survive that long."

None of them argued.

James sat in the room only with cursory awareness of the people around him, turning over the President's speech in his head. The rest of the room was quiet. The smell of charred steak permeated the air and James realized how hungry he was.

Dinner was an uncomfortable affair. James mulled over the President's speech, still trying to piece together what had happened. His dad only made eye contact with his plate while his mom stared out the window, taking small bites and chewing slowly. James made eye contact with Mar across the table and shrugged. Caitlin and Michael were oblivious to the tense atmosphere.

"It's simple. I can beat you. You're a girl," said Michael matter-of-factly, sticking out his tongue.

"I will sneak in your room, and I will break each of your toes in your sleep if you keep talking," Caitlin retorted, raising a forkful of steak menacingly. "I mean it."

Michael smirked. "Still won't be able to because you're a—OUCH!" His mirth disappeared instantly. "Mom, she kicked me."

It was Caitlin's turn to smirk. "I warned him. I said I would get him."

"You said you would break my toes, not kick me."

"I took an easier route."

"Enough!" James's father banged his fist on the table and glared at the two of them. "Will you two shut up? I'm tired of this damned bickering." His father glared at the two younger siblings while James bit his lip to keep from laughing.

"Sorry, Dad," the two said in unison, hanging their heads.

James's father went back to eating his meal in silence.

After dinner, their parents walked out to the back porch and talked to one another in hushed voices while James and his siblings did the dishes.

"What do you think they're talking about?" Mar said, handing him a plate.

"Might be about the draft. But they were acting strange even before," replied James, trying to sound indifferent.

"Yeah, they were in the living room talking while you were outside mowing earlier."

"Huh," he said, letting this strange calm continue to wash over him. Since the announcement, a nervous energy trickled under his skin and his parents' reactions confirmed he was not the only one who felt something was afoot.

20

They washed the dishes in silence until their dad called James's name.

"James," his dad yelled from the porch, "would you come outside? Your mother and I would like to speak with you."

James gave Mar a puzzled look. His sister nodded.

"Don't worry. Cinderella can finish the dishes all by herself," she said.

Outside, James's parents were sitting in chairs on the patio, their faces illuminated by the floodlight. James picked up a chair on his way, placing it in front of them. They sat in tense silence for a moment.

"James, we have always known you are a very smart and talented young man, and aside from a few lapses in judgment, you have matured incredibly fast," James's dad started. His face was more serious than James had ever seen it in the past. His mother gazed blithely into the backyard, and he could not see her expression in the dark.

"Am I in trouble?" James asked, clasping his hands together. Sweat slicked his palms and he dried them on his pants.

His father took a deep breath and began. "Do you know those tests you take each year? The standardized ones?"

James nodded. How could he forget? They would give them these stupid tests at the end of the year, right as kids were getting ready to take a mental checkout for the summer.

"You have thirty minutes to complete each section. If you cannot complete a section, you may not go back after time has expired. If you look at someone else's paper, your exam will be taken from you, and you will receive a grade of zero for the exam. If..."

The list continued and James shook his head to get rid of the monotonous hell playing over in his mind.

"These tests were IQ and EQ examinations. They were administered to all the students in the country between the first and twelfth grade. We were all told they were tests designed to see if a

21

student was able to move onto the next grade level. And in a way they were. The answers and grades were always kept highly confidential. The only indication of how a student did on the exams was a pass or fail notice. When this started, it was controversial, but as time wore on parents worried less and less about the tests."

"By the time you started school, the process turned into a normal routine for students."

James looked puzzled at his father, "Yeah, I remember all of this, but why does it matter? I passed the exams." Why was his father going on about all this? All it did was rehash memories of sweat, boredom, and the itch of freedom waiting on the other side of a page.

His father continued, "We didn't think anything of it until you were in seventh grade. We received a call from the principal who asked us to come into his office for a meeting. Principal Joseph told us he was contacted by a group from the test board. They mentioned they were associated with intelligence agencies around the Federation—CIA, FBI, NSA, and others. Apparently, they were inquiring about you based on your test results. This was the first time in his thirty years of teaching and administration he received interest from the government in a student your age. He assured us there shouldn't be any significant alarms, but he thought as parents we should know."

James was confused more than ever. Where was all this headed? Why was he being given a backstory on tests he took in elementary school?

"We decided it wasn't a big deal. The government couldn't do anything to you, and you were happy. So, why worry? Still, your mother thought it would be a good idea to investigate, so I called my college roommate, Carl Jackson. You remember Carl?" his father said.

James nodded, remembering the first time he met his father's friend. He was a big guy with a form-fitting military

22

uniform. They were at a reunion for his mom and dad's college friends and Carl escorted in a beautiful, brunette woman walking picturesquely with a delicate hand resting gently on his arm. When his father introduced him, he gave James a high five engulfing James's hand with his palm.

James was shy and grabbed tighter onto his mother's skirt who patted the back of his head.

"All good, he's just a little nervous. Hey, buddy, how would you like to come for a ride?" Carl said, bending down.

Carl put out his hand and James laced his small fingers into the man's giant paw and led him to the silver convertible parked outside. The car was so cool. James had never been in a car worth bragging about in his life.

He let James sit in the front on the brunette woman's lap, enjoying every second. They flew around bends and wind tore through his hair. He was in heaven. When they got back, James wouldn't leave Carl's side. He was ecstatic when Carl accompanied them home to read him a story before bed.

After that, James was connected to him for life. Whenever he came by, they would hang out in the backyard, throwing around a ball or taking a ride in one of the new cars Carl seemed to swap out each month.

He had not seen the man in years but nodded at his father. "Yeah. What's he got to do with this?"

"He works in military and government intelligence so we thought it would be a good idea to ask if he would keep an ear out for us. He had no problems with it and assured us we shouldn't worry until he looked into the matter."

James glanced over at his mother. She was still silent, not uttering a word since they sat down. Her indifference to the conversation worried James, but he kept his mouth shut as his father continued.

"Well, we waited and began receiving invitations for you to visit military academies once you hit the end of middle school.

Once again, we brushed it off. Lots of kids get these invites. Two more years flew by and one day I got a random voicemail from Carl. He told me he needed to talk immediately. He asked the usual questions, family, work, friends, etc. And he asked about you. He wanted to know your plans for college, friends, sports, hobbies, all of it. I asked why he wanted so much information and after a fair amount of avoiding an answer, he explained he learned the government issued those tests as the initial push to find an elite group of soldiers." James's father stopped. He took a sip from his water before continuing.

"The military and intelligence agencies were looking for the best and brightest *of all time*. There was a doctor or scientist who found what he thought were convincing indicators pinpointing the most highly evolved human beings on the planet between the ages of six and eighteen. The next year the United States began its testing which was expanded when the Federation was founded. They discovered the doctor's evidence accurate and moved forward with creating recruitment plans.

"Your class was singled out because of the strangely high scores for children born in 2017. In the end, it turned out 2017's children had the highest scores from each year of testing and not by a small margin."

James was taken aback by the information. What's he talking about? James thought. He knew Mar should have scored higher than him. None of this made sense.

"After this, they compiled all the children born in 2017 with the top scores and the military was granted access to the list along with other intelligence directors. They took it and whittled down the names to find those with the strongest potential. Carl told me you were on the list. Not only on the list but in the top percentile."

James's stomach burned with anxiety and his mouth filled with cotton. He was nervous, but he didn't know why. However, while his nerves built and the pit in his stomach expanded, a new reaction washed over him. His eyesight was razor sharp, his hands were steady and dry on his kneecaps, his breathing normal and his heart rate even. He absorbed the fear and angst, drawing it internally to fuel and tend his inner substance.

"He assured me they were not doing anything more than keeping the list with no future plans, but he thought I should know. I told your mother about my talk with Carl when I got home, but there was nothing we could do. We waited for more information.

"Two weeks ago, I got another call from Carl to meet. He told me there were rumors the Federation was reinstating the draft and would recruit the top percentile. However, recruitment was not like it was in the past. Recruitment means drafted and mandatory entry into the military. The government is ready to do whatever it takes. James, you will be pulled."

James looked at his feet. His head spun with questions. Why 2017? Who was this doctor? What happens now? He looked at his father who stared back at him with a painful, empathetic expression. He turned his head to his mother who was still staring into the backyard.

"Can I see him? Carl?" James asked.

"I asked, but he said he couldn't until they officially recruit you. And only if he is your recruiting officer. He pushed his boundaries already. We can't ask him to get in any trouble."

James's head bobbed numbly. He was interrupted by his mother who wrapped her arms around him tightly while he sat holding his face in her shoulder. When she released him to walk back to the house, she paused. Her hand rested on the banister of the stairs, her head bowed. "I'm sorry all of this has to fall on you." With that, his mother walked up the steps and closed the door.

James and his dad sat silently, not knowing what to say next.

James's dad spoke first. "Do you have any other questions?"

James looked at him, "No, I think I've heard all I need to."

"All right." His dad spoke softly. "If there's anything you need or want to talk about, your mother and I are here for you."

James stood up. "Thanks." He walked upstairs to his room, flopping on the bed and staring at the wall. He lay there for an hour going through his father's words, thinking about his future, what he wanted, what he aspired to be. He shut his eyes, reliving his seventeenth birthday until he fell asleep with visions of his last good time welcoming his dreams.

CHAPTER 4

James had been in a daze since Saturday night after he spoke with his parents. They had not received any formal notice from the government, but he assumed it was only a matter of time. School was a welcome reprieve. He left the house, concentrated on something other than himself, and most of all stayed out of the eyes of his mom who was far more sensitive than usual.

It was Wednesday and the whole school seemed to drag along with him. The teachers were even having trouble keeping focus, distracted by the gorgeous weather outside. There was a palpable longing for the sun and breeze, so cruelly separated from the students by a pane of glass. Each time James walked by an open door or window, he smelled the fresh spring air.

The heat made James regret his choice of jeans. Drips of sweat rolled down his rib cage. James made his way to his afternoon classes, fighting off the natural drowsiness following lunch, when he felt a pinch on his elbow. He turned and saw Kaylie walking casually next to him, eyes forward, indifferent to his presence.

Her hair was in a ponytail tied up in a blue band, and she had on a pair of black yoga pants accentuating her curves. She wore a light gray hoodie with a small, manufactured tear at her neckline, exposing her collar bone. Her casual dress was accompanied by strappy, brown sandals, her toes colored cherry blossom pink to match her fingernails.

He grinned. "In the habit of assaulting people for attention, are we?"

"Only when they can't get their head out of the clouds," she said, grinning back, looking at him with her half-moon eyes. "You seem off."

James wasn't sure what to say, "Just busy. Got a lot going on, I guess."

Kaylie didn't ask him to explain anymore as they rounded the corner. They walked through the door to their history class and James glanced at the poster on the wall:

"Culture defines us, but our education connects us to the world." – *First Lady, Jennifer Tawles*

James remembered reading it for the first time and having it explained to him by his father when he was twelve. He sat on his porch on a cool fall evening, early in the school year. His father's legs were stretched out on the ground, leaning back with his elbows against the steps.

"You see, James," he said, taking a sip of his beer, "after the Joining, some major questions arose. Who taught what history? How do you create learning requirements for two separate continents? Is there a better way to rule in one country versus another?

"The immediate answer was to force the US education system on all the new countries." He took another sip. "It was a *spectacular* failure.

"Instead, they decided to focus primarily on science and mathematics. Students needed to be fluent in both Spanish and English, and history would be taught as it related to your locale. Students were required to take a year of North American history, South American history, and local or country history. After these were completed, more in-depth, topical classes were offered depending on your area."

James understood the gist, and his father continued at length about the strengths and values instilled by the new system. After his second trip to get a beer, James remembered his father looking at him quizzically, asking if James understood. Upon

28

nodding in response, somewhat confused, his father patted him on the shoulder, "Good boy. Now, go on."

James was not entirely sure what he sat through back then but learned more and more from his father's rambling lessons as he grew older.

James enjoyed the less rigid learning structure. He also liked history and was usually a present, vocal participant, but this week was a slog, even in Mr. O'Brien's US History: WWII class.

Mr. O'Brien was an old history buff. He loved talking about subjects from before the Melt and thrived off questions involving the military. There were times when the class would begin talking about a subject and finish playing videos of released footage from the 1940s of the US testing their nuclear arsenal in the middle of the ocean. Bikini Bottom, as Mr. O'Brien would say and chuckle. James did not get the joke.

James was drifting off and dug his thumb into the palm of his hand, forcing himself awake. He felt a nudge from Kaylie. She was looking at him expectantly, leaning her head in the direction of Mr. O'Brien who stood five feet away, propped against his desk at the front of the class. He was looking at James with a smile curling up the side of his mouth.

Mr. O'Brien was a well-groomed older man with shocking white hair and bright blue eyes. He always wore a suit to his classes and was never seen around town in anything less than a button-up shirt and tie. However, with all his pomp, he possessed an approachable manner for students.

"Mr. Coffey, how may I help you?" Mr. O'Brien asked.

Mortified, James tried to think of an excuse, when he realized he may not need one. He thought for a second, before he spoke carefully. "I was wondering, since I think we're all thinking the same, if you would tell us a little about the BlankZone?"

A look of surprise flashed across Mr. O'Brien's face and disappeared before James added in a rush, "I asked my dad and

29

other people, but they don't know anything. And I thought because you know so much history you could clear it up for us?"

The room shuffled and the mood changed. He had hit a nerve. Mr. O'Brien's brow furrowed, and he pushed off his desk, pacing across the front of the class, cracking his knuckles. James's mouth dried with anticipation. He pretended not to notice the other kids in the class glancing in his direction and did his best to keep his expression neutral.

Mr. O'Brien stopped pacing and James's heartbeat slowed to match the breath in his chest. Mr. O'Brien looked at James and in a measured tone said, "Well, Mr. Coffey, what is it you want to know?"

The eyes of James's classmates were boring holes through his skull. He shifted in his seat and asked, "What's really happening with the BlankZone and how don't we know more?"

Mr. O'Brien's face morphed into its thoughtful scowl while he resumed his pacing. An intense silence followed for what seemed like an hour while he sat there holding on for Mr. O'Brien to answer. Mr. O'Brien finally stopped, and his expression changed.

He looked at James with an odd face, like he knew deep, dark secrets and owned answers to all their questions in his back pocket. His eyes held an air of mystery and James instinctively leaned forward in his desk while chairs creaked in the anticipatory silence.

"The BlankZone border started at the point where the power grids changed from the beginning of the Asian continent at the edge of Eastern Europe and stretched through to the Pacific Ocean. The shared infrastructure was erected to maintain peace throughout the continent, share costs, and create a sense of unity in an intensely diverse population.

"Now this was not to say the companies and governments were forced to participate in some sort of centralized government structure. Quite to the contrary. Multi-national corporations, power suppliers, financiers, governments, and independent energy contractors took part gladly and sparked an economic revolution in Asia not seen in centuries. The entire endeavor was a resounding success promoting an almost Silk Road effect, spreading ideas and people while building a truly global society. The entire world was connected and thriving. There was certainly conflict, but we were in peacetime. Then came the Melt.

"To this day no one can get a straight answer on what happened to kick off the Melt, but it was as if the Asian continent disappeared. Border countries were destroyed, and the world was thrown into chaos. Entire economies collapsed within hours. Governments ground to a halt and every military in the world was on high alert. The bottom had fallen out of the tightly wound international ecosystem we relied on and all we could do was stare at a black hole filled with questions."

Mr. O'Brien paused scanning the faces in the room, letting the severity of his statement sink in for effect.

"As I said, no one knows what triggered the collapse or what happened on the other side, but we can make a few assumptions about their position today. Based on their pre-Melt resources they must have repaired some of their infrastructure. However, they have not tried to contact us yet. Why? No one knows. But as far as we know, they still do not have power, and we are doing our best to get to them and help them in any way possible." He paused again, gathering his thoughts.

"Now there are rumors of violence, military forces growing, and potential for mass unrest. Still, our government tells us a different story. We are told everything is okay and all our leaders' actions are merely precautions. It's up to you to decide who to trust and when. It's not my place to teach about the BlankZone, but it's what I know and have heard. There are matters beyond the grasp of even my expansive knowledge, Mr. Coffey."

Mr. O'Brien sat back at his desk.

James wasn't satisfied. The answer wasn't finished, and the way Mr. O'Brien looked at him made James feel as if a piece was missing. He cautiously raised his hand again. "Sir?"

"Yes, Mr. Coffey?"

"Do you believe it? What they say? The people in charge."

James would never forget the smile on Mr. O'Brien's lips and the covert knowledge shrouded behind his gaze as he looked at James and answered in a low voice. "No, James. I do not buy it for a second."

CHAPTER 5

James was in the living room, surrounded by his family with his packed bags sitting by the front door. No one knew exactly what to say. James left the room, needing an escape. He walked to his bedroom and sat looking out the window.

The day after his class with Mr. O'Brien, two men in military uniforms came to his house and delivered him a summons letter.

He was requested by order of the government to attend basic training for his "recruitment" program. The men said they would be back in seventy-two hours. He was expected to pack what he needed in the green canvas bag they provided. No list, just a simple directional point.

He met with Kaylie the night before to say goodbye. She picked him up in her beat-up, gas-powered, blue sedan to get ice cream. She dressed casually wearing a pair of workout shorts with her usual light gray hoodie. He noticed her lack of makeup and thought she looked beautiful in her simplicity.

"You look good," he said, feeling his nerves.

"Thanks," she replied smiling sweetly. "Ready to go?"

James hopped in the passenger side, kicking himself for not being smoother.

They drove to an ice cream parlor in a nearby town next to the waterfront, casually flirting while they parked and bought their cones.

James savored his time with her, walking down the streets watching people pass by, eating their ice cream and giggling while avoiding any discussion around their inevitable goodbye. When they returned to James's house, neither one was ready to leave yet and they walked around the block, their conversation subdued. They strolled quietly for some time and James was worried she was getting bored when he felt her fingers slip through his. His stomach tightened in excitement, and he was surprised by the sudden rush of sadness, knowing he was leaving.

Don't think about it, he thought. Nothing you can do.

They stayed quiet the rest of the walk around the block, and James ingrained each footstep in his memory. They stopped at her car, and she let go of his hand to open her door. James stood back, ready to wave goodbye, when she turned around and pulled his shirt, kissing him deeply.

Kaylie's lips were soft and tasted like her caramel nut ice cream. They stayed there for only a second, but it was a moment of pure happiness. She pulled away and looked at him.

"Don't leave us all behind, okay?" she said.

He grinned back. "I couldn't."

Kaylie smiled one last time from the driver's seat and pulled away, her caramel ice cream lingering on his lips.

James sat quietly remembering the night when he heard a knock at the front door. He walked to the top of the stairs to watch as his father welcomed a tall, well-built, officer in his dress uniform. He took off his hat as he entered the living room and shook his father's hand.

"Carl Jackson, how the hell are you?" James's father said, gripping Carl by the shoulder.

"Fine. Glad I could come. How's it going round here?" James heard the distinct, booming timbre of his father's friend's voice.

"Not bad. Let me grab my wife. She's been waiting to see you."

James watched his father leave through the swinging door, and Carl walked into the living room. He sat on the couch, settling deep into the cushions.

Carl sported a military crew cut and his face was shaved smooth. His dark eyes soaked up the living room, scanning the area methodically. James decided it was time to make his presence known.

He walked into the room. "Hey, Carl."

Carl stood up. "James, how's it going?" He shook James's hand, the strength of his grip apparent during the brief handshake. "Been awhile, huh?"

James grinned. "Yeah, we haven't seen you. What've you been up to?"

"Military's got me running all over the place. You know how it is." He shook his head, exhausted.

James's father came back into the room followed by James's mother who immediately hugged Carl. She stood on her tiptoes to get her arms all the way around his neck.

"Where the hell have you been, Carl? We've been more worried about you than our kids," she said sarcastically.

"Well, I'm sorry to disappoint Julie. Just my incommunicado lifestyle nowadays," said Carl, grinning. "I've definitely been keeping myself busy these last couple of years."

The room was quiet as the four of them looked around uncomfortably when Carl broke the awkward silence. "James and I have someone else to pick up. I can give you all five minutes alone to say goodbye. Then I have to take him. I'm sorry it can't be longer." He gave an apologetic look to James's parents and then spoke to James. "I'll leave you alone. Meet me out by the car."

James's siblings strode into the living room as Carl walked out through the front door.

Mar kicked off the ceremony by walking up and giving him a hug. "Don't do anything stupid out there," she said as she pulled away.

Caitlin followed suit, hugging him briefly, never one for extended physical affection, and pulled away. "Good luck," she said.

35

Michael was the last to go and struggled with the weight of the moment. James made it easy on him, giving him a quick hug and patting him on the back. Michael's eyes dropped for a second before he looked at James, blinked, and turned away. James grinned, not wanting to embarrass his brother, and patted Michael's shoulder while he shuffled with his sisters back to the family room, leaving his parents to say their farewells to James alone.

A stillness hung over the three. James's mom put her arms around his neck while she tried to speak but was unable to. James heard words slipping away from her tongue and hot tears ran down his neck. He pulled her in close and she kissed him on the cheek before letting go.

His father shook his hand. They looked each other in the eye for a moment, not sure what to do or say next, when his father reached in and hugged him. When he released James, his father reached into his jeans pocket and pulled out an envelope.

"Don't open this until you have no direction left and need guidance. You're one of the few hopes I have in this world, and I wouldn't feel safe with anyone else taking care of my fate. There are going to be times that test you, but never abandon what you have learned and never leave behind what matters. Remember, I am always here to talk. This is simply a reminder." James's father handed him the letter. "Good luck, James."

James put the envelope in his pocket and picked up his bags. He glanced at his mother, who was looking at him with swollen eyelids and tear-stained cheeks.

"Good luck, James. We love you."

James was surprised by the strength in her voice and hugged her again.

"I love you, too," he said, before stepping back and smiling at both of them.

He pushed open the screen door and made his way over to the car.

36

"You ready?" Carl asked, standing by the car patiently.

"Yeah, let's go," James replied, his voice trailing off.

Carl nodded and turned toward the car. The man in the passenger seat emerged and took James's bags, depositing them in the trunk. James and Carl waited as the man came back and opened the door for them.

After they settled in, James looked back at his house. His family stood on the front steps, watching his departure. James wondered when he would return and under what condition. Visions of birthday parties, Easter egg hunts, Christmases, Halloweens, and first days of school flashed through James's mind in vibrant colors. His throat was thick as the car pulled away and he waved as his home was swallowed by the street.

Carl turned to him from the front seat. "You hungry?" he asked.

"Nah, I'm fine. Thanks though," James replied, still looking out the window.

"Are you sure? We still have to get one more kid and then it's another drive to the airport where you won't be able to eat until you're on the plane," he said.

"I'm all right. Dad made breakfast this morning," James said, giving him a limp thumbs-up.

"Sounds good. We'll be at the next kid's house soon. I think you'll like him. He's an interesting person and a more… *colorful* recruit," Carl said, emphasizing colorful with air quotes.

They pulled off the highway and stopped outside a blue and white colonial house. There was a kid roughly James's age, slightly taller and thinner sitting on the front stoop of the house with, James assumed, his parents on either side of him.

Carl turned to James. "Wait here. I'll be back in a moment."

James watched as Carl walked toward the house. The kid stood and shook Carl's hand. Carl motioned at the car and the driver got out to collect the kid's bags.

Two girls came out to give the kid hugs, one at a time. The kid gave one last wave before walking to the car. James slid over in the back seat, and the new person crawled in next to him.

Carl motioned in James's direction. "Declan, this is James. James, Declan."

James held his hand out to Declan who did the same. "Nice to meet you," he said, shaking Declan's hand.

"Same. And you can call me Deck. The name Declan makes me feel like I got caught coming home drunk."

James instantly liked him.

Deck's long sandy hair pulled across his forehead in a sweep, shadowing his brown eyes. His movements suggested an athlete, with an undercurrent of teeming energy disguised by a practiced facade of effortless grace apparent even while he sat buckled in the back of the SUV.

"Where you from?" asked Deck, reclining in his seat, trying to get comfortable.

"Oak Park neighborhood, down the road," said James, relaxing.

"Know anyone from around here? The New Ro area?" said Deck opening the window and fussing with the buttons on the door.

"A few but not many. What about you? Anyone from Oak Park?"

"Not well enough to remember their names or even leave enough of an impression for them to remember me."

"Yeah," said James, deciding to look back out the window.

"Hey, Carl?" said Deck leaning over the middle console. "Where are we going and when will we get there?"

Carl turned around and replied, "We're headed to the airport where the other recruits are waiting. The jet will take you to your training facility where the rest will be explained."

Deck nodded and looked at James. "They come and kidnap you to become a soldier but can't give you specifics on anything. The hell is up with that?" he said, putting his hands in the air.

James chuckled and Carl smiled. "Calm down, Declan. All will be explained after you land at the training facility."

"And where exactly is our training facility, may I ask?" said Deck leaning forward.

"I am not allowed to discuss that at this time," said Carl, putting up the blocker between the seats.

Deck leaned back and pointed a thumb toward the front seat, making a disappointed face at the back of the headrest. "Bunch of bull," he muttered.

When they arrived at the airport James watched in wonder as they drove through an opening in the chain link fence topped with razor wire surrounding the tarmac. He was more excited with each passing moment. His stomach tightened into a ball of anticipation, his heart stringing together steady beats. They arrived at their gate where a brightly painted white jet stood with a Federation star gleaming proudly on the tail.

Guards stood on either side of the staircase to the jet with rifles across their chests.

Carl walked in front of them toward the plane and the men snapped to attention, saluting him. Carl returned salute and waved his hand, allowing the men to return to their former positions.

Carl faced James and Deck. "These guys will get your bags. If you need anything from them for the trip, say it now. They can bring it to the cabin for you before takeoff."

Both Deck and James shook their heads.

"Let's go."

Carl walked up the staircase followed by James and Deck.

At the top of the stairs, two more guards stood on either side of the doorway. They did not move when James and Deck walked past them.

There were two rows of wide, spacious seats. The seats were a beige leather, and the plane hinted at an underlying scent of old cigarettes, further evidenced by the brown smoke stains covering the cabin walls.

James counted ten others on the airplane. They all glanced at him and Deck but lost interest looking back out the windows or at their HOLOs instead.

Two seats remained up front. James sat in the one next to the window and Deck followed.

Carl shut the cockpit door. He motioned to the two men standing guard on the tarmac and they pulled away the stairs, readying the plane for departure.

Carl walked to the back of the aircraft checking each set of seats. When he was done, he turned back and made his way up the aisle to the front of the plane.

He addressed the group while he walked. "As you all know, my name is First Sergeant Carl Jackson. I will be the commanding officer aboard this airplane. I am not here to be your guidance counselor. I am not here to be your babysitter. Nor am I here to befriend you in any way, shape, or form of the word. I am here because the Federation has chosen me to train you to be the best soldiers the world has ever seen. There will be no easy breaks, no simple tasks, and no redos. You are supposed to be the best. Therefore, I expect you to act as such."

James looked at Carl, hiding the knots of excitement tying together in his stomach with a placid expression on his face. He was learning to love the slow boil mixed with the anticipation of the complete unknown.

"I am here for one reason and one reason only," Carl continued. "To train you to deal with every possibility of combat you can imagine. You will be in a facility consisting of 188 other trainees. You will receive further instruction when we land. Until then I suggest you get some rest because the next few months will not offer any such opportunity." Done with his speech, Carl turned around and walked to his seat in the front cabin.

Deck leaned over to James. "I don't think he's very friendly," Deck whispered. "In fact, I think he truly means he's not going to be my friend. I can't imagine how well he did sharing in kindergarten." He shook his head in the direction of Carl's back.

James nodded. "I'm guessing block time was a bit of a hassle for him growing up."

Deck grinned.

The plane was silent. The white noise of the engine was all James heard as the airplane rose smoothly into the air. The sun melted in the sky behind the city. Shades of red, orange, yellow, and pink reflected off the steeply angled buildings creating pools of brilliant color in the clouds. The spires of the skyscrapers pushed ever upward poking through the atmosphere. James smiled bittersweetly as the plane carried him away from the glistening forest of metal and glass.

PART II

CHAPTER 6

"GET UP! GET UP! LET'S GO! LET'S GO! LET'S GO!"

James lay in bed for another second, taking a deep breath before slapping Deck's lifeless leg hanging from the bunk above him.

Over the last couple of weeks, James was ready to go a full hour before their "alarm." While waking early before call wasn't exactly desirable, it was far more relaxing than the alternative.

James rolled over, pivoting out of bed. He used the metal frame to pull himself up, cracking his neck side to side. He pulled his tousled sheets flat, yanking the covers over his pillow and smoothing out the wrinkles from the head of the bed to the foot.

James threw on running shorts before starting the next part of his day: waking up Deck.

Deck's breathing was heavy. His leg hung dead on the other side of the bunk. James stepped carefully onto the metal frame of his bunk and pulled his shoulders to Deck's level, balancing on the balls of his feet. He steadied his legs and pulled back his cupped palm and came down in a hard slap on Deck's ear, making a popping noise. He ducked and jumped off the bed, narrowly escaping a swinging paw aimed at his head.

"Sonofabitch," snarled Deck, sitting up. "Every fucking morning, man."

"Got 'im," Jerry's bodiless voice called out from the other side of the bunk, and James smirked.

Deck continued grumbling, rolling out of bed, legs tangled in sheets, his body sloth-like.

James grabbed his shirt and walked to the yellow line in the middle of the room. The other early risers were gathering for their morning run. James gave a thumbs-up to Jerry who nodded in return while he pulled his short bulky arms over his head in a stretch.

James sniffed sleep all around him. The scent of musty dried sweat, emanating from hundreds of teenage bodies, hung in the poorly ventilated air.

"Morning, bud," James said, pulling his arms behind him stretching out his chest while Deck approached with heavy steps.

"Is that what you say after another 5 a.m. wakeup call over a goddamn loudspeaker?" mumbled Deck shaking out his legs. James had quickly come to realize Deck was not a morning person.

"Come on, you have to be used to this by now. We've been here more than eleven weeks and it's the same every day. Besides it's 5:30," James replied, winking at Deck.

"Exactly why I shouldn't be used to it. I feel like I'm in an insane asylum the way they keep the clock ticking around here," replied Deck gruffly, ignoring the jibe.

Jamie and Marissa were in front of them in line. Jamie was stretching out her long, tanned legs, her running shorts stretched tight against her thighs. "Can't handle the mornings, Deck?" she teased, batting her eyelashes.

Deck shot her a nasty look and Marissa giggled, pulling her auburn hair into a ponytail. "Go back to bed. Nothing will happen," she said sarcastically.

Deck turned to James, seeking validation. James shook his head and Deck's face dropped back to a scowl.

The doors to the barracks lifted steadily toward the still dark sky, and Sergeant Jackson walked into the room. He wore a white t-shirt and black running shorts with nondescript, gray running sneakers, the same as everyone else.

"Let's go, people," Jackson said, his face a mask of unemotional drive. "Five miles."

James turned back around to Deck as the line snaked out the door. "Come on, cheery. Let's go."

Deck cursed under his breath as he followed James out the door. "Dumbass early hours. I can run after ten, ya know."

They started their morning like every other in camp, winding around the edge of a field, the floodlights powering down as the horizon lightened. The grass was still soaking wet, but they were on a beaten dirt path almost immediately, their feet methodically pounding the compact earth. The air was crisp, and the dew was fresh, bathing them in a sweet aroma.

No one spoke on their runs. It was not a rule, but more of an unsaid agreement across the camp in which they decided on solitude in the morning.

James saw the long, low fences as they came upon the rolling, green pasture, a sparkling white from the water condensing on the blades of grass. He followed the rest of the group, hopping easily over the low wooden stake walls connected with iron wires before continuing.

They had been sent somewhere in the Midwest for training. The base they trained on was enormous. It spanned miles of land creating ample room for the Federation military to teach them appropriately. The hills went on continuously across the prairie broken only by the occasional patch of forest or stream.

When they had arrived at camp eleven weeks ago, James was lightheaded contemplating the journey before them.

Leadership placed them in groups of nine or ten, sorting people standing next to each other on the ground off the tarmac. This, James learned, meant nothing more than a way to choose unbiased training groups. They were all on the same footing with no knowledge of the military, little understanding of their situation, and their most common trait was confusion.

Deck and James were standing next to each other and were placed in the same group: Group K.

James and the rest of K. followed Jackson to the barracks, which were housed in a converted airplane hangar.

The building had seen better days. Its original forest green paint was nearly invisible between the swaths of gunmetal gray breaking through to the exterior. As they walked through the doors, the rough gravel of the tarmac gave way to smooth, cold concrete and their footsteps echoed off the aluminum walls. The floor shone in the dimming sunlight with residue from past oil spills, and the rafters still sported heavy iron chains used to hoist propellers off planes when they underwent maintenance. James heard the creaking of the building on the windless day and smelled decades of engine grease saturating the dank, dry air.

He looked around at his surroundings curiously with the rest of the camp, trying to establish his bearings. On either side of the hangar were rows of metal bunks with what looked like a four-foot-high filing cabinet fitted with two drawers between each bunk set. Above each set of bunks was a different HOLO receptor with glowing letters in random order running up and down the walls, ten letters per side.

First Sergeant Jackson, as James knew him now, stood in front of the camp and gave them a rundown of what to expect in their day-to-day. James remembered it well.

"You will be woken at 0530 every morning. The summers here get fucking hot, so we like to run early. We will give you two minutes once the doors open to ready yourselves and stand on the yellow line in the center of the barracks." He pointed to a two-foot-thick yellow line running from the back of the hangar to the opening.

"We will begin our days with a five-mile run. Afterward, you will be expected to clean up and report to the mess hall. Showers and bathrooms can be found on your left. Mess hall can be found in the hangar next door. We don't have the luxury of individual bathrooms for men and women, so you'll be sharing."

James blushed and he glanced at the other trainees in the room who were turning a similar shade of red or concentrating intently on their feet. Might be awkward, James thought before turning his attention back to the Sergeant.

"You will find your group's bunks indicated by the HOLOs on the walls. There's a clock on both sides of the barracks which you will need to pay close attention to. We run on a fucking schedule here.

"After you eat breakfast, you will report back here, ready to go by your bunks where an instructor will either come get you or will send instructions on where to go depending on the training for the day.

"The first week you will be trained together so we can get you used to the system and in shape. After, we'll begin more technical group trainings. Any questions?" Jackson looked around the room. They shuffled in place, letting their nervous movement fill the air.

"Good. See you all in the morning." Sergeant Jackson left through the opening, leaving them to their own devices for the night.

James looked around numbly. Well, what do I do now? There was a light tap on his shoulder. He turned to find Deck standing behind him.

"Wanna grab a bunk?" asked Deck, nodding toward the section of beds with a giant, glowing, blue K suspended over them.

They walked over to the bunks, and James looked around at the other groups as they met next to their respective letters. The other people in Deck and James's K group followed, making their way across the expansive barracks, light filtering in through the hangar door.

They examined their new "rooms." Each bunk was eight feet long with a slim cot stretched between the wireframing. James sat heavily on the bottom bunk and was surprised at the spring's strength. He ducked, missing a nasty gash on his head from the bunk above him.

Deck threw his duffel on the top bunk while he inspected the drawers. He opened the top one and peered inside shaking his head sullenly.

"Quite the intro, huh?" he said to James.

"Yeah, you really feel the love around here," James said.

Deck looked at the bunks next to them. "Hey, you," Deck said loudly.

A slim girl with purple bangs obscuring her forehead turned around on the bottom bunk near theirs. James thought she looked familiar but could not quite place her.

"Where you from?" Deck asked.

"Florida. You?" she said, a slight accent drawing out the i.

Deck pointed a thumb at James. "We're both from New York. Flew in with a bunch of other people from there. Thought you might have been with us."

"I was," she said, her face blank, unamused with Deck's attempts at friendship. That's it, James realized, suddenly recognizing the bangs.

"Oh," said Deck sheepishly, "Well nice to meet you."

She turned around coldly, getting off her bunk and walking to the drawers inspecting them, ignoring Deck and James.

James and Deck gave each other a look before they noticed a face pop up from the top bunk.

"I'm from Massachusetts. Kinda close I guess!" The kid's voice was fast with a heavy city-bred accent. A body dropped swiftly and a short stocky teenager with a mohawk appeared in front of them holding out a rough callused hand covered in freckles.

"I'm Jerry," he said, shaking their hands.

Jerry turned around, hopping back up to his bunk. When he reached the apex of his jump, he turned around in midair with a swift twist, bouncing lightly on the mattress as he landed.

James was impressed by the effortless acrobatic agility.

"Were you on our flight, too?" asked James.

"Nope, I was on with a bunch of other guys, but between unloading the planes and moving all around I lost them when we got here. Happened to fall into K, I guess."

"They give you any more information on the flight?" asked Deck.

"Nope, I'm guessing the same as you guys. Told to wait until we got here," said Jerry shrugging. "Didn't get much yet though."

"Sounds familiar," said Deck, rolling his eyes.

James pushed himself up, walking to the end of his bunk to get a look at the whole camp.

The steel topped lamps hanging from aluminum coils flickered on as the sun set. The doors were still open, and a breeze blew in causing the chains draped overhead to swing.

James realized how tired he felt, ready for a long sleep to prepare for what would surely be a busy morning.

He turned back around to find Deck rooting around the file cabinet and Jerry breathing heavily, asleep on the top bunk next to them.

James pulled back the covers on his cot and took off his shirt.

Deck turned around. "By the way, shorts, shirts, and shoes in here. Not much else though. I'm guessing we're wearing these tomorrow morning."

"Thanks." James nodded and laid down, feeling the weight lift off his feet while his head hit the pillow.

"Anytime man," said Deck as he jumped into the top bunk.

James saw a shirt drop to the floor and he looked at the digital clock on the far side of the room: 2104. Damn, thought James, I'll have to get used to military time.

Just then, a noise erupted overhead, and he sprang up out of bed.

48

Deck jumped from the top bunk and rolled into a crouch next to James.

They knelt next to each other as the grating noise continued and looked around at others in similar positions or sitting up in their beds, confused at what was happening. James plotted their exit when he noticed the entrance to the hangar growing smaller. The gaping darkness in front of them was shrinking and James looked at the ceiling.

He patted Deck's shoulder who was still scanning the room intently. James stood and pointed at the ceiling, suddenly embarrassed at their initial reaction.

The door to the hangar was moving sluggishly toward the entrance, closing for the night. The old gears created a screeching sound as the decades of rust scraped violently against the metal chains releasing flurries of oxidized metal.

"It's the fucking door," James said as he crawled back into bed.

"Dammit," said Deck. "That's embarrassing. Welcome to the military, I guess."

James grinned, turned over on his side, closed his eyes, and fell instantly asleep.

James was knocked out of his memory as they came upon a stream cutting through their running path. He moved carefully, stepping deftly through the maze of mossy rocks littering the shallow water.

During the first week or so it seemed like everyone in camp was constantly falling, crouched on the side of the trail vomiting from exhaustion, or stretched out on the ground trying to knead their way through crippling leg cramps. Minor cuts and abrasions appeared regularly on arms and legs, welts swelled in places where young sapling branches whipped shins and unprotected faces.

First aid kits were on their bunks when they returned from the first run. James peeled off his blood and sweat soaked socks, and dirt and pebbles poured onto the floor when he tipped his shoes upside down. He smeared antiseptic cream on his blisters, wrapped his foot carefully with an ACE bandage, and pulled on a fresh pair of socks. He hardly had time to take a breath before a bell rang calling them to eat.

When they trained, the emphasis was on the quality of the exercise, doing things correctly. Form was important above all else and was stressed by all their instructors to the point of insanity. Granted, they were expected to work hard and learn fast, but had to do it right, a sentiment James appreciated.

After the first week in camp, the showers were standard. It was impossible to be embarrassed in front of hundreds of other people enduring exhaustion to the point of collapse.

James's body heat elevated at mile two. The morning breeze cooled his sweat-soaked brow. They finished cutting through the small path in the woods and arrived at another field where high stalks of grass created the walls of an old cow path. James watched the other trainees disappear from the waist down in the high grass, their torsos bouncing rhythmically, their backs drenched wet with sweat, and the sweet smell of dry earth mingled with decomposing grass in the air.

Technical trainings started faster than James realized, especially after two weeks of grueling physical training. Their days were broken into different segments ranging from small weapons training, language lessons, explosives walkthroughs, skydiving, and rappelling. They learned how to operate the majority of the Federation's vehicles and navigate through any landscape using stars or improvised compasses. Survival kit creation and all the different ways to build a fire were taught extensively along with different plants safe to eat in any environment.

Classes were taught as groups with each individual responsible for their own threshold until the group passed.

When it came to physical challenges, Jerry was ahead of them all, and Maria was a nearly perfect shot with any weapon.

They learned the easiest way to finish was to pool their efforts. James and Deck moved quickly through most of the exercises, using the time remaining to help others in their group who did not pick up the lessons as easily.

The camp entered an easy rhythm. They awoke before dawn, trained through the day and lights were out when the clock hit 2200 hours. James developed a comforting sense of assurance from the grating, rust-filled movement of the closing hangar doors.

They finished their run at the doors of the barracks. James slowed to a jog and kept moving with decreasing speed toward his bunk. Without breaking stride, he grabbed his towel and headed into the showers.

Most people showered immediately after their run, but as time wore on some people chose to hit the weight room or do yoga afterward. James preferred to do a heavier workout later in the day and showered after their run.

He walked through the bustling post-workout frenzy to the lockers where he found an empty shower head. He turned the dial to freezing cold, letting the nozzle spray frigid water down the back of his neck, lowering his body temperature and revitalizing him.

He closed his eyes, wiping his mind into a blank state when he heard the showers to the side of him sputter.

He listened to Marissa and Jamie chatting, the steam from their showers more pronounced as it got closer to the cold water James was running.

"That one was a bitch today for some reason," said Marissa, rubbing shampoo into her cropped, Federation-accepted hair. "I was struggling."

"It'll happen," said Jamie. "Each day is different."

"I guess," replied Marissa. "Did you see the geese this morning?"

James tuned out their conversation, still enjoying the quiet from the morning and finished his shower, nodding at them when he walked back to his bunk, his towel wrapped around his waist.

There was a note pinned to the end of his bunk and Deck was pulling on his training attire for the day.

"Map work and an afternoon with Folm," said Deck to no one in particular, reaching for his shoes.

"Great," said James sarcastically, "another day of looking at wind currents." He rolled his eyes, thinking of how inane morning class would be.

Deck stood slapping him on the chest playfully. "Relax, bud. You get to blow shit up later."

James nodded, realizing an afternoon with Folm would be a perfect pick-me-up after staring at maps of coasts and oceanic pressure currents all day.

The girls returned a few minutes later and changed while the rest of the group hung around waiting to go to class. When Jamie came around the bunk, pulling a piece of military-issue ribbon around her short ponytail, the rest of the group did a mental headcount making sure one last time the rest of K was present before heading off to training for the day.

They finished their day quickly, running through map work and explosives training like clockwork, preparing and blowing up complex, improvisational devices used by Federation soldiers.

"Yep, guys, I tell you. This will get you out of anything." Folm paused and spat out a long strand of tobacco juice. He wiped his lips with the back of his hand, rubbing the excess liquid into a growing stain on his pant leg. "You wanna blow a hole through concrete, metal, or the freakin' moon—there ain't any better way." He chuckled.

James heard rumors Folm was the top explosives expert in the Federation and the military obtained most of its techniques from Folm's personal instruction manual. He was a giant man with bear paws for hands and a bulging stomach beneath a tobacco and food-stained shirt. James was skeptical at first of such a sloppy guy who was supposed to handle some of the most delicate explosives in the world. However, Folm's hands moved with the dexterity of a surgeon. His fingers flitted with the wires and coils of the various devices like a hummingbird and at a nearly unattainable level of precision. James could not help but be impressed by Folm's undeniable, natural talents.

Folm dismissed them early giving James time for a quick nap before dinner.

He awoke to Deck standing over his bed staring at him dropping water on his forehead. "Isn't that creepy?" Deck's face was no more than a foot away from his and James pushed him back.

"The hell is wrong with you?" he said jokingly, getting out of bed.

"Nothing," replied Deck coolly. "Was hungry and didn't want to go to dinner alone. I'd look like a loser."

"Yeah, you would."

"Ouch," said Deck, clutching his heart dramatically "Now hurry up, man. I'm starving."

James jumped out of his bunk to get dressed. Jerry walked in from the bathroom in his boxers, a towel draped on his shoulder. "We ready to go?" he said to Deck.

"Hold your horses, pal," replied Deck. "James has gotta put his pants on. I don't think the COs would like it much if he showed up sans pants." Deck scanned Jerry up and down.

"Speaking of, you could do with some clothes, too."

"No shit," Jerry retorted, walking over to his side to change. "Give me five."

Deck looked back at James and put his arms up exasperated. "Or maybe they wouldn't mind, I dunno. But I wouldn't want to be the one to test it, you know. Some advice from a friend."

James shook his head, smiling. "Thanks. I'll remember."

"Anytime, man, anytime," said Deck, clapping a reassuring hand on James's shoulder.

Meals were James's favorite times in camp. All 188 trainees ate in a banquet hall of five tables with long benches crammed with everyone sitting shoulder to shoulder. It reminded him of home, people joking and laughing, able to relax after a long day. The main difference was how gluttonous nearly 200 people were after training fourteen hours a day.

James entered first. The room was packed with lines of other trainees flooding the tables and buffets. Some ate in silence, listening to the dim roar, while others chatted over their meal. James spied the ones waiting impatiently with plates licked clean, eyes darting around furtively, looking for seconds.

James grabbed a tray and jumped in line. He spotted Marissa on the other side of the cafeteria waving to him, pointing to the seats she saved. He gave her a thumbs-up and focused on his points of attack.

James stopped for his protein first, the smell of freshly cooked meat wafted from a long line of steaming dishes. He got to the grill in the center of the line, grabbed a cheeseburger and stacked onions, bacon, and tomato on top of the burger before slathering a mayo-horseradish sauce on the bun. Next was the salad bar where he piled romaine lettuce on a plate and heaped a generous portion of croutons on top with a drizzle of olive oil. At the end of the table, he grabbed a bowl of fruit, balancing it between his burger and salad. He capped it all off with a baked potato lathered in butter and salt. His plate probably weighed four pounds and his mouth watered when the potato, onion, and burger hit him at the same time.

He balanced it all with a glass of milk, and he made his way to the table through the crowd of hungry trainees eagerly traveling to and from the food.

By the time he got to the table, Deck and Jerry were scarfing down their food as fast as possible. Jamie walked up to the table. Her face matched Marissa's as they looked at the two young men, shaking their heads in disgust.

James looked at Deck and Jerry. "That's semi-disturbing. Have you breathed?" he asked. Jerry took a second to lift his middle finger in James's direction before diving back into his food. James chuckled, while he mashed the potato on his plate, making sure the butter seeped into every crevasse.

"How can you eat like that?" said Jamie, not trying to mask her obvious displeasure.

"Li' wha'?" asked Deck through a mouthful of what looked like potatoes and pork.

"Like an animal," said Marissa with a look of self-righteous condemnation gleaming in her eyes.

Deck finished his bite swallowing painfully. "What? I'm starving. And besides, we're chewing with our mouths closed." Deck waved his fork emphasizing his points. "So, I don't see the problem." Deck dug back into his meal, gorging an oversized forkful of mashed potatoes and gravy to prove his point.

The girls, not amused by his answer, ignored it and turned to talk with one another.

"Hey, James!" a voice called through the crowd in front of him, hidden by a line of other trainees. Teresa busted her way through the shuffle of bodies and set her tray next to Jerry's.

"What's up? How've you been?" James said, looking at the diminutive yet curvy figure sitting across from him.

Teresa was in group D, small, fierce, and easy to get along with. They met at the med-station one day after James received a nasty cut rappelling a rock wall during an obstacle course. Teresa came in, her arm covered in blood from her shoulder to her wrist and waited patiently in the back of the line with him until it was their turn to get treated.

He remembered she used her torn uniform as a makeshift tourniquet, cutting the blood flow off below her shoulder. Her face was pale and the piece of cloth she clenched in her teeth made conversation a nonstarter. James was impressed by the determination it took to wait patiently for her turn.

When the time finally came for James to see the doc, James, trying to be a gentleman, offered to let her go in front of him. However, she refused with a forceful shake of her head.

He walked in through the swinging tent doors, relenting to her silent pressure only to be pushed out ten seconds later when Teresa passed out and fell through the flaps.

Ten minutes later the medics were hooking her to an IV and waking her with smelling salts while James was getting his arm sewn shut. Her first words when she woke up, to no one in particular, were "See, I'm not a fucking pussy." James laughed and walked her back to her group afterward, striking an immediate friendship.

The plus side of their friendship was her influence over Deck, who stared whenever she walked into a room and developed a nervous edge when she was around.

When she sat at the table, Deck looked like he was going to throw up as he tried to swallow the massive amount of food still in his mouth. He choked, letting out a brief cough, before coolly tipping his head at Teresa.

Teresa either pretended not to notice or was trying to be nice ignoring Deck.

She took a bite of her burger before she replied, "Good. Ya know, tired. Can't wait till all of this is over."

"Three more days."

"No. Tomorrow, stupid."

"Wait, seriously?" asked James, putting down his fork.

"Yeah, seriously. Tomorrow is the last day of training and then who knows what happens? I mean we know, but we don't know, you know?" she said.

It was one of the more confusing lines James ever heard, but he still understood what she was saying. They were never given any sort of guideline on what was going to happen to them after their basic training was done. All they were told was there would be eliminations.

"I guess it's real now, huh?" he said, thrown by the news.

"Yeah, feels weird," said Jamie picking up her tray. "We're gonna get dessert. You guys need anything?"

James replied, "No, I'm fine, thanks."

Deck and Jerry shook their heads, their plates cleared, unable to speak.

James finished his meal chatting with Teresa and when he finished, left Deck at the table with Jerry, both groaning in pain holding their stomachs.

The next night, after another day of repetitive training, the mess hall was filled with delicious foods. The trainers and officers were congratulating them all on making it this far, holding a final meal as a celebration.

Deck was visibly elated at the sight of roast beef, cocktail shrimp, hanger steaks, ham, pork roast, turkey, and an assortment of appetizers, sides, and desserts to accompany the feast. For the first time, the mess hall was silent, save for the movement of plates, muffled belches, and squeaking chairs sounding around the room when people returned for seconds.

James finished his third plate of food and was watching Deck consume his fifth when Captain Hartsman walked to the head of the room.

Hartsman looked like the typical military man. His short hair was parted neatly, and his uniform was pristine. A pair of reading glasses dangled from his breast pocket, and his perfectly shaven face never had a single smudge.

Deck was poised to continue his meal, about to dip his shrimp in cocktail sauce when James knocked it out of Deck's hand.

"What the—" Deck started to say but James pointed to Hartsman. Deck gave a thumbs-up acknowledging James's quick save and turned toward Hartsman as he began to speak.

"Ladies and gentlemen, I wish to congratulate you on making it through the last twelve weeks in the Federation's Elite Soldier Training Program. You have all performed well beyond what we thought capable, causing us to change our training regimen within the past eleven weeks to accommodate your speedy development.

"However, as you may remember, the next step here is elimination. We will grade you in a series of mental and physical tests beginning tomorrow where we will eliminate 50% of you on the spot. It has been a privilege working with all of you, but now the best will move on. The rest will be sent to other training regimens until you are old enough to officially enlist.

"Tomorrow we will come get you at 0500 hours. We expect you all to be awake and dressed in full gear. Congratulations and good luck."

Finished, Hartsman walked back through the doors on the side of the cafeteria. The mess hall was hushed. They were about to go through hell, and they all knew it.

Someone needs to step up, thought James scanning the room. He caught Deck's eye and nodded at him. James stood up, took his tray, and walked toward the trash. Deck jumped up, following his lead along with the rest of K. James threw away his garbage, placed his tray on the dish line, and headed straight to his barracks.

He felt others watching him but refused to turn around as he heard the familiar scrape of cafeteria benches pushing back from tables.

James made his way to the barracks with what seemed like the entire camp following behind. He went to his bunk, finding two unassembled rifles waiting. James looked over at Jerry and Maria who discovered the same setup waiting on Maria's bunk. Deck was on the other side of the bed and brought two rucksacks out opening them and unloading their contents, placing them heavily on the bed next to the rifle parts.

In each bag were two extra magazines of ammo and an empty twenty-ounce steel canteen. Deck picked the rucksacks back up. "These are damn heavy," he said.

James knelt and patted the sides of each pack, locating the weights sewn into the sides.

"Fuck," said Maria, sitting on her bed. "These probably weigh twenty pounds." James saw the concern on the slender girl's face, contemplating the strain this would put on her frame. He worried about Teresa for a second before brushing it aside, deciding to focus on assembling his weapon instead.

Deck pulled a fresh set of fatigues out of his drawer and laid them on the floor, setting his boots next to each leg.

Group K was silent. Even Marissa and Jamie who normally kept a steady flow of conversation were quiet.

James finished his routine preparations and climbed into bed. He pulled the sheets up to his neck while the natural light dimmed outside the hangar. He lay on his back, staring at the bunk above him, preparing and silently praying to nothing in particular as the rest of camp sank into an uneasy sleep.

CHAPTER 7

James's hands gripped the sides of the wash basin cut into the long plank of steel stretching the length of the blue tiled bathroom wall. The dull gray metal from the bathroom "mirror" reflected glittering light when the swinging fluorescent bulbs hit one of the divots on its surface. He splashed cold water on his face, preparing for the day.

Sleep was contentious. He had tossed throughout the night in a cold sweat thinking he would miss his wakeup. Each time his eyes opened he willed his heartbeat to slow and wrangled in his nerves. He was awake early and rather than lie around letting his stomach churn itself to pieces, decided to jump in the shower.

He patted his face dry with a towel, leaving some of the moisture on his forehead cooling him down while he walked back into the barrack's main room, depositing his towel in one of the canvas laundry receptacles. He became more alert with each step. James jogged back to his bunk keeping his knees high, his blood moving more freely through his joints.

When he arrived at his bunk, James pulled on his shirt and threw the weighted pack on. He clipped the extra mags to the straps across his chest and secured his canteen over his rib cage, careful to make it tight enough not to jostle about.

Deck stood in front of him with his arms spread, motioning to the unhooked straps on his chest. James hooked them together, pulling them taut and looking over the rifle gripped in his hands before he spread open his arms for Deck to do the same for him.

Most of the other trainees were lined up in the center of the barracks. No one was talking. An urgent disquiet beat through the room. The cords of iron in James's stomach tightened. He took deep breaths, willing himself past the interminable hell of the wait.

Focus on now, he repeated over and over in his head, taking his place in line behind Marissa and Jamie.

James smelled the angst in the air around them. People's hands clutched the straps across their chests, their knuckles white and cheeks tight with strained tendons visible in each jawline.

Maria was pulling the straps of her backpack as tight as she could, the nylon creating grooves in her skin. Her face was emotionless, but James sensed the undercurrent of apprehension.

The exception in the room was Jerry, who stood a few people behind him and Deck, lithely waiting as if the pack was not even on his back. He lazily checked his weapon a few times, unconcerned.

"Gotta make it through, my man," Deck said suddenly, his voice toneless, not hinting at anything other than complete focus.

James reminded him, "Tall order, bud."

"True, true… very true," Deck replied before going silent.

The doors opened and the darkness outside filtered in, the artificial lights in the hangar creating long shadows from the bodies at the front of the line.

A vehicle approached them and Captain Hartsman drove into the wide-open doors of the hangar, riding shotgun in an off-roader.

All the trainees stood at full attention as Hartsman drove up to inspect the camp. The COs followed on foot, sweeping the line in twos, checking each person. One would check uniforms while the other looked over weapons and gear. The COs gave the go-ahead signal to Captain Hartsman from the back of the line.

Captain Hartsman stood and put a loudspeaker to his mouth. "Today is the first day of eliminations. We will begin with a run."

Hartsman's driver started the vehicle and headed up the path toward their normal running fields.

That was it? No more explanation? James thought, doubting the difficulty of these eliminations.

The line started easily. They were hardly in a jog.

He was confused but did not speak up, keeping the same rolling jog during the morning along with the rest of the camp. The bodies in front of him bobbed methodically, each footstep tamping down the dew-sodden grass. His breath was even and rhythmic. His heartbeat was steady and the blood flowing through his legs warmed his lower body.

The morning sunlight filtered through the dull clouds overhead. James was enjoying the day, forgetting for a second, he was at the beginning of eliminations from a military training program with a twenty-pound rucksack strapped to his back and a semi-automatic rifle gripped in his hands. Well, short-lived moment, he thought, the items on his person ripping him back to reality.

At mid-morning, the pace quickened, and James sprinted to keep up when the person in front of him pulled away without warning. He caught up and maintained the new pace, taking a sip from his water, the liquid splashing up his nose when he tilted the canteen to his lips.

His legs were tiring, and he was working harder to control his breathing. The rucksack weighed on his shoulders and the blood coursing through his body caused a steady, throbbing beat in his extremities.

They continued their pace until the sun hit noon when the person in front of him picked up speed again. His legs burned and the muscles in his back tensed under the weight of the rucksack. His hamstrings were losing feeling and his thighs felt like jelly. Streams of sweat created slick rivers down his back and legs. His senses were overrun with the stickiness of his t-shirt and salt stung his eyes.

The heat increased rapidly by midday and the sun remained solid above them. James waited for the next bounce in speed.

James focused on his feet, moving steadily one in front of the other. With a jolt, he realized, the person in front of him was at least four body lengths ahead. James gritted his teeth and, pooling his energy, sprinted to close the gap.

When he reached the person in front of him, his legs throbbing from the quick burst, he was startled by the new scene before him. What the hell happened? he asked himself, wondering why Marissa's hair was a light golden hue instead of its normal black. Maybe the sun and salt in his eyes were affecting his vision, he thought. He shook his head and when the same ponytail bobbed before him, he realized it wasn't Marisa. She must have fallen out of the line. He uttered a silent goodbye.

The sun was starting to fall in the sky and the strain on James's shoulders from the rucksack was more noticeable. They must have been running for close to twelve hours at this point James realized and with no break in sight from what he could tell. He shook his canteen, the final remnants of water sloshed around in the bottom.

As they ran, broken bodies littered the sides of the path, lying on their backs or in a fetal position on the ground, cramps and sores affecting their decimated limbs.

James stumbled, knowing it would not be long again before he would need to catch the newest set of bobbing shoulders in front of him.

James risked a glance back at Deck whose eyes were doggedly staring ahead, churning his legs through the flattened grass. James put his head back down, focusing his mind on the next step, keeping a keen eye on the distance between him and the closest trainee.

James lost all track of time and the sky around him was nearly dark when the person in front of him slowed their pace.

At first, James thought it was a mistake and maneuvered around him, ready for the other person to fall when he noticed the long line of COs waiting for them under a flood of lights. The COs stood with their backs straight and faces emotionless. They walked out in pairs to support the remaining runners stumbling forward into a brick building.

When James finally came to a stop, his body seized up with cramps, and the muscles in his legs were close to tearing. He dropped his rifle and bent over with his hands on his knees as two of the COs reached him, gripping him under his shoulders. Blood flowed to his legs, swelling his joints, sheltering them from the pain.

His mind was in a fog as he felt one of the faceless COs pour tepid water on the nape of his neck. The COs held his arms firmly while they half-walked, half-dragged him into one of the training buildings. He lifted his face and heard the rasp of his voice making a feeble attempt at asking for water.

The COs pushed James against a wall, propped him up, and left without a word. His knees shook with the strain of his own body weight and his legs were about to buckle. He forced the pain out of his mind, focusing on the moment and, with a monstrous amount of effort, forced his legs to push one last time while he locked his knees in place. He barely kept his eyes focused on the room. His head pounded and his mouth was bone dry. Each time he breathed, his lungs only pulled in hot air creating a scratching sensation in the back of his throat, making him nauseous.

When he was finally about to pass out, two more faceless COs, holding small lights inspected him. James noticed the blurry red patches sewn to their chests. He was guided to a chair and sat roughly. There was a prick in his arm and the two COs left as quickly as they arrived.

After a few minutes, James's senses returned, and he was able to observe the room lucidly. He was sitting at a desk with an IV sticking in his arm. Clear fluid moved through the transparent tube into his veins. The dense cloud obscuring his thoughts let up with each passing moment. There was a group of trainees in the room with him, each hooked to an IV.

A slow trickle of trainees supported by COs continued to filter through the steel frame door. All of them were treated the same as he, leaned carelessly against a wall where they were attended by a two-man medical team. After the medics finished their inspection, clear plastic tubes were shoved into the trainees' arms. The medics would wave over one or two of the waiting COs who dropped each of the recently IV'd trainees in one of the remaining desks. He wondered who else made it from K when Captain Hartsman walked to the front of the room. He spoke clearly with his hands clasped behind his back.

"Excellent job. There are ninety-two of you who made it. Now you will be taking a test."

James's glazed eyes stared out of focus at the captain. He could hardly move his legs and his upper body was stiffening rapidly. He struggled to comprehend the captain's instructions when he spotted a familiar face close to the captain. Deck sat kitty-corner a few rows in front of him, staring dully at Captain Hartsman. Deck's face, or at least the side of it James saw, was slack with exhaustion.

Is that what I look like? James thought, self-consciously touching his face and pulling up the skin he was convinced hung loosely off his jaw.

COs walked around the room depositing white bubble sheets and blue test booklets in front of each trainee.

Captain Hartsman's instructions continued. "Fill in all answers. If you do not know the answer, guess the best possible choice. If you skip a question, it will be considered an immediate fail." He turned on his heel and walked out of the room. The COs administering the exam closed the door behind Hartsman with finality.

An instructor James did not recognize walked to the front of the class and sat at the desk. "You have three hours to answer 750 questions. You may begin."

James was not registering directions. He was exhausted, dehydrated, and his legs were on fire. His head spun as he reached for the pencil in front of him. He opened the booklet, tearing through the tape on the side and read the directions.

They were given three hours to answer 750 questions? James took a deep breath, his mind raced as he turned the page to the first set of questions in the test booklet. The problems were simple, but James could not concentrate. He struggled to formulate cogent thoughts from the numb signals firing through his brain.

"If Jill is older than Maggie by two years, and Maggie is older than Katie, and Katie has a five-year difference from Jill, how much older is Maggie than Katie?"

James answered the questions one by one.

His mind raced through the sludge sticking to each thought. He was depleted of strength. He muddled his way through each question, not even noticing or keeping track of pages or numbers.

The questions kept coming. He barely noticed the medics making their rounds, checking the IV bags. The tape on his arm pulled on his skin when they changed the fluid bag.

After an eternity, James heard a whistle and looked to see Captain Hartsman standing in front of the room, wordlessly gesturing to his medics and COs standing in the wings.

James did not protest when two sets of arms lifted him like a rag doll. He was vaguely aware of the IV bag, handed to him by one of the medics. His body was led through a set of doors and staircases into a square room lined with cots. The room contained a whiteboard spanning the horizontal wall across from the door. It must have been intended for classes. In his delirious state, James smelled the dry erase markers, once the primary aroma in the tiled

66

space. Now the air was steeped with a musty scent of sweat and palm.

James collapsed on a cot once the COs guiding him let go of his arms. He felt a moment of relief when he saw Deck enter. He was draped over the arms of two medics and placed a few cots away.

James's legs were numb aside from the throbbing muscle spasms in the husks that used to be his thighs, and hot coals rolled down his windpipe when he took a breath.

He only recalled passing out when he woke up to another whistle accompanied by yells from the COs bouncing off the walls in the makeshift barracks.

"GET YOUR ASS UP! WE'RE NOT DONE YET! LET'S GO!" The COs ran around the room verbally attacking the tenant in each bunk, yelling at them to get on their gear and move.

James opened his sticky eyelids painfully and looked to his side still lying on his back. He found a new pair of boots, a vest, and a .44 Magnum with a chest holster in a pile by his cot. He got up, unsurprised by the stiffness in his muscles, and he struggled with the haze clouding his mind. He pulled the vest over his head, wondering how long he was asleep. The khaki vest pulled on his shoulders, putting a new strain on his aching body. He latched the straps across the front and a piece of tape lingered on his inner arm from the IV. He tore it off, noting the lack of sting from the hairs ripping out of his skin. Only so much the body can comprehend, I guess, he thought, waving his hand to get the tape off his fingers.

James knelt to tie his boots and blood rushed to his head while he strapped his laces. His mind swam, trying to keep up with the activity around him while his numb fingertips fumbled with the long, black strings wrapping them one by one around the metal studs, securing his feet in the dense, leather boots. He finished, grabbed his gun, and checked the chamber absentmindedly.

He slid the sidearm into its holster and looked over at Deck. When Deck saw James look at him, he motioned toward the door.

James looked around the room while he walked out, searching for anyone else in K still standing. The exhaustion obscuring his senses proved too much and he gave up.

The other trainees strained while assembling their gear. They were incessantly berated by the COs, but most of the remaining trainees were barely awake at this point.

James saw one trainee he did not recognize. The CO had singled him out to push the boundaries. James was at the door when he turned back, brushing past Deck on his way.

James stepped in front of the CO and lifted the vest in front of the trainee.

"Hold your hands up," James instructed.

The other trainee looked at him blankly and did as he was told. James dropped the vest over his head

"Sit down." James knelt, grabbing the boots next to the cot. James pulled them over the trainee's swollen feet and tightened the straps. While he laced the boots, he noticed a lull in commotion come over the room.

The CO, quiet when James came over, snapped out of his initial shock, and laid into James.

"What do you think you're doing?! Get the hell outside into formation!" he screeched in James's ear.

James pretended not to hear, handed the trainee his gun and assisted the next trainee, undergoing his own barrage of insults. Deck followed his lead, helping the other trainees in the room, receiving the same treatment from the COs as James.

The pair of them approached each cot, helping the lagging trainees until they were the only two left in the room. They followed the last of the stragglers outside making their way through the now quiet COs.

When they arrived outside, a group of leftover trainees stood at attention in front of Captain Hartsman leaning against the same vehicle as the previous day.

Captain Hartsman climbed in the passenger seat without a word. His driver pulled away at a quick pace.

James and Deck took the front, ignoring the single-file formation from the day before and trailed the four-wheeler shoulder to shoulder. James's legs warmed quickly at the brisk pace, and he was surprised by the initial lack of pain. His lungs flowed easily while the lactic acid in his body dissipated with each step. The day was cloudy, and a breeze gave them some relief from the baking sun they encountered the day before.

"Wish it was this way yesterday," Deck muttered.

James nodded, worried he would upset his equilibrium by talking.

They cut through the pastures and were mounting one of the ridges on the east side of the compound. Thin paths crisscrossed the hilltops with skate park-like half-pipes in track grooves at the top of each ridge.

James realized where they were headed when Hartsman's driver veered downhill, where the hills converged into an unnatural valley.

The lake on base came into view as they made their way into the valley leading to the man-made monstrosity occupying the east end of the base.

The lake was three square miles and 175 feet deep. James and the rest of K spent hours in and on the lake practicing boat maneuvers, underwater demolitions, one-man submersible trainings, SCUBA, and zero-oxygen operations. James could not imagine what they were about to do and readied his body for another grueling excursion.

Hartsman jumped off his four-wheeler and walked toward the small motorboat perched on the grassy shore. His driver followed and started the engine.

Hartsman picked up his megaphone and put it to his lips. "There are only thirty-nine of you after yesterday." He stopped, letting this sink in. "Today we will swim across the lake." His words were firm and unforgiving.

Hartsman stepped aside, pointing to the gear organized into neat piles along the bank of the lake.

"Each person should take a pair of goggles and a suit. You can leave the rest of your gear."

James stripped off his vest with no complaint, pulling the straps over his head. He yanked his boots off his feet, glad to be done with them.

It was the first time he looked at his feet since yesterday. Seven of his toenails were gone leaving behind a soft, red underbelly on the tops of his toes. Two were cracked in half and one was attached at the cuticle. He lifted the tip of the nail and pulled back, swiftly tearing it from his big toe. There was no pain.

He picked up his suit and immediately felt the weight of the material. He stepped into the legs and pulled the rest of the body up over his torso.

When he was done James walked to the edge of the water. He dipped his toe in cautiously and was taken aback by the frigid temperature. He looked around at the other trainees, their faces cast down, eyes blank, and bodies drained.

James glanced at Hartsman who put his hands calmly behind his back and stepped into the boat tied to the side of the dock. Once situated, he brought a whistle to his mouth, and blew, releasing a shrill sound penetrating James's core. The boat took off, guiding the group to the edge of the wake zone.

Without a second thought, James stepped into the water. He waded out with Deck at his side until the depth reached his waist. The cold water forced him to take short quick breaths.

The water lodged in the material of the suit, dragging him down with each step. Meanwhile, his feet trudged through the muck on the bottom, he could practically hear the mud sucking his toes, the muck climbing up his ankles with each step. He was nearly to his shoulders when he took a deep breath and sank under the surface of the water. James floated for a second, acclimating to the liquid environment. He collected his legs beneath him, finding himself on the edge of the lake's drop-off point. James planted his feet and sprung with all his might cocking his arm to come out with a strong stroke when... WHAM! He ran into a hard object and plunged under the surface.

His brain was assaulted by water. The scent of algae plugged his nose and the brown, frigid liquid ripped him to the bottom.

His lungs begged for air and when he looked up, the surface was gone. He reached his hand down, hoping to grab a handful of mud to gain his bearings, but there was nothing.

His mind raced, the water around him closed in and his vision dissipated. James kicked his legs with all the energy he could rally, pulling his arms to his sides in long broad strokes, propelling his weighted body swiftly through the water when his shoulder collided with a spongy surface.

Come on, James, fucking move, he cursed and tried to get his legs under him to push off the bottom of the lake. But it was too late. He had nothing left. His vision was gone and the icy tentacles from the water extended into his mouth and down his throat.

His grip on reality slipped, leaving James at the bottom of the lake, fighting for his life in frozen, black isolation.

CHAPTER 8

James was going to die on the bottom of the lake.

It pulled him lower, leaching the last remnants of strength from his arms. The muck created dusty clouds and his legs kicked out for a hold, burying themselves in the silt floor before losing their grip. His hands clawed at the water, but his fingers slid through the dusty murk.

James swallowed the same pocket of oxygen he recycled through his mouth dozens of times, holding off the water inching through his lips each second. His lungs burned while his mind fought the murderous impulse to breathe with every fiber of his being, intense fear blinding his decisions.

Scenes and sensations from childhood flooded his mind. The smell of the citrus mix his mom made at Christmas, buying his first bike, losing his first tooth in kindergarten, the antiseptic smell of the hospital when Michael was born, Kaylie's lips brushing against his. He was getting ready for a final push when a hand grabbed under his armpit and pulled up sharply.

His body was being dragged to the surface. He did not try to help. Let the COs do it all, he thought selfishly, allowing his body a second of rest. He kept his eyes closed when they surfaced and deflated the minuscule amount of oxygen left in his lungs before sucking in a gulp of air. It was the first time he realized the true joy of a simple breath.

He floated with his head tilted back, body limp in the water still relying on the CO to keep him afloat. He let the knowledge of his shortcoming sink into his conscience.

Fuck, he thought, I wanted to make it. He was annoyed at his failure, feeling the dull ache from where he hit his head when a sharp *thwack* buffeted his ear.

It wasn't the first time a CO hit him or any of the other trainees, but now? His eyes blinked open and the first thing he saw was Deck's grinning face struggling to keep him above water. Hartsman's boat purred toward the far shore off in the distance, the blue light on its stern flickering off the water illuminating the swimmers splashing behind him.

"You done dreaming yet?" Deck said.

James was stunned.

"What? How?" James stammered, still trying to get a grasp on what happened.

"You mistimed your push off the ledge and went smack into the back of Hartsman's boat. You sank like a fuckin' stone," he laughed, shaking his head. "You looked pretty stupid."

James shook his head, grinning now, still in disbelief.

"I guess I owe you a thanks, man."

"Time for that later," said Deck, waving him off. "Let's finish this shit, and then you can blow me."

Deck pulled his goggles back on and swam away with a smooth, long stroke. James shook his head, happy to still be in it.

He cleared out his goggles and caught up to Deck, swimming behind his lead. They followed the blue HOLO under Hartsman's boat across the lake. The light underwater brightened as they neared the churning wake.

Every few strokes James saw Deck peek under his arm back at James. James shook it off, glad someone was watching, but embarrassed at his near fatal mistake.

When they reached the other side, James realized how drained he was and surmised the cold water and lack of oxygen sucked the life from his bones. He forced himself on shore, stripping off the top of his bodysuit. His skin was cold to the touch, and he rubbed his chest to get the blood flowing faster. His head throbbed where he knocked it on the bottom of Hartsman's boat. He reached to touch the affected area. He expected some sort of sharp pain or a bump but got nothing. He shook his head, mumbling under his breath, "Water's cold enough to act as an ice pack. Go figure."

He made his way on land and saw Deck sprawled out on his back basking under the blanket of clouds on the faux beach, breathing deeply, his suit peeled off from the waist up.

James put his hands on his knees and bent over to catch his breath while he evaluated their surroundings. Hartsman's driver was parked at the edge of the beach landing. Hartsman stood with his hands clasped behind his back, watching the water and the trainees behind James and Deck.

He and Deck were followed by only seven others who were dragging themselves onto shore. They looked at one another with exhaustion, their eyes ringed and faces contorted in a mixture of semi-bewilderment and apprehension.

James looked out over the water to see if any more trainees were trying to make it ashore. Instead, small, high-speed rafts zigzagged across the surface of the lake, braced with COs and medics. The two-man crews were outfitted for lightweight dives with masks perched on their foreheads.

A boat pulled to a quick stop two hundred yards offshore. The CO and medic on board were efficient. They pulled on their breathing equipment and were over the side in an instant.

James waited with mounting anticipation for the diving crew to resurface but was interrupted by Hartsman's bark. "LET'S MOVE!"

James turned reluctantly from the scene, making his way to the line of remaining trainees.

Hartsman's face was a passive mask of authority while he calmly inspected the line of survivors in front of him.

James kept his face emotionless, ready for the next step. He wanted to get a better look at the others in line with him to check out the competition but resisted the urge.

"This is the final stage of eliminations. At the top of the hill, you will find packs of gear waiting for you. Once you put them on, head north. After a five-kilometer run you will encounter an obstacle course and will be engaged by enemy fire. Good luck."

James waited to see if there was more but realized it was all they would get when the captain turned around to walk toward his idling vehicle. They watched Hartsman take off, making his way back around the lake. We're in for the worst of it, James thought.

James and the other trainees kept to their line, thrown off by Hartsman's sudden departure. They waited at attention for a few more seconds before looking at one another, confused.

One of the trainees at the end of the line spoke up. "Fuck this," she said tiredly, her tone matching her attitude. "I'm going." She walked up the hill. James turned around long enough to see a short, stout body and cropped, brown hair bouncing up the slope with each step. Ballsy, he thought, worried the trainers were listening.

Other trainees followed, making their way up the grassy slope and James caught Deck's eye who shrugged before following them. James made his way after the rest of the group, shaking his legs as he jogged, working out the soft bursts of pins and needles in his calves and thighs.

When he reached the crest of the hill, he looked around, taking stock of the situation. Everyone was in different stages of dress, pulling off their wetsuits or pulling on the uniforms left in the piles for them.

The uniforms were a breathable, flexible fabric with sections molded to fit them snugly. The stomach, chest, and upper-back areas were a padded gelatin substance. The legs had similar pads over the thighs, hamstrings, and butt. James examined the suit

75

and remembered a class where they reviewed mobility and the uniform of a soldier. They learned about the different prototypes for combat suits, and he recalled a bulletproof gelatin substance.

Looks like we're the guinea pigs, James thought, holding the suit to the sky to get a better look at it. It was a relatively standard set of fatigues, but as he moved the jacket from the land to the sky, he noticed a slight change in the appearance of the material. The camo was color-absorbent, allowing the wearer to potentially disappear into the background. So cool, James thought, folding the jacket while he continued to dress.

James finished taking off his wetsuit and pulled on the gelatin skin. The upper body of the suit tightened over his torso while leaving his arms and shoulders flexible. He took a deep breath, feeling the fabric constrict slightly on the first breath and expand as the stitching adjusted to his body. It smelled like one of the plastic balls from the grocery store James played with as a kid, and he tasted the sour rubber engulfing his senses.

He put on the rest of the camo, pulling together the pieces as he did.

When he reached to pick up his sidearm, he saw his pants take on an earthy green and his sleeves were whiter with a hint of gray. They were mimicking the backgrounds from his vantage point, he realized, watching his arms change as he stood up. He clipped the sidearm on his belt trying to not get too distracted from the shifting fabric and picked up the rifle, checking its safety, before clipping the extra magazines into the loop across his chest.

When he finished checking himself, he looked around for the rest of the group. The remaining trainees were standing in a circle next to a cooler, occasionally breaking to dip their cups into the orange basin for water.

James made his way to the group, unconsciously licking his lips.

"Any other ideas?" a deep voice came from one of the trainees standing in the closed circle of faceless bodies.

James ignored them and grabbed one of the cups next to the cooler. He dipped his hand into the ice-cold water, enjoying the odd feeling of relief mixed with horror left over from the lake. He drank the water in one gulp, relieving his parched throat.

He took his time, filling his cup and taking another sip. He closed his eyes, floating through the darkness.

"We should move as a unit, fanned out in a single line to cover as much ground as we can," James heard the same deep, level voice say and snapped out of his reverie.

"I agree. We need to act as a unit, but we should stagger ourselves," a higher-pitched, familiar voice spoke. James sensed an edge to her tone. "I say one up front with a column approach. Lead gets replaced with next in line, fluid changes, and avoids holes in unit coverage. I'll take point first."

James heard the murmured agreement of the crowd while he reviewed the strategy in his head, silently commending the unknown speaker.

He finished his water and tossed the cup into the plastic bin on the ground, wiping his mouth with the back of his hand.

All right, ready, he thought rolling his shoulders, working out the residual knots in his back, let's do this.

He walked to the circle of trainees, edging his way between two uniformed backs. He started to take his initial assessment of the others when his eyes stopped on the face across from him.

Teresa stood, her back straight, eyes sharpened into a cunning glare, almost challenging anyone in the circle who dared look back at her.

James grinned. It was her on the beach. Should have known, he thought.

While she continued her death stare around the circle James caught her eye, smirking.

"It's agreed." The deep voice spoke again, and James connected it to the squat body across from him.

77

"Move with a staggered approach. Fill positions as needed."

James bobbed his head along with the rest of the group.

"I'll take second," Deck said.

"I'm with you," said James catching Deck's eye.

They walked toward the front, checking over their weapons while the rest of the group took their positions in line.

Teresa was in front, going over her ensemble. James stood in his place in line. He kicked a pebble at Teresa who looked up when the rock bounced against her foot.

"Good to see you, too," he said.

She grinned, giving him the finger. "Welcome to the party."

"Good to go," a shout announced from the back of the line and Teresa set off at a quick pace headed north.

The sky was still and overcast with mountainous clouds moving in swiftly to challenge the gray blanket obscuring the heavens. The wind picked up on the ground, matching the speed of the darkening sky above them. Long prairie grass dipped to the earth with each sweeping gust of wind. Invisible swirls of humidity broke across James's skin. James looked to the west and saw a wall of rain coming at them. He scanned their surroundings, seeking cover, but nothing stood out to him.

They needed to get out of here and fast, he thought.

Teresa had the same idea as they picked up their pace, now close to sprinting as the storm whipped random droplets of water through the air.

James looked to the hills in front of them, keeping his internal compass aimed north but edging east away from the storm. He squinted, trying to make out what looked like an overhang under a hill when he heard a sharp whistle.

Teresa turned around and without breaking stride put her two fingers between her lips letting loose another screeching whistle. She pointed straight ahead at the bottom of the hill to the tree line belonging to one of the forests on base.

"Let's pick it up!" she yelled, but James barely heard her voice from beneath the weight of the wind and was certain no one in the back could understand her.

Droplets flew into his eyes and the clouds took on a forest green hue with cavernous holes of black interspersed throughout its landscape. The clouds sparked with light at closer and closer intervals with neon tinged lightning, giving a definitive density to the squall overhead.

James smelled the moisture in the air and dust whipped into his face while he sprinted behind Teresa.

His breath was steady and the adrenaline coursing through his veins seeped into the rest of his body.

A lone rumble came from the west. Deck was running head down in an easy gait following Teresa's sprint. The land lit up and a clap of thunder crashed overhead.

James guessed they were about a hundred yards away when the storm started. The wind tore his face with pellets of rain and hail stinging his fatigue-reddened skin. He took one last look before he hit the tree line and then... nothing.

The world was darkness and trees.

His eyes adjusted to the lack of light. Teresa stood in front of him taking stock of the densely canopied forest.

James looked around, checking the treetops, feeling a sense of unease tense his stomach lining.

"That's weird. Rain stopped," said Deck, his voice trailing off, his eyes squinted.

Deck was right, there were no more droplets of rain. James's clothes were already dry, and the lack of any sign of weather made him uncomfortable.

James nodded. "Keep an eye out."

"Yep," said Deck, turning toward Teresa. "Let's get on the move. We need to find the obstacle course."

79

"Give it a minute. Let everyone regroup. Then we move out."

James circled the clearing. His gut churned each time he took a breath. His heart quickened with each beat, the fresh scent of the bare earth under the trees flooded his nose.

As the other trainees joined them, they took defensive positions looking at the eerily lit tree limbs spreading in all directions.

James scanned the woods, his gaze able to penetrate deeper each second.

Teresa spoke up. "Let's spread out, three wide. I'll lead."

"Can we take a two-second break?" the largest of the group asked, his voice exhausted and frustrated. James glanced over to find the trainee leaning his rifle against his legs with his hands clasped behind his head.

"No, we should keep going," the deep-voiced trainee said, picking up the rifle and handing it to him. "Come on. Let's move."

"Fuck, man. Two minutes," he said, pushing the rifle away.

James spoke up. "We should move."

The large trainee grunted, shaking his bald head. "Screw it."

He grabbed his rifle from the trainee with the deep voice who mouthed a thank you at James before moving back to his spot in the line.

James saw movement out of the corner of his eye. He was standing next to another trainee who was idly tightening the straps on her pack.

He instinctively pushed the trainee out of the way as a loud bang resounded and a white light blinded the area.

CHAPTER 9

White noise enveloped James's senses.

His eyes were closed, but the crumbs of soil in his mouth told him he was facedown in the dirt.

Getting to his hands and knees, James opened his eyes to a world of darkness and indistinct shapes. He let the light filter in through his pupils as the edges around him regained their sharpness.

An unknown body lay with its back turned to James, shoulders slumped forward like it was pushing a cart, its neck at an angle reserved for those asleep.

James kept his body low, trying to ascertain his position when he caught movement in front of him. James tensed ready to spring when Deck's face came into focus.

Deck held a finger to his lips and beckoned to James with his free hand.

James crawled to Deck's position.

"Where's your rifle?" asked Deck, scanning the area around him.

James had not thought about his rifle, happy to be moving more than anything. "No clue. Man, what the fuck was that?"

"No idea," replied Deck, his voice low. "You see anything?"

"A flicker of movement and then the light," said James, checking over his shoulder.

"Must be another test," Deck said dully. "Freakin' a. Or we found that obstacle course. Different than the other ones, huh?"

James did not answer, unclipping his sidearm before patting Deck on the arm. He motioned toward the body and signaled he was going to move it. He approached the body on the ground with Deck taking a knee behind him, eyes trained on the walls of vegetation around them.

James pulled the shoulder of the crumpled body to him, and the rest of the trainee's limp torso flopped over, settling with a thud.

James made a quick inspection of the neck, finding a pulse. Her chest was rising and falling. Her eyes were open halfway, the whites a gray dish soap.

"How is she?" Deck asked.

"Stunned but alive," said James, checking for broken bones.

"What's the move?" asked Deck.

James made up his mind about the next steps and was not looking forward to his decision.

"I'll carry her first. You lead," he said, half-hoping Deck would step in and be the chivalrous one.

Instead, Deck agreed. James knelt to get his hips under the body, leveraging her over his shoulders before hoisting the dense collection of skin and bones onto his back.

He stood, his legs unsteady beneath him for a second before they took off into the brush, Deck leading a few paces in front of them.

The trek was slow-going, and the heavy package James carried weighed on his exhausted body. Deck kept a solid but steady pace, so James was able to keep up. When he needed to, James would lean against a tree, taking some of the weight off his shoulders while Deck scouted ahead before motioning him the all-safe signal.

James was resting against a tree when Deck dropped into a crouch. James followed suit, hitting the floor of the forest with a thud, the trainee's body fell heavily on top of him. His hamstrings

82

screamed, struggling under the weight, and Deck disappeared into the underbrush. James waited, counting each second with the heartbeats in his legs.

Still covered by the foliage, James moved the body against the tree, easing the access to his sidearm if anything happened.

Suddenly, he heard a familiar giggle in front of him followed by a gruff-voiced Deck. "Don't give me the finger. Fuck you! You should have said something!"

"Oh, please, you're better than that," Teresa snapped. "You look so serious."

"Little help here," called James. He needed to get this damn body off him.

The shorter trainee with the deep voice showed up a few seconds later followed by Teresa. They pulled the trainee off James, immediately relieving the strain in his legs. Blood flowed through his sore muscles, providing a temporary respite from his cramps.

The shorter trainee hoisted the body easily over his shoulder walking away from them.

"Show off," James grumbled while Teresa helped James off the ground.

"Any idea what happened?" she asked while he brushed the dirt off his knees.

"Nope," said James, shaking his head. "A white light, face in the dirt, and all I know is I'm following Deck through the woods with a body on my back."

"At least it's not you."

James nodded, knowing how close he came to his moment earlier that day.

"Where'd you all end up?" James asked, now seeing the rest of the group emerging from their hiding places.

One of the other girls spoke up, her ponytail swinging behind her head. "Saw the light and hit the ground. We were all around each other and partially blind. Pumped into one another and made our way using the brush as cover."

James nodded. "Weird you missed us."

"We figured you guys were done," said Teresa in a matter-of-fact tone. "Instead, I see you were forced into carrying someone else by your supposed friend," she said, pointing a thumb over her shoulder at Deck.

"He wanted to!" said Deck incredulously. "James tell her."

"Is this true, James?" said Teresa, looking at James, faking concern.

"Well…" James said, playing into it.

"Un-fucking-believable," said Deck. "Don't carry one goddamn body," Deck grumbled bending to retighten his boot. "Well, what's the move from here?"

James spoke first. "Take turns carrying the casualty and get through the woods."

He glanced around at the group, appreciating the soldier-like nods agreeing with him.

"We'll take point," he said, indicating himself and Deck. "The rest of you fan out behind."

He found the biggest guy in the group and pointed at him. "Can you take carry duty?"

The big man nodded and walked over to the body, slouched against a tree where the other trainee left her.

James waited until they were situated in the middle of the group before he moved.

He kept the pace slow and steady, wading through the brush, sidearm poised in front of him, his body tensed ready for whatever was coming next.

"What the fu—" a random voice came from behind him when it was cut off by a sudden flash of light and a shattering of bark.

James dove for cover as more volleys of white light flew overhead. The noise was deafening, and the ground lit up as noise crashed around him.

When James turned around, he counted at least three more bodies on the forest floor.

"Let's go," a voice spoke, tugging his shoulder upward.

James stood hastily and moved after the person in front of him. James and the unknown leader huddled for a second behind a tree.

"You good?" James recognized Deck's voice.

"Yeah, I think we got lucky." He scouted their surroundings, expecting another volley of white light to pounce on them at any time. "We should go back."

"No way, man. They're out cold."

"Deck, it's what we have to do. We go back. Now, come on."

James pushed his way off the tree and ran back to the group, not waiting to see if Deck followed.

The bodies of the remaining trainees were strewn about the ground in awkward positions. James knelt by the first body he encountered, pulling it into a sitting position. It was Teresa. Her head hung down on her chest, her eyes half-lidded and unfocused. Deck appeared at his side and watched the dark forest surrounding them.

"She's out," James said, looking around at the rest of the bodies. "They all are."

He laid her back gently.

"We've got to get out of the fucking woods. Nothing we can do in here."

"Let's go," James said, standing up, eyeing an invisible path through the undergrowth to the north.

The two sprinted through the woods giving everything left in their bodies. White light exploded around them, and falling

85

leaves blurred their path. They ran frantically, fighting to get out of the hell they found themselves trying to escape.

James was more alert than any other time in his life. Each blast of light ignited the shadows and pathways ahead. He was at a new level of survival mode, and he was going to make it out of the woods if he needed to crawl out on his elbows, dragging Deck across the forest floor.

Finally, relief—light seeped through the foliage. James's breath ran ragged. His chest burned along with the woods surrounding them as smoke tendrils appeared out of the corner of his eye. With all his remaining energy, he broke through the edge of the forest.

James kept sprinting, blind from the sudden change in light. He was void of emotion or feeling, his body's primal fight sense took over.

He put his hands to his face, and they came away wet with blood, smelling like iron.

What the hell is happening? he thought, turning to find Deck who appeared as a stumbling blur.

Suddenly, he ran into a wall of bodies.

He was wrapped up by multiple sets of arms and smothered to the ground by a gang of others.

"Whoa, whoa, whoa! Easy there," a voice counseled.

"You're done, gents."

James did not recognize the voices. He swung his arms, his hands shaped in gnarled claws. His knees buckled and his head hit his chest before he lost consciousness under the crowd of bodies.

James didn't know how much time had passed when he blinked awake lying on another cot. The IV and tape on his arm was too familiar. He sat and leaned his back against a cool concrete wall.

"Morning, bud," Deck said, characteristically happy in another joyless situation. "You're finally up."

"How long was I out?" James asked, realizing this was the same room they slept in after the first day of eliminations.

"No clue. I got up about two minutes ago and been trying to figure out what the hell is going on."

A door opened and shut outside of the room followed by approaching footsteps.

"Visitors!" Deck said with mock enthusiasm, and James watched the doorway not sure what to expect.

Hartsman entered followed by two medics and his driver.

The medics approached James and Deck, taking out their IVs and doing routine checks.

"Easy, bud!" Deck exclaimed when his medic ripped the tape off his arm.

The medics were mute during their examination and James felt less like a person and more like a robot being prodded.

When the inspections were finished, the medics gave an all-clear signal to Hartsman who motioned for everyone else to leave the room. James, Deck, and Hartsman were the only ones remaining. The tense atmosphere was tangible. Even Deck remained quiet.

Hartsman did something uncharacteristic. He took off his hat, brushed back his short, cropped hair, and took a deep breath. James read the look on his face as a mixture of intense relief and immense stress. The fact that Hartsman kept such a placid expression the rest of the time was even more impressive given his current state, James thought.

"Man, am I glad this is over," Hartsman said more to himself than anyone else in the room. "I told them this was too much."

James was confused and glanced over at Deck who furrowed his brow, his head cocked to the side.

Hartsman put his cap back on. "At ease, gentlemen. Follow me," Hartsman said before he made his way through the doorframe.

James swung his legs gingerly off his cot, following Hartsman, tailed closely by Deck who was still shocked into silence for, what James assumed, was the first time in his life.

Outside James forced his feet to move as stiffness and lactic acid teased the muscles in his exhausted body.

A preternatural silence enveloped the training campus. A few groups of COs milled about performing chores, but most of them appeared to be packing the camp. There were groups of soldiers carrying bags of supplies and leaving them outside. When they walked by one of the buildings, anyone outside would stop and stand at attention saluting Hartsman until they passed, occasionally holding their position to get a good long look at James and Deck before they turned back to their activities.

James did not know if the stares were good or bad. Deck nudged him, dropping his voice only for James's ears. "Where is everyone else? We weren't out that long, right?"

James shrugged. "No idea. Don't know how they could have moved them so fast."

"Yeah," Deck said, nodding distractedly.

James pushed the problem aside and followed Hartsman to one of the administrative buildings.

Hartsman held the door open and motioned for them to enter. They stood in the foyer of the barracks and followed Hartsman down a hallway to a door with "Captain E.J. Hartsman" stenciled in bold letters across the semi-transparent glass.

"Gentlemen, please, take a seat."

James and Deck sat in the wooden chairs facing the desk in the office. James was still confused. Why were they sitting in Hartsman's office and where the hell was everyone else?

Hartsman sat behind the desk and leaned back in the chair, casually observing the two of them over the polished wood surface. "How do you feel?"

They did not know how to answer. Deck started with a "fine sir," but Hartsman cut him off, obviously upset.

88

"I was pretty pissed off they had you all go through this bullshit."

James nodded absently, now even more confused than earlier.

"I tried to change the rules, but they said this was the only way it would work. In a way, I guess it was," Hartsman said bitterly.

"You have been selected to join the other six who passed. You will be sent to a training facility where they will explicitly work with the eight of you to become an elite military unit. You have a week to rest and recuperate. Part of the time will be spent here to make sure you are all good medically. The last two days will be at home with your families. Afterward, you will be flown out to join the others. Any questions?" Hartsman looked back and forth at them both.

Deck went first. "Wait, so we made the cut? We're the only ones in the entire camp to make it?"

"Yes."

James's mind drifted to the other trainees, picturing Teresa's face in particular and looked steadily at Hartsman. "What's going to happen to the ones who failed, who got cut?"

"They will be brought to a separate training facility. Like this one, but they're Federation military now. Simple as that."

James remembered the original story alleging they would be sent home to enlist or get drafted but held his tongue. He was not sure what else to ask. What do you ask in a moment like this? James wondered.

They sat quietly until Hartsman broke the silence once again. "If you have any concerns or questions, talk to your COs. But if not, feel free to do whatever—lounge around, eat, read, watch TV, or sleep for a few days. I'm sure you're looking forward to seeing your families. Afterward, I don't have…" Hartsman paused rethinking his statement. "*No one* has a clue as to what you'll be up against."

James and Deck nodded, numbed into silence.

He waved toward the door, dismissing them. They got up to leave while Hartsman turned around to look out his window.

James and Deck headed to the empty barracks. They mulled over the events of the last few days and the uncertainty of the future in their heads.

James was still trying to grasp what occurred. He was going to be one of the elites. They reached the barracks and slumped against the opening to the hangar. The last rays of sun elongated the shadows of the trees beyond the tarmac. James and Deck were content sitting there not speaking, lost in their thoughts while they looked across the color-soaked grounds, embracing the present with such an uncertain future.

CHAPTER 10

Early evening light filtered through the multi-colored treetops lining his parents' block.

Neighbors he knew since childhood halted what they were doing to watch the armored SUV glide down the street. It stopped in front of his parents' house and James saw Michael looking out the window. He opened his mouth in an inaudible shout letting the whole family know James had arrived.

James grinned and hopped out of the car, taking a deep breath, happy to be out of the recycled air and dark interior.

"Here you go, man." Tim, the driver, brought James's bags around the side of the car and dropped them at his feet. "Have a great trip. See you in a few days."

"You got it. And let me know how you like the bar. My only perspective is as an underage jackass."

Tim laughed. "Will do. Later, man." Tim waved and jogged back around to the driver's side.

James watched his family eagerly pile out the front door, his mother and Michael leading the way.

"Did you get to shoot a gun?" asked Michael making a beeline for his bag and pulling the zipper back on the Federation-issued duffel.

"I did, and easy there. I've got all my crap packed in that bag," said James, smacking his hand away playfully.

"Hi, honey," his mom said, draping her arms around him and pulling him into a close embrace.

"Hi, Ma."

"Good to have you back," his dad said, stepping aside to let James greet his sisters. "How long did they give you?"

"Only a couple days. Got the next part of training coming up. Should get some more time after."

"Where are our presents?" asked Michael from the ground, who managed to unload James's bag on the front lawn.

"Michael!" his mom scolded.

James laughed. "When would I have time to get you presents? There isn't a gift shop at boot camp, bud."

"I was just wondering." Michael's face dropped and James reached into his bag and handed him one of his training t-shirts.

"Here, you can keep this."

"Thanks!" Michael said and promptly took his shirt off to try it on.

"Jesus, Michael, go inside first," said Caitlin as James and Mar followed their parents into the house.

"Mind your own friggin' business," Michael retorted.

"No change, huh?" James said to Mar.

Mar rolled her eyes. "You have no idea."

James's parents kept his room the same although cleaner, neater, and better arranged than he remembered.

She wasted no time getting in here, James thought imagining his mother sprinting to his room after he departed. Must have been a hell of a cleanup.

He picked up the HOLO on his desk and with the swipe of his finger and a quick retinal scan he was back online.

His messages were filled to the brim with well-wishers who missed him before he left. He could go back to those, he thought while he typed in Kaylie's name and pulled up their latest thread.

He wrote her a quick message:

Hey, in town for a few days. Would love to see you if you're around.

92

He was about to write a few more people when he thought better of it and put the HOLO back on the desk. He unpacked, his ears hyper alert for the sound of his HOLO's next notification. After hearing nothing, he left the room and showered. He threw his towel on the sink and entered his first private shower experience in months.

He could not stop thinking about Kaylie and how she hadn't responded yet. Maybe she moved on. Maybe she was not interested in seeing him again. Maybe she changed her HOLO tag. It happened on rare occasions. He hoped she was busy with school. Or maybe she didn't know how to say "no" without hurting his feelings. Or worse, maybe she didn't care and was ghosting him.

By the time James finished his shower, he was convinced Kaylie was messing with him the entire time and only found him interesting at all because he was a disappearing commodity. He also decided she should go screw herself and he would find another girl. Deck and he could "scoop up a couple broads," as Deck loved to say, whenever they wanted.

He hung his towel on his door handle and peeked over at his HOLO where he saw a message notification from Kaylie.

It took all his willpower not to dive across the room to read the message. James forced himself to calmly open his HOLO and read her response:

HOLY CRAP, YOURE BACK!!!! I would LOVE to see you!!! When are you free?!!??

That sinking feeling of rejection James had self-projected vanished.

His fingers had trouble keeping up with his mind as he responded.

Aespme! Are you free tonigh o Tommmorow?

93

He read his text back in his head, realizing he looked like a dumbass when Kaylie's message popped up underneath:

Haha, I am definitely free Tommmorow.;) Let's meet up.

James wrote his next message, more carefully this time:

Great, can't wait to see you!

He put the HOLO on his desk facedown and sat there for a second, grinning at the wall. His mind was racing. Less than twenty-four hours ago, he was sitting on his bunk chatting with Deck, enjoying their daily IV drip. Now, unconsciously rubbing the spot where the needle punctured his forearm, he was home before he shipped out to endure months of rigorous training.

"Weird world it is," he muttered.

He arrived downstairs to find his family ready for dinner. They ate in the dining room and James was sure neighbors heard them from three blocks away with the amount of noise they made. After dinner, James and his siblings cleared off the table. He noticed Michael pulling his weight in helping.

"I see some things have changed for the better, huh?" he said, nudging Caitlin and nodding at Michael who was putting all his muscle into carrying the cutting board with leftover chicken on it back to the kitchen.

"The second you left he began stepping up," Caitlin said offhandedly. "He looks up to you. Does everything like you and about cried when Mom said he couldn't sleep in your room."

"Sounds about right," James replied, under his breath.

"Be careful," Caitlin whispered. "He sneaks in there sometimes to sleep and makes the bed in the morning."

"Little room thief," James said in mock affront.

"I'll say."

James finished with the dishes and went back to sit with his parents. They talked about how life was going on around there. James said he couldn't talk too much about training, but he assured them he was safe, even if he harbored his own doubts.

"Well, what's the plan for tonight?" his dad asked, pouring his mother a glass of wine.

"I'm not too sure. I reached out to Kaylie and we're going to hang out tomorrow, but oth—"

BANGBANGBANGBANG

James dropped to the floor, his heart in an immediate panic while he grabbed a butter knife and rolled against the wall closest to the bursts of sound.

What the hell? He peeked over the ledge when he heard another set of explosions, accompanied by a long hiss and a colorful *pop* in the sky.

HISSSSS POPHISSSSPOPHISSSSSPOP

"What the…" James stood and looked out in the yard to see his friends standing there with a case of beer shooting roman candles and bottle rockets above the house.

Ed saw him through the window.

"James, you made it! Welcome home, man!" he shouted and sticking his arm in the air, set off another barrage of colorful flames.

The rest of his friends shouted congratulations and welcome backs, punctuating it all with a fresh salvo of explosions. James laughed as they ran around the front yard, occasionally stopping to light their handheld explosives and fire them in the air.

"We didn't mean to scare you but thought you may want to see these guys when you got home," his dad said, patting him on the shoulder.

"You all can hang out in the backyard. Try to keep it down for us, okay?" his mom added.

"Thanks," said James and walked out to meet his friends shouting a chorus of mistimed holiday cheers beneath multicolored blasts of light.

"HAPPY NEW YEAR!"

"IT'S YOUR BIRTHDAY!"

"MERRY CHRISTMAS!"

Conor walked up and handed him a beer. "Welcome home, man."

James took a sip and let himself soak in the moment, relishing each second. "Great to be here."

James awoke the next morning expecting a blinding hangover. His shades were open, but the normally caustic morning light was welcome, and he felt refreshed and ready, restless even.

This is new, he thought, getting out of bed, and heading downstairs.

The kitchen clock read 6:15 a.m., and he was the only one in the house awake. He glanced in the backyard and saw the remnants from last night's party picked up. He went out back to collect a few stray cigarette butts still littering the ground outside, and took a deep breath, enjoying the momentary freedom to stand alone in the morning air without being forced to do or say anything.

James got the strangest feeling. He did not understand where his motivation came from when he walked up to his room and put on his running shorts and sneakers. It was like he was in a dream. He returned downstairs, loosened up with some stretching in the driveway and took off at an easy pace.

They broke me, James thought. I'm one of those lunatics who runs in the morning, dammit.

He reached the top of the hill and decided to go to his old high school. He remembered Chris talking about it the night before.

"Yeah life's different now," he said, burping under his breath before continuing. "Not like the city's taken over and people are out goose-stepping or some shit, but the high school is basically becoming a processor for the Federation to take care of business. You should check it out. They've got temporary buildings going up all over the place on the fields."

James passed through his neighborhood streets with practiced ease, meandering through the cool fall air looking for differences. From his vantage, home was the same as Chris said. People's lawns stopped growing and colorful piles of leaves spilled off into the road. The odd soccer ball or football was lying on someone's front lawn and fall decorations, along with forgotten ones from last year, popped up randomly throughout the neighborhood.

It was all the usual until he arrived at the high school.

He stopped in his tracks at the sight of a massive tent engulfing the upper lot where the teachers parked. The entrance, normally unassuming, was fortified with guard towers on either side.

What are they doing out here, James wondered as he turned into the lot and nodded at the Federation security guard sitting with his feet on the wall.

The blacktop was touched up with Federation military symbols James recognized as troop directions from camp. He made his way to the back buildings where another tent spread ominously across the grass.

James approached the tent, pulled back one of the transparent gray plastic sidings and peered inside. All it contained were desks, chairs, and boxes stacked all over the place.

Still moving in, I guess, James thought. He continued down the hill only to be greeted by the same heavy gray canvas tops peering up at him. The soccer and baseball fields were also covered by sprawling tents. The football field and the track had smaller tents organized in neat rows.

James stood at the edge of the high school more confused than ever. He made his way back home, his mind lost in his thoughts trying to decipher what the hell the Federation was up to.

The rest of the day passed in easy form with his parents taking the family on a hike an hour north of their home. James thought to ask one of them about the high school but did not want to go into anything near military discussions. Better to be with them for the moment, he thought and tried to get all he could out of the hours he was allotted.

At the end of dinner, James felt a buzz in his pocket and read a message from Kaylie on his HOLO:

Still want to hang out?!

James replied quickly:

Definitely! What time are you free?

He started to put the HOLO back in his pocket but received another haptic alert seconds later:

Whenever you are. I'm at home so tell me when you're on your way.

"Hey, Ma, can I borrow the car?" James asked, unassumingly picking up his plate and his father's.

"What for?" she asked as James took her plate.

"Nothing. Wanted to see Kaylie."

"Oh, sure! You two can hang out here if you want."

"I think we're good," James said, avoiding eye contact. "Might grab ice cream, I dunno."

"Sounds good. Don't be too late. I want you up for breakfast."

"All right," James said, giving himself a mental high five. He whipped out his HOLO a second later and messaged her back:

Be there in a half hour.

James's heart pounded in his chest. He couldn't wait to see her. Before he knew it, James was driving to Kaylie's house. His hands tapped on the wheel as he drove through intersections and stop signs until he pulled onto her street and into the driveway.

He opened the car door and put one foot on the ground before he thought, shit, was I supposed to bring her something? He considered running to the store nearby to grab a little gift for her and made up his mind to leave when the door of the house opened. Kaylie stood in the doorway, smiling at him and waving.

James grinned and waved back, turning off the car and shutting the door, letting the auto locks click while he walked away.

Kaylie pushed the door open for him and he walked inside where they stood awkwardly for a second.

"Hey," she mumbled before lightly kicking his shin and grinning at him.

James grinned in return. "Hey, yourself," he said, kicking her lightly back.

"Ouch, that hurt!" she said mockingly, which made James laugh and the tension drifted out of the room. The muscles in James's back relaxed and he took off his jacket, hanging it on the coat rack next to the foyer.

"So, how's life?" he asked, bending to untie his shoes.

"Same old around here," Kaylie replied, leaning against the entrance to the living room. "Have you seen the high school though?"

"Yeah, took a run there earlier today," James said, thinking he might be able to elicit some information. "Seems like a lot's going on with all that popping up out of the blue."

"I mean, they've been setting it up for months now. Pretty slow going project, but all our sports are relegated to rec center fields in the city. Bizarre," Kaylie replied, unfazed. "Must not be too weird for you to see though, Mr. Federation Man," she said playfully, pushing him on the shoulder while he slipped out of his boot.

"You'd be surprised," James said offhandedly, looking to steer the conversation away from topics he wasn't able to discuss. "School's going well?"

"Oh, you know how it is," said Kaylie, making her way into the kitchen and motioning for him to follow her. "You saw how the seniors were last year. We're all in the same boat, but with the looming potential of a draft notice on our eighteenth birthday rather than our first legal beer."

"Sounds exquisite," James said sarcastically.

"You bet." Kaylie rolled her eyes. "But I have my sights set somewhere else I think."

"Yeah?" James sat at the counter while Kaylie opened the fridge and tossed him a water bottle. He caught it expertly and noticed the flash of a mischievous grin from Kaylie, trying to catch him off guard.

Kaylie leaned her back against the fridge, looking out the window. "Yeah, I may try to go the med route in the Federation military," she said casually, twisting off the top of her water. "They're going to get me through the draft. Why not beat them to it?"

James was surprised. He never pegged Kaylie as a Federation military girl, but, in a somewhat shameful truth, before training he rarely thought of women in the military at all. Why couldn't Kaylie join and be as successful as anyone he trained with? he thought.

"Good for you," he said, lifting his bottle to toast her. "To getting to the point."

Kaylie knocked her bottle against his. "Clink," she giggled.

They each took a beat enjoying each other's company. James felt comfortable, but there was a sudden and new tension he had never experienced before with another person.

He cleared his throat. "Any cool classes?"

"I mean, what classes aren't exciting?" Kaylie said with exaggerated eagerness.

She spent the next hour or so talking about high school, the students, teachers, classes, latest gossip, town news, state news, and Federation whisperings. James was fine sitting there listening to her, occasionally stopping her with a joke or a question. He was simply happy to let her talk. This was better than even the most basic fantasy he envisioned lying in bed at training camp.

"Anyway, that's about all going on here. How about you? Can you talk about your training?" Kaylie asked. James jumped. He had not been paying attention for a second and was knocked off his mental balance.

Kaylie grinned. "What? Can't say anything?"

"Not really," James said. "But no. I was realizing how much I liked this, sitting here and listening to you. Better than I imagined." Instantly, he was self-conscious, realizing he admitted to thinking about her while he was away.

"I thought the same. Sorry I've been such a blabbermouth," she said, smiling in return.

"No, it's been nice." James felt like the stupidest person in the world. It's been *nice*? He could have said nothing at all, and it would have sounded better than *nice*.

"Good."

They were quiet again and the same tension filled the room. James's heart raised in his chest, his face warmed, and he was about to start talking when he pulled himself back to earth. He remembered being in the forest, the thunder pounding overhead, and bodies strewn about.

101

He stood and every muscle in his body prickled with apprehension, but he forced himself to relax. He leaned back against the fridge with her, and she looked up at him.

He bent and kissed her on the lips. She hesitated for a second before kissing him back, the tip of her tongue seeking out his which spurred him along.

Seconds later, they fumbled their way through the hall to her bedroom, awkwardly pulling off each other's clothes and scattering them in the hallway until they were lying in bed with Kaylie on her back. James kissed her softly on the neck and face, letting the moment carry them from the world.

An hour later, James got in his car and shut the door while Kaylie stood behind the window watching him with the corner of her mouth curled up in a smile. He waved as he pulled out of the driveway. His mind was still in a fog, unable to fully comprehend the last couple of hours while he wound his way back home.

James awoke from his HOLO phone buzzing. He turned to see a flash reminder from his Federation calendar: *Pickup at 1100 hrs.*

He took a deep breath before pulling himself out of bed, not before shooting Kaylie a quick good morning message and getting a smiley face in reply.

He made his way downstairs to find his entire family up and about with breakfast in full swing. He checked the clock. It was only 7 a.m. What were they doing up? He looked around at the faces and, other than his parents and Michael, realized this may not have been a voluntary activity.

"James!" his dad bellowed. "Morning! Do you want pancakes or eggs?"

"I'll take eggs," said James, sitting at the counter in the kitchen.

Mar looked at him through heavy-lidded eyes. "They can't pick you up in the afternoon?" she asked.

"Cheer up," James said, patting her on the shoulder. "I'll be gone, and you can take a nap as soon as I'm out the door."

"Might start before," she mumbled, taking a long sip of coffee and melting into her chair.

"Bacon?" he heard as a plate filled with crisp brown bacon over a bed of paper towels appeared in front of him. Michael looked around the side of the ceramic plate expectantly.

"Thanks, bud," said James, popping a piece in his mouth savoring the greasy gratification.

"How was last night?" his mom asked, placing a steaming mug of coffee in front of him.

"It was good. She says hi, by the way."

"Nice girl. Glad you got to see her."

"Eggs and toast!" James's dad said plopping a plate of three eggs and two pieces of toast in front of him along with a portion of hash browns and two sausage links.

"Wow, thanks," said James. "I'll have to get a good nap during the trip."

"That's the goal," his dad said. He turned around working on the next plate.

"Do you know where you're going yet?" asked Michael, pulling up a chair.

"Not yet, but they didn't tell us the last time until we got there so probably won't know until I land."

"Are you nervous?" asked Michael.

James thought about for a second and realized he was not. Not like the last time. This time there were expectations. They were low and he doubted for a second he would understand what was happening until it did, but it didn't make him nervous. He was ready to accept his fate.

"Ready to go, I guess."

A buzz in his pocket distracted him and he pulled up his HOLO screen. It was a message from Kaylie:

What time do you leave?

James replied:

At 11 this morning. Eating breakfast now.

Kaylie:

Can I come see you off?

James:

I'd love that.

James's mom interrupted him. "Who are you talking to?"

"Kaylie. I think she's going to stop by to see me off. Is that okay?" he added tentatively, not wanting to text her back rescinding his invitation.

"Of course!" his mom said.

"All right. Cool." James finished his meal and hung out chatting with his family for the next couple of hours until it hit ten and he rushed upstairs to get ready.

He was downstairs in half an hour, showered, packed, and ready to go. He put his bag in the living room in time to see Kaylie pull up to the front of the house. He opened the door and walked up to the car to meet her.

As he walked, James realized he wasn't sure how to approach her. Hug? No hug? Kiss? He was lost in self-doubt when she stepped out of the car. When he met her eyes, he forgot what he was worried about and kissed her on the lips.

"Hey," he murmured.

She smiled back at him. "Hey."

James took her hand and they walked back toward the house where James caught a glimpse of Michael and Caitlin's heads ducking under the windowsill.

"Hi, Kaylie!" James's mom said, emerging from the kitchen and hugging her before his dad came out and introduced himself. As they made small talk, James kept his eye on the street. After a while, a black SUV turned into the driveway and Tim hopped out.

The room quieted, and James shouldered his bag.

"Come on. We've done this before, guys. Don't worry," James said, trying to be cheerful, but he knew what was going through their heads. He took Kaylie's hand and walked out the front door.

"Tim, how you doing?" he said, handing his bag to Tim's outstretched hand.

"Good, man, good. We've gotta get a move on, but I can give you a few minutes to say goodbye."

James once again went through the process of saying goodbye to his family, but this time it seemed harder for them than his first exit. There were more tears, and even Michael was more vulnerable, holding onto James's waist a little longer when he hugged him.

James hugged Kaylie last, kissing her lightly on the lips. "I'll miss you," he said softly.

Kaylie pulled him in and kissed him one last time. "Come back."

He smiled at her and with a final wave got into the back of the SUV.

"You ready, man?" Tim said, looking at him from the rearview mirror.

"Let's go!" James said with false enthusiasm.

They pulled out of the driveway and James rolled down his window, waving once more at Kaylie and his family before driving up the street.

James had the benefit of being the one who got to leave. He was responsible for his risks. The hardest part about loving someone in his position was the absolute lack of control. They were about to undergo the same all over again with even less knowledge than the first time but with the hope he would come back home. How many more times could that happen?

CHAPTER 11

Waking up from the jolt of a plane's tires hitting asphalt is getting old, James thought, duffel in hand standing on a random tarmac next to Deck, watching yet another plane fly away.

He checked out their surroundings. The air was dry and crisp with a bite of cold but no breeze. They were in a cleared-out valley, neatly forested to make it inconspicuous to overhead traffic. They were deep enough in whatever mountain range where smaller planes would have a difficult time getting through the airspace without crashing from turbulence and big planes would not even bother to pass close enough to the ground. Intentional seclusion, James thought, eyeing the wall-like peaks.

"Another paradise, I guess," Deck said, turning in a circle.

"We have different versions of paradise," James replied, putting down his bag and taking a sip from a water bottle.

"You'd think we would get some nice service at this point. A couple of elite training studs like us," Deck said, sitting on top of his Federation issue bag. "But noooo, can't make anything easy."

"Can't disagree."

The last few days were a nightmare. They transferred planes four times at five different bases, were picked up, dropped off, and turned onto so many false trails they gave up trying to determine where the hell they were.

James was even surprised by the sun when they emerged from the back of the latest cargo plane where the red glow from the exit signs were their only source of light. Now they were sitting alone again, no clue what was happening next, on a hideaway base in the middle of a mountain range.

James heard the purr of an engine and nudged Deck who was staring dejectedly at the ground shaking his head and mumbling under his breath.

"Look sharp. We've got a buddy."

Deck groaned and made a show of getting to his feet but straightened out with a twist and crack of his back. They waited shoulder to shoulder, standing at the ready.

A vehicle, like the one Hartsman used, driven by a man wearing desert camo came into view. The man's face looked well-weathered but was defined by the sharp angles old men develop when they spend their days in a gym. He had a strong jawline with a heavy brow and a receding stretch of silver hair, fashioned in the traditional military crew cut. He pulled up, turned off the ignition, and stepped out.

James and Deck stood at attention. James was not sure what to make of the man as he circled them, inspecting their stance, their bags, and their clothes. His eyes were pervasive, and James would not have been surprised if he walked up and sniffed them.

His initial review complete, he faced the two of them, his upper body rigid, lithe, and predatorial.

They saluted and Deck spoke first. "Sir, Private Whelan reporting for duty."

"Private Coffey reporting for duty, sir," James said.

The man did not say a word. His deep, cold, gray eyes could have been mistaken for stone. James was committed to return the glare without awakening the animal he sensed lurking beneath the surface.

Finally, the man broke eye contact and walked back to his vehicle. He spoke in a deep, clear, authoritative voice. "My name is General Croyton. I will be your CO while you're at Elite Training Camp. The others are waiting for you in the barracks." He

108

turned the ignition and looked back at them. "Grab your gear and fall in line."

Without another word, he pulled away. James glanced at Deck who looked equally puzzled. They threw their packs over their shoulders and ran after their new commander.

They followed him off the stretch of asphalt onto the hard-packed dirt next to the runway. Croyton led them on a hidden path into the forest. The woods on either side were practically impenetrable, and James smelled the decaying earth mixed with the fresh scent of late seasonal flowers blooming through the dry mountain air.

They sped through the trees, coming across trailhead offshoots, and winding their way along the path. They even crossed an immensely wide runway. James looked to see the trees intertwined, creating the illusion of a naturally occurring forest beneath its branches. Where am I? he thought, shaking his head in wonder at the world revealing itself around him.

They came to a clearing where three buildings of varying sizes stood in stark contrast to the rest of the wooded encampment. James determined one of them was some sort of hangar because of its wide, unobstructed front and the array of machinery organized within. A grounded silver Airstream with a metal chimney sat in the middle of the clearing. The final structure was fashioned in a similar style to the trailer with stainless steel plates connected crudely by iron bolts and soldered seams but was wider and had two spouts at opposite ends of the building. James slowed as Croyton stopped his vehicle ahead of them.

The ground was barren with a layer of dry dirt covering the open areas, and grass sprouted along the edges of the buildings. The air smelled used, and the occasional wafts of motor oil gave a distinctly human aroma to the space.

"These are the only buildings in the compound."

From his vehicle, Croyton pointed to the warehouse structure. "This is your armory. In there you can find everything from a pocketknife to a Jeep Wrangler mounted with a rocket launcher. He stepped off his side-by-side vehicle and walked toward the larger of the two buildings next to the hangar. "These are your barracks. There are eight of you. The rest got here earlier today, so take the remaining bunks." He pointed to the Airstream in the middle. "Those are my personal quarters. Any questions?"

James and Deck shook their heads and walked behind Croyton to their new bunks. He stopped outside the barracks and motioned for them to go inside. "Get yourselves settled. Orientation will be in an hour." With that, he left them.

Deck entered first. The room contained eight beds, four to a side. Next to each bed was a small desk with a chair, a dresser, a nightstand, and a lamp. In front of each dresser were canvas bags with, what James assumed, were new training fatigues.

The other six people in the room looked at them calmly and James got his first glimpse at the squad of handpicked elites. There were five boys and one girl. The girl sat on a bed near the door at the front of the room while the rest of the trainees milled about their bunks casually.

Deck sauntered across the floor and took the last bed available on one side which left James the bed directly opposite. He dropped his duffel at the foot of his cot and stole another glance around at his new crew before he unpacked.

This is awkward, James thought while he took his folded clothes out and filled the top drawer with his boxers.

When he turned back around, a tall well-built almost-man with dusty hair, intense brown eyes, and a five o'clock shadow stood before him. His stance was so straight James wondered if he wore a brace for a second.

The stranger stuck out his hand. "My name's Kyle." Kyle pointed over his shoulder to the tall, black-haired trainee standing behind him. "That's Kevin. We came from the same camp."

James reached out his hand to Kevin and was greeted by another powerful grip. "I'm James. That's Deck. Same deal."

110

Two more in the room approached the gathering. The first was shorter than James with a shaved head and a stout upper body. His voice had a southern twang when he spoke. "My name's Clint, and this is Bob," he said, pointing at the thin blond trainee standing next to him. "We got the beds surrounding your boy over there."

"I'm Jon by the way." A trainee with curly black hair and a Latin accent poked his head around Kevin reaching a hand across the circle.

Deck moseyed over as introductions continued.

James was overwhelmed but got more comfortable while talking with the rest of the group.

"Yeah, so I ended up telling colleges I would play and next thing you know, here I am," said Kyle, leaning against James's dresser. "Who knows. Maybe nothing happens and I can get back into the recruiting cycle."

Deck snorted. "Don't count on it."

"I'm ready to get this show on the road," Clint said, unconsciously shuffling his feet, "Where were y'all training?"

"Out on the plains," James said. "You?"

"Shit, somewhere in Mexico."

"Damn, I didn't know they were shipping kids there," said Jon, throwing his hands in the air in frustration. "Would have been an easier place to send me rather than fucking Canada for training. Traveling from the Southern Federation up north was brutal."

"Gotta suck to leave paradise," Clint said, looking dreamily in the distance.

"You've never been to some of our cities…" Jon replied, sitting at the end of James's bunk. "Beaches are beautiful but the city?" He shook his head. "No es bueno."

James nodded as if he understood, trying to hide his ignorance. He looked at Kevin. "Where're you from?"

"Louisiana," he said, his voice deep and laconic, almost like he spoke in song. "Kyle and I were in the desert somewhere for training.

"Damn, they threw us all over," Bob jumped in, the pace of his voice was hyper but focused at the same time. "I'm from Michigan and ended up in the deep south. Must have been Florida or Georgia. Either way, too hot for me. Sounds like they had eight or nine different places with all of us."

James nodded, musing aloud, "Wonder how many of us they pulled?"

"As many as they needed," said Deck, which put a brief pause on the rest of the conversation. James drifted back to the eliminations, practically feeling the cramps in his legs and burning in his lungs.

Kyle broke the silence. "We should probably head out."

They all made their way to the door. James started to follow them out of the room but stopped and unzipped his duffel taking the letter from his father out and placing it in the top drawer of his dresser.

As he made his way out the door, he noticed the only girl in the group walking towards the armory alone with her hands at her sides, her wavy dark brown hair cut off above the shoulder.

He caught up to her and reached out his hand. "My name's James. You?"

She looked over, took his hand in a quick shake, and smiled. "I'm Stacie. Sorry, didn't want to interrupt things earlier."

James grinned. "Nah, don't worry," he said reassuringly. "We're all in the same boat. It's nice to meet you. Where'd you come from? You know, training-wise," he added.

"Texas. Hot as hell," she replied. "*Not* something I'm used to," she added hastily with emphasis.

"Damn," James commented. "Where're you from? Home-wise this time."

"Canada. On an island off the East Coast."

"Nice. Never been but love the oysters."

Stacie laughed. "Well, you're alone there."

"You don't like them?" James asked with mock incredulity

"No. They're disgusting," Stacie said, making a face and fake gagging.

"Looks like you're the only girl who made it."

Stacie sighed. "I was hoping the last two would change the balance a little bit," she said, bobbing her head in Deck's direction and back to James before shrugging. "Guess it's up to me."

They stopped talking when they saw Croyton standing rigidly next to eight chairs in two rows of four inside the mouth of the armory. Apprehension and intrigue swirled in James's gut as he took a chair in the middle of the back row. Deck sat on the aisle next to him as the rest of the chairs were filled in by the team.

The group waited as Croyton stood silently in front of them. He held them there, letting the moment build into an uncomfortable standoff, their combined breathing and haphazard chair creaks were the only sounds in the room until he finally broke the silence. "You have been picked to become the first Elites trained by the Federation."

Croyton paced in front of the group. "Because this has never been done before I have devised a training program that, in my opinion, is only possible with your specific skillsets. However, there is one reason and one reason only you are all here today. The Federation has received information we will be attacked in a unified effort by our enemy and their newly acquired countries."

James was not shocked by the information but was surprised by Croyton's offhand manner in sharing it. He listened carefully as Croyton continued. "The Asian Republic, or as it's known by the rest of the Federation, the BlankZone, is still, as far as we know, in charge since the Melt. We know when the Melt began, and we know it happened for a reason. However, I can tell you right now we don't know *how* or *why* it happened. Nor do we understand how they managed to keep an electro-chemical border stable for so long."

What the hell is an electro-chemical border? James thought while Croyton continued.

"Our sources indicate there are growing signs of militaristic development within the BlankZone.

"It seems the Forgotten World has built an empire behind this impenetrable curtain. We'll talk more about them as we dig deeper during training, but to summarize they started as a low-level group with no particular strength focused on using extremism to create a different world arrangement by any means necessary. Their vision was along the lines of global unification, but they never got a foothold. Shortly before the Melt, they went silent. Their activity was non-existent, and we thought they were killed off by a different organization that didn't like their ideals. Our intelligence now leads us to believe they found a way to amass power, consolidating it within the Asian Republic, and using it to throw more than half the world's population into stark isolation for over four decades.

"Now, we think they are going to come for us. They've managed to take over all of Asia along with the remaining parts of Eastern Europe still standing after the Melt. We can assume whoever reigns over the BlankZone will work on expanding its reach. The difference is this time they don't have the benefit of a cataclysmic power outage or nuclear blanket knocking out the resistance."

Deck's hand went up and James was surprised when he heard Deck still decide to speak under Croyton's icy silent response. "Why not? They've done it before. Why can't they attack us with a nuke this time?"

"We don't think they did," Croyton replied, an edge of annoyance in his voice. "They need people, bodies. Their goal is to take over, not destroy, and, given the population currently under their control, they can."

"But wha—" Deck was cut off by Croyton holding up his hand.

114

"We can dive into the details when the time comes. But for now, shut up and let me finish." Croyton's voice was controlled rage and James exhaled as Deck sunk back in his chair.

"This will be the first war for the Federation, the first external war in the Americas since the United States gained its independence in 1776, and the largest attack on our soil since Pearl Harbor," Croyton continued. "The government has decided to do what it can to prepare." He paused. "That includes all of you."

James wondered about the other moves. The general rested his gaze on James. "Now you are all fully aware of the situation we are dealing with, I'll go over your training."

Croyton broke eye contact and James shook off the stare, wondering if anyone else noticed.

Croyton picked up a stack of HOLO emitters and handed them to each person. James held it on his lap while Croyton finished his distribution and walked back to the front of the room.

He put on a pair of steel wire glasses while initiating the HOLO screen and thumbed through the electronic pages explaining the contents. "In here you will find the training regimen I have scheduled for us. As you can see, there will be a heavy emphasis on physical fitness, hand-to-hand combat, tactical guerrilla warfare, and knowledge of each BlankZone country's former battle systems. To understand how they fight now, we need to know how they evolved.

"By the end of all this, you will not only be the most physically prepared soldiers to touch a weapon, but you will also be the smartest. You will truly be an elite class."

Croyton stared hard at the group, threatening them to challenge him. "You will follow the orders of the Federation and because of your efforts, we will win this war." James's skin pricked and his hair stood on edge as Croyton finished.

The room was quiet, and Croyton nodded. "Read these over tonight and be ready in the morning. We wake up early."

Deck started to raise his hand, but James caught his arm on the way up before Croyton noticed. He gave Deck a subtle shake of the head and Croyton walked out the armory entrance.

The others got themselves up and headed back toward their barracks. Deck and James shuffled out of their row, following behind the group.

"I was gonna ask if we can ask questions because he hadn't exactly made his point clear," Deck said sarcastically.

James grinned. "I don't think he would take your brand of humor as well as Hartsman and Jackson."

"Well, at least we're getting some information now," he said, absentmindedly picking under his nail. "Do you think they'll keep the info coming?"

"Enough to keep us interested," James said with a shrug.

"Ahh the predictability of it all. Yank us around the country and back again until we're too numb to ask anything."

"I don't plan on relaxing," James said, eyeing his surroundings before he continued in a lower voice. "Did you see Croyton? The way he looks at everyone? It's different, like he's sizing us up, but not the way they did in basic. It's more...severe."

Deck shook his head. "Can't say I noticed, man. Don't worry about it for now." Patting James on the shoulder, he walked through the barrack doors.

James took a second to clear his head. Could he be making it up? Was it all in his head? He looked at the red clouds and darkening skyline. He needed to put it out of his mind like Deck. He made a promise to try and ignore his inner monologue.

The rest of the team was quiet and self-reflective so James sat on his bed and pulled out the HOLO, unlocking it with a scan of his palm.

The home screen displayed different folders and James tapped on the one titled "Physical Regimen" in bold letters. He perused through the program, studying the exercises and tests they would undergo shuffling back and forth to the other bold headings with titles like "Battlefield Study" or "Explosives Training" until he got to the section "Specialist Tactical Simulations."

Intrigued, James read through the section. Each of the simulations had a leader, two operatives, three mechanics of varying skillsets, a medic, and a scout. Guess we know the grading curve, James thought, closing the HOLO with a swipe across the screen. He stretched in his cot looking at the ceiling as the lights shut off, wondering what the next months carried in store for them.

He must have drifted off because he was awoken by a crude blast from an air raid siren.

James jumped up and began making his bed. Croyton barged into the room and flipped on the lights to find them all awake mimicking James's actions.

Croyton yelled, "Everyone, stop!" He planted three swift steps landing in front of James. "What are you doing?" he asked, pointing at the bed.

"Making my bed, sir…" James said, confused. This was an activity they did every morning in basic training.

"Well, we're not going to be doing that anymore. No more making beds or doing dumb crap. Here you are learning to kill, not how to be a goddamn homemaker."

James nodded and continued looking straight ahead.

Croyton stared coldly into his face. "Do I make myself clear, Private Coffey?"

"Sir, yes, sir!" replied James.

"Good, let's move. Get your gear together. You have two minutes."

James scrambled to change as fast as possible throwing off his shirt and pants. When he pulled on the new gear the underarm to the suit separated, leaving a gaping hole running up his side. Panicking, he pulled it on, hoping to reattach the seams in the next thirty seconds when the pieces glued together and morphed to fit his body.

"Damn, that's cool," Bob muttered across the room, having made the same discovery, watching while the clothing zipped up the side of his pant leg.

James pulled on his boots, they employed the same auto-fit functionality as his suit zipping up the seams instantly. He glanced around the room to see where everyone else was in the process. Stacie finished dressing first, and James followed her out the door. They stood abreast at attention while Croyton waited for the others to join.

When the rest of the line filled out with the remaining six team members, Croyton began his explanation.

"We will begin each day for the first three weeks with a five-mile run and one-mile swim followed by a course. After the first three weeks, we will double our distances." He walked over and sat in his four-wheeler, turned it on, and looked back at the group over his shoulder. "You will all be able to maintain a mile with full gear in five minutes and a mile swimming in under fifteen. Your course goal will vary day to day with objective times depending on the design I choose."

Even with a cursory review of the numbers Croyton mentioned, a pit grew in James's stomach. Muscle cramps from eliminations came to mind while phantom pains spread through his legs. He tasted the acidic breath of oxygen-depleted air seeping out of his lungs again.

Croyton faced forward on his vehicle and raised his voice over the dull purr of the motor. "Let's go."

He followed the command with a long shrill whistle and made his way down the path to the landing strip.

James and the group followed in a staggered formation behind the vehicle.

At the beginning of the path, Croyton made a sharp turn onto an invisible trail. James did not think Croyton's side-by-side even fit on the narrow strip and was unsurprised to see bare

118

branches with their stripped leaves lining the ground on either side of the trail.

The group of trainees entered single file and James filled in behind Kyle. The pace was difficult, but mercifully consistent and James found a nice rhythm.

The woods were one of the most mysterious phenomena James witnessed in his life. It was both jungle and forest at the same time. The pathways contained the bright greens James saw in movies and documentaries about the rainforest, while the plants he grew up with mixed in seamlessly. The pathways, though thick with vegetation on either side, were well-maintained without branches crossing their way or impeding their running progress. James wondered how all of this was even possible. I wonder where we are, he thought, realizing the only person they knew about on base besides the trainees was Croyton. The staff must be huge. Who else was here? He puzzled at how this perfectly camouflaged mecca of military training existed as its own Eden without interference from the outside world.

They followed Croyton for close to an hour winding through the intricate pathways in the forest when the trailhead stopped, and they came to the edge of a body of water. The scene in front of them was breathtaking. Crystal blue water was nestled between barren, pine-dotted mountain slopes.

James walked to the edge of the lake and kicked off his boots. He took a step into the shallow edge of the lake and the icy water gripped his foot, but the sensation stopped at his ankle where the pants to his training suit began. Croyton stood at the end of a bare wooden dock. Two buoys floated in the still water, one closer to them, the other off in the distance, its neon green markings glowing eerily across the glassy surface.

Croyton yelled, his voice carrying naturally over the distance. "There are goggles in the box at the end of the dock," he said, pointing to a cardboard box sitting on the ground. Kyle ran over to retrieve it while Croyton continued. "Swim around the far buoy, come back, and do the same. Ten laps are a mile."

Kyle returned and handed James a pair of goggles.

"Thanks," James said, pulling the plastic rims over his eyes.

"You got it, man. Good luck," Kyle said before walking to the next person in line.

James waded into the water, and once he was up to his waist took a long, smooth stroke out into the lake, pulling his weight easily through the flat surface. His hands and feet were still cooler than the rest of his body, but he warmed up, swimming through the increasingly choppy waters from the rest of the team's wake.

He hit the last lap before he knew it, keeping a steady pace, but his body was tiring. The wear and tear from running five miles settled into his legs and the threats of a cramp were sneaking into his muscles. This is going to be a rough few weeks, he thought, pulling past the buoy, finishing his last lap, and striding onto dry land.

Croyton waited with his arms across his chest while they waded out of the water and pulled back on their training boots.

"Bizarre," Clint mentioned under his breath, looking to the ground as his boots molded to fit his feet.

"Spooky," agreed Kevin.

"All right," Croyton said, his hand resting on the front of his transportation. "Now you have your first course, a three-mile path in the forest. Interspersed throughout you will find red glow sticks marking where you should go. I'll watch your progress."

Croyton slid behind his steering wheel as he finished his instructions. "You will hear a whistle. Then you can begin. Rifles are racked at the head of the course's trail." He peeled off in a puff of dust

James did not bother to track his route into the woods. Instead, he followed Kyle and Kevin to the edge of the forest where they were picking up rifles and turning them over in their hands.

James took one and checked the chamber. Ensuring it was empty, he turned it over, acclimating to the weight and balance. He picked up two magazines, inserted one into the bottom of the rifle, and racked a bullet in the chamber. He flicked on his safety before pocketing the extra magazine and turning around to see the rest of the group finishing the same process.

"Odd day," said Kyle, standing next to him, holding the butt of his rifle in the sand, and balancing his hands on top of the muzzle.

"Too reminiscent of basic," James said.

"No kidding. I guess this is how they treat us now. Travel to an unknown location, learn how to use a weapon, and then we're going to run you into the ground."

James snorted. "Could be worse though."

"I guess," Kyle said before walking away to inspect the trailhead.

James felt antsy and caught Deck's eye. He nodded at the trailhead, ready to get going. Deck wordlessly followed James to the edge of the course.

They walked past Kyle and into the forest. James glanced at the rest of the group trailing behind them, eyeing the walls of the forest path for any signs of movement.

The path eventually forced them to walk in a single-file formation with James taking the lead. All light from the late morning sun was blocked by the dense foliage above and James wondered again how they managed to sculpt the world around them in such a unique fashion.

There was a pat on his back and Kyle motioned at a junction ahead. As they approached, they found a rock face looming before them. The whole climb was probably fifty or sixty feet straight up. James rubbed his hands together approaching the rock face, about to grab on and climb when Stacie came to the front of the line, attached her rifle to the front of her suit, and started her ascent. Deck shrugged at James and followed Stacie up the rockface.

Bob stood behind him with Kyle. "You two go ahead. I'll keep an eye out here with the rest of the crew. We'll follow when we get the all-clear signal."

James grunted and gripped the first handhold, pulling himself up as Kyle followed.

The rock was lined with small ledges, suitable for grabbing with fingers and toes, but perilous once more than fifteen feet off the ground.

James turned back to see the rest of the group concentrating dutifully on those climbing while they kept an eye on the forest around them. When James looked forward again, Stacie was no longer visible, and Deck's legs were disappearing over the edge. James quickened his pace. As he climbed, the path at the top narrowed to the width of the trail and he edged his way toward the center. When he reached the top, he dug his foot in for one last push over the edge when he realized he was pushing on air. His foothold had completely disappeared.

"Holy crap!"

He heard a yell from behind him.

James's body slipped backward. He shifted all his weight to his shoulders, slammed his upper body on the top of the ledge, and swung his feet around. Completely breathless, he turned to see Kyle hanging with one hand a few feet from the top.

"It disappeared," he said, his face painted in exertion while he strained to keep his body steady.

James reached out his arm. "Grab on."

Kyle swung his other arm up and James braced to take the weight.

Kyle let go of the wall. His heavy frame was entirely supported by James holding him off the edge of the cliff.

"Come on, man. Dig your legs in to get up." James gritted his teeth and held on while Kyle rappelled the rest of the way up the slick rock face using James as his rope.

When Kyle reached the top, James fell onto his back while adrenaline filtered through his body. His breath was still shallow and his ribs hurt, but he knew how lucky they were.

James pushed the doubt out of his mind, checking over the rest of his body and propped his elbows beneath his torso to sit. He lifted his shirt and saw a bruise beginning to form.

"What happened?" Deck said from behind them. He glanced at James's stomach and winced. "Damn, that looks bad."

"Seriously, what was that?" Stacie said, pulling Kyle to his feet.

"The holds disappeared. One second, I'm moving up the rock about to hit the top, the next second my hand is the only thing holding me fifty feet above the ground," He looked over the ledge at the group standing on the ground below huddled and staring at them questioningly.

James leaned over the ledge and cupped his hand to his mouth shouting to those waiting on the ground, "Little bit of difficulty up here. We're gonna figure out a way to get you up!"

Bob gave a thumbs-up and James looked around for a way to get them to the top without having to risk them scaling a rock face with disappearing footholds.

Spanish moss hung in thick folds from the branches, interspersed with long green tendrils of ivy. James walked to the tree and pulled the ivy with a sharp tug. It came loose, but it was tough. It didn't break at the top where the youngest vines hung tenderly to the bark. With a couple of hard yanks, James managed to bring down a few cords along with a clump of Spanish moss. He pulled off the moss and twined the vines together. When he got to the end, Stacie was ready with string she spun using the moss from the trees.

"Here, use this to tie it all together," she said, applying it to the end.

"Smart idea," James said. He turned to Kyle. "Tie this around your waist. We'll use you as the base."

Kyle nodded and Deck grabbed the ivy cord and looped it around his waist while Kyle held his arms out to the side.

"Good we've got a big fucker like you, huh?" Deck said conversationally as he measured around Kyle's torso. "Must have been a hit in tug-o-war."

Kyle chuckled. "Best anchor in the third grade."

"No way to talk about yourself, pal," Deck said before slapping him on the back and giving James a thumbs-up. "He's good to go."

Kyle was braced on the ground while Stacie and Deck stood back from the ledge, ready to pull the rest of the cord taut in case of emergency.

James threw the rest of the ivy down, watching it uncoil itself ten feet or so from the ground.

James cupped his hands again and yelled. "Climb up to the bottom of the rope and rappel the rest of the way!" he shouted. "We've got you up here!"

Bob nodded and motioned for Kevin to go first.

Smart, James thought. Heaviest guy first. Kevin situated himself on the wall and pulled his body up to the first hold. Kevin reached for the rope, testing its strength.

"Here he comes," said James, and Kevin put all his weight on the ivy straining the makeshift rope with a stomach-dropping groan. James's body tensed, waiting for a snap and a hopefully light fall at the bottom of the cliff.

But it held. James took a deep breath, gritting his teeth.

He gave a thumbs-up and motioned for Kevin to climb. Kevin moved his feet into position and made his way up, hand over hand, body horizontal to the ground behind him.

In a few minutes, he reached the top and James grasped his forearm, pulling him over the edge with a final heave.

A collective sigh of relief escaped from the team at the top.

"Thanks for the lift, folks," Kevin said with a grin. He sat with Deck and Stacie in front of Kyle, helping to keep the line strong while the other three made their way to the top of the ledge.

When they were gathered at the top, James wrapped the cord into a ring and looped it over his shoulder. "Let's move, but keep an eye out."

"Yeah, no more surprises. Next you know the goddamn path's gonna turn to lava or some shit," Clint said, eyeing their surroundings warily.

"I'll lead," Deck said, making a show of walking his way to the front of the line where he promptly fell over a root and into the side of a tree, barely catching his balance. He turned back, embarrassed.

Stacie shook her head and walked in front of him. "Genius. Truly genius," she muttered, as the rest of the group filed into line behind her. All of them were on high alert, ready for even the trees themselves to reach down and pluck them off one by one.

The rest of the course was relatively non-threatening with a few basic water crossings and a rope bridge, which would have been more treacherous if not for the insurance rope they kept.

They reached the end of the course in anti-climactic fashion, exiting the woods to find Croyton leaning against the edge of his side-by-side with his sleeves rolled up and arms across his chest.

James eyed Croyton from the trail, the rest of the group surrounding him. Sweaty, beaten down, scraped, scratched, bruised, and exhausted, they must have looked like they went through quite the ordeal. But Croyton simply stood there, leaning against his car. Almost serene, his placid demeanor more an insult than anything, and blood rushed to James's ears.

125

Before he knew what was happening James took a step in front of the group, his mind racing and heart pounding against his sternum, but the steel in his stomach gave strength to the surge of adrenaline coursing through his veins.

"How you feeling, Private?" Croyton asked offhandedly, scanning their faces without emotion, "You look a bit pissed off. Tired but pissed."

"What the hell did you just do to us?" James said, the quiet around him unsettling, and the depth of his voice surprised him.

"What was what?" replied Croyton.

"The rock, sir." Heat rose in his body, pulsing with each heartbeat.

"You didn't like it?" Croyton said, pushing off the car with a lazy swagger, "Couple of surprises too tough for you?"

"You could have killed us."

"Well, you're here, aren't you? How do you feel?"

James was thrown off by the questions.

"Pretty pissed"

"Good, you passed the first step. Next time you won't be so stupid." Croyton stepped back to his vehicle.

"I'm pissed we've got you telling us what to do, and apparently, you're fine passing our lives off without a second thought. I'm pissed I keep getting thrown all over the goddamn country without a fucking clue as to where I am. I'm pissed because every time we go somewhere, people almost end up dead, and all anyone seems to care about is putting a bandage on us and sending us back out there." James's breath was heaving with the ferocity of his words. "So, yeah. I'm pissed."

Croyton slowly turned toward him. Croyton's mutated before their eyes and the seething anger, animalesque intensity, and pure fury Croyton bottled up surfaced.

"You're pissed at me? Let me get one thing straight for you," he said, taking a step in James's direction. "I don't give a flying fuck how angry you get. I don't care how much you tell me

126

you're ready for this to end or that I should give a shit whether any of you live or die. You are a tool. A machine for me to engineer, to program, and to release into the world." Croyton was less than a foot away from James's face and his hot coffee breath assaulted James's senses.

"You should *never* be pissed at me because never fucking forget. I do not relent. I do not stop for anything, and I will drill you to fucking death with this. I am here to turn you into a human being you will never recognize. Go ahead and blame everyone else. Blame the Federation, the President, the fucking world for all I care. Because at the end of the day, there's a war coming, and you're part of it. This is how I turn you into a goddamn weapon. *Never* get angry with me because you might as well be screaming at a brick wall. The best you can do now is get mad at yourself, at least you'll get somewhere." Croyton eyed the rest of the group behind James. "Does anyone else have a problem?" Croyton asked.

In unison the group said, "No, sir."

Croyton stepped closer to James. "And you, Private?"

"No, sir," said James breathing deeply. The instinct to hit Croyton raged inside his head, but he managed to tamp it down. It isn't worth it, he thought, letting the anger settle.

Croyton nodded. "Good, we can begin examining battle formations you can use in surprise situations. Let's get back to the armory."

James followed, but ignored the rest of what he said, going through the motions of training still burning with anger.

Why the hell did they let this ridiculous old man train them? They were only seventeen, but for some reason he got the go-ahead to possibly break their necks and it would be their fault. James's ire continued until Croyton called it a day.

After classes, they headed back to their barracks in a slow jog. When they arrived, Croyton carried in a cardboard box filled with bars of some kind and bottles of water.

"The military has made these specifically for your consumption," said Croyton holding a bar up in the air. "One of these is designed to give you the proper vitamins and nutrients sufficient for three square meals. Don't worry if your stomach feels empty. You'll get used to it."

He threw the bar to Deck who opened the recycled plastic and took a bite. He munched loudly. "This is the most tasteless thing I have tried in my life," he said swallowing his first bite and chasing it with a sip of water.

James, realizing how hungry he was, tried his. It was about five or six inches long and brown. There was a slight crunch, but Deck was right. There was no flavor at all. He chewed on the morsel, swallowing painfully before taking a deep swig of his water.

Croyton walked back to his barrack, "Be ready to head out tomorrow bright and early. You have six hours to rest."

They walked back to their barracks. The group sat on their beds, catching their breath and eating the bland bars they were given for their dinner. There were two showers in the barracks and James waited for his turn. Afterward, James looked back through his HOLO checking what they would be working on the next day.

"Hey, how you feelin'?" Kyle stood next to James's bed.

James shrugged. "I'm good now. I wasn't expecting him to catapult us off a rock on the first day. I thought we'd ease into the neck-breaking exercises."

"Yeah, no one saw that one coming," Kyle said and patted him on the shoulder. "Nice grab by the way. Next time I've got your back."

James tried distracting himself by reading their schedule for the next few days but found it hard to concentrate, constantly replaying Croyton's unforgiving stare.

He stopped reading and put the HOLO on the dresser next to his bed. He shut his eyes and pulled the blanket at the bottom of

128

his mattress to his shoulders. He turned over, facing the door, waiting for sleep to carry him to the next day.

CHAPTER 12

James's eyes were glued to the woods around him. Each step held the threat of an impending mine about to blow him sky high, but he kept moving.

Deck padded ahead, stepping lightly, methodically placing each foot on the path. James followed, careful not to step out of turn, expecting the worst. His senses were heightened, his heartbeat steady but tight. The shifting scents of nature mixed with sweat seeping from his pores after their morning run.

Croyton introduced them to the gym earlier that morning, an iron focused corner of the armory with a wide range of dumbbells, some benches, and a squat rack. A couple of basic machines for shoulders, chests, and legs were sprinkled through the area. James suspected Croyton would not emphasize their use judging by the inordinate amount of time he spent walking around to the various iron implements in the rest of the weight room.

Now, they were back on a course. They entered at the same point, or near it at least. James could hardly tell the difference between the constantly shifting gateways to the interior woods. When they ran in the morning, they were on a new path. Or at least that's what James thought. The residue from Croyton's vehicle was cut fresh from the surrounding greenery and there was no indication of trampled leaves from the previous day.

"What's up there?" Stacie whispered from behind him.

James glanced past Deck where three men with rifles casually patrolled the route. Deck noticed them too and threw up his hand motioning them to stop. He walked backward to them, crouching to remain unseen, keeping his eyes on the guards.

Stacie motioned to the rest of the group, and they huddled in the center of the pathway.

Deck knelt, checking over the tops of the brush before he spoke in a hushed tone. "Looks like we have three guys ahead. All of them are armed but not showing any interest in us. Yet."

"We should make our way up there," Kyle said. "Get them to surrender. Numbers mean a lot in this world."

"Too easy," said Stacie shaking her head. "There's gotta be a catch."

"She's right," James agreed. "I think we need a closer look first."

"I've got it," said Deck who, headed into the woods, and vanished behind the foliage.

Clint grinned and shook his head. "He's a wild one, huh?"

"Pain in the ass is more like it," Stacie said, shaking her head, decidedly not grinning at the situation.

"Let's disappear, split sides, and wait until we see something ahead. Try to give ourselves a good vantage point," James said. He pushed his way into the shrubbery on the side of the trail and Stacie and Bob followed. He crawled on his hands and knees to avoid moving any brush while he made his way forward.

There was a break in the conversation from the men up front. James picked himself up slightly to see if he could spot what was happening.

The voices were muffled, and James barely heard them from behind the dense vegetation.

"Something moved," one of them said.

"Yeah, I swear, it was over here."

Two of the men walked over and scanned the far side of the trail. He dropped flat to the ground and watched their feet shuffling about.

"Maybe it was the wind?"

"No way. Wind doesn't move like that."

131

"Shh, there it is again." The man who stayed on the other side of the trail was moving toward James, Stacie, and Bob. His feet followed in perfect lines across the dry earth beneath his boots. The air in James's lungs froze as the feet stopped within feet of his position.

James tensed his body, ready to spring forward when one of the other men yelled, "It moved again!"

The feet in front of James disappeared and James relaxed. He stopped himself from sighing too deeply.

That was Deck, James thought.

He turned around to find Stacie and Bob looking at him expectantly. He motioned up the path at the men, trying to indicate moving around them when he heard a loud crash.

"Got him!" yelled Deck, followed by four gunshots and silence.

James's heart raced and he sprang up, his rifle ready and his finger practically pulling the trigger, but all he found was Kyle, Clint, Kevin, and Jon searching the area, confused.

James walked out of the woods onto the path where Deck frantically searched the ground on his hands and knees like was looking for his glasses.

"What the hell happened?" Deck asked, kneeling back on his heels.

"Where'd they go?" Jon asked, equally perplexed, "I hit them and they... vanished."

"What do you mean vanished?" Stacie said, pushing her way onto the path.

"Vanished, poof, gone, no more," said Kyle, pulling Deck to his feet.

"Who fired?" asked James, turning in a circle and scanning the trees around them.

"I fired three shots at the guy on the far side of the trail," Jon said, his voice unsure of itself. "He turned once Deck made his move as if to shoot and so I took him out, two to the chest and one to the head, but by the time I tried to shoot the other two… nothing was there anymore."

"You see the other two, Deck?" asked Stacie who bent to the ground, inspecting the path's floor.

"I got myself in a good position. They were next to each other with their backs turned. I figured I would jump 'em from behind, but the second I hit them…" Deck trailed off.

"More we don't know," Clint said, shaking his head. "Croyton said this shit would keep happening."

"He can't make people disappear," James replied, but he was not so sure. What the hell was going on here? he thought, looking around at the surrounding forest.

The group's anxiety was palpable. The tense exchange and resulting human disappearance put them on edge and James knew they needed to move on, but how? How were they supposed to get over the unexplainable, again and again?

He was about to tell the team to keep moving when Stacie spoke up. "There aren't prints."

"What?" said James, looking down.

"Prints. Look where Deck would have hit them. Not a single boot or rifle impression anywhere on the ground. It's all ours." She stood and brushed the dirt off her knees. "I don't think they were real."

"Are you saying they were some sort of fuckin' HOLO?" asked Deck, incredulous.

"I think so."

"What the…" Bob said quietly under his breath.

"No fucking way," Kyle said shaking his head. "You need an emitter to create those, especially something so concrete."

"It's the only thing that makes sense," Stacie said, picking her rifle back up off the ground, "Not saying I know how, but it's what I think happened."

James's mind was spinning now. The Federation, Croyton, or one of the unseen minions who worked here figured out a way to create standalone HOLOs with the ability to mimic human beings. Where the hell were they?

"We won't know until the end of the course," James said, moving his rifle back to his chest and walking to the front, "I'll take lead for now. Croyton will tell us what we need to know when we get back."

"I highly doubt it," said Deck.

For the rest of the course, James kept going over the situation in his head. He could not figure out on his own what the hell happened, and Stacie's hypothesis was the only option that seemed like a reasonable explanation. If that was the case, James reasoned, it would explain yesterday's cliff fiasco. If they could manipulate a standing image to interact with humans, why couldn't they do more? They could manipulate anything they wanted. Here they owned the environment. The thought made James's stomach tense up. He narrowed his eyes at the forest around him with a renewed sense of suspicion. The last thing they needed was another piece of the environment they could not trust. The problem was that *thing* happened to be the entire world they lived in for the time being.

When they reached the end of the trail, without further run-ins or obstacles, they found Croyton standing with his arms crossed again, but this time a grin hovered on his lips. The attempt at humor looked awkward on his face.

"So, what'd you think?" he asked expectantly. "Pretty impressive."

James kept his face impassive. "Yes, sir," he replied coolly, unwilling to betray the confusion and questions swirling around his head.

"They finished developing those a couple of weeks ago. They'll be a big part of our training to help you all get used to more real-life situations," Croyton said.

He walked up to James, who, thinking he was about to get read the riot act again, tightened his stomach muscles bracing for the verbal assault, but Croyton made a turn at the last second.

He stood in front of Jon and poked his chest.

He stared at Jon's chest loud enough for the group to hear and said, "Right about there."

He let the statement hang in the air. James waited for more dramatics to follow but Croyton simply stepped back, his finger still glued to Jon's chest.

He looked around at the group, "You see this spot? Right here, where my finger is?"

James nodded apprehensively while his brain sent signals of utter confusion up and down his spinal cord.

"He's dead," Croyton said, the lack of emotion in his voice lessening the impact of the statement before he removed his finger to point it in Jon's face. "You. You are dead. No more. That's it. You're dead."

The rest of the group looked around at each other puzzled when Stacie muttered, "Four shots. Sonofabitch."

"Say it again."

Stacie looked up and, unaware she had spoken out loud, repeated herself loud enough for everyone to hear, "Four shots."

"Four shots… what?"

"Sonofabitch?" Stacie replied.

"Four shots, sonofabitch!" Croyton's hands were on his hips. "Three shots go off from your gun, one more from the HOLOs"—he pointed back at Jon's chest—"where it found its home."

Jon was perplexed. "I didn't feel anything."

"You wouldn't if you were dead either. These suits will track everything, including shots from the weapons the HOLOs have so don't play stupid. A kill by them is the same as a kill in the field. At least here you don't need to be Lazarus to walk around again.

135

"Right now, they're apparitions. But soon they'll be able to do more. Soon they'll be able to hit back a little harder." He stared at Jon. "You'll feel it. Don't worry."

Croyton turned around and waved for the group to follow. This is going to be fucking weird, James thought.

They returned to camp walking directly to the armory where chairs were set up in the same way as the last two days. This time foldable trays were attached with HOLOs, displaying rotating globes above them.

James took a seat in the middle of the group, trying to be inconspicuous.

Croyton tapped his HOLO, and another globe popped up in front of the room. Croyton waited a few seconds for it to grow while he commanded the image from his emitter, zeroing in on the border of the BlankZone.

"These satellite images are confidential and also incredibly difficult for us to get," Croyton began. He motioned with his hands and the wide shot of the border flipped to a satellite view and the screen turned into an image of what James assumed was the border of the BlankZone.

"This is the BlankZone's front. The other side runs smack into the ocean so it's easy to see, but their western flank is on land so it's more indistinct," he continued, zooming in to give them a closer look and flattened the map into a broad rectangle.

There were no distinctions to tell the two sides apart.

It appeared to be a standard town from above with square, cement municipal buildings, drab gray streets, and unremarkable tar rooftops. HVAC systems and the occasional stairwell scattered the roofs, but the buildings had no other identification. Even their sizes were relatively uniform.

Stacie spoke from the back. "How can you tell where the border is?"

"Good question," said Croyton. "You can't because it's all the border. Notice any people walking around? No? Good, there aren't any and if there were, they would die in minutes without the proper equipment. Even then it's an extremely limited amount of time one can stay within a mile or so without feeling the effects of the biotech and electro-chemical enhancers they're using to protect the boundaries."

"Has anyone ever tried crossing?" asked Kyle.

"Yes, but it was unsuccessful. Before the BlankZone officially enacted their border we tried. Now though, not only is it inhospitable and deadly for humans, but robotic sentinels patrol the area. They'll kill at a moment's notice," Croyton finished maneuvering the video through the town.

"Why don't we have any shots of them?" asked James. "The sentinels." James felt stupid saying sentinels and almost used air quotes when he said it.

"We do. Not in this shot. This isn't a live feed. In fact, we've never been able to get a live feed in there. Whatever they're using to keep up the boundary blocks most satellite images. This type of border or satellite protection exists over the continent extending through Africa. They've managed to keep any sort of view from here over the Indian Ocean to the Pacific Ocean essentially invisible. We sneak images whenever we can, but it's a crapshoot and pure luck." Croyton waved his hand, sprouting a new image before them.

A flat metal disc with a round top appeared. The disc had a few different angles offering James some initial theories about its power source but looked like a cartoonish flying saucer.

"This is one of the sentinels. The top part is the equivalent of a brain. Don't let their simplicity fool you. They are both incredible pieces of technology and extremely deadly forces in the future of warfare."

James was still studying the top view of the sentinel trying to figure out how they carried out their offensive capabilities when three indistinct dark shapes against a blue backdrop appeared.

"This is what set everything in motion. We pulled these images over a year ago and are pretty damn certain they're transport ships. To give you an idea of how big these ships are, we're taking this shot from the stratosphere without a zoom. The ships are in the Mediterranean Sea now. We believe this is how they're going to send their initial forces to our coasts."

The breath rushed out of the room as they stared at the ships. They must be the largest moving objects ever created, James thought. Each one was practically its own landmass. They were clear, distinct, and horrifying.

"Now it's our job to figure out when they're going to hit and where. Then we can mobilize properly. Understand?" Croyton looked around the room. James nodded, his eyes still fixed on the HOLO.

"Good. Let's begin."

The next six hours were spent reviewing all the satellite images of the ships and the area they occupied. Given the size of the ships, James assumed the Federation's satellites would have been able to get multiple angles or detailed scans of the behemoths, but there were only four sets of shots, all of them the same. Stagnant objects sitting in the Mediterranean off the coast of the country formerly known as Turkey, now another blank box with lines around it behind an impenetrable, toxic curtain.

Great, James thought, more questions with no answers. At least we're all in the same boat now.

"Let's break for thirty. Grab a bite to eat and meet me back at the armory doors." Croyton walked out the gaping mouth of the armory in the direction of his standalone bunk.

"I'm starving," said Clint, standing up.

"Same. Too bad all we have are those stupid vita-bars or whatever the hell you call them," Deck said, jumping to his feet and following Clint to their barracks.

James, hungry but more curious about the map, decided to take another look at the HOLO. He walked to the front of the room and touched the seemingly solid image in front of him. He made a motion pulling the object apart and the screen zoomed in on the ships. He stood back and studied them trying to wrap his mind around their enormity.

"Floating Death Stars." A voice came from behind him startling James. He turned his head sharply to find Bob and Stacie.

"God, I hope not," Stacie said. "Planet destroyers sitting in the middle of the ocean. Doesn't seem like a smart idea."

Bob snorted. "We've got plenty of planet destroyers all over the Federation, nukes galore, ready to pop at any moment."

"Fair point," James said, his face glued once again to the screen.

"But I don't think that's what these are at all," Stacie said, moving closer to the image.

"Neither do I," James agreed.

"What do you think?" Bob asked, rotating the picture around to get a better view of one of the ships.

"Like Croyton said, transport. If they planned to attack us with a nuke, they would have by now."

"Right, but they're coming here?" Bob asked skeptically. "Seems a bit far-fetched for them to travel across the ocean, right? I mean, they have the advantage of the cover from satellites."

"They still have the whole continent of Africa they've left alone and don't want us to see. Why?" Stacie's voice was flat, almost careless but James sensed she was unraveling a thread.

"Guess they decided they could go there whenever they want. Take what they need when they need it. Not take on more than they can handle."

"Maybe..." Stacie chewed on the word. "Or..."

"Orrrr?" Bob asked, looking over at Stacie expectantly.

"Or the reason those ships aren't in the ocean isn't to hide them from us. It's to test them." Stacie took a breath and started to continue, but James interrupted.

"And they aren't expanding their forces. They're going to hide the whole ocean from us. They needed the real estate to make it happen."

"Bingo," Stacie said, her eyes still scanning the ships. "They're going to use the continent as their recruitment and then some. They get the added benefit of testing their force before they try it here, too."

"And we're waiting for the shoe to drop."

"Holy shit," Bob said. "There has to be something we can do."

Stacie motioned at the armory and the training compound. "We are something." She chuckled morbidly and walked out of the armory doors leaving Bob and James to contemplate the power of the enemy they would have to be prepared to face one day.

The weeks wore on and each day was structured much the same as their previous camp. They would wake up and go on their run, which now turned to ten miles, they swam for two, and afterward jumped on a course. They spent the remainder of their days in classes building their knowledge base.

The weather changed, and mornings were cold with frost adorning the grass struggling to stay alive before winter set in. The nights started earlier, and daylight began later, but it did not deter their schedule. When it was time to wake up, James knew Croyton expected them ready. If they were not awake... well, no one risked trying to find out the result.

Croyton focused on a different subject each week, building their education piece by piece. The classwork spread from military history to technical schematics of electrical grids or city water infrastructure diagrams. The breadth of what they would learn in the classroom seemed to spread across an infinite range of anything Croyton perceived as important to their function as soldiers.

During basic, they learned the skills Croyton needed them to use during their training. It was only thirteen weeks in, but

140

James already noticed how Croyton built his training regimen. The classroom lessons gave direct insight into the courses each week. They were expected to leverage their technical skills to conquer the challenge. James begrudgingly respected the method, but he still did not like Croyton as a person.

Outbursts of yelling were not infrequent, and he did not relent during physical training. He knocked a few of them out during combat training and even put Kyle to sleep during a particularly intense jiujitsu session.

Along with the physical and mental challenges James noticed camaraderie growing within the group and skillsets emerged organically. Specializations became apparent as time wore on.

The easiest to distinguish was Clint. He was an absolute master of vehicles. He put together and took apart every engine, rearranged the propellers on helicopters, flew, drove, and maneuvered moving objects through the trickiest of spots. His skill for sensing the space around a moving vehicle was unparalleled. He claimed it came from growing up the son of a gearhead, but James sensed it was natural instinct.

Then there was Kevin. His resting heartbeat must have been twelve beats per minute because in the face of an imminent explosion James trusted no one more than Kevin. He had no problem walking up to a lit fuse and carefully disarming it with precious seconds left before his body blew into thousands of pieces of human confetti. James thought of him as a bit insane, but he was jealous of Kevin's approach to life. He was perpetually calm and did not speak unless he thought it added value. His personality fit well with someone who came in such a substantial package. James remembered his uncle's saying, "Walk tall and carry a big stick." Suffice to say, Kevin did not need the big stick. He had filled out considerably since arriving at the training camp putting on close to fifteen extra pounds of bulk. After the first two weeks, Croyton placed a light machine gun in his hands, telling him he would be the cover fire for the group. James trusted him more than anyone to hold the line.

Bob and Jon were the two smart ones in the group, or as Deck called them, the "killer nerds." Jon was the only one from the Federation's Southern Territory. The small village he grew up in took part in little to no communication with the outside world and when he was a boy, he found a way to set up the old cell phones sent from the north to work with the same data centers as the newer HOLOs. While this did not entirely solve their problems, at least they received the same information as the rest of the world. To top it all off he did everything using his dad's tools for working on the family's bikes. Simply put, he was a technology genius.

James often thought of the time in a course when Croyton sent blinking lights by the thousands, blinding and confusing them into retreat. While this happened the HOLOs on the course fired at them with charged particle blasts sending electric shocks through their bodies. James thought they were done for as HOLOs circled their position, but Jon whipped out the HOLO emitter he stashed in his training gear. He hunched in the middle of the pack while ionized charges erupted around them. In thirty seconds, he hacked into Croyton's system turning the lights off and shutting off the HOLOs allowing them to make it safely through the rest of the course. The electric burns and pain from the shocks still resonated, but they were overjoyed at the new loophole they found. The next day Croyton banned HOLO emitters from entering the course.

Meanwhile, Bob was the kid who loved to learn. He would sit down and pour over the literature Croyton gave them at night. James would skim through the various topics, focusing on the parts he found interesting or important, but Bob knew absolutely everything. It was no surprise to anyone when during their week focused on field medicine, Bob kept calm under pressure while he wrestled James's skin back together after pulling a piece of razor wire from his shin bone. The resulting injury would have been a setback in any other setting, but the new biotech salve Croyton slapped on him stitched him back up good as new. Bob was fascinated by the techy medicine and spent the next three weeks reading extra material on the topic solidifying him as their field medic.

The team grew to enjoy Deck's company more and more. He would relax the group with his jokes. He called the bars of food they received at night "poop tubes" because of their brown color and odd texture and, unsurprisingly, their likeness to poop. Some mornings Deck would coo to his training gear while dressing. "Are you ready to go to hell for the day? Yeah, you are!" It was a morbid ritual, but one James found oddly calming for the day ahead.

Deck was the fastest in the group, and most eager when it came to attempting dangerous, ridiculous stunts. Since the first course, Deck acted as their main scout. He would enter the field first, moving through the tops of trees or between pressure mechanized obstacles. His ability to predict dangerous situations and his nonchalant attitude toward death-defying acts coupled with a rash decision-making process made Deck a perfect fit for the team.

Kyle was the most physically talented in the group. His speed and size were intimidating to everyone, especially when they were going round for round in martial arts. This especially became clear when Deck, trying to be cocky after watching a bit too much MMA in his free time, thought he could flip Kyle during a Krav Maga session. He tried to take out Kyle's knees and instead flew through the air landing face-first on the mat, his nose exploding in blood. Deck was quiet and sullen for a few days until all of them got beaten by Kyle, too. It seemed the validation of everyone else's embarrassing loss improved Deck's mood immensely. The reaction was not lost on James.

Finally, there was Stacie. She was an enigma in the group and competent at anything she tried, but her ability to transform before your eyes was incredible. She premeditated every move she made, morphing to situations with natural ease. Stacie possessed the uncanny ability to decipher the next steps of an opponent making her a strategy guru and irreplaceable in every aspect of their training. She was strong and owned a knack for absorbing information faster than the rest of them—it served her well as the group's intelligence junky. Bob knew information and could parse it, but Stacie read what the information actually was and read things differently than the rest of them. She was truly an assassin.

Going through their veritable strengths and determining their special skills made James doubt himself. What did he bring? It was the conversation he came back to in his head. Stacie was intelligence and strategy. Clint was a mechanical genius, and Kevin handled explosives. They all had a specialty that helped them stand out in the crowd. What about him? He would often try to push the question out of his mind, but he drifted back to it more and more as training progressed.

James lay awake, as always, a half hour before everyone else. Each night consisted of four hours of sleep, but James was conscious before the whistle blew. He would stare at the stainless steel molded together above his bed. His thoughts focused on home, working to grasp a sense of normalcy he tried to retain since Jackson picked him up from his parents' home.

Darkness enveloped the room save for the hazy blue light shining from the HOLO next to his bed. He reached over and picked up the emitter balancing it on his stomach.

While he could not contact his family, friends, or Kaylie regularly he developed a habit of checking the news while lying in bed, trying to get a sense of what the rest of the world was going through. He thought there might have been some sort of leak or information shared with the outside world about them, but found nothing.

The news never mentioned anything remotely correct about the BlankZone either. Even the conspiracy sites the media regarded as on track were silent regarding the ships he knew existed. Instead, they kept positing their far flung theories about alien craft being the true driver behind modern technology or alleging cabals of secret government organizations manipulating the Federation for their nefarious means. While James knew the reports were inaccurate, and even damaging to the people's impression of the world around them, what was the actual harm? Let them think about all the lizard people they want. It was the easiest option at this point. Once those ships moved, there would be nothing to focus on but the immediacy of war.

He heard movement and glanced up to find Kyle rubbing his eyes and making his way back from the bathroom at the opposite end of the barracks. James shut his HOLO, placed it back on his bedside, and took a deep breath. He let the air out in a long smooth exhale, his lungs depleting themselves of oxygen before he braced himself, swung his legs off the bed, and stood up. He walked over to the sink with his toothbrush, and absentmindedly brushed his teeth while he relieved himself, spitting in the metal bowl when he was done. He flushed, getting a few groans from the rest of the room, before returning to the sink washing out his mouth, and splashing cold water on his face.

He flipped on the pre-set coffee machine, the one luxury item they were allowed in their barracks, while he walked back to his cot. He hit Stacie's feet playfully as he passed her and was met with a feeble kick.

He changed into his training gear, throwing on his boots hardly noticing the form-fitting technology at work anymore. He kept the top half of his suit at his waist choosing to remain topless while he filled a ceramic coffee cup and walked outside. He let the door stay open long enough to get a muffled "fuck off" from Bob who rolled over and buried his face in his pillow with practiced defiance.

Snowflakes fell in long straight lines from the sky. He let the frigid air fill his body before he exhaled steam into the dark morning. His upper body was cold as he leaned against the metal barracks and sipped his coffee, the hot, bitter liquid warming his chest between breaths.

There was not a touch of wind in the compound's enclosure. It was strange seeing so much tropical green mix with the flaky snow dropping around him. James held out his hands and the light bounce of snowflakes hit his skin, the frigid blossoms evaporating instantly, leaving behind only a memory of ice.

The compound was still and quiet at this point in the morning. The only light penetrating the darkness came from their classroom inside the doors of the armory, the lamps flicking on behind him, and the single bulb illuminating the hovel of metal Croyton called home. James had not verified it was actually a single light bulb but judging by the spartan lifestyle Croyton displayed so far it was as good a guess as any.

Croyton was the ultimate creature of habit and war. He was awake at an almost unacceptable hour in the morning, well before James and the rest of the team even thought about opening their eyes. James had started his early morning coffees a few weeks ago and was outside in time to see Croyton walking into his bunk with sweats on, a towel over his head, and his drenched gray gym shirt.

A half hour later, he emerged, shaved, clothed, and looking as if he stepped out of an audition for the commando they used to model toy soldiers and action figures.

There was nothing out of order in any sense about him and his adherence to precision stretched to all aspects of their life in the compound. Croyton worked on a clock and there was nothing out of place, which was both monotonous and worrying because while Croyton was keyed in on the schedule, the others were not. He was five steps ahead while James felt like he was an extra four steps behind. The only activities James was sure of anymore were running, swimming, courses, and classes. But they kept adapting, just not fast enough for Croyton's liking, which brought out his ire.

146

James learned to take the harsh reality of his commander's high expectations with practiced calm.

The snow left behind a powdery residue. The light from the armory was blurred by snowfall, and the tree line surrounding them stood out in sharp green contrast to the white world.

James put his coffee on the ground and pulled his training suit top over his shoulders. The seam stitched up instantly, providing a warm shield to the wintry air. He picked his mug up and sauntered back in the room to find the rest of the group in varied states of dress.

"Cheer up. It's gorgeous out there," James said, clapping Clint on the back and getting a weak bow in response.

"Jesus, James. How the hell are you this awake?" Kyle said, his voice stuffy. "It's not even light out."

"Won't be today, I'd bet," James replied. "Snow."

A unified grumble arose from the group.

"Looks beautiful though," James added, carefully taking a sip from the steaming liquid.

"*Looks beautiful though*," Deck mocked playfully.

"I'll bet," said Bob. "You're a real masochist James."

"Just a morning person"

"Same shit," Clint chimed in, cracking the door open to confirm the weather report.

Deck looked outside over Clint's shoulder. "That is unnatural," he said. "I've never seen snow and green leaves before."

Kevin pulled his top over his shoulders and looked out over them. "Looks like wildfire ash. Scary shit."

"Well, I can confirm it's not," James said tipping the last of his coffee into the sink. "Croyton'll be out there any minute. Let's move."

He walked outside once more and stood at attention, waiting for Croyton. The rest of the group filled in the empty space

147

around him, and their CO stepped outside. He barely acknowledged the snow existed.

He stood in front of them for a moment, searching their faces as he did each morning. James never knew what he was looking for exactly, but whatever he wanted to see he must have gotten it.

He finished his inspection and walked over to the armory where a minute later the low rumble of his side-by-side fired up. He pulled out swiftly leaving two lines of black dirt in the snow cover behind him.

He parked in front of them. "Come on." He pulled away and the day began.

The next two hours were par for the course. By now, James possessed the physical tools and memory to deal with all levels of their morning exercise. No matter what, the first mile was a bear, but afterward he hit his rhythm, each step falling easily into the next.

The swim was similar, but he hit the same rhythm faster. He thought it was due to his controlled breathing, stroke, stroke, breathe. He did not gulp in air as he did when they ran which helped him stay more balanced.

When they finished, James shook himself off and followed Stacie and Kyle onto the land. The shin splints in his legs ebbed into their standard dull throb at this point, the rehab, albeit strenuous, from kicking for an hour helped stretch the tendons. Not to mention, the suits kept the water out and the heat in, but the cold was still present and the temperature of the lake combatted his internal thermometer.

He pulled on his boots, shaking each foot to get the heel in place before they formed seamlessly around his ankles.

He stood in line, shoulder to shoulder with Stacie and Kyle, waiting at attention as the rest of the group fell in line around them. Croyton stood back in his usual pose, straight back, arms across his chest with the blank stare of someone who was watching houses pass by from the window of a train car.

Croyton waited for a few more minutes, once again inspecting them pensively. This is strange, James thought. Normally Croyton waited for them to fish themselves out of the water, turned heel, and walked away.

Instead, Croyton ambled over to the line. He moved with his hands behind his back, not saying anything until he stopped in the center and faced Kyle. He was no more than a foot away from Kyle's face when he spoke.

"Do you know what day it is?" he asked with a monotone voice. Kyle kept his mouth shut, waiting to hear Croyton answer his own question.

"I asked, do you know what day it is?" Croyton reiterated, his tone the same as it was before, almost serene in the way he spoke, but more forceful. He was focused entirely on Kyle who, glanced into Croyton's eyes and looked away quickly before he replied.

"It's Thursday, sir."

"Do you know the significance of this Thursday?"

"No, sir."

"You don't know the significance of this specific Thursday?"

"No, sir. I do not."

"Hmmm, okay."

Croyton turned around and walked back from the group, standing in front of them with his legs apart, addressing them at large now, stopping his scan every few faces to emphasize a point or to intimidate one of them with his gaze.

"Today is Thanksgiving. Although I made the point that half our population does not celebrate the holiday the Federation has requested we limit training." His heart skipped a beat. No way, he said in his head, but fought the instinct to show any recognition of the words on his face, silently hoping the rest of the group would do the same.

"Given we've been here for over three months and all of you have improved to a somewhat acceptable level in my eyes, I decided I will accept the order from Central Command. You have been granted the rest of the day off."

His back tensed.

"We'll end our day here but meet me in the armory at 1700 hours."

Croyton climbed onto his side-by-side and drove away from them.

"Nope," Deck said. "No way. You have got to be kidding me. I do not trust it."

James recognized the hushed agreement along the line and bobbed his head. "I hear ya, but we have to go tonight," James said, trying to reassure himself everything would be ok.

"He's going to poison the food," Clint said, leading the way back to their barracks.

"He's not going to poison us," Stacie said exasperatedly.

"You don't know that," Deck said. "This is an experiment for machines, remember?"

"Yeah, and if he poisoned all his machines? Not an effective solution."

"Fair point," Deck said, his face scrunched in thought.

"We'll be fine," James said. "This is all in our heads." He did not believe his own words though. This was exactly what Croyton would do to throw them off.

"Let's enjoy the day off, get some rest, and be in the armory on time."

A bit before 1700 hours, James and the rest of the group were in the armory. Sitting in the folding chairs without an agenda was more anxiety-inducing than James realized. The afternoon had dragged and flew by all at once. They were all in their heads. Even Deck was quiet.

The door to the side of the armory opened and a cart emerged with two serving trays on top. Croyton wheeled them to the center of the room standing in front of the group awkwardly. He reached to the bottom tray and pulled out a set of paper plates and plastic silverware, placing them on the table he normally taught behind. He took the top off the two aluminum pans revealing a turkey in one and a stack of potatoes in the other.

He stepped back and with an unceremonious presentation motioned to the pans. "Eat."

The word was a forced invitation and James bit his lip to ensure he did not utter a sound. The group looked around at one another, carefully gauging the situation until Stacie stood and made her way to the table, picking up a plate and helping herself to a portion of turkey and potatoes.

James glanced around, awkwardly half-standing above his seat before he made eye contact with Kyle who shrugged. Kyle made his way to the front of the room grabbing a plate and filling it prodigiously with helpings from both pans. James stepped in line behind Kevin, whose plate sagged when he was done loading up his meal. James heaped two piles of food on his plate and walked back to his chair.

The rest of the group continued to take their cues from Stacie and ate, shoveling food in their mouths. James found Croyton watching with the same amount of interest a child would have listening to the evening news.

James stabbed his first bite of shredded turkey. The bird was a little dry. Some gravy wouldn't have hurt, James thought, but anything was better than their tasteless ration bars. James ate like there was a hole in his stomach. Before he knew it, he was up from his seat getting seconds, falling in line behind Deck this time.

While he filled his plate, James noticed Croyton sat behind his own ample serving of dinner, shoveling the food into his mouth at a pace reserved for refugees. He even eats like he's training, James thought, making his way back to his seat to finish his meal.

151

Five minutes later, James looked up, realizing he had not said a word to anyone since Stacie led the charge with dinner. In fact, no one said anything since Croyton invited them to eat.

The pans filled with potatoes and turkey were empty, save for the leftover juices floating on the bottom.

James sat patiently while Croyton collected the trays and placed them in the trash. He did not utter a word as he wheeled the cart to the doorway and opened it. James thought he would not say a word to them at all. However, he surprised them all when he opened the door, turned back to them, and, with his hands clasped behind his back said, "Happy Thanksgiving."

He did not wait for a response and there was an awkward smattering of hushed "thank yous." Croyton disappeared, the door latching shut behind him.

James was in a stunned silence, almost scared this was a trick when Deck spoke from the back row.

"Well, I'm not saying it wasn't a treat or anything, and I do not know how anyone else has Thanksgiving at their house," he said, "but that was the weirdest dinner in my life. The silence though… kinda nice."

James grinned and Kyle and Clint gave Deck friendly shoves, ping-ponging him between them. They walked out of the armory, stomachs full, happy for the first time in months, walking back to their barracks ringed with snow covered trees as green as they would be in the summer.

CHAPTER 13

Slush broke against James's waist leaving an open trail of water in his wake. The team's faces reflected a grim determination and James battled the compulsion to run back to the compound and sit in his cot wrapped in every blanket in camp. Just the thought sent a longing for heat through the pit of his stomach to his toes.

James's feet, numbing under the icy shallows, gripped the ground, his body poised to make a one-eighty and give in to the urge to turn back. But he couldn't or simply wouldn't, he thought. A nagging feeling deep in the recess of his conscious, rooted in an unknown source of stubbornness told him he would never get out of the water.

"Not today, I guess," he mumbled. He took a breath of frigid air and plunged face-first into the icy water.

The cold battered his senses, forcing James to direct energy to simply move his arms in long strokes. His body struggled to acclimate, fending off the stiffening effect of the freezing liquid. He pushed through the painful sensation that came with shoving his head in water no human does unless they are drunk or going for a record in a ridiculous Nordic challenge.

James concentrated on each movement, getting his legs into a rhythm. Once warmed up, he pulled through the water, actively deterring thoughts of a warm shower.

Emerging from the icy water was rough, but when the wind cut across the surface of the lake behind him, James nearly doubled over from the effects on his exposed body parts. He gritted his teeth, shaking his hair, realizing it was probably time for another cut from Croyton. He slipped on his boots while his suit evaporated moisture and returned to its pre swim slack, the arms and legs providing room to move.

Thank God for these suits, James thought, running a hand through his iced hair. He broke off a small chunk from the back of his scalp and tossed it to the side nonchalantly, a routine he was accustomed to over the last few weeks.

James waited, standing abreast with his team while Croyton inspected them, his hawklike glare scrutinizing them head to toe. When satisfied, he pointed in the direction of the course entrance for the day, marked by the rack of weapons next to a nearly imperceptible break in the tree line.

James waited for Croyton to turn away and hop on his side-by-side before following Stacie, Clint, and Kyle to the head of the trail. The thought of a warm blanket still hovered in the back of his mind.

All week the team learned evasion and chase techniques. They were taught from the perspective of the one doing the chasing and the one trying to evade. James was happy to remain the chaser whenever possible, but given their future field of expertise, he assumed evasion was a far more necessary skill. Judging by the courses Croyton put them on all week, leadership agreed.

The HOLO display fixed to the gun rack, a regular part of each course, read:

You have narrowly escaped from a maximum-security prison with only the weapons you took off the guards.

James looked around and realized they all carried a different firearm—a rifle, a few shotguns, another submachine gun like himself, and a pistol. James turned back and continued reading:

154

While escaping, you tripped an alarm, and the woods surrounding the prison are now swarming with guards and reinforcements are en route. You have a half hour to make it through the woods before your escape is cut off. Move north, but you must not be seen or heard, or the guards and militia will be able to target your location.

"Fun stuff," Deck said, casually inspecting his shotgun.

"Quick and quiet," Kyle said, looking around and racking a magazine in his rifle. "Make it so we don't have to sprint out of there."

Without further discussion, they made their way into the woods.

The path stopped as soon as they entered the initial brush. James checked the compass on his arm to ensure they were moving in the right direction before he concealed himself in the brush, avoiding the leaves and branches spread underfoot.

The woods were unnervingly silent and artificially dark. Heavy cloud cover limited the amount of sunlight reaching the top of the forest which meant James and the team were walking through an eternal dusk. Each step James took was a full heel-to-toe plant using maximum surface area to avoid crunching the dying leaves falling from the branches above them. To make matters more difficult, some of the underbrush lost its green for the winter, so ground cover was impossible to rely on.

Like this ecosystem exists anywhere else in the world, James thought, pushing an icy vine out of his way. A breeze ruffled the green leaves around him and a branch snapped unexpectedly.

He shot to the ground.

James's ears were primed. His heartbeat pounded in his chest followed by the sounds of more footsteps coming toward them.

155

It's not us, James realized, trying to peek up front at Stacie, Kevin, and Kyle. Stacie was signaling to Kyle and Kevin, her back against a tree while she peeked around the side of the trunk.

James read her hand signals.

At least five, armed, walking this way, spread out in a line.

Dammit, James thought, looking for a way out when he spotted a briar patch near Kevin and Kyle. He signaled to the briar patch and got a thumbs-up from Stacie. He made his way back to the rest of the group and indicated for them to follow, waving his hand, and listening in the direction of the HOLOs.

The group moved past James, following the tube of disturbed snow Kevin, Kyle, and Stacie had made heading into the briars. James found a branch on the ground and used it to cover their tracks, brushing the prints behind him as he walked backward. He got on his hands and knees, still sweeping the ground until he backed into the guiding hands of Clint. He placed the fallen branch over the mouth of their hiding place, and took a slow deep breath, letting the mist from his frozen breath fill the dark air.

James's heart beat in a steady rhythm while two groups of HOLOs came up the path. He felt a tap on his shoulder and saw Bob point up and exhale. James realized he was pointing at the steam. He took in a deep breath, hoping the heat from their bodies would not give them away.

The heartbeat in James's ears grew louder waiting for the last of the HOLOs to make it past them. He desperately needed a breath and when the head of the last HOLO disappeared he let out a rush of air along with the rest of the group. James removed the branch he used to cover their escape before he crawled out to scan the area.

He turned to cover the rest of the group when a crack from a branch behind him sent him spinning as a HOLO emerged from behind the briar patch.

James reacted instantly, pulling the knife from his boot, and leapt to cover the distance to the HOLO. He shoved the knife in the throat of the HOLO who disappeared.

James waited, the seconds ticking around him. How much noise had he made? Would they have heard his kill? Should they run?

He was answered a second later when a whistle sounded from the direction of the HOLO troops. James saw a HOLO standing on the path, lifting his rifle. James took him out with three quick shots.

"RUN!" he shouted diving for shelter behind a tree.

Projectiles blasted around him, and he waited to cover the group scrambling to exit the briar patch. Kyle and Kevin waited with him, and James waved the others past shouting at them, "Rotate cover fire! Go, go, go!"

He waited thirty seconds taking out HOLOs until he heard the whistle from behind him and watched the rest of the team's fire take out HOLOs in front of him.

"Let's go!" he yelled at Kyle and Kevin who jumped up and raced through the woods on either side of him.

Gunfire echoed off the trees and bark exploded in showers of pulped wood. Ahead, clouds of snow with the occasional reflection of muzzle fire glittered in the crystalline air.

He whistled at the group in front of them. Kevin and Kyle found similar positions and provided cover fire for the team sprinting through the floating splinters and tattered green leaves.

How much fucking farther do we have? James thought as the team streamed past them up the line.

There was another whistle behind him, and an explosion of pain erupted in his shoulder. He stumbled to one knee, gripping the ground with one hand and his gun with the other, his knuckles white from cold and pain.

It was as if someone stuck a live electric cord directly under his skin and it was all James could do to stop from collapsing in shock.

Fucking move, he said in his head while he clenched his teeth. Kevin held out a hand and pulled him to his feet, swinging him forward effortlessly.

It's like following a bear, James thought, running in Kevin's wake and looking around for Kyle who emerged from the woods, jumping over a fallen log.

They sprinted and were about to settle in for a cover spot when Kevin continued running in a full sprint. "Clearing up ahead!"

Thank God, James thought, the searing pain in his shoulder residing but the effect of the electric pulse still very real as he struggled to remain upright.

Before they reached the clearing James let out a shrill whistle and finding adequate cover with a rest for his gun, began taking out the horde of HOLOs running after them.

When Clint finally made it past them, James turned around and threw himself through the end of the course, lying on his back staring at the slate gray sky.

His lungs were gasping for air while lactic acid streamed in and out of his internal organs, making each breath more agonizing than the last. Meanwhile, his fingers twitched from the pulse effects in his arm and the familiar numbing sensation spread out from the impact site near his deltoid.

Not vital at least, James thought as he pulled his body to a sitting position.

The team was in varied states of disarray, their hands and faces torn from whipping branches and exploding bark. Jon was massaging his leg, and Bob knelt next to Stacie.

"Take a deep breath," he said, holding her elbow and tricep with both hands.

Stacie's face was a mask, the muscle in her jaw tight. "Do it."

"Relax," Bob said. "One... two..." *Crunch!*

Stacie took a deep breath through her nose before letting a long steamy breath out through her mouth.

"Try not to move it too much until we can get you a cortisol shot back at the barracks. Gotta reduce the inflammation."

"Thanks," she said through her teeth while she flexed her fingers and tried lifting her arm. She grimaced and held it at her side instead.

James waited for the inevitable purr of Croyton's side-by-side to come disrupt the stillness at any moment.

Wind, cold, and miserable, gray skies were all they knew.

Since the first real snowstorm, James and the group endured utter crap for weather. The days were incredibly short, so James knew they were in the Northern Hemisphere. Hardly much of a relief given how little he knew about where the rest of the world was in relation to him, but he took comfort in the fact he was still at the top of the world, at least from his vantage.

Although they performed the same fundamental daily activities, Croyton switched their classes around. There were days when they ran front to back until the sun was gone. Or Croyton would have them sprint to the lake, swim at top speed for a half hour, and then put them through a course where they were chased by a mass of HOLOs with trip wires set throughout the trail to physically maim them with pepper spray, rubber bullets, small explosives, and other harmful objects. Enough to hurt but not seriously damage.

The days were mentally and physically exhausting, but James sensed new growth and strength in himself. As much as he might hate them, Croyton's methods were working.

What set his mind wandering was the lack of intervention needed to maintain the purity of the world where they lived. While mud and snow could not simply be cleaned up, the broken leaves, greenery, odd mix of plants, and winter all perplexed James and his fellow trainees to no end. The best theories they agreed upon were only found in sci-fi novels they read or movies they watched. Stories where humans terraformed distant planets, took over other galaxies, or became interstellar travelers and galactic pioneers. James only imagined the possibilities if that was already happening in this strange biodome of militant perfection.

He sat in bed, finally warm, with his HOLO propped up on his lap. James was reading through a political history regarding the Argentinian government's battle with authoritarian dictatorships in the mid-twentieth century. As boring as the subject sounded, he was fascinated by the various implements governments used to control the people who entrusted them with power. From Hitler to Milosevic, there were incredible examples of humanity brought to the brink by those who simply thought of others as lesser. Argentina's struggle was not as singular in mentality but held parallels to the mass death carried out by the other two men. James put his HOLO down and looked across the room blankly, comparing the three stories in his mind when the door opened.

Croyton stood in the doorway, his back rigid. The snow sticking to his crew-cut hair and eyelashes gave James the impression of a lost hiker in the Alps.

"They moved." He said the words with such calm gravitas James did not know what he was talking about for a second.

"We aren't sure when yet, but we got in the first images. Be in the armory in ten." He finished in a rush and closed the door with an air of finality.

James stared at the place Croyton stood a second earlier, letting his words sink in before he made eye contact with Stacie, her eyes a mirror of painful knowing.

James spoke up. "Come on." He pulled his boots on and mentally prepared for what was going to be a long night.

When they entered the armory Croyton stood in front of their instruction screen blown up to its largest possible dimensions with his hands on his hips staring at the image in silence.

They did not bother to sit and stood gawking at the displayed image.

The screen was broken into multiple squares focused on Northern Africa. Instead of the differentiated plains of grass, earth, and water with settlements sprinkled throughout, there was a sprawling web of interconnected buildings, roads, and a brand-new infrastructure spanning the width of the continent and trailing off the screen to the south.

They completely took over.

They weren't practice. They were their base, James thought in terror of the army that required an entire continent to operate.

As the images filtered in, the web of settlements grew throughout the landmass. There were entire squares filled with what looked like long, lean barracks neighboring full towns of armories, each covering the same square mileage as a major city.

Harbors along the coasts were filled with ships and docks, while airfields were strewn throughout the flatlands displaying gleaming rows of chrome weaponry perfectly arrayed, wing to wing.

"How the hell did they pull this off?" asked Stacie. "It's just... *wham*, an entire continent disappeared and in its place... this."

"We have no clue. We're having trouble determining exactly when all of this happened, but it must have been months ago."

Months?! James's mind was spinning, thinking of the physical demands and resources it would take to build infrastructure of this magnitude. They were looking at a decades long project at the least. If whoever ran the BlankZone accomplished all of this in a matter of months, what else were they capable of?

He kept scanning the area when he noticed clouds were blocking some of the images. He moved closer and realized they were moving in an odd pattern, flowing over the land, and petering out along the southwest coast. He looked around trying to find where they started, but the originator was offscreen.

Is that smoke? He wondered what source of fire could be so widespread it caused clouds on such a grand scale. His mind drifted to pictures of volcanos he studied in high school.

"How did we get these?" James asked, trying to wrap his mind around the enormous scale of the base.

"Same as before. A break in their satellite protection and constant attempts to hack through," Croyton replied. "Different this time though."

"How so?" asked Stacie from the other end of the line.

"They meant us to see these shots."

"A warning," James said quietly.

"A threat," Croyton replied stonily. "They want us to know what they're capable of, how easily they can assert control without blinking an eye. The ships were a warning. This…" He shook his head, unblinking. "This tells us how ready they are."

James turned this over in his head, realizing the severity of the situation. They were coming sooner than anyone would have thought. He bit his lip while the images filtered through the evidence of pure militaristic might.

"Is there any way to get an estimate on their numbers?" Bob asked.

"Millions. This was the final piece of the puzzle for them. We can expect more to happen soon. We need to pr—" A beeping sound coming from the HOLO cut him off and Croyton's head snapped like a hawk targeting its prey.

He walked up to the HOLO, and James took a step back along with the rest of the team, watching their commander.

162

Croyton minimized his inbox to a corner of the screen and scanned the message.

James exchanged a glance with Deck, who shrugged. Searching for hints on the back of Croyton's head in those next ten seconds was excruciating. James's stomach churned with anticipation until Croyton made the first uncalculated movement James witnessed in his months of training. His shoulders dropped, and for three seconds, James saw Croyton as a human being. The moment disappeared when Croyton turned around throwing new images onto the screen. "They burned Europe."

What? James thought. He did not understand what Croyton was saying. The images loaded in front of him, and his jaw went slack.

The entire Iberian Peninsula was a black scar of land jutting out like a dead limb from the rest of the continent. The countries comprising the middle of the country were bathed in vicious flames, their cities non-existent.

Northern areas of France were completely missing, and the coast looked like a massive beast swept at the hind legs of an animal, tearing gashes of flesh from the earth. James's eyes kept going north, searching for the British Isles.

"Sir, where are Britain and Ireland?" he asked Croyton, still searching and trying to see if it was a trick of the smoke.

"Gone."

The simple reply sent a wave of fear through James. They made what once was the world's greatest empire disappear.

The images continued to load, giving them more views of the continent. They destroyed everything.

"How goddamn big is this army?" asked Clint. "And what did they use to erase them?"

Croyton stood with his back to them, his entire body tense. He did not answer as he scanned through the images and pulled them to different corners of the map until they managed to get far

163

enough under the haze of smoke to find the image he was looking for.

He pulled the square to the center of the screen and expanded it, turning back to the rest of the group, and pointing at the screen.

On it, a square brick building with a demolished rooftop was visible. The picture was clear enough they could see inside where rows of beds sat under the rubble. Small bodies were scattered on the ground with larger ones sprinkled throughout.

Deck and Kyle looked away from the image.

"Look closely," Croyton said, his eyes boring holes in their skulls. "This is what we're fighting. Never forget it."

Without another word Croyton walked out of the room slamming the metal door behind him, allowing the rest of the group to stare in stunned silence at the morbid scene.

How were they supposed to fight against a power like this? What hope did they have versus war machines capable of razing continents, leaving blackened fields of death visible from space?

CHAPTER 14

The HOLO propped against the lamp on his nightstand read 0417. He still had thirty minutes to get going. His thoughts drifted back to his friends from home. He wondered what he would be doing had the government not scooped him up for training. Probably getting ready to lifeguard or caddy at the golf course where he worked the previous summer. He wondered how his friends were taking his absence if he was missed among the group. He didn't like to think they didn't notice so he happily imagined them sitting in a circle around a fire lamenting about how he was not there to get in trouble with them.

A snore jarred his concentration and the group of friends he knew his entire life drifted away in a haze of memory, leaving him inside a metal box surrounded by a new group of friends handpicked by the military for their elite skillsets. Still friends though, James thought.

James pushed out of bed, slipped on his training boots, and poured a steaming cup of coffee. He pushed the door open and stood outside in the cold, watching his breath dissipate in a cloud of smoke. He took a sip of the coffee and the shock of boiling water hit his teeth, giving him an instant jolt.

The remnants of snow still lined the edges of the buildings where drifts found shelter from the wind and sun. The remaining ground was a frozen patch of mud. James looked at the chalky sky. The clouds were so low the mountain tops were hidden from view.

"Pretty fucking miserable around here," he said, realizing he had not spoken to anyone outside of their compound for months. There were longer and longer stretches of time when he stopped thinking of home, his whole mind occupied by his current life, the inevitable war in the future, and what was expected of him and the rest of his team.

He sipped his coffee, examining their surroundings, drifting away for a second when his ear caught a sound he had not heard for some time. It was faint, almost a whisper, but it sounded like air buffeting against the blades of a helicopter. He held his breath, wondering if what he heard was real, willing himself to steady his heartbeat to listen, but in the end nothing came of it. He leaned against the cold metal staring blankly at the mountains in the distance.

Figures, he thought, no one's coming to save us.

Learning about the BlankZone's attack left a significant impact on the group. It was almost two months since the news, but their training meant more, carried more weight, and gave them an actual reason to train as hard as they did. Seeing the power of their enemy built an animosity and protective instinct inside of James. It provided a laser focus on all aspects of his life.

He sensed the same feeling in the rest of the group. Courses were sharper in execution, classes were the back-and-forth teachers begged of students in school, and their physical routines were above and beyond the call of duty. The unfortunate trade-off was the stories of home and life outside training were far fewer. James rationalized this was them growing up, finding the purpose the Federation carved out for them. There was no more time for holding onto old thoughts. They had to be ready because if there was one thing he was certain of, the other side was coming for them—and fast. Less personal happiness was an easy sacrifice to make with the challenges they were expected to face.

He tipped his head back, draining the rest of the now lukewarm coffee in one gulp.

When he pushed back through the door, he found the rest of the room dealing with the morning in their own ways. The same whistle Croyton used to wake them before was no longer necessary. They were all up and moving well before the wake-up call.

James put his cup next to the pot and made his way over to his bunk, patting Clint's shoulder on his way.

Bob, Deck, and Stacie were talking while they drank their coffee and pulled on their training suits.

"How the hell do you think they're gonna hit us, Stace? With a ton of bricks, right on the coast. *Wham*." Deck slammed his fist into his palm emphasizing his point.

"Too easy for them, Deck. Do you think they did that to the entire Sahara? No way. They planned it for years." Stacie shook her head. "They're too careful to throw away decades of planning for a smash and grab."

"Oh, come on. You saw what they have out there."

"I did. Not convinced it's more than a show of force to make us think that's what they'll do is all."

Deck threw his hands in the air, annoyed. "Well, I don't know what to say at this point. Bob, what do you think?"

"She's got a point Deck," Bob said, trying to stay out of the thick of the argument.

"What? I…" Deck stammered as Kyle clapped him on the back.

"Sorry, man. She's got you beat."

Deck made as if to argue more, putting his index finger in the air, but lowered it and shook his head. "Well, I hope we figure out how they're going to attack using your plan sooner than later."

Stacie grinned. "So do I. But in the meantime, I'm happy being right." She winked at Deck before finishing the rest of her coffee. She walked to the door, placing the mug on the ledge of the coffee maker.

The rest of the day passed like any other. A few times James's mind would take a turn, imagining the same propeller beats he heard in the distance earlier that morning, but he brushed them off as hopeful distractions.

The course was no more difficult than normal. They were run-of-the-mill lately. It was difficult to gauge their battle prowess when all the HOLOs shot back at them were temporary stunners and the occasional flashbang grenade. Beyond that, the "damage" they took was recorded on their suits and other than a few scrapes and bruises, they ended up with no mortal wounds—at least as interpreted by the suit's tech. James was not convinced the suits were able to tell if a wound would kill them or not, but it was at least a gauge of immediate death. The measurement they used did nothing to comfort his thoughts of real battle.

After the rest of their classes were done and the others slept or relaxed in bed, James, Jon, and Kevin were the lone holdouts in the gym. Jon and Kevin were working on their bench press while James was going through a leg and shoulders routine he developed a few months earlier using kettlebells and platforms. He was on the final set, and his legs burned with each step count onto the platform. His forearms were about to give out from the fifty-five-pound pieces of iron in his hands.

Two more, he thought, struggling to hold onto the bell as he stepped from the platform swinging his arms forward and placing them down with a thud. The immediate release of the weights was almost more painful in those first few seconds than holding them. James kneaded his knuckles into his forearms breaking up the building lactic acid.

"One more! Come on! One more! Come on!" Kevin shouted as Jon pushed through the final phase in the lift and planted the bar above his head.

Jon sat up, deftly tucking his head under the bar as he did.

"Nice work, man," Kevin said, pulling a forty-five-pound plate off the end of the bar.

"Did you touch the bar?" Jon asked.

"Nope, all you."

Jon did a fist pump to himself. "Hell, yeah, 315!"

James turned away from them, preparing to take on the next set. He picked up the kettlebells, straightened his back and, before he could stop himself, stepped on the platform.

The nightly ritual of coming to the gym was a mental bonus. Whether he was there alone or working with a partner on deadlifts or benches, simply focusing on the motions of lifting and staying in control of items heavy enough to crush his skull was enough to force any negative thoughts from his mind.

Ever since the first night when they saw the devastation of Europe, he could not stop thinking about what was coming for them. That was the primary reason he kept going back to the gym. To escape the images filtering through his mind like a never-ending scroll.

The days after were a mirage of casualty numbers and images showing towns, cities, and villages across the continent smashed and burned to the ground. Churches, castles, government buildings, and old country mansions wiped off the face of the planet. Structures that survived the bombing of London and Berlin in WWII or villages with scarcely a population still intact after the bubonic plague were gone. Only a cloud of smoke and fire-blackened bones remained. The images were stuck in his head no matter how hard he tried to erase them. But here he was able to distract himself.

He placed the kettlebells back on the platform as he finished his last step. One more, man, he thought, putting his hands on his hips walking around the rubber mats, willing his body to go again in the next thirty seconds.

"We're heading out," Kevin said from across the room.

James did not even bother to look up, focused on finishing his workout. "See you back there," he replied with an offhand wave returning to the iron bells and gripping them, his forearms catching their weight before he took a step onto the elevated board.

He did not even hear their footsteps when they left the room. His mind was locked in a zone. His last step was almost in a delirium of pain and happiness with both emotions running through his mind in parallel. He slumped against the platform, his legs burning and his forearms pulsing.

When he was finally ready to move again, he gripped both kettlebells and put them in with the others. He picked up the step platform and stacked it between its two mates, one short, one tall, off the side of the mat.

He liked this time of night when it was only him, post-workout and in a state of happy exhaustion coupled with a feeling of accomplishment.

He flipped the lights off and walked outside, darkness blanketing the world around him.

He stood outside the barracks. The stars danced around in his vision. Incendiaries billions of miles away provided a light show worthy of the gods. Lingering steam from the showers drifted across his line of sight taking the lights in and out of focus. He took a deep breath of mountain air, letting the cold settle in his lungs before he expunged it again.

He began to step inside when the faintest beat of air caught him off guard.

Again? he thought. It was like something was breaking through a barrier to the point where he could determine its source before it disappeared into the ether.

James stood stock-still, waiting for the world to respond around him. Nothing.

He gave up and made his way inside, deciding he would ask the group about it tomorrow morning. Not worth causing them any worry.

He rinsed off in the shower and flopped on his bed. Last awake in camp, he realized, looking around at the rest of the group in their beds.

He reached out for his HOLO and scrolled, sifting through older material to continue reading a paper he started earlier in the week. The soft rise and fall of breathing surrounding him created a relaxing atmosphere. He dove into the text, finding where he left off when an uncharacteristic squeak of their door distracted him. Confused, he looked up and saw a crack open by the doorjamb, wide enough to see clear sky above the tree line. He put his HOLO on his chest and squinted his eyes trying to make out what was happening when an object arced through the air as the door slammed shut and the room exploded in light with a *BANG*.

James, blind and deaf, rolled off his cot, to hide under the bed, but three pairs of hands ripped him off the edge of the mattress before he hit the ground. His ears were ringing as metal shackles clamped around his wrists and ankles.

His vision returned, and a blurry sketch of human bodies outlined themselves in front of him. Dozens of hazily shaped people moved swiftly inside the tiny space of the barracks clamping bracelets on everyone else in the room.

James's captors wrenched him from his bed and held him with grips like steel vices, moving him outside. A cold wind blew through the training camp and the shock of dark and cold sent James's senses spinning. He was forced to kneel on the frozen earth, his bare knees scraping the ice-layered ground. His face was pushed in the mud, and he felt a sharp stab in the side of his neck.

High pitched ringing reached a crescendo in his ears while thoughts and memories swirled together in a kaleidoscope of color, and his lucidity slipped. James cried out with a scream tearing through his mind.

CHAPTER 15

James's nose was pressed into a damp, spongy surface. His ears felt filled with cotton and a drawn-out bell tone echoed in his skull. He opened his eyes but shut them immediately as his brain exploded in a jumble of needles. Reevaluating, he sniffed at the air, his only useful sense, trying to get a feel for his surroundings.

The musty scent of decay pervaded the atmosphere. His hand groped the ground, and he grasped a fistful of fine grain earth too wet to be sand, too soft to be dirt. The ringing dissipated, but his hearing was still sensitive. He pushed his body to a crouching position and leaned back on his heels.

James opened his eyes again, slower this time letting the light shutter in through his eyelids. He found himself in a jungle clearing rife with bright greenery filled with banana leaves, palm fronds, and thick vines rooted in black soil. The rest of the group lay around him in various states of recovery, crouching or pushing themselves off the ground. He looked up expecting to see the sky, but only caught a brief glimpse through the dense leaf cover of the world outside.

Another one of Croyton's tricks, James thought, finding some comfort in the routine nature of his new world. He made a second sweep of the team, ensuring the group was complete.

He pushed off his knees, standing for the first time, feeling the cracks from long periods of inactivity ripple from his back to his kneecaps.

He looked at his body. He was dressed in his suit, but his boot knife was missing from its ankle sheath along with the compass normally embedded in his forearm. There was a military truck with taut canvas stretched over its cargo hold parked behind him. In front of the truck bed stood two men in jungle camo, rifles crossing their chests. A third man came around from the front of the truck, dressed similarly to the other two, but only carrying a holstered sidearm. He leaned casually against one of the wheel wells.

"Private Coffey, how do you feel?" the man asked, observing the group with disinterest. "My name is Captain Fletcher. There's a hostage situation in the jungle roughly three miles west. We need you and your squad to take out the enemy combatants and rescue the six hostages."

James flexed the muscle groupings in his legs to both steady himself and root out any surprise cramps. "Where are we, sir?"

"Don't worry. Get your crew moving. You leave in two minutes."

James walked over to Deck. He picked him up off the ground. "Get the team up and ready. We have a hostage crisis."

Deck looked at him in shock. "What the hell?" he said. "Where are we?"

James shrugged. "Beats me but wake up the others. We leave in two."

Deck let out a sigh as he cracked his neck before pulling Kevin to his feet, straining under the weight.

"God, you're big, Kev," he grunted.

"Thanks, bud," Kevin said, dusting himself off and looking around the clearing. "Jungle?"

"Beats me," James said, walking to the truck, convinced this was a place of Croyton's making.

James kept his face blank and stood in front of Fletcher and the other two men, hands at his sides, ready to pounce if they made a move.

"You have any gear for us?" he asked.

173

The taller of the two unnamed soldiers motioned his head to the bed of the truck. There James found two black canvas duffle bags. James grabbed the bags in both hands and dragged them off the truck. The bags dropped heavily to his sides. What the hell is in here? James thought. He swung back around toward the group, his shoulders straining.

The team convened in a semi-circle facing him. All were stretching or loosening themselves up while they recovered from whatever toxin they were force-injected with back in the compound.

"Anyone happen to get a look at the people in our barracks?" Stacie asked, holding her shoulder as she rotated her arm in a circle.

"It was too dark, and I was out cold," Jon said, standing up from touching his toes. "James, you were in the gym later. Were you still up?"

"Yep, but those flash bangs got me. Couldn't see or hear anything," James said, dropping the duffels in front of the group. "Sounds like there's a hostage situation in the jungle about three miles west of here."

"Where is west? I can't see anything through this tree cover," Kyle said, peering up at the dense canopy blocking any incoming light.

They were in the middle of what looked like a tropical jungle with tree cover too dense to tell the time of day, instructions from a man he never met with two other soldiers he could not address by name if he wanted to, a killer headache from dehydration after being pricked with a drug cocktail he did not know, and a hostage situation they needed to handle.

Par for the course, James thought, unzipping the bags revealing rifles and handguns outfitted with suppressors and red dot sights. He picked up one of the rifles, inspected it, and inserted a magazine from the other bag. He racked a bullet in the chamber before flipping the safety off and back on. He bent back over to find their boot knives on the bottom of the magazine bag. He took one of them out, tucking it into the empty sheath on his ankle.

"This has Croyton written all over it," Deck said, placing his handgun in the holster on his uniform. "No direction, plenty of confusion, and non-descriptive objectives."

"Better than the same courses we've been doing," Clint said, checking the sight on his rifle. "Now we get to chase HOLOs somewhere else."

"Yeah, that's what I wanted to do—chase HOLOs somewhere else," Deck said sarcastically.

"Stop it," Stacie broke in. "Enough focusing on what we don't know. Let's get moving and figure out what we need to know."

"I got it," James replied and walked back to Fletcher and the other two soldiers. "Which way are we going?" he asked. He kept his face placid and unemotional, hoping to come off more like an automaton soldier than the teenager he was asking for directions.

Fletcher glanced at the two men flanking him before shaking his head and grinning. He said nothing but nodded over James's shoulder before shifting his weight and leaning against the back of the truck with a smirk.

Creepy asshole, James thought, wheeling around to the group.

"This way," he said, pointing through the team into the dense fringe of jungle. "I'll take point. Keep your eyes peeled.."

Humidity and heat were the first to assault him followed by an onslaught of insects. The mosquitos were in such dense swarms he thought he was going to swallow a mouthful of them by accident. He held his breath until he finally hit a part of the forest floor that was not ten-foot-tall banana leaves or horse sized ferns. He spit pieces of bug from his mouth and gulped in the brutally hot air, his lungs barely recognizing it as breathable. Pieces of bug flew down his windpipe, causing him to choke and cough.

175

Hands on his knees James got his breathing under control when Deck, Kevin, and Kyle came sputtering out behind him, tearing at their faces and mouths.

"What was that?" Deck cried in a muffled yell rubbing dead mosquitoes and smears of his blood from his cheeks. "I did not see that coming."

Bob and Stacie came out a second or two later, much calmer and grinning, with a crowd of gnats assaulting their faces. Why are they not reacting? James thought, grinding his teeth over his tongue to rake insect limbs from his mouth. As they approached, James saw the cloud of supposed gnats turn into a thin veil of netting cast over their faces.

"Must have been rough," Stacie said, grinning and walking over to Kyle.

"It was awful," Kyle said. "Did they not go after you? How do you sound so normal?"

"Relax a second," she said and pulled on the back of his collar, unfurling a thin piece of netting at the back of his neck. She proceeded to stick it to the suit via a magnetlike strip around the underside of Kyle's collar until his face was covered by the same bubble sported by Bob and Stacie.

James touched the suit behind his neck and found the netting at the back of his collar. He pulled it around his neck, attaching it to seal the seam.

"What the…" Deck said, his face still covered in wings and smears of insect organs.

Bob walked over and helped him. "You'll need to get some antihistamines. Probably have a dozen or so bites on your face."

"I'll keep it in mind what with the extensive med kit we were given," Deck said. "But thanks, doc," he added.

James blinked and a magnified mosquito leg tumbled from his eyelash. "Now are we ready to go?"

There were a series of nods from the team.

James headed through the thankfully lighter underbrush, listening to the sounds of gnats, mosquitos, and flies buzzing around his head. From the middle of the pack, he heard a grumble from Deck. "God, I hope there aren't any bees…"

A stifled chuckle rippled through the group and the mood shifted in a more positive direction.

Sometimes you need the first mistake, he thought, get the jitters out. At least it was a swarm of bugs and nothing worse, he reasoned.

Mammoth spider webs glittered in the few rays of sunlight sneaking through the leaf cover. The spiders themselves swung around, impressively large. James peered into the canopy, where birds flitted among the branches. He occasionally caught sight of what he thought might be a snake happily basking in the wet jungle heat.

"Gross," he murmured, realizing this was the nightmare version of a stroll through the woods. Sweat dripped down his face in rivers despite his dehydration. The salt stung his eyes and created pinpricks of pain from the bug bites on his cheeks.

What a miserable place, he thought.

"I think that's a road up there," Jon said in a hushed voice and pulled James into a crouch. The rest of the group took notice, following their lead while Stacie shifted closer to the two of them keeping her eyes glued on their surroundings while she listened over James's shoulder.

"My abuela lived in a tiny village on the coast and we would play in a clearing by her house. The plants were hacked by machete twice a year to let us into the jungle." He pointed at the vegetation twenty yards before them blocking the route. "That's what it looked like before they cut it."

"Thanks, Jon. Good looking out," James said. He turned back instinctively to call over Deck who was sitting rubbing his eyes through the bug netting and blinking.

177

That won't work, he thought, searching the group for someone else when he realized his scout was already there.

He turned back to Jon who had taken a defensive position watching the area around him like a hawk.

"Jon, let's scout this one out. Deck's... not in a good place," James said, getting a thumbs-up from Jon who checked his gear while James turned to Stacie. "We'll go and inspect the tree line a bit closer. I'll signal back when you should move. Sound good?"

Stacie checked her mag and flipped off her safety. "You've got it."

James motioned to Jon, and they made their way to the edge of the supposed road, approaching in a belly crawl.

James pressed his hands to get himself into a plank and brought his knees under his torso, careful not to disturb the leaves and dead reeds on the ground. He pushed through the first layer of jungle shrubbery and peered onto a dusty dirt path cutting through the woods. It was just wide enough for a single truck. The cut greenery drying and decaying on the side of the road gave James the impression there was not a whole lot of traffic. He looked at his suit, surprised by his lack of torso, forgetting for a second the camouflage technology.

More confident, he edged forward, scanning the opposite side of the road. He looked to his right and searched back to his left when he caught movement out of the corner of his eye. A man walked up the road with a rifle in his hands. The strap hung loosely around his neck. His dark hair was pulled into a greasy ponytail. As he neared, James leaned back into the shrubbery and not a moment too soon as another man walked two feet in front of James's face, his eyes focused forward, searching for signs of movement on the road.

Close one, James thought, not daring to move until both men disappeared. When the coast was clear, James let out a hiss of air, unaware he was holding his breath.

He let the sentries do two more rounds of inspection, mapping their route back and forth.

Comfortable with the timing, James nudged his torso out of the fronds on the road and looked to see the backs of both sentries walking toward a bend in the road where a clearing lay waiting, hidden within the darkness of the jungle. He backed out until they were a safe distance from the road.

He whispered to Jon, "I'll take out the guy on the road close to us. At the same time, I need you to hit the sentry on the other side of the road. The bend should hide him from the view of the encampment, but make sure he falls in those reeds. Otherwise, it might trip the rest of the HOLOs in that camp."

Jon nodded and checked his scope, ticking off his safety deftly with his middle finger. "You got it, boss. I'll go farther up the path to make sure I hit him at the right angle."

"Good, we'll get 'em on the comeback."

"Roger that."

James signaled the basics of the plan back to Stacie who gave him a thumbs-up in reply. Readying for action, James took out his boot knife. The weight of the blade balanced easily in his grasp, the finger holds were molded perfectly to fit his hand. He shifted the knife to a stabbing grip and got back into a belly crawl until he was in position.

The wait felt like an hour as the two guards ambled up the path, taking their time analyzing the foliage surrounding the roadway.

After they passed, James gathered his legs beneath him, ready to spring when they returned. He held his breath. His heart beat a steady rhythm through his sternum, flushing his body with adrenaline as the seconds ticked by until finally, the guard's foot came into view.

James reacted swiftly, springing up and putting a gloved hand over the HOLO's mouth, plunging the blade in across the opposite side of his neck and sliced with a smooth pull of the knife.

Normally the body would slump, and he would need to push it to the side. Sometimes they would disappear in a field of static giving James or anyone else on the team the opportunity to drop back into cover.

This time was different. The blade snagged when he pulled through his cutting motion and the body contorted as a stream of bright, hot liquid squirted from the neck of the HOLO. The man's mouth was open on his hand, his tongue pressed against James's palm. Saliva and blood coated his arm from the wrist up.

James tasted iron and the front of his netting was bathed in a dark liquid. James shrugged off his natural revulsion and pulled the still writhing body through the fronds and back into the clearing where he got a look at the torn skin on the neck of the dying man. A face stared back at him contorted in horror. The eyes were spread wide with terror as the man realized he was dying, gasping for air, and choking on his own blood. His hands were covered in the slick liquid as he clawed at the gash severing his neck. Flecks of saliva mixed with blood fountained sporadically from his mouth, leaving raindrop-like markings on the man's face. Finally, his eyes lost all distinction of humanity and the white orbs turned gray, staring at nothing.

James gaped at the man he killed. The torn neck was splayed open, the ends of the severed carotid artery visible through the fleshy gash.

What the hell? James thought, his mind racing, his stomach roiling at the broken body before him.

He heard someone approach and a voice spoke.

"What was that?" James mumbled, still in a haze when a slight push knocked him out of his reverie.

"You okay, man? Hey," Jon said urgently. "They aren't HOLOs. This is the real deal."

James nodded. "There's so much blood."

"I know. We've gotta move."

James nodded as he stood up, unable to stop staring at the body, his gaze stuck on the man's face looking into a blank eternity.

"Come on," Jon said more forcefully, and James tore his eyes away from the body, the image burned in his memory forever.

They made their way back to the rest of the team and James wiped the blood from the knife on his pants, the net soaked up the blood from his kill. He looked at the blood smears across his torso. James was nauseous. Unable to control himself, he turned to the side, ripped the netting off his face and vomited on the jungle floor. Spitting the remnants of the foul-tasting juices from his mouth James reapplied the magnetic seam.

He did not break stride and walked up to the rest of the team trailing Jon.

"Umm…" Deck sputtered, looking at the two of them, the muzzle of his gun drooping to the ground and his mouth opened in surprise.

Stacie approached them, her jaw tight. "What happened? Are either of you hurt?"

"No more training. We're in it," James said in a steadier voice than he anticipated. James examined the faces of the rest of the group. The emotions they were willing to display ranged from mild shock to determination. Were they ready for this?

"Stacie, you lead Bob, Jon, and Kevin," James said, his mind working in a mechanical rhythm as he spoke, planning each stage in steps, "set up a base of fire along this side of the camp. Jon can guide you but keep an eye out for sentries along the tree line."

Stacie nodded and checked over her gear.

"Kevin, when you're in position, find a decent clearing where you can pop up to lay down cover fire. Kyle, Clint, and I are going to make our way across the road and come at them in a pincer formation."

"How about me, boss man?" Deck said, walking up to the group.

181

James looked at him. "Do you think you're good to go?"

Deck put the sight of his rifle to his eye checking his vision through the scope, "You bet. I could pass a driver's test with this fucker from a thousand yards right now," he said confidently.

"Good. Get up in the air. You're sniper cover and relaying comms for us," James replied. "Find a good place that gives you enough cover from the camp until we move, but make sure we can see your hand gestures from both of our positions."

"Roger," Deck said eyeing the tree line ahead, searching for his operation's nest.

"All clear on the plan? Deck, you need to identify where those hostages are as quickly as possible. We need to move like lightning to get them out," James said, looking at the oddly calm faces of the soldiers surrounding him.

"Rules of engagement?" Kevin asked quietly, his tone conveying the forthcoming response.

"Neutralize all threats," James said without hesitation, surprised at his certainty.

A series of nods and unblinking eyes greeted him in return.

"This is what we've been working on for months," James continued. "No more HOLOs, no more tablets, no more sprinting from lightning in the woods. This is life and death. Let's get in and get out. Good luck, all."

James took a final look at his team, his friends, his soldiers in arms, trying to remember the moment for a time he was not sure would even exist in the future. The nausea was gone. His hands were steady and the familiar sensation of iron coursed through his body. He was ready.

"Let's go."

The group split in three directions. Stacie and her team followed Jon along the side of the road through the brush to close in on the left side of the encampment. Deck made a beeline between them and the road, swinging his rifle behind him as he walked, his nesting tree already chosen.

James took off straight for the road trailed by Clint and Kyle. They passed the broken body of the guard James killed, already covered in insects, the heat from the jungle doing nothing to help the leakage from the body. James's eyes were drawn to the fly-covered wound in the man's neck, the tear where the serrated bottom of his blade ripped a jagged line through the flesh. Forcing himself to look ahead, James lowered into a crouch and moved up the road.

He dropped to a crawl, throwing his rifle over his back as he dug his elbows into the earth until he came to the dusty edge of the path. Pushing back into a crouch he looked left and right, listening for any sounds, and poised for the slightest movement in either direction. He motioned back to Clint and Kyle, letting them know he would tell them when the coast was clear from the other side.

After a final sweep he sprang across the narrow dirt road and slunk into the brush. On the other side he made as little noise as possible, scared of alerting someone in the village before they even started the attack.

He took a few tentative steps on bent knees into the forest before he was satisfied no one else was around. He gestured for the other two to join him.

Seconds later all three were hunched over walking parallel with the road through the jungle. James made a quick detour pulling the other sentry's body deeper into the brush in case anyone came by during their raid. The back of the head was a bloody pulp covered in leafy fragments. The two shots in the chest propagated a crowd of insects looking to feast on a human meal.

James ignored the emotions flowing through his head and dropped the body unceremoniously on the jungle floor before he continued to the encampment.

They followed the line of brush as it jutted out from the encampment until they found their spot.

Smothered ashes mixed with human waste and burned plastic wafted through the air. The occasional break in the shrubbery gave glimpses of the encampment where five thatched-roof huts stood in the clearing. One of the huts was placed strategically in between the other four and three guards milled about the area, rifles in hand, searching the tops of trees or scanning the edges of the encampment. James pulled back a few yards looking for Deck when he caught a disembodied hand demanding his attention. Recognizing the signals James signed back exchanging information silently to the treetop. Deck signed:

Ten men visible; middle hut contains hostages; three on guard at hut; four others on guard, one at each corner; two men eating; one making his way with rifle toward huts; move now

James relayed the message back to Clint and Kyle who did a final check of their rifles before flipping off their safeties.

James signed back:

Signal the attack; take out closest to the hostages first; on your go

Deck replied with a thumbs-up and James moved his team into position. He fixed his scope on one of the three sentries circling the hostage's hut. They trained for this. Deck knew what to do: trust the team.

James counted the beats of the moment under his breath "Three, two, one…"

The second the last syllable left his lips, a red mist popped out of the back of the sentry closest to the entrance by the hut and James squeezed the trigger in two rapid motions, a similar spray erupted against the side of the center hut behind his mark.

He heard the suppressed fire from both Clint and Kyle on either side of him and walked forward as the sentries at the other corners fell lifeless to the ground in quick succession.

He reached the edge of the camp, where two bodies were sprawled out on their backs, their legs slung over the rocks they had occupied moments earlier. The final man stood with his mouth open, speechless and confused.

James made eye contact with him before he squeezed the trigger three times, *tap tap tap*. The body fell backward, its head splashing a dark red burst of liquid when it connected with the ground.

Stacie, Bob, Kevin, and Jon emerged from the other side of the encampment, rifles at the ready.

Stacie nodded at James.

Deck motioned the all-clear signal from the treetops. James gave him the affirmative and crept toward the center of the camp. They checked the four surrounding tents first finding nothing but bedding and supplies.

Satisfied, James pulled at the wood slat door to the central hutch, nearly ripping it off its hinges.

The stench was inhuman. James clenched his jaw fighting the urge to vomit as saliva flooded his mouth. Once his eyes adjusted to the lack of light, he saw six hostages lying flat on the ground or seated cross-legged, hunched over. Their captors had covered their heads in canvas bags and the ones seated swung unconsciously from side to side.

He bent to the one nearest him and lifted the cover to find a woman with ragged dark hair and half open eyes not registering the removal of the hood staring blankly at the ground. She wore a soiled dress, and her arms were bound behind her with wire cutting into her wrists and thick rope wrapped around her ankles.

"My name is James. I am part of the Federation military," James said softly while he motioned to Bob. "What's your name?"

The unseeing eyes looked at him with no sense of recognition. The pools of darkness showed only the faint acknowledgment of sound, nothing else. Disturbed, James looked around the room.

"Bob, take a look at them. Let's get them out of the hut and we'll figure out what to do next. Might need to carry them through the woods. Looks like they've been tortured."

"No shit," Stacie said, bending to another one of the hostages on the floor before she gently removed the hood.

James was suddenly anxious to get outside and he called for the others. "Kyle, Kevin, Jon, give us a hand. Deck and Clint, I want you two on watch."

"James, come over here," Bob said from the other side of the tent.

James stepped over to him, kneeling next to Bob who was crouched over one of the bodies, the head still half encased in its bag.

"This one's dead. I don't know what this is honestly. This is, I mean..." Bob stopped his voice cracking before he uttered in a whisper, "What the fuck?"

James agreed. "I know, man. Let's get outta here. Help me carry her out to one of the other huts. Don't let the others see," James said, pulling the hood back over the dead woman's face, not interested in the prospect of seeing another pair of blank eyes.

Bob, Stacie, and Clint tended to the women while Deck circled the edge of the encampment checking for anything they may have missed during their initial raid. Kevin and Kyle were out of sight wrapping the corpse of the dead hostage with a mosquito net they discovered in one of the surrounding huts. The bodies of the men they killed were piled on top of one another next to their fire. James and Jon collected their first two kills from the woods to add to the corpse pile.

Dragging the body of his victim, stiff from rigor mortis, James stumbled and bent while he unhooked the body's left foot from a root arching above the ground humming "*Clean up, clean up, everybody everywhere*" like his mother sang when they picked up their rooms. It's strange where the mind can wander, James thought continuing his trek to the burn pile.

They poured a can of gasoline on the bodies and walked back to the center of the encampment. They would ignite the pile with a match before they left, careful not to attract attention with unnecessary smoke signals.

James knew they needed to finish their plan, but all his focus was on the sheer horror these hostages endured during their imprisonment. None of them spoke but they were tentatively accepting water from the team, preferring to interact with Stacie whenever they could. The hostages were all women, probably between the ages of twenty and forty. Their bodies were so broken, malnourished, and covered in grime it was impossible to do anything but feel empathy for them. Empathy and rage for their captors. Simmering hatred boiled in James's stomach as he outlined the type of revenge he would have liked to carry out. His murderous thoughts were interrupted by a tap on his shoulder, and he jumped slightly.

"What now?" Deck asked, pretending not to notice James's reaction.

"We've got to get out of here," James said. He looked around the area nonchalantly to hide his startled response. "There's enough equipment here to host another ten or twenty men. They might come back at any time."

Deck nodded. "And they probably will."

"We're going to have to carry them," James said, absentmindedly looking into the woods. "Get some bug netting and let's get moving. Quicker the better."

"You got it," Deck replied, ambling off to one of the huts for netting.

James walked across the circle of women and knelt next to Bob. "Do you think we can move them?"

"Move them? You mean now?" Bob looked around at the women, calculating the risk in his head. "Not on their own."

"I figured as much. How about on our backs?"

187

"They're fragile, but they should be okay. Slow and steady is the trick."

"Let's start," James said, waving over Kevin and Kyle walking back from their burial task.

Minutes later the women were covered in bug netting on the backs of Kevin, Kyle, Clint, Stacie, and James.

Bob did his rounds and final medical checks while he tried to settle the women down to monitor their vital signs. When he gave the go-ahead, Deck took off into the woods through the narrow footpath Stacie and her team had forged an hour earlier.

James stepped through the high grass. He gripped his rifle tightly and adjusted the arms of the woman on his back to help her hold herself more securely while he walked. Her lack of weight shocked him, enforcing the realities of their forced depravity.

The interior of the jungle was so dark James barely saw Deck walking stealthily in front of him searching for signs of danger. James flipped the switch next to his safety illuminating the dim glow light at the tip of his muzzle.

Jon trailed them, wiping their path to disguise their escape route. The more we appear as ghosts the better, James thought.

Floodlights suddenly flashed in front of him illuminating the depth of the jungle in elongated shadows. He whirled around, dropping to a knee ready to ream out one of his team members for being a fucking moron when the searching lights crawled over the rest of the team carving a solid pathway of light through the thick vegetation.

The chug of a diesel engine hummed through the brush muffled by the jungle.

Dammit, James thought calculating the next move in his head. How had they missed that? They let a truck sneak up on them until they were in the darkest part of the woods. Now their pursuers were sitting behind them with light on their side and far more knowledge of the terrain. Not only that, but they were motivated, they wanted their hostages back.

James heard voices speaking in a tongue he could not place. What is that? The volume of the voices pitched higher and lower in volume depending on the speaker's location.

We've got to move, James realized and tapped Deck on the arm to keep moving ahead.

Deck crouched low, moving farther into the jungle. James followed silently hoping they were going in the right direction. Last thing they needed was to get lost out in a dense jungle with a group of armed hostiles on their tail.

James adjusted the woman hanging on his neck. Her legs were wrapped around his waist, ankles crisscrossed near where his belt would buckle. Her hot breath brushed against his ear and down his cheek where her face was buried near the base of his neck. Her heartbeat was like a rabbit's, drumming fast against his spine. The realization of her helplessness motivated James, his body strengthened with each step.

The gunshot he heard pushed him into full battle mode. James dove behind a tree and whipped the rifle he clutched in his hands up, sighting one of the men running at them through the woods and taking him out with a quick double tap on his trigger.

More shots rang out, interrupted by the muffled gunfire from the team's silenced weapons. James stayed hunched over behind the tree when he felt a tap from behind and saw Jon who had come up from the back of the line to yell in James's ear.

"There's at least a dozen of them, man. We've got to go! They're going to have us surrounded!"

James had already made up his mind and slapped Deck on the shoulder before shouting, "Move!" in his ear.

The next second they were sprinting through the woods. James turned around to get a headcount of the team, but the darkness made it impossible for him to tell who was behind him. The feeling of training hit while he ran in absolute darkness save for the light bobbing from the muzzle of his rifle.

He crashed through the woods with reckless abandon while rounds erupted behind him sporadically. He had no idea where they were or how far they needed to go when he burst into a clearing where the two trucks remained. Captain Fletcher and his buddies were nowhere to be found.

"Where the fuck are they?" Deck yelled, circling the trucks feverishly.

"Motherfucker," Clint said, jumping into the back of one of the trucks and checked the covered bed. "They ditched us."

A rage boiled beneath the surface of James's skin. He put down the woman from his back and sat her against one of the truck's tires.

"We'll figure it out. Everyone ammo—" James never finished his sentence, distracted by a familiar pinprick sensation on his neck. His body fought with him, his heartbeat slowed, then the world turned into a kaleidoscope and the bottom of a pit came up to meet him once again.

CHAPTER 16

James was careful when he regained consciousness. His mind was less fuzzy than the first wakeup and he lay prone on his back. Sensations waded through the drug induced fugue and the distracting bell tone was absent this time. Probably due to the lack of a flash bang going off before he was doped like a wild animal, James thought. Kicking only the toxins made for a more pleasant, albeit unchosen, way to wake up from an unintended nap, James surmised wryly, finishing his assessment.

Determining his body whole, he turned his attention to other matters, his team. His current situation limited the scope of his ability to check his immediate surroundings. James was worried about them. Where were they and what shape were they in? Had they all succumbed to the drugs, too? How were they drugged in the first place? And most importantly, had anyone else woken up yet? He half-expected, half-hoped to hear Deck curse while slapping him awake, but after lying still on his back a few moments longer he gave up on that outcome.

He kept his eyes closed enduring a scratchy dry sensation, reticent to open his lids and expecting another harsh exposure to light. James reached out to the world around him with his other senses.

The low hum of an engine or fan churned in the background. The air tasted sterile, recycled. There was no natural scent to his surroundings other than the dried sweat covering his body. This was a different environment compared to the rich, moist atmosphere of the jungle where each breath was filled with blooming plants, traces of animals, and all manners of life in various stages of decay. That air was rife with what James could only describe as nature. This was fake, cleansed, and human. James was on alert.

James gently brushed the surface he lay on with his palms. Soft linen greeted his skin. The thin fabric betrayed its years of wear and tear, but it was dry and clean. That's good. Not laying on a burlap sack, James thought. Or another body, he shuddered internally at the thought.

Bracing for the worst, James peered through his eyelids letting his lashes absorb the light filtering into his sensitive pupils. He was careful to hide his state of wakefulness, wary he was being watched, but he needed to figure out where he was.

The world above him was made of metal plates machine-welded together. Attempting to keep his head still, James saw a long light hanging above him. He turned his eyes as far as they would allow without budging his chin to maintain the illusion of unconsciousness.

He peeked to both sides finding the room encased in steel walls.

James knew it would be unwise to lift his head for a more panoramic view of his surroundings, so he did his best to concentrate on the sounds. He focused to separate each of the mechanical hums, visualizing their originators, defining their owners and if they were remotely human. However, the dull engine noise was too overpowering, and James gave up.

James heard a swooshing door behind his head and closed his eyes. He calmed his heartrate taking even breaths through his nose, begging the monitors not to betray his state of wakefulness.

He counted in his head to keep his heartbeat steady, breathing in and out between the even and odd numbers.

One, breathe in, two, breathe out, three, breathe in, four, breathe out. His eyes tired as he did so. He would need to fight against the hooks the drugs still held in his bloodstream at the same time as he pretended to be asleep. Difficult little balancing act, he thought.

He hit 426 seconds, and his eyes were rolling back farther in his sockets when he sensed a person standing next to him.

A set of smooth, strong, and small hands checked his pulse and the connection to the IV stuck in his arm.

Medic? He thought. They fiddled around for another fifty-two breaths before leaving his bedside followed by a beep from the monitor next to his head.

James was patient, counting his breaths, still praying the monitor was keeping his secret. After another minute of their presence James heard a swoosh and waited ten more breaths, before he opened his eyes.

Straining his ears for further signs of human activity, James took the risk and turned his head.

Kyle lay next to him splayed out on a hospital gurney. Dirt smudged his cheeks and a five o'clock shadow grew along his jawline. A HOLO hung from the ceiling behind his head pointed toward his face and an IV drip dangled from a rack with a bag of clear liquid. He was taking deep even breaths, the same as the ones James mimicked moments earlier.

Hardening his resolve, James tilted his head, so his chin rested on his chest. There was another row of gurneys and James ID'd the heads of Stacie, Clint, and Bob. He lifted his head and peered over Kyle to find Jon. He turned around to come upon the enormous feet of Kevin directly over his shoulder and, finally, Deck parallel to him. Above the two of them, James made out the edge of the sliding door.

All accounted for, James thought settling his head back down and counting to thirty, waiting for the cavalry to come busting through the door, pricking him with another shot of poison.

While he waited James developed a plan. He knew someone would come back and check on them according to a schedule, but he didn't know when. He would have to be patient and make his shot worth it.

Until they returned, all he could do was wait.

He lay on his back, enjoying the solitude, or illusion of it, for a few moments before visiting people in his mind. His thoughts jumped around wondering what was happening with his family. He had not seen them in months. Holidays passed, but they were so consumed with training and preparing for an impending world war he forgot all about it.

On Christmas, they spoke for ten minutes, checking up on each other, but James felt distant. Not distant in terms of actual miles, that much was obvious to him, but more in his mind. He wasn't with them when they spoke, and it disturbed him throughout the conversation until they stopped talking and he forgot about the feeling. His drive was concentrated on his team, his mission, and their objectives to keep the Federation safe. It was all that mattered.

Realizing he was headed down a rabbit hole, he shrugged off the thought and moved on to Kaylie. He wondered what she was doing, if she met anyone else, or if she tried to contact him since he arrived at their new camp. He imagined how events might have gone if he was able to stick around town. He drifted off to their little time alone together, getting ice cream while walking through town, the scent of her bedsheets. Maybe one day, he reasoned, letting the memories wash over him.

Lost in a sea of nostalgia, James almost missed the swoosh of the door. He closed his eyes. He measured his breathing, slowing his heartbeat and waiting for his moment, forming the iron in his stomach.

He counted until he hit 420 seconds and, lo and behold, a person stood next to him, with what he assumed were the same pair of hands inspecting his arm, body, and monitors. He counted to sixty in his head, determining the stranger's gaze based on how their hands interacted with his body. They were methodical, going from left arm to right arm, to right leg and then left. Final check of his throat and they were finished. He counted out the seconds creating a timestamped checklist in the back of his mind for the next part of his plan. He knew they would move to Kevin next. He needed it to happen. His life from this moment hinged on that assumption.

They left and he started a fresh count. When he reached thirteen seconds, if he was right, they would be at Kevin's legs. Within thirty seconds they would be checking his IV.

Five seconds later, James began his move.

Lifting himself to a sitting position, James turned and placed his feet lightly on the ground. He braced his arms on the bed and pushed off. James turned to find a woman with slim shoulders and brown hair tucked into a neat ponytail wrapped in a black headband poking at the HOLO above Kevin's head.

Forty-two seconds. She tapped an unseen pad before her. James wrapped his IV cord in his hands, lifting the bag off its stand, leaving slack between his fists.

Forty-eight seconds. Her head was still down, her back to James, and he stood behind her.

Fifty-two seconds. She lifted her head and took a step back, bumping into James's chest.

Fifty-three seconds. James wrapped the cord around her neck and secured it behind her back with enough pressure to control her movement but not enough to cut off breathing. Meanwhile, he brought up his other hand, still covered in dried blood and grime, to cover her mouth.

Her heartbeat, induced by fear, slammed into his chest, her muscles went rigid. He had complete control over her life. It terrified him.

"I need you to listen to me carefully and answer all my questions with a nod for yes, a shake for no. Do you understand?" James whispered, his voice low and deliberate in her ear. The woman nodded and a pool of her tears formed on the top of his wrist.

"Good. I am not going to hurt you. I need information. Am I still in the Federation?" James asked, getting a nod in response, "Okay, am I in the north?" A slight shake of the head told him south.

"Are we on land?" he asked, piecing together the situation in his head. Another shake further filled out the picture.

"Air?"

Another nod.

"Are there other people on board?"

Nod.

"Are there other military on board?"

Nod

"Is one of them named Croyton?"

A hesitation before a shake. James was surprised but forged ahead.

"Fletcher?"

Another nod.

"Are there two other men with him?"

Another nod.

"Are there other armed military personnel besides them?"

A shake in response and with it, James's plan was solidified.

He released the cord from the IV, letting it drop around her shoulders like a broken necklace.

He placed his palm out flat in front of her. "Give me your access method. Nothing else."

He felt a slight hesitation. James hoped her sense of self-preservation would eliminate the option to fight.

After a few seconds of internal debate, she reached to her neckline and pulled out a lanyard from inside her top. She pulled the cord over her head and hung it around his outstretched palm.

196

James peeked at the card and saw the picture of a young woman with deep blue eyes looking back at him. He unclasped the ID from its chain with one hand and stuffed it in his pocket.

"I'm going to take my hand off your mouth now. I want you to sit where I was and do not say a word, understand?"

A final nod gave him the go-ahead to release her. He took a step back, raising his hands above his head as he walked around her, not daring to turn his back.

He stood with his side to the door, watching the woman lean against the gurney with her arms hung loosely by her sides. Her face was fixed on the floor.

"Go on. Sit down," he said gently.

She glanced up at him, her eyes wells of fear, confusion, and distrust.

"It's okay. Sit down. I'm going to leave. All I ask is you give me thirty seconds before you sound the alarm."

She looked back at him wordlessly. She placed her hands on the gurney and lifted herself onto the cot, her feet dangling in the air, her eyes never leaving his.

James tossed the lanyard on the bed next to her, battling a deep well of shame, regret, and anger. He wished he had a different option rather than intimidating and forcefully taking someone's key card from them. This was it though, and he kept his face stoic while he turned and opened the door waving her card over the receiver next to the entrance.

He stepped into the hallway and looked back at her still staring at him. Her eyes were red and puffy. The tears dried, leaving streaks on her face, causing her eyelashes to meld into one another.

"I'm sorry," he said, and the door closed.

Got to keep moving, James thought and looked up and down the hallway. Both ends stopped in sliding doors. The sign outside of the room where they were being held indicated a mess hall to his left. James went right, stopping in front of the door at the end of the hallway.

James put his back to the wall next to the entryway and scanned the access card over the receiver. He was greeted with a swoosh when the doors opened.

Natural light poured into the room, and James gritted his teeth before taking a swift step through the door where he found one of the guards from the jungle sitting reading a book on his lap.

"They still sleep—" The guard started speaking but gurgled out the rest of the sentence as James hit the side of his throat.

The guard fell to his knees, clutching his neck with one hand. James lifted him and sat him back on the bench before relieving him of the sidearm attached to his hip. The guard was unconscious when James checked his vitals before he finished inspecting his surroundings.

James stood in a narrow hallway with windows encompassing either side. Another set of doors stood in front of him, and James, removing the weapon from its holster, stepped up to the doors. With the muzzle of his gun pointed at the doors, he took a deep breath and pressed the access card to the receiver.

Another swoosh and James found himself in a packed cockpit where four heads turned to greet him.

James recognized Fletcher first whose arms were crossed in front of him, and his mouth opened in shock.

Before James said anything, he saw movement out of the corner of his eye and ducked in time as the butt of the other soldier's rifle whiffed over the top of James's head. James, using the attacker's momentum, scooped his arms through the legs of his attacker and slammed the man's head into the doorjamb behind him. The soldier slumped to the ground unconscious, and James whipped around to find Fletcher with a hand on his sidearm.

James spoke, careful not to point his gun's barrel directly at Fletcher. "Don't move."

Fletcher's hand stopped.

"Hands behind your head and step back against the wall behind you," James said, keeping his weapon still pointed at the ground, but in the captain's general vicinity.

Fletcher complied, moving his back against the wall, his placid face now tense.

James, knowing he was running out of time, scanned the rest of the room.

The cockpit was one of the more modern aircraft James had ever seen with sleek panels and lights flowing gracefully within the dull silver interior. There were two captain's chairs occupied by pilots, one of whom still flew the plane. The other turned around in her chair, with her hands above her head. The rest of the room was barren save for the four jump seats facing each other on either side of the cockpit.

James was mesmerized by the windows encompassing the room flooding the metal surfaces with brilliant light. He would have loved to take a closer look around or sit in one of the pilot seats while they flew, but time was of the essence.

"So, what's the move James?"

James looked at Fletcher first who looked back unblinking, the muscle along his jawline popping from the side of his face.

"I said, what's the next move, James? You broke into a military plane's cockpit and have taken hostages. So, tell me. What's the fucking move?"

James searched the room, trying to determine who was speaking, even turning around to check the unconscious soldier still sprawled out on the ground behind him, when he suddenly recognized the voice and realized it was coming over the intercom.

"Croyton?" he asked, looking around him suspiciously.

"About time. Up here on the dash."

James peered between the two pilots and was met by Croyton's piercing, predatorial gaze staring back at him. His expression defined serene rage.

"I ask again because you clearly didn't hear me the first time I asked. What's the plan now, James?" Croyton's voice was even, but the edge in it could cut diamonds.

James looked back at the last year of his life— taken from his home, thrown into training, dragged around the world, until he ended up with a team he grew to love and trust as much as his own family only to watch them get dropped off in the middle of the jungle and thrown into an unchecked situation, putting their lives at risk before they were drugged again like animals who escaped from the zoo. He wasn't their pet. He made his own decisions, and this is where it was going to end.

"Fuck you," James said under his breath, before speaking louder to make sure everyone heard. "Fuck. You."

Croyton's eyes remained the same flinty balls of iron.

"You think you can do this to people? Kidnap them, drug them, and drag them into the jungle? Then what? Tranq us when we're leaving to go do your bidding somewhere else? Let me ask you. How did those women get in the village, huh? Was this a sick game you were trying to play with us? You think holding a war over our heads is enough to make us your fucking pets?"

James heard his voice rising but continued, knowing he was done for. At least he would make a final stand. "For months we've done what you asked, worked in the freezing cold, watched friends fall over from heat strokes, dehydration, or worse. Broken our bodies and our minds to become your tools. We've given all we have to become what you wanted us to be. Then you pull that crap on us. No warning, no sign, nothing. All our loyalty, all our sacrifice.

"You betrayed us, General. Plain and simple. Do what you want to me. I don't care anymore. But this is not the war we're here to fight and it's not the way we're going to fight it. We'll call the shots now. We're done with you."

James breathed harder now. He felt it in his chest. His words flowed easier than expected and he watched Croyton's face, anticipating a visceral, violent response.

Instead, Croyton did not react. He remained passive. James clenched his teeth, ready for the backlash.

"Training complete. Good luck, Coffey."

The monitor clicked off.

James stood for a second, unsure of what to do next. His hands still gripped the hilt of his sidearm, his knuckles white from squeezing.

Did he say done? he thought, still not sure of what he heard when his thoughts were broken by another voice in the room.

"Would you help me pick him up?" Fletcher asked, looking at him questioningly and pointing to the guard still laying on the floor. "I assume we'll need to get Donny, too."

James nodded numbly and flipped on his safety before tucking the gun into his suit's holster.

He bent and lifted the soldier to one of the jump seats, buckling him in.

"Sir, where should we land?" the pilot still turned around asked, her question aimed at James.

James looked out the window, his mind processing what happened when he heard himself say, "Take us back to base. We'll get our orders from there."

With a nod the pilot turned back around in her chair.

He helped Fletcher with the other soldier going through the same process of strapping him into a seat before James headed to check on his team.

He opened the door to their room and found the medic doing her rounds, finishing up with Clint as he walked inside. The door swooshed shut behind him, and tense silence filled the room.

The medic stood up straight and looked him in the eye. Her tears were gone, replaced by a steely resilience and the same shame as before welled up inside of him when James looked at her.

201

"You can go back to the cockpit now," James said pointing over his shoulder

She nodded and walked past him with her head down.

James swiped the key card over the access panel and as the door opened, he spoke. "I am…"

She turned around and looked back at him, her eyes connecting with his.

"Sorry. I really am. I never meant to hurt you or scare you I…" James's words trailed off and the unspeakable strain he had been put through for the past year came crashing on his shoulders. He looked at the ground ashamed.

"I know."

He looked up in time to see the doors slide closed. The medic lost from his vision.

James walked around the room, checking each one of his teammates before he found his bunk and lay back on the soft linen sheets, staring at the ceiling, finally feeling a semblance of control in his life.

PART III

CHAPTER 17

Damn it, James thought, swinging his legs off the side of his bed. He propped his elbows on his knees and stared at the worn carpet. He glanced at the HOLO leaning against the lamp on his nightstand. He groaned out loud: 0400, again.

He had not slept past four since they arrived on campus, and he hated it.

James swiped up on his HOLO ignoring the early headlines from the day, most of them still left over from yesterday. Instead, he checked his mailbox swiping away the never-ending newsletters, advertisements dressed up as personal mail, and other junk he received more of with each passing day. When he finished his cleanup, he noticed a message from Kaylie, and he opened it briefly:

Hey! Long time no talk. You free for a call sometime? Hope you're doing well! xoxo

James pressed the reply button, his fingers poised over the light-based keyboard ready to type out a message. After a moment he decided against it and pushed the message back into his unread folder.

He didn't think of her the same way as before his first stint of training. She was still on his mind, but he couldn't focus on her like he did when he used to lay awake in his bunk.

His brain was elsewhere these days. Even talks with his parents were different and their conversations ended up stunted, leaving both parties feeling even more estranged. His team was what mattered to him. His family understood, right? James stopped questioning himself, realizing he would get nowhere at 4 a.m. staring at a HOLO.

He moved toward the door when he stepped on a soft and gooey pile that squished between his toes. He jumped, slamming his knee on the desk he shared with Deck. James scowled and rubbed his knee, the initial pain subsiding to a dull ache. His eyes fell on a peeled banana smushed into the thinning carpet. What's that doing there? he thought. He shook his head, blaming Deck as the obvious culprit. Cursing his roommate under his breath, he hobbled to the living room.

James gasped at the carnage in front of him.

"Dear God," he whispered.

Beer cans covered the room with pools of condensation gathering at the bottoms of their aluminum cylinders. Cigarette butts littered the space or were crammed into the top of a can poking out the opening like a vase of disgusting petal-less flowers with trails of ashes snaking along the countertops. Plates with partially consumed food were scattered about and flies buzzed above their greasy remains. Empty and nearly empty bottles of liquor stood like soldiers on tables and countertops, their caps strewn about carelessly. Ants and all manner of insects were crawling around, picking at the leftovers in pizza boxes and Styrofoam to-go containers.

James was struck by the smell. A putrid mix of stale beer, cigarettes, and cardboard-dry microwave pizza. Realizing he needed to get the hell out of there, James rushed into the bathroom where he found a similar alcohol-fueled scene covering every inch of the cramped room.

This is animalistic, he thought, pushing Solo cups out of the sink, actively ignoring their contents, before turning on the faucet and splashing his face with cold water. He walked cautiously across the bathroom floor and lifted the lid of the toilet, relieved to find an empty bowl greeting him.

Ten minutes later, he was walking down the dark street, the pale glow of early sunlight only a thin sliver on the horizon.

The air was wrapped in a misty, humid blanket. Thick enough to notice but cool enough to be comfortable. No matter how much he wished to sleep in, James enjoyed these moments in the morning. It was refreshing, especially when he woke to a scene best suited for a frat house.

He reached in his pocket and pulled out a bent cigarette from a crumpled pack. He straightened it out, stopping a moment to light the tip. A plume of smoke trailed behind him as he walked to the deli where he got his coffee.

The last three months since making it to the city were a blur. After they landed at the training compound, James prepared to be met with trouble from Croyton, but their commander did not even stick around to say goodbye. Walking the gangplank of their transport James watched a prop plane taxi down the runway and take off into the sunset. Fletcher stayed with them instead, proving to be an okay guy. Even still, James held a healthy skepticism of Federation authority, one he knew he earned during their latest ordeal and Fletcher was no different in his mind. James was not about to trust so easily.

In the meantime, they were told to wait for their next set of orders and relax while they recovered from their recent mission. They simply enjoyed the freedom none of them had known for a long time.

The word eventually came for them to report to a university campus on the East Coast for the upcoming summer.

Not one to argue, especially when James knew he should be facing criminal charges for his act of mutiny, James went with the flow.

They ended up in Midway, a city on the water located in the mid-Atlantic region of the Northern Federation. Their orders were to wait for the Federation to move military personnel into the area, handle reconnaissance for an attack and, most importantly, stay alert.

James looked back at their first few days here as a distant mirage of responsibility. They woke up early, ran together, and finished the day reading diligently from their HOLOs. That level of dedication was short-lived once Deck learned his military ID could purchase booze at almost any store in the city. They quickly combined their discovery with the generous stipends granted by the Federation.

The party had started.

It started simply enough, getting a case or two a few times a week. However, moderation proved elusive. Next James knew they were buying cases of beer nightly with a few bottles of liquor and cartons of cigarettes each week. Nightly trips to local bars in the area were an unspoken destination each night. James realized the partying escalated to the point of a problem when Bob began fashioning homemade gravity bongs from the liquor bottles piled high in their overflowing recycling bins.

That continued for the better part of two months until the cops showed up one night because of constant noise complaints. A noise complaint at a college dorm is not a big deal and would not have been a problem, but the team was placed in a nearly empty dorm apartment on a busy street in one of the larger metropolitan areas on the eastern seaboard. They had no neighbors, and the cops were called from three blocks over due to Deck and Kyle hanging out on the rooftop blasting Led Zeppelin at 3 a.m.

After that, they realized it was time to cool it and the bender came to an end.

James stood outside the glass doors of the deli and stubbed his cigarette in the ashtray next to the entrance, throwing his trash in the solar powered compactor. An automated *ding* sounded when he walked over the store's welcome mat.

He smiled with a quick wave at the woman behind the register. A muted HOLO hung suspended above the woman with news headlines scrolling along the bottom while three heads talked, their mouths moving simultaneously. James ignored them, seeking the continuously scrolling feed instead. The words fell off to the side when they finished their progression.

"*Draft continues, close to 30% of population chosen, total expected draft numbers to reach over 40% by the end of the year. European refugees flooding Federation cities. Search for survivors hampered by dangerous levels of radiation in Eastern Europe. Federation military continues troop presence on coasts increasing deployments to bases. New protests breaking out in the Capi—*"

Tense, James thought, going over the words written in white, hazy light. Troop buildup from the ring of fire to the polar caps, increased worry from media correspondents predicting imminent war, and unrest in major cities protesting the draft. Meanwhile, the Federation kept insisting they were merely taking precautions, and nothing was wrong. Hard to make that argument when the ashes of Europe snowed off their coast. The logic sounded exactly like the Federation, James thought, remembering his treatment over the last year with a grim smirk.

James arrived at the counter and smiled at the attendee.

She gave her standard courteous nod, no smile, before sliding her pointer finger up the face of her HOLO, the blue light creating glowing orbs of her pupils in the dimly lit store.

James grabbed one of the cups standing next to the coffee machines and placed it under the regular roast, filling it using the auto-sensor while he grabbed a sleeve and a cap from the other side of the counter.

He pulled out a crumpled twenty and nodded at the cigarette display behind the woman. "Pack of Camels, please."

She did not look at him as she turned around, taking the cellophane wrapped rectangle off the stand, and rang up the coffee and cigarettes, pushing him the change.

James dropped his coins in the tip jar, and walked outside, throwing the refuse in the compactor while a *ding* echoed upon his exit.

James hit the bottom corner of the cigarette box, popping a filter up from the twenty cigarettes tucked snugly together. He lit it in stride, savoring the fresh tobacco flavor missing from the mangled cigarette during his walk to the deli.

He ducked off the main road, cutting through the side streets back to campus.

The houses in the neighborhood surrounding the school were modest. They defined character. Owned and cared for by the people living there. On the other side of the main street bordering the rest of the campus, existed one of the wealthiest neighborhoods in the region. Sprawling mansions lined the streets with gaudy cars and misplaced stone archways. Just a roadway separated them, one area on the fringes of a ghetto, the other a model of what money can buy, a socioeconomic paradox James did not understand.

When he arrived back at the dorms he challenged himself to sprint up the stairs but backed out when the elevator was already waiting on the ground floor. Easier than eight flights, he rationalized, entering the cramped, carpet-covered interior and pressed the button to his floor.

He walked into the apartment, hoping someone else would have cleaned up, but the demolished scene he left was even more disheartening, the trash mocking him while he stood in the doorway, getting up his courage to step fully inside.

He let the door close behind him. He did not want to clean. It was always him. Where the hell were Deck, Kyle, and Clint, anyway? They should have to do this, too. Clenching his fists, James walked up to Clint and Kyle's door and was about to knock when the door swung open. James was pushed by a muscular body to the side, falling unceremoniously over the arm of the couch.

James landed in a puddle on the couch cushions while the shirtless torso of Clint disappeared around the corner of the hallway running to the bathroom. A feeble attempt to close the door was followed by violent retching sounds as Clint dealt with his decisions from the previous night.

Serves him right, James thought, smelling the hand he inadvertently placed in the puddle, hoping he was not about to play "guess this bodily fluid." He was relieved to discover the yeasty aroma of stale beer.

James rolled off the couch and looked around the room cursing his roommates before he took out a roll of garbage bags, paper towels, and a full bottle of anti-bacterial spray from under the sink.

Clint came out of the bathroom and, after a slow start that involved a few more trips to the toilet, helped James remove the debris from the room. They sprayed the soiled surfaces, and threw the garbage out behind the building where dumpsters overflowed from the trash their team accumulated in the last week.

When they returned, they fell into the couch breathing more heavily than they should have and inspected their work. The garbage was removed along with most of the spills. Some of the stains in the carpet were there to stay, James thought, but at least they weren't living in filth.

"Goddamn, I feel like hell," Clint said, bending over and putting his hands to his face. "I gotta get something to eat. Wanna come?"

"I'm good," James replied, putting his feet on the freshly scrubbed coffee table. "Drank some coffee so gonna wait a bit."

"Suit yourself."

Clint returned to his room and James synced the communal HOLO to his emitter, expanding the screen while he searched for a movie on one of the Federation's streaming services.

He flicked absently through the 3D titles popping out from the HOLO, opening film trailers one by one until he landed on an old comedy he knew well enough to quote. He needed to distract his mind and in minutes he was sleeping peacefully on the couch.

He awoke to the door swinging open and Bob walking in with a glass bowl in his left hand and a bag of weed in the right.

"Hey," he said, closing the door behind him and holding up the items in front of James. "Do you mind? Stacie's trying to take a nap on the couch and asked me to get lost."

"Help yourself," James said groggily, still waking up. Bob placed the bowl on the coffee table and broke up sticky pieces of weed into the glass smoking apparatus. Bob sat on the couch and as was customary in the group, offered up the first hit. James waved off the offer and looked for another distraction to play on the HOLO.

James landed on another old show he knew and sat back as the first exhale of smoke expanded, giving him the impression of a cloud of electricity with the bright colors from the HOLO shining through the indistinct haze.

They sat in relative silence watching an old Christmas episode where members in an office were playing yankee swap. They were laughing together and now that he was more awake, James was about to ask Bob to pass the bowl when there was a rap at the door.

Bob shrugged as he brought the bowl to his lips. "Hope it's not the RA kid again. Deck's made him cry at least five times by now." He lit the bowl and inhaled deeply while James sat by him, choosing to let the person at the door wait.

Bob let the smoke puff lazily through his mouth and nose. He was handing the still smoking bowl over to James when another more forceful knock rang through the apartment.

James got up from the couch, "All right, all right. I'm coming!" he said, annoyed. "Hold on."

He opened the door and found himself face to face with a middle-aged, well-built man in camo with a lieutenant's stripe on his chest.

210

"Are you James?" the man said, putting his hands in his pockets and cocking his head to the side. Cold dread seeped into James's body.

"Uhhh… yes, sir," James stammered, immediately regretting Bob's presence as well as his decision to present a full view of their compromised apartment.

"Private James Coffey, sir," he said, saluting and standing at attention.

The lieutenant brushed by him walking into the room without further questions. James began hating his decisions over the past few months. He turned around to see the officer standing in the middle of the room while Bob sat on the couch his mouth puckered with wisps of smoke escaping from his lips.

The lieutenant stared as Bob turned and let the smoke out, attempting to hide the cloud rising above his head.

James prepared for the blitz of hell they were about to face as the lieutenant turned away from Bob and walked into the kitchen where he stopped in front of the fridge.

He pulled the greasy handle to the fridge and looked at James over his shoulder. The Natural Ice cans gleamed iridescently, delivering a stark contrast to the fridge's otherwise bare shelves.

"Is this what you drink?" he said.

James barely registered the question, his mind packing the bags in his bedroom, explaining his failure to his parents. "Excuse me, sir?"

"Is this the crap you drink?" he repeated with a serious face.

"Yes? Yes, sir?" James said, confused.

"Well, it's crap," he said, turning back around and taking one out. "Do you mind?"

"No, sir."

"Good. Want one?"

"Um… yes, sir. Thank you, sir."

James's confusion mounted as the beer came flying. He caught the can, tapping its top unconsciously to relieve the pressure inside.

The lieutenant turned to Bob. "And you?"

Bob stared, his eyes turning deeper shades of red by the second. He glanced at James who shook his head mutely before he faced the lieutenant and mimicked James's response.

The lieutenant grinned and closed the door of the fridge, popping open his beer as he walked over to the counter and helped himself to James's cigarettes.

He took one out and put it behind his ear before walking to the patio door and sliding it open.

James and Bob watched in stunned silence while the lieutenant lit his cigarette and leaned over the edge of the patio.

He turned back to both of them. "Well, what are you two waiting for?"

James made his way to the door. Bob stood too quickly and spilled the glass of water at his foot on the rug. While he fetched a rag from the kitchen, James stepped outside.

The lieutenant was not as old as James had thought at first glance. However, the lines of experience etched in his face contained an indefinable edge James only witnessed in seasoned soldiers like Jackson or Hartsman. His eyes were a deep-set brown and his light brown hair was cropped close to his head. His jaw was strong, and a scar ran down the side of his neck from behind his ear to his collarbone. He wore an easy smile and a five o'clock shadow.

The lieutenant turned to him and stuck out his hand. "Name's Luke. Luke Brandt."

"Nice to meet you," James said, cautiously offering his hand.

Brandt grinned at him and turned back to lean over the edge of the balcony. "I thought you were gonna shit yourself when I walked in here," he said, peering at James out of the corner of his

212

eye. "Figured I would play the aloof military brass until you relaxed a bit."

Brandt glanced back at Bob, who was still mutely watching the two of them. "Your buddy is pretty baked. Bob, right?"

James didn't know what to say. Who was this guy and why was he the first senior military member to make him feel relaxed?

"Yeah that's Bob, and I'm not sure what you mean, sir." James took a quick sip of beer as he finished, hoping Brandt would let the conversation drop.

Brandt ignored him. All James's comment did was egg him on. "Hey, Bob!"

Bob's face perked up like a puppy.

"Me?" asked Bob, still attempting to maintain his composure.

"Yeah, you, dummy. Can you grab me another beer? Also, come and join us on the porch."

Bob's face sank. "Yes, sir."

Bob turned back to the kitchen. He kept his knees against the coffee table, bracing for movement before taking his first steps.

James eyed the porch next door, envying the lack of beer cans converted to ashtrays. He envied a lot about the apartment next door. From Jon's ripe red tomatoes to the still passable seating on their balcony, an overall healthier lifestyle existed one door to his left.

When they first arrived, the rooms were chosen for them by F.E.S.T. This was the acronym stenciled on the info packets and it stood for Federal Elite Soldier Training. When James first heard of the room assignments, he was excited to live with Deck again. He had no experience living in close quarters outside of boot camp with Kyle or Clint, but he assumed it would be fine. Fast forward three months and here he was, waking to shocking displays on a daily basis, usually the work of Kyle and Deck, but James was not completely innocent.

To make matters worse, Clint was constantly bringing home old engine parts to put back together and fix up so grease stains covered the apartment. They eventually forced Clint to keep all the parts stacked in bins in his bedroom, but bolts or bits of metal were a hazard whenever James stepped outside his room barefoot.

The apartment next to them was the complete opposite. While Jon brought home old computer parts, they were significantly neater than the greasy carburetors dragged in by Clint. On top of that, Kevin was an amazing chef which was not surprising when James saw how much he ate, and Bob developed the habit of getting baked and cleaning their entire apartment top to bottom at least twice a week. To top it all off, Stacie kept their gear organized and ready to go in the apartment, making sure their go-bags were always well stocked.

Simply put, they operated the correct way while James's apartment looked like a bombed-out college dorm room in a part-time chop shop.

Brandt looked behind him and sat heavily in one of the lawn chairs on the porch. He put his feet on the railing and motioned for James to join him.

"What's your endgame here, James?" Brandt asked looking at him quizzically. "Your next step? Ever thought about that?" Brandt's eyes turned into a piercing gaze.

James had not heard that question since Croyton posed the same one to him during his mutiny at the end of training and answered shakily. "I'm not sure yet, sir." Suddenly realizing he never thought about this James added, "I actually have no idea."

Brandt nodded and sipped his beer. "Make sure you know your next step."

James didn't know how to respond so he took a sip of his beer, hoping Brandt would go back to smoking his cigarette and staring out at the view.

Bob finally arrived, pulling open the doors while he steadied himself with noticeable effort and handed out their beers. James expected Bob to fall flat on his face walking back in, but before Bob was asked to do anything else, he lit the cigarette stowed behind his ear, leaned against the wall behind him and attempted to look casual.

Brandt was amused, almost impressed with the newfound stability Bob found in the last five minutes.

"Thank you, Bob," he said, tipping his beer. Bob managed a nod before he turned away to stare in the distance, smoking in silence.

"So, what have all of you been up to around here?" Brandt asked, directing the question at James.

James thought over his answer.

Brandt was aware of the drinking, smoking, and other extracurriculars Bob took part in, but to explain *everything* to date would be awkward. Living in a new city for three months, away from home and outside of any real control was jarring for all of them, and there had been a few run-ins with locals during their brief stint in the area. James knew he would have to soften the message.

"Maintaining a presence in the area while we await further orders, sir."

"Glad to hear it." Brandt paused to sip his beer. "And all the partying?"

James's stomach dropped. His eyes grew wider as Brandt glanced at him with a blank stare.

In that split second, James had two options. He could maintain the admirable position Brandt offered or deny everything until he knew Brandt meant business.

"Sir?" James said hesitantly, peering off to the side of the building avoiding eye contact.

215

"Well, from what I hear, life's settled down a bit. So, let's keep it that way." Brandt glanced out of the corner of his eye and James looked at the floor.

The lieutenant finished his second beer and set it on the table. "It seems like you're all doing fine, for the most part. Just stay out of trouble, you good with that?" He gave James a hard look who nodded in response. "My wife and I wanted to invite you to our house for a cookout. We're having a barbeque for the command and thought it'd be good to get you all out of this dorm for a little while. Interact with real people."

"That would be great, sir. Thank you."

"Awesome." Brandt waved while he started his exit. "See you tomorrow and tell the crew we're here now, too." Brandt winked at James who again felt his stomach drop. James worried if he would have those nausea inducing moments when he ran into Brandt in the future. Before he got hung up on it, he walked over to the fridge and cracked open another beer.

CHAPTER 18

James sat on the couch in the living room mindlessly watching another TV show with the volume low. He sipped his beer, thinking about the meeting with Brandt earlier in the afternoon, pondering their current circumstance.

About an hour earlier he received word from Captain Lopez via his HOLO that James and his group would still be the leads for "maintaining area security." If the military was moving in, then that's great, but the phrasing implied something different. What did it mean? Why did a new officer show up out of the blue? What was going on? Brandt mentioned the rest of his command. If James's instincts were right, a group of trained, experienced soldiers were stationed in the same city. He was in the dark again and needed answers.

While James puzzled over their situation, Bob shuffled about in the kitchen, cooking hot dogs in a skillet while his toast let off the acrid smell of burned wheat.

The door swung open in a rush of voices. Kyle and Deck came stumbling heavily into the room, their faces flushed and their shirts drenched in sweat.

"Damn, it's brutal out there!" exclaimed Deck walking over to the kitchen sink and shoving his mouth under the faucet as he flipped the handle to cold water. "Ten miles feels like a thousand."

Kyle peeled off his shirt, throwing it in a crumpled pile by the door to his bedroom and tromped through the living room to stand beneath the HVAC vent in the corner. "Yeah, we almost didn't make it through the first five miles. Stopped for a refresher."

Deck mimed taking a shot. "Nothing like a little liquid courage to keep the juices flowing," he said, putting his face back under the water stream.

"Never been wrong," Kyle replied, stretching his arms over his head

James got up from the couch and walked over to the fridge. "Humid, huh?"

"Yep," said Deck. "Hot as the devil's taint, but what can you do?"

"Well, it would make it easier if you ran earlier in the day," Bob mentioned offhandedly, looking around, noticing something was off about his meal.

"Why in the world would I put myself through that?" asked Kyle.

With his hot dogs done and forgetting his burned toast, Bob plopped on the couch and poured a pile of ketchup on his plate before methodically devouring his meal.

Deck turned off the burner Bob was using and opened the fridge. He grabbed two beers and tossed one to Kyle, who kept his spot under the vent.

"New commander in town. Came by to say hello," James mentioned casually, picking up Kyle's shirt and throwing it in the room he shared with Clint. Even in the darkness, James discerned the heaps of clothes and engine parts scattered about.

"What did he want?" asked Deck, rummaging through the cupboards taking out random packs of ramen and bags of chips.

"Not sure," said James. "Nice guy though. Seemed pretty cool. Bob?"

Bob nodded, his mouth full of hot dog, ketchup staining the corners of his mouth.

James continued, "He wanted to know what we've been up to if there have been any issues. You know, the usual."

Deck, not paying any attention, boosted himself up to kneel on the counter. "Aha! Gotcha!" He jumped from the counter with a jar of Nutella in his hand. "So that was it? A check-in?" he said.

"Yeah, what it seemed like at least. But it was different, they're not telling us something again."

Deck, after noisily banging around the utensil drawer, dug through the dishwasher. He held up a spoon for inspection and, after a quick wipe on his pants, dug into the jar eating a heaping spoonful of the rich hazelnut spread. "As long as he doesn't try to fuck up a good thing when he sees it."

Kyle snorted. "You think you're going to have a say in what happens?"

"I would make our time unpleasant for everyone," Deck said between scoops of Nutella.

"What's the Federation doing moving them in here though?" James asked, entering the kitchen for another beer.

"Relax, man," Kyle said, walking to his bedroom. "They're beefing up military presence all over the country. You know that."

"Right, but why not tell us a new commander is in town?" James asked.

"I woo-ent woowy." Deck swallowed. "Classic Federation all over again."

"Exactly," said Kyle, walking out of his bedroom with a towel around his waist. "I read the other day they've mobilized an entire fleet in South America. The conspiracy sites are going bonkers about it," he added, closing the bathroom door behind him.

"See," said Deck, screwing the top back on the Nutella and throwing the spoon in the sink. "You're overreacting for nothing. At least we know the whole story."

James didn't say anything. He knew he was oversensitive when it came to the Federation's treatment of them and his mistrust ran deep, but he was the only one who saw his teammates helplessly sedated, laid out on gurneys in the back of a plane. He did not need another reason to question motives.

"So, where'd you all go today?" asked James, sitting on the couch next to Bob who was characteristically quiet, zoned out staring at the HOLO screen in a food-induced coma.

"Went to the waterfront and ran around a few of the local college campuses. New crop of students arriving."

"Don't you mean the only crop of students you've ever known?" James said, rolling his eyes.

"Yes, technically, but my way sounds a lot cooler," Deck said, sitting on one of the barstools next to the kitchen counter. "What else would you have me say?"

"Literally anything," James replied.

Deck waved off his comment, looking at the HOLO screen.

"Brandt invited us to a barbeque, by the way," James added, remembering the main reason for bringing his visit up in the first place.

"Who?" Deck asked, still watching the screen.

"The new lieutenant, Brandt. He invited us to a barbecue tomorrow. Might be a good way to get to know them and learn the inside scoop on why they're here."

Deck nodded absently, taking a sip of his beer.

The bathroom door opened, and Kyle walked across the floor wrapped in his towel, steam trailing behind him.

"Well, this is all fine and dandy, but we should get ready," he said to Deck, walking into his room.

"Ready for what?" asked James.

"To meet the fine young women we met on our run today," Kyle said nonchalantly, closing the door behind him.

"Yeah, they were running in the park, and we happened to stop and need a stretch break at the same time," Deck said, winking. "Care to join? I'm sure they can convince a friend to come along."

220

"I'm good, thanks," said James. "Don't cause any trouble."

"I am offended," Deck retorted making his way to their bedroom. "I have been nothing but on my best behavior."

"Ha! My ass," said Stacie, walking in through the front door. "You are an adult Dennis the Menace."

Deck gave her the finger and closed his door.

"What's up, nerds?" Stacie said. She walked over to the fridge, took out a beer, and leaned casually against the kitchen's bar ledge. Her red nails contrasted sharply with the aluminum of the can.

"Nada, Serial," said Kyle, coming out of his room. His hair was significantly longer since training and he wore it loosely behind his ears.

Stacie rolled her eyes. "If it isn't the ass."

Kyle grinned, blowing a kiss in the air. "There's my lovely."

Shortly after their arrival, Kyle came home early one evening and found Stacie sorting her clothes. He was not thrown by the perfectly folded shirts and pants, but by the unbelievably intricate pattern breakdown and color coordination of the whole process. He commented how she was like a serial killer with her hyper-organization. Ever since then, he called her Serial which she leaned into with aplomb. Stacie just called him ass. James thought it worked.

Deck walked out of their bedroom, holding a towel around his waist. "Kyle, you almost ready?"

"I am ready," said Kyle walking over to the fridge, helping himself to another beer. "Get in there already."

"I'm going!" Deck yelled.

James heard the curtain rings slide against the shower's metal rod as Deck stepped into the shower. He turned to Stacie. "What have you been up to today?"

"Reading a little bit. Trying to see if I can get some more info from the Federation database. All these reports about troop movements are weird."

James nodded. "Funny you should mention—"

"Hurry up!" Kyle interrupted. Seconds later, he was greeted by the shower turning off.

"I am. Hold on, hold on. Christ, I'll be two minutes. Relax. It's barely even happy hour," Deck retorted through the bathroom door.

"I'm going out for a smoke," Kyle yelled back, pulling a cigarette from James's pack on the counter.

He walked to the patio door and stepped outside, shutting the sliding door behind him, a cloud of smoke breaking against the glass behind his head moments later.

Deck, still soaking wet, scurried from bathroom to bedroom, not bothering to shut either door.

"So, where are you meeting these girls?" asked James loudly from the kitchen.

"The little dive up the road," replied Deck.

Stacie's head whipped up. "You are *not* taking them to that place where the guy got stabbed last week, are you? That *little dive*." She capped off her comments in air quotes, her face incredulous.

James knew the place well. A few blocks away, past the storefronts advertising "Checks Cashed Here" and discount cigarettes, there was a small, dark dive bar. It was a single entrance bar with cheap pitchers of beer, pool, and darts. Almost every week James and the group heard about a different stabbing, murder, or shooting in, around, or connected to the bar. It was also known to have a loose hand when serving patrons, frequently resulting in its customers pouring out into the night sprawled on the sidewalk.

"You have got to be kidding me," James said, exasperated. He knew the last thing they needed was Kyle and Deck getting in trouble with two local college girls.

"What?" asked Deck innocently, pulling on his jeans while he came out of the room. He had not expected this kind of reaction.

"There was a stabbing there two nights ago," said James.

"One last night, too," said Clint walking in the front door. "You know I can hear you in the hall? Shitty walls in this place." Clint made a beeline to the fridge, pulling out a beer. He cracked open his can and rested his elbows on the ledge of the counter next to Stacie.

Deck waved them off. "We'll be fine. We can avoid the pool area. That's where it all happens."

Kyle entered the room and threw his arms in the air at the sight of Deck. "Finally!"

Deck thrust his face back under the faucet, chugging water before he stood up, wiping his mouth with the back of his hand.

"Let's go!" he said with a flourish. The two of them walked out the door without another word.

Clint sat next to Bob, shaking his head. "He may have given himself giardia from the towel."

Stacie laughed. "At least chlamydia."

James grinned. "I don't think he's ever washed it."

"I know he hasn't. I took his spare," Clint said, getting laughs out of James and Stacie.

Clint pulled the HOLO out of his pocket and took over control of the monitor from Bob. Clint found a college basketball game on and put his HOLO on the coffee table.

"I didn't know you liked basketball," said Stacie. "You play?" she asked, moving from the kitchen to the armchair next to the TV.

"Nah, we worked," replied Clint. "Too much happening at the shop to play for real, but my brothers and I had a hoop out back to shoot around."

Bob got up unsteadily, walking into the kitchen. He put his ketchup smeared plate in the sink, poured a glass of water, and walked sleepily toward the front door. Standing in the entrance he turned around, bobbed his head in a feeble attempt to say good night, and walked out into the hall swinging the door shut behind him.

"Has he been sober since we got here?" Clint asked the room, shaking his head at Bob's exit.

"I think once he smoked, he found his groove," James replied, grinning. "At least we know our medic has plenty of patience and the Zen attitude we need."

Stacie laughed. "Yeah, but what if he's too stoned to do the job?"

"He'll figure it out," said Clint. "Kid's good at his shit. Needs a break every once in a while." He picked the bowl off the table Bob used earlier and repacked it with some of the weed still sitting in the grinder.

"Do you smoke, Stacie? I don't think I've ever seen you burn," he asked, lighting the bowl with a lighter from his pocket. The flame licked the top of the plant, and he alternated his finger on the carbs, pulling in thick white smoke.

"Not a fan," she said. "And not my lane. When I wasn't at practice or playing in a game, I was at home helping my mom in our store. Didn't have time to get stoned. Basically, a poster child for any rec center's success story," she added, leaning back in her chair, her eyes focused on the game.

Clint held the bowl out to James. "What about you man?"

"I'm good tonight," James said tiredly. "I'll be worse than Bob if I do."

Stacie chuckled. "Doubt it."

"What'd you play, Stacie?" James asked. "Track wouldn't surprise me." James thought back to her burning the team during their group runs.

"What didn't I play?" she said, rolling her eyes. "Track, swimming, lacrosse, basketball, you name it. But last year I had to stop. My mom needed more help at home."

"Impressive," said Clint, letting a small cloud of smoke blow out from his nose.

"Thank you," she said in reply with a quick bow. "What about you, James? Any sports? Any fun?" She walked into the kitchen, throwing her beer in the recycling and poured a glass of water.

"Mostly fun and some sports," James replied. "After the unification, our lives stabilized, and we were better, I guess."

"Lucky, man," said Clint. "My mom died after the unification. I had the pleasure of getting raised by four older brothers and a dad who knows machines better than people. But wasn't too bad. Learned how to fight early," he added with a grin, the scar above his eyebrow wrinkling as evidence to his statement. "Why'd you have to quit all your sports?" Clint asked Stacie as she sat back in her chair, popping open her beer while she did.

"My dad died," Stacie said coolly. "Heart attack working in our hardware store late one night."

Her eyes were glued to the HOLO. James was taken aback by the lack of emotion behind the words. However, he recognized the self-defense and tried to move past the topic.

"I'm sorry to hear that, Stacie," James said, unsure of what else to say. Stacie nodded back and they let the silence hang in the air for a moment.

"What do you think our families are doing now?" asked Clint, lying back in the couch cushions, his voice aimed at the clouds.

"My dad's probably getting home from work and either eating or about to eat. My sisters are getting home from practices or doing homework and my brother is avoiding my mom like the plague as his bedtime gets closer," James said, looking at his reflection in the window. He drifted to a dinner table hundreds of miles away.

"I'd be finishing up at the store, and one of my younger siblings would be putting dinner together," Stacie said. "We used a chart that said who was in charge of what. My mom had six kids on her hands, a Type A personality and an energy drive meth-heads would find off-putting. She put together this massive chart, organizing exactly where we needed to be and what we were expected to do. Washing dishes, making dinner, vacuuming, garbage, laundry—hell, even taking animals to the vet was a chore," said Stacie. "Made living easier but I hated it. Couldn't get away with anything."

"Damn! That's intense," said Clint. "I don't think my dad would even have the concept of a chore chart or whatever you call it. We'd all still be at the shop probably, eating take-out. Or grilled cheeses—a staple in our house. We didn't have many rules," he added. "Good grades and a well-run shop—all my dad cared about. Simple guy."

James reached out and grabbed the lighter off the table, pulling his cigarettes from his pocket. "Anyone care to join?" he said, flipping open the top of the pack.

Stacie and Clint both shook their heads, caught up in their family daydreams.

James walked out onto the porch, lighting his cigarette and leaning over the railing, watching the world below change with dusk. He loved Midway at night.

It was a unique moment of the day when the rays of sunshine turned into long streaks of ever-shifting color. Reds, yellows, purples, and oranges intersected across the horizon, bathing the street in a soft even glow. The city shifted, a weight lifted, a breath of air injected it with a renewed sense of calm. People crisscrossed the busy streets, making their way home or on to a happy hour or the grocery store. So mundane but James felt a twinge of jealousy at their normalcy. A myriad of scents flavored the air—from the corner flower stand to the wafts of the evening's appetizer courses from nearby restaurants.

He let his mind drift, getting lost in the white noise bubbling up from the city, thinking about his life from his family to his friends and their place in his new reality.

Over a year ago he was in school, learning history and basic electrician training, deciding on a future path, and readying for the world after high school. He would sit in his friend's basement, talking excitedly about the world beyond their own, trying to discern what would happen later in their lives, making plans to do whatever the hell they wanted.

Now, many of his friends were probably drafted or volunteered. He thought of Kaylie, training to be a field nurse somewhere on the southeast coast, stomaching the brutal heat and torrential rain that plagued the area. He slipped into dread and stopped before he dug any deeper in his mind.

Knock it off, he thought. Focus on what you can change and what you can control.

He took one last drag on his cigarette and stubbed it out on the rail before flicking it down to the street.

He walked back inside where Stacie and Clint were arguing over a movie to watch.

"But it's a classic," Clint was saying. "And I haven't seen it in years. Can we please watch it?"

"Fine, but I choose next time," said Stacie.

"You got it, girl," said Clint, grinning.

"What are we watching?" asked James, returning to his seat on the couch after pouring a glass of water from the kitchen.

"*Stepbrothers*," said Clint. "Ever seen it?"

"I don't think so."

"Well, get ready for the time of your life." Clint pressed play on his HOLO, and the screen responded jumping to life.

"You're gonna love this." Clint leaned back, an anticipatory smile hovering on his lips.

Stacie rolled her eyes at James and mimicked a face of mock stupidity. James stifled his laughter and settled in to watch the movie.

After an hour, Clint was passed out on the couch snoring loudly and James dozed off.

When he awoke, he was alone on the couch and someone was jiggling the door handle. He heard the auto-lock open, and Kyle staggered into the room. He calmly pulled himself together before he walked over to the sink where he proceeded to throw up voluminously.

James left the couch and walked into his bedroom, still hearing Kyle's retches, while he closed the door behind him.

CHAPTER 19

Kyle and Deck were in rough shape. Their pain was evident from the dull glassy-eyed stares they shared focusing on nothing. A thin sheen of sweat clung to their faces, and their splotchy skin emitted a sickly glow. Serves them right, James thought ruefully.

James predicted a painful experience for the two of them given Kyle's immediate reaction to seeing a sink and Deck stumbling into their room at 3 a.m. only semiconscious. He proceeded to bump into every object around him except his own bed, eventually finding a home on the floor, close to where James stepped on the banana the previous day. Now, the three of them sat in the back of a taxi, winding their way to the address Brandt sent over earlier in the morning.

James turned his attention out the window, watching the trees whir by in long, broken blurs of brown and green. The heat had attacked with a vengeance and their cab's broken AC barely cooled the rear seat of the four-door sedan. James was tempted to shove his head out the window to escape the sickly aroma of spoiled milk and loose change filling the stale air.

James made eye contact with the cabbie, hoping he had not noticed the state of his fellow passengers. He did not want the driver to make them walk because he was nervous about two teenage lightweights ruining his upholstery.

They crossed over the cement bridge, entered the restaurant district, and stopped at the red light. Droves of people crossed before them walking the main street heading to the curbside restaurants or milling about shopfronts. Even the oppressive heat could not keep people away from an outdoor brunch, James thought, impressed at their resilience.

The light changed and they drove up the steep incline, entering the honeycomb streets zigzagging through the neighborhood nestled on the side of the hill overlooking the river. Houses on either side of the road were stacked on top of one another, and a sense of vertigo overcame James looking at the precariously structured architecture.

"Thirteen bucks," the cabbie said, addressing James through the rearview mirror as he pulled over to the side of the road where a police barrier blocked the entrance to the street. James pulled a twenty out of his pocket and handed it to him.

"Keep the change," he said.

The cabbie nodded his thanks and James scooted out the door meeting the rest of his friends standing outside the barrier, looking at the festivities. Young families and unaccompanied tweens walked up and down the sidewalks with face painting, balloon animals, and make-your-own candy stations scattered along the street. Aromas of barbecue and carnival food filled the air creating a sticky sweet sensation on James's hands before he even saw a funnel cake.

"Where are we?" asked Kyle, his eyes bloodshot.

"Brandt told us to come around now. I didn't think it'd be… this," James replied, thrown off by the vast array of food and entertainment.

James checked out their surroundings while they walked. The homes were nearly identical to the rest of the row houses throughout Midway, but were freshly painted and worked on in the past few months. Each house hung a Federation flag somewhere on the property and every stretch of sidewalk was packed with kids running and playing.

The street was never-ending, the crowd only growing thicker as they walked. James thought this was going to be a small barbecue, but this was a professional event, more like a mini fair than a neighborhood block party.

When they crossed what seemed like the tenth cross street blocked off to the rest of the public, James noticed a familiar face in the crowd. Brandt stood in a group of people holding a kid on his shoulders with a beer in his hand. He waved James over when he caught sight of them over the crowd.

"Down with you. Dad's gotta entertain." Brandt swung the kid from his shoulders eliciting a giggle from her.

He bent and got a kiss on the cheek before the little girl ran off to one of the yards, joining in with an ongoing water balloon war.

Brandt stood casually in front of the group. James did not know why, but he was suddenly nervous, realizing he was showing off his team to their new commander.

"James, how are you?" he said, clapping him on the shoulder.

"Good sir," James replied.

"You must be Stacie. Pleasure to meet you." Brandt stretched out his hand to Stacie who returned the shake.

"Likewise, sir."

"Bob, good to see you again. Seems like you've got all your senses together this time," Brandt said with a wink.

Bob looked at his feet sheepishly, his face deepening a shade.

Brandt introduced himself to each one of the team members. James was impressed by how easily he talked with everyone and was more impressed by his good humor at the state of Deck and Kyle shaking their hands longer than necessary when it came time to meet them.

When he was done, Brandt addressed the team as one. "I know I'll get to know you all in time, but before I do let's get you all some food. If I don't, my wife will kill me."

He guided them to the backyard avoiding the side of the house where the water balloon war raged. He led James and his team through a wooden gate and down a tight alleyway. At the end of the alley was a compact backyard with an impressive display of hot dogs, bratwursts, sausages, burgers, brisket, ribs, and every type of barbeque James could think of.

Brandt waved to someone through the back door of the house and was joined moments later by a lean, blond woman carrying two trays of steaming cornbread. Her face was marked by sharp cheekbones and piercing gray eyes. She had a thin but clearly defined jawline. She looked so familiar to James, but he could not place her. She looked accusingly at Brandt with a sharp gaze.

"What the hell, Luke? Why haven't you gotten them fed yet?" she said in a stern voice.

"They just got here, Riley," he replied, grinning at her. "This is my wife." He said over his shoulder to the group.

She didn't even notice, his introduction. "Well, take these. They need to eat. Probably been living off boxed potatoes and chicken fingers." She offloaded the cornbread into his arms and grabbed Clint by the wrist, pulling him over to the buffet line near the stacked paper plates.

"Eat as much as you want. We have plenty of food, so don't hold back. You are welcome to whatever."

"Thank you" was all Clint could say as she pulled Kevin's arm to the line next.

"Don't be shy, people! We've got food. You're hungry. Get to eating."

James looked over to Brandt who nodded toward the food line, still grinning.

"What the hell are you grinning at? Go put those at the end of the table."

"Yes, dear," said Brandt in a mock fawning tone, receiving another glare from his wife.

James piled his plate until it sagged with its greasy load and walked to the long picnic table Brandt's wife had set up for them.

He took a spot next to Jon who was working on ribs slathered in barbecue sauce.

"Mmm, these are good," Jon said, his voice muffled. "I'm gonna need to throw up before we go home."

"Go around the side of the house," James replied dryly, picking up the burger on his plate.

"No way. Right here, man."

James elbowed him playfully before taking a big bite, the mayo and onion falling off the sides and juices pooling on his plate. Steamy flavor lines rose from the plate causing his mouth to water while he chewed. He was in heaven.

The group spent the next half hour in silence devouring the contents of their plates. Kevin and Bob were the first to go back for seconds followed closely by the rest of the team. No one wanted to see the ribs disappear before they had a chance to grab their second set.

"Dessert, anyone?" Riley came over with two tubs of ice cream, balancing bottles of chocolate syrup, and a jar of butterscotch. Her husband followed close behind with cans of whipped cream, cherries, and three different types of sprinkles.

"Diabetes, anyone?" he asked playfully, getting an elbow in the stomach.

"Don't listen to him," Riley said, throwing a paper bowl in front of each place before delivering two healthy scoops of ice cream to each member of the team.

When they finished gorging, the team lolled around the table, clutching their stomachs. Brandt invited them to a firepit set up on the front lawn.

James followed him while the others cleaned up and threw out their plates. Brandt pointed him toward the cooler and James grabbed a cold beer taking a long sip.

He sat in a lawn chair next to a group of younger guys who were talking loudly.

"Jesus, Bill, have you seen your QB throw the ball? It's like his eyes are looking at the ground when he lets go. Throwing on a wish and a prayer. What in God's name makes you think you can do anything next season?"

"What's he supposed to do with no o-line? He has to look at the ground, he's getting pummeled every other snap!"

"Excuses, excuses…"

The sun was setting behind the houses across the street casting shadows across the lawn. Kids played in the road with some of the older ones arranging teams for manhunt.

Stacie, Jon, and Bob were talking on the front step with Riley, watching the kids play, Kevin and Kyle were already engaged in a cornhole match on the lawn across the street. Clint and Deck walked out from the backyard and were bombarded by kids.

"Want to play manhunt?" asked the girl who had been sitting on Brandt's shoulders when they arrived.

"Sure," said Deck, stretching out his hand. "I'm Deck. What's your name?"

"Shannon," she replied, hitting his hand with the energy only a child can muster.

"This is Clint," Deck said, pointing at Clint who extended his hand for a similar low-five from Shannon.

"Can you show us what to do?" Deck asked. Shannon practically jumped out of her sneakers with excitement.

"Okay! Follow me!" Shannon sprinted away and Deck and Clint took off at a jog to keep up with her.

James grinned as they disappeared behind the house resulting in a series of shouts from other members of the game.

Brandt came up, pulling the cooler behind him and sitting next to James. He pulled out a bottle, shaking off the ice. The white plastic lawn chair creaked under his weight when he leaned

234

back. They watched the cornhole game across the street intensify as Kyle gave double guns to the other team after sinking two bags in a row to send the game into overtime.

"Nice throws," Brandt said, impressed.

"He has a way of doing that," James said, remembering many games when he thought he had Kyle beat only to bring out the competitor in him sinking bags, hitting a bullseye, or burying the eight ball each time.

"So, how you feeling, man?" Brandt asked offhandedly, taking a sip from his beer.

"Not bad. That was a great meal. Thanks for having us," James replied.

"She's a damn good cook and a better wife and mother. Not to mention the toughest woman I've ever met."

"Well, she made fans out of all of us."

"Good to hear."

James leaned forward. "So, which ones are yours?"

"Kids? Well, the one sitting on Jon's lap over there is Danny. Little spitfire but a good kid. He's our youngest at two. The little towheaded girl running around is Shannon. She's six and talk about wild. Finally... *oomph!*" Brandt let out a gust of air as a small body landed across his shoulders. He grabbed at the newly arrived torso and whipped it onto his lap holding him in a tight body embrace.

"This is George." He took George's arm by the elbow and extended his hand. "Say hi to James, George."

"Hi, James George," George mimicked with a hollow voice. Brandt grinned and squeezed his sides causing George to howl in laughter.

George wriggled his way free, sprinting off laughing when his feet hit the ground. Brandt picked his beer back up off the ground.

"He's four and is more spirited than I need."

"Sounds like they all are."

"Ain't it the truth,"

They clinked bottles, settling in their chairs while streetlights blinked on. James took a breath and sensed his moment, realizing now was better than ever to ask the questions he needed to answer.

"Lieutenant, how'd you pick this neighborhood?" James asked.

"Same as we usually do," Brandt said with a shrug. "High up, plenty of space for kids, enough houses, close enough to protect, easy to get in and out of, etc., etc...."

"How long ago did you all start looking here?" James asked.

"About a year ago. Didn't decide until a few weeks ago though."

"Strange," James said aloud, looking around. "So built up already. Seems weird."

"What's weird?" Brandt said, still not fully invested in the conversation.

"An entire neighborhood was redone and moved into by a couple hundred military families, and no one said anything." Brandt's jaw tightened.

"You know, when we were driving here there was a lot that struck me as odd. The fact that a new lieutenant shows up out of the blue who surprisingly doesn't care about anything we do in our free time. Before that, strange rumors running around about major cities getting special attention from the Federation, more military supplies, and whatnot. In addition to it all, we haven't gotten updates from central command in months, even while we were still in our specialist training or whatever you want to call it. We were analyzing the same scenarios over and over again, piecing together the attack bit by bit."

"James—" Brandt started, but James continued.

"All of that was strange but understandable. I mean, no one knows what's going on here, but I don't know if that's true

236

anymore. I think there's a plan going with our team playing a central role and no say in what happens." James took a sip of his beer. He knew he was treading a thin line but kept talking.

"Here's the thing. The Federation's spent millions training us to be the top soldiers the Federation has, supposedly, ever seen. We can analyze troves of data with Jon's computational algorithms and processing shortcuts. Put together operational plans with Stacie's and my understanding of battle strategy. We've been dragged around our whole career. What I'm trying to say is, start using us. To do that, we have to get information. For now, we have none."

"How'd you know something was up?" Brandt asked, his voice betraying nothing.

"You have ten blocks of military families living here. That's a lot of men to go under the radar. Not to mention, those soldiers are all senior enough to have families, too. Indicates seasoned vets, not a bunch of fresh recruits.

"Now why would a command of roughly 300 experienced military personnel move into a city where the Federation happened to place their newest experiments? I don't know about you but sounds like we're getting pulled into another plan again and haven't been told about it. This time I want to take the reins before it all gets out of control." James looked coolly at Brandt.

Brandt met his gaze and took another sip of his beer, condensation dripping on his chin from the glass neck. James shut up. Whatever Brandt said or did next would define how they would work together for the rest of their time.

"Fair enough," Brandt said finally. "Let's meet to talk another time."

"All right, but we want to know not just what *you* think we need," James said sternly, trying to make sure his point was made. "Consider us a need-to-know on *everything*." James knew he was asking a lot, but this had to happen. How else would he and the team make it in the Federation if they didn't have information to make decisions? This was their moment to step up.

"Everything. Give me two days, okay?" Brandt said, extending his hand. James accepted it.

They sat in silence, sipping their beers.

"Damn, feels like I was in your shoes yesterday," Brandt said, looking at the dappled purple and orange sky. "No wife, no kids, no responsibility other than myself and where I needed to be in that moment. There was no concern about school or my five-year plan. I just... did."

"You've got it pretty good now," James said, leaning over to light a cigarette in the flames leaping over the edge of the brass pit.

"I wouldn't trade it for the world."

They were quiet, James contemplated how Brandt would have been when he was a younger soldier. Probably a wild side to him and eager to travel the world. Ready for what got thrown at him. Not like James who still wasn't sure what he was here to do.

"So, you guys have a pretty good handle on Midway?" Brandt asked.

"I think so. Have a detailed mental map of the area at least."

"Good," Brandt said, letting the topic trail off again.

James was about to press his earlier conversation further when two small bodies flew out of the darkness and landed on top of Brandt who dropped his beer on the grass. A spray of hoppy foam squirted up between them.

"Jesus," he laughed, pulling his sons up over his shoulders. "Couple sacks of potatoes."

"I'm not a sack of potatoes, Dad!" George yelled gleefully, his head swinging wildly over his father's shoulder.

"You sure?" said Brandt, winking at James, "James, what do you think? Potatoes or not?"

238

"Potatoes, definitely," James said, nodding his head solemnly.

Brandt sighed. "You heard him, potatoes. Off to the peeler."

The two boys howled and fought to get off his back while he brought them over to the edge of the kiddy pool in the corner of the yard, threatening to drop them in.

"Gotta clean you before we peel you."

Cries and screams were interrupted by Riley who came over and picked Danny off Brandt's shoulders.

"It is not time to peel you, but it is time for a bath."

This elicited further howls, protesting the end of their night.

"Let's go with your mom boys."

James and the rest of the group grinned as the three children ran circles around the front yard, avoiding the deft grabs of their parents until it was Shannon versus Brandt who managed to grab her after he lunged over some shrubs to execute the takedown.

"Come on," Brandt said, holding her over his shoulder with one arm and keeping George in a firm grip with his other hand. "More time to play outside tomorrow."

James looked around at the group who all caught his eye. "Okay, I guess…" James started to say when Brandt cut him off.

"Hey, you all want to wait here? There are more beers in the cooler, and the wife and I are going to stay up a little later. Give us a half hour?"

James shrugged. "Sure."

"Great. Be back in a few."

The team walked over to the circle of lawn chairs and sat, pulling over new seats to make room.

Clint and Deck returned with their faces streaked with lines of sweat and covered in pieces of grass and smudges of dirt.

"Have fun with the kids?" Stacie asked.

"A blast," said Clint, rubbing dirt from the lines on his kneecaps. "Best exercise I can remember since leaving home."

"Agreed, real fun time. Although *best* exercise, I don't know…" Deck said with an exaggerated wink, which made Stacie roll her eyes.

"I didn't know you came from a big family, Jon," she said, ignoring Deck's comment.

"Twelve brothers and sisters. I was the middle of the pack. All of us lived under one roof at one point, too. Talk about hectic."

"I can't imagine," said Kyle, chiming in from across the flames. "One older brother and we fought constantly. Dealing with twelve would be unfair and would have caused a lot more stores to close after the soup aisle got destroyed."

"Please, let us come back to that sometime in the future," said Clint.

"Come back to what?" asked Kyle, oblivious.

"Never mind." Clint shook his head.

The sound of objects falling came from the house and indiscernible yelling from both Riley and Brandt came immediately after, followed by silence.

"Someone's in trouble," said James.

"Oh, definitely," replied Clint.

A few minutes later, Riley and Brandt came out of the house and took a spot on a bench across from James. Kyle tossed them each a beer that they opened with a muted hiss as the carbonated air escaped from its glass prison. James thought they looked like parents are supposed to—tired.

"So, how'd you two end up together?" asked Jon, stirring the fire with an iron poker.

"Not a long story honestly," Brandt said, eyeing his wife.

"Nope. He was a dumbass trying to hook up with anything that moved, and I got snared in his web." Riley nudged him in the side.

"Yeah, very romantic."

240

"But seriously, I used to work for a defense contractor. Traveled around the world helping different parts of the military construct their emergency preparations. It was a stressful job but a lot of fun to travel so often. I ended up on a base outside of New Orleans. My company assigned me there to help institute a plan for both the military base and the city. It was a huge job, would've been impossible without the might of the military.

"I was there for a few weeks, working day and night trying to get some sort of first draft of a plan in place when I was invited out to dinner by the other women on my team. We ate a nice dinner on Decatur Street, some of the best gumbo I ever had in my life. Afterward, we went out for a couple of hurricanes, because back then you couldn't go to New Orleans and not get a hurricane. We were drinking and having a great time when a group of dumb, drunk soldiers walk in and start hitting on anything they saw."

Brandt grinned and shook his head. "That's not how we looked."

"Yes, yes, it was." She tapped him playfully on the arm. "Now let me finish my story. Where was I? Bar, drunk assholes, one in particular… right. As we're finishing our drinks, this guy comes stumbling over trying to be slick and introduce himself. He took a sip of his beer, and it must have been a little too much too fast because that's when he spit it all over me."

"I didn't puke if that's what you're thinking," Brandt said, holding his hands up to defend what remained of his diminishing honor in the story.

"It would have been better if you had. I was covered in wet, beery saliva. It was disgusting."

"I felt pretty stupid," Brandt said.

"And you should have. But he felt even dumber the next day when we met in the afternoon and learned he was replacing my military liaison for the rest of my time in New Orleans."

She looked over at him and lifted his chin with her hand, looking him in the eye, "And here we are married, three kids later, and living in a city hundreds of miles away from the swamps."

"Better for it."

There was a pop in the distance and James looked up to see a bottle rocket explode against the night sky. A few more volleys echoed off the houses on either side of the street and their circle was bathed in light from the amateur fireworks launched from behind one of the houses. James took in the sulfur as it washed over him, bathing his senses in nostalgia.

When the show ended James looked around at the group. "Ready to head out?"

A few mumbled yeses came from around the fire and James pulled up the cab company on his HOLO, ordering them rides home.

They stood and thanked Brandt and his wife for the invite.

James approached last. "Thank you again," he said, hugging Riley. "Truly incredible. Exactly what we needed."

Riley patted him on the back and released him. "You are welcome back any time. Who knows how long we'll all be here."

"I'll take you up on that," he said and shook Brandt's hand. "Let me know when you want a tour. We're more than happy to show you around."

"Works for me. You eat my wife's food. The least you can do is give me a tour."

James grinned and walked away, carrying one of the gallon size Ziploc doggie bags Riley made for all of them.

In his cab, he was greeted by a silence that lasted the whole ride. Kyle and Deck stumbled their way to bed when they arrived home. It was only moments later Kyle's snores echoed through the living space.

Clint plopped on the couch, throwing his head back, exhausted.

James grabbed a cigarette from the pack sitting on the table. He walked outside and sat in one of the lawn chairs while he smoked, watching the skyline reflect the light of the city.

His mind drifted back to his first days in training on those grueling runs, landing on the tarmac in the mountains to carrying a woman on his back through the jungle, her hot breath on his ear, her heart beating rapidly against his shoulder. He did his best to push it from his mind.

The air from the street mixed with the smoke from his cigarette, creating a comforting aroma he grew to love over the past few months. The night cooled considerably. A breeze wafted through the air, signaling a return to school, the end of summer fun. Homesickness crept into the back of James's mind. The smell of new paper, new clothes, rubber erasers, floor cleaner, and bus exhaust flooded his senses. The fear of waking up early tempered by the promise of a new year, stepping forward into a brand-new world. James realized he would never experience that sensation again.

A sudden buffet of wind forced the smoke into his eyes.

He swore and rubbed his face, tears streaming down his cheeks while he gritted his teeth through the sudden sharp pain.

"You got a light?"

James, startled, turned to Deck with a cigarette in his mouth, leaning against the railing.

"Jesus! When did you get out here?" James said. He handed his lighter to Deck who took it, lit his cigarette, and lowered into the other chair looking out over Midway next to James.

"A second ago. Couldn't sleep," Deck said, his voice tired.

"Surprising, especially considering your nightly adventures," James said sarcastically.

"Give a mouse a cookie," Deck said, "and he'll ask for a beer to go with it."

James chuckled and the two of them sat in silence for a moment, smoke wafting above them before disappearing in the darkness.

"Finally got some goddamn say in our lives. Guess I relish it," Deck said suddenly, skipping ahead in the conversation he was having in his mind. But James understood. The constant pressure the Federation put them under for the past year was unimaginable in James's previous life. From drafting him, training him in the most controlled environment in the known world, drugging, and dropping him in the middle of the jungle. James felt the same release when they first arrived.

"I hear ya," James said.

"Yeah, I know you do. It's …" Deck trailed off. "It's that you and I are different, James."

James was surprised. This was a turn he had not expected.

"How often do you think about those women in the jungle? Or the men in that truck? Or the men we killed?" Deck said, his voice almost pleading before he turned to James. His eyes were clear but sad, even scared.

"I don't know," James replied, realizing how long it was since he consciously thought about the jungle. Memories flitted through his mind on occasion, but he squashed them before they bloomed. It was over three months ago, but to James, it all took place in another lifetime.

"I guess I try not to think about it," James said, wondering where this was coming from.

"Yeah, well, I can't stop thinking about it," Deck said, his voice wavering. "The mist from the back of their skulls when I pulled the trigger. The heads toppling to the side. Knees buckling when they fell. It's a lot."

Deck grew quiet, leaving James in a place that felt like he was infringing on his privacy.

"Listen, man…" James began.

"Nah, don't worry about it," Deck said gruffly. "It's in my head, I know. I'll figure shit out eventually. Needed to ask, I guess."

James nodded, still unsure of how to respond.

"Enjoying the ability to decide what I do now."

"I get that. You're off to the races," James said, careful not to sound judgmental.

"Yeah, I know. It's …" Deck shook his head. "You know what, forget about it. Glad someone else saw something in you, I guess."

"What're you talking about?" James asked, confused.

"You don't find it odd how you were the only one who woke up on that plane, James? Hell, we were all in there and somehow you magically arise. All without serious disciplinary charges?"

"What are you saying, Deck?" James asked slowly.

"I'm saying someone found what they were looking for in you, James. Why else would we be here? We should be flying around being dropped off at various locations with little to no guidance accomplishing missions with vague goals and outcomes."

"What? Deck, I woke up randomly because someone messed up." James was scrambling. What was he saying?

"Sure, you did."

"Deck, what are you talking about?" James asked, his voice serious now, almost defensive. He was a part of the team. That was it. Nothing different about him.

"All I'm saying is ask yourself, is it possible someone intervened? Were you meant to wake up?" Deck stubbed out the rest of his cigarette and stood up, looking at James with a hand on the railing. "Think about it, James. I'm just happy I can piss when I want to."

Deck clapped James on the shoulder and slid open the patio door, leaving James to sit in silence questioning what he had not seen while the cigarette in his hand burned to the filter.

CHAPTER 20

James heaved for breath outside a coffee shop down the hill from the neat rows of military houses.

He and Kevin had just finished the equivalent of a half-marathon and the burn in his legs and lungs dissipated uncomfortably while he regained composure of his diaphragm.

"Why the hell do we do this to ourselves?" James asked, stretching out his side.

"Because we have to. Otherwise, we lose it," Kevin replied, his voice muffled as he bent over to touch his toes. "If we don't, we aren't enjoyable people." He stood back up, his face flushed. "At least that's what they tell us."

"They're all jackasses," said James, remembering how the two of them fought with each other and the rest of the group constantly upon their arrival on campus before they realized how much they needed the release.

"Agreed," said Kevin, opening the door to the coffee shop. "Iced?"

"Yeah, that works," said James.

"Cool. Want to grab a seat out here?"

"Will do."

James slung the shoulder straps of his drawstring bag over the back of a chair at an empty table. Assuring their spot was saved he walked back to the entrance of the shop and poured ice water from the cooler by the door. He drained it and poured a second, the recycled plastic cup melting in the humidity. Some of the icy water fell onto his chest, a reprieve from the suffocating heat.

Kevin joined him moments later, handing James an iced coffee wrapped in a saturated napkin.

James took a sip, the bitterness and cold melding together perfectly.

Kevin shook his head at James disapproving. "Don't get how you do that. Iced coffee isn't actually coffee without milk in it."

"Never liked it. Too many liquids mixing for my taste," James replied.

"You're disgusting is what it is," said Kevin. "Damn, it is hot out. Feels like summer in the south."

"Yeah?" asked James

"Yeah, absolutely brutal," Kevin continued. "It would get above a hundred for weeks on end. The sun just a blip on the horizon but the humidity..." Kevin paused shaking his head while he stirred his coffee. "The second you stepped outside your breath got knocked out of your body. Made you want to sit and do nothing. Can't even imagine what it was like before air conditioning."

"How long were you there?" James asked, sloshing melting ice cubes around in his glass.

"My whole life. Dad worked for the city and my mom worked at a bakery. She was a classically trained pastry chef. When I was old enough, she went back to work to pay the bills. I grew up in those kitchens learning how to mix a beignet, raise a baguette, and all that. She taught me all she knew. So did the other people who worked there, but my mom drove my love of baking."

"Your dad?" asked James.

Kevin shrugged. "He lived nearby. Big guy, big temper."

James nodded, reading Kevin's silence.

They finished their coffees and continued their self-prescribed torture. James needed these runs to keep his mind clear and get the ever-present anxiety off his back. The exercise itself was far from his favorite, but he loved exploring Midway's neighborhoods. Whether they were going through the harbor area where tourists were a constant obstacle or the business district where people in suits walked with their HOLO screens hovering before them, James enjoyed it. This was the first time they were running this neighborhood and attempting such a big hill. Even though they were here a few days earlier, James was still intrigued by the houses and their precarious positioning on the steep slant.

Yards were practically hewn into the concrete like steppe farmers in ancient Mayan culture. The streets running parallel to the incline boasted bay windows giving them a bird's eye view of the city and the river.

After a soul-crushing twenty minutes running straight uphill, they reached the end of Brandt's street. Kevin pointed in the direction of their destination, unable to speak as he turned with James following close behind.

James mentally prepared stepping onto the block, slowing his pace, his skin hot, breath heavy, and sweat dripping from his pores.

When they arrived at Brandt and Riley's house, they found their commander with his shirt off, lying on his stomach, pulling clods of grass out from underneath the lawnmower.

He stood as they got closer, wiping his hands on his pants, leaving oily streaks on the denim fabric.

"Well, look who showed up," he said with a smile.

Out of nowhere a bolt of blond hair came flying from behind Brandt and landed on his back. He let out a guttural *oomph* from the impact and flipped the tiny body over his shoulder.

"What do we have here?" Brandt said, tickling Shannon who howled with laughter.

"It's me! It's me!" she cried, before rolling herself under her father's legs and positioning herself in front of him again. The little girl dipped into a crouch, her face serious, ready to attack.

Brandt held up his hands, recognizing the signs of an imminent tackle.

"Whoa, whoa, whoa," Brandt warned. "Your mom is gonna kill me if you do what I think you're going to try next. Get the soap bucket from the kitchen and fill it up for me. When I'm done with these two I'll wash up out here and you can help me put some of this away, sound good?"

"Fiiiiine," said Shannon, stomping away.

Brandt turned to them, a grin on his face while he flipped the lawnmower back over.

"I assume you got my message?" asked Brandt, waiting to speak until he heard the door close.

James nodded, glancing at Kevin who was as stoic and silent as ever.

"Good, glad you decided to come by. Let's go to the backyard and chat a bit." Brandt turned around before they could protest.

James was unsure what to expect. The team was aware of his conversation with Brandt from the night of the barbeque. Reactions ranged from Deck blowing it all off as completely natural to Stacie insisting this was a full-blown military operation in progress with the Federation planning a major move. James, reluctant to cause any problems decided Kevin, the least dramatic member of the group would be the best to join him. The last thing they needed was a heated Stacie fighting with a new commander so soon after his arrival to the area.

They followed Brandt around back sitting at the picnic table. Brandt placed two waters in front of them and sat on the opposite side of the wooden planks, taking a deep chug of his own.

"Ahhhh," he said, beads of water dripping down his chin. "Sometimes nothing beats ice-cold water." Brandt leaned back on his bench using his arms to brace his upper body from toppling backward. "You've been here for a while now. Three months?"

"Almost exactly," James replied.

"And you all know the city pretty well at this point between the eight of you, I'd imagine."

James nodded.

"Good!" Brandt said loudly. James jumped at the sudden burst of energy, "I need that. Hell, we all do. As you correctly assumed, we're here to help prep Midway in case anything happens. Take stock of the space, feel it out from a military perspective. We get told by the Federation to prep an area all the time and the best way to do it is working with locals to figure out how they would protect themselves." Brandt spread his hands out in front of him, gesturing to James and Kevin across the table. "Lucky for us, you are acquainted with the area. So, what I'd like is for you all to come up with a plan. Some way to give us a complete picture of the city. The weak points, strengths, places of high value, places of low value, hidden gems, population numbers, population spread, and density by neighborhood. You know, the works."

James followed, mentally outlining ways they could give Brandt what he needed. Kevin and Clint would be able to examine the structural foundations of the city, determine how to maneuver vehicles, and protect more critical areas like bridges and tunnels against attack. Jon and Stacie could get a better understanding of electric infrastructure to help plan for eventual power needs and any cyber requirements to maintain communications with the outside. Meanwhile, Kyle, Bob, Deck, and James could focus on the population. First question to James's mind, how do you move millions of people succinctly and efficiently? Next up, where do you move them?

Running through the various scenarios led him down more disparate paths, his brain picking up increased layers of complexity while he devised plans to accomplish all this when he stopped.

Ask yourself why.

It was a question he needed to ask more often. Deck did so without effort. James needed to do the same. Instead of paying attention to the synapses firing in his brain, connecting the pieces of this newly presented puzzle, James forced himself to stop.

250

"James. James. Hey, James!"

James was so caught up in his planning and self-questioning that he completely missed the conversation's progression.

"You good, man?" Brandt asked, grinning at him.

James nodded. "Yeah, sorry. Lost in thought for a second."

"Good, exactly what I want to hear. Jumping to work," Brandt said, standing up. "I'll let you two get to it but let me know if there is anything else you need from us. When you're done, come find me. We'll talk through next steps."

Kevin and James stood in unison, finishing off their waters and leaving them on the table after being waved off by Brandt when walking over to the bins.

"Thanks, Lieutenant. We'll be in touch soon," James said, stretching out his hand. It was accepted enthusiastically by Brandt who nodded and shook Kevin's hand.

"Glad to have you two. Glad to have all of you. I mean it."

James nodded and turned around, walking to the gate followed by Kevin, his shadow towering in front of James.

Why did Brandt want their help? Or better yet, why did James feel this whole arrangement was off? He couldn't put his finger on it, but he knew he needed to keep mulling it over.

"That went well," Kevin said, sidling up next to him.

"Yeah, I guess so. Got what we wanted. More control over our time here and all," James replied, letting his ideas rest for a moment. "You know what you want to do?"

"I think I've got a pretty good plan. Gonna need to work with Clint. Bob, too," Kevin said, his face reflecting the concentration of his brain firing on all cylinders.

James was impressed at the way Kevin's mind jumped to the same ideas as his own, unraveling the plan like a piece of twine, teasing the strings apart one at a time.

"Kev, I got a question for you," he said.

"Shoot."

251

"When we were on the plane, you know, when I woke up—"

"Who planned to wake you up?" Kevin interrupted, glancing at James.

James hid his surprise at how quickly Kevin was able to finish his question but nodded.

Kevin walked in silence for a few seconds before he spoke again. "I don't know who woke you up. I can't tell you how any of this happened to us. All I know is I woke up on an airplane with one hell of a headache and you were there looking out the window like we were headed home for Christmas.

"It's strange. All I wanted during our training, our brief exploit in the jungle, and over the last few months was some semblance of control over my life. Now I think we may have inherited the weight of the world without knowing it." Kevin looked back to James and shrugged. "I don't know who's pulling the strings. But I know it wasn't a mistake."

James was not sure how to respond, but he got his answer even if it wasn't the one he wanted. All he needed to do at this point was figure out what was in store for them next.

CHAPTER 21

James, Stacie, and Jon stood with their arms crossed in front of six HOLOs displaying a seamless aerial image of Midway. James glanced at the time in the corner of the image, and 1510 changed to 1511. Damn, this only took five hours, James thought, admiring their handiwork.

"I have to say, this is… really goddamn good," Jon said. "I mean, we figured out a way to dissect an entire city in an afternoon."

He swept his finger in a circle on the control HOLO which flipped the view of the city and sent the 3D image spinning like a top across the light-based screens.

"We've got a long way to go," Stacie said, turning away from the map to fiddle with one of the other HOLOs on the coffee table before them.

James was excited by their progress. Putting together a war room in a college dorm was no easy task, and they managed to do it in the span of an afternoon. But Stacie was right. Now they would have to put it into action.

"Hey! You real—wow," Deck said, walking into the room and stopping short, causing Clint and Bob to bump into him as he did.

"Looks good, huh?" Jon said, looking endearingly at the screens. "Once we get those plans from the city office, we'll be able to map out a detailed breakdown of all Midway has to offer from bike paths to fiber optic cable networks. We'll have a full view top to bottom, inside and out. It'll be… beautiful."

"I think someone's impressed with himself," Clint said, walking over to the front of the screen and shoving Jon's shoulder.

"Bet your ass I am," Jon replied.

"Nice work. Seriously," Deck said. "This is gonna be awesome."

"Only if we add to it. We've gotta run downtown before they close for the weekend," James said, pulling on his sneakers and heading to the hallway.

"Right behind you, man," Deck said, following him out the door.

"Good luck. Don't fuck up!" Stacie shouted, her voice carrying into the hallway. "The whole plan kinda revolves around those blueprints!"

"Don't remind me," James mumbled while he pushed the button for the elevators.

A bell chimed and the doors popped open.

"Don't worry," Deck said confidently, winking at James. "I got this."

It all started three days earlier after Kevin and James's conversation with Brandt. When they arrived home, the rest of the team was waiting for them in the other team's living room.

"So? What's the word?" Deck asked, resting an elbow on the kitchen counter where he was perched, unable to hide the desperate need for answers from his tone.

"Yeah, how'd it go?" Kyle stood next to the doors to the patio while he stretched his leg behind him bumping into the chair where Clint sat.

"Do you have to do that, man?" Clint said, turning around perturbed. "You're making me nervous."

"It's how I relax," Kyle retorted.

"Well, stop moving."

Stacie cut them off. "Stop." She held up her hands at the two of them. "We're all on edge. Let's hear what happened." She nodded at Kevin and James to continue. "The floor is yours, gentlemen." She leaned back in her seat on the couch.

"It went well," James said. "Or we think it did. Brandt wants us to run their whole reconnaissance mission. Get all the specs for the city and report back to them."

The group exchanged glances, and an odd silence hung in the air.

"What didn't he say, James?" Stacie asked, breaking the quiet.

"He didn't say why."

"Sounds right," Deck said, sipping from his bottle of water.

"At least it's what we expected," James said, the wheels turning in his head. "No one's going to give answers to us. No one's even going to hint there're plans we don't know about. That much we've found out so far. This time we know. We need to tell them what they're not telling us."

"Ummmm…" Bob said skeptically.

"What I mean is we have to find out for ourselves why the hell they're here. They're not leaving any time soon. It's time for us to take control." James let the momentum build and carry him. "We have to look at this like a puzzle. Piece by piece. Let the story unfold in front of us. In order to do that, we need to be meticulous. Kevin and Clint, I want you two to get us a full run down of the city's infrastructure. Clint, you should be able to tell us what kind of vehicles can be used in an attack or evacuation. We should prep for both. Kevin, highlight the weak points. Where could we be hit the hardest? Stacie and Jon, let's start working on the tech side. Electrical grids, cable lines, fiber optic wiring, the works. We need to know how this city runs inside and out. Got it?"

"I've got ideas, man," Jon said bobbing his head.

"Good. The rest of us should figure out the demographics. How many people are here for work each week? How many people leave? Total residents? Citizens? Active military presence?

Population density? We need an entire simulated city top to bottom. We arrange all our edge pieces. Then we fill in the middle. Once we do that, we'll have the picture we need to answer our questions. It's exactly what Croyton taught us."

James paused, looking around the room seeing calm faces surrounding him. There was strength in their silence, their features chiseled with hardened lines of resolve beyond their years.

"Let's get to work."

By the time they reached City Hall, it was 1500 hours. James and Deck walked through the looming brass doors. They flashed their Federation IDs to the cadre of security guards who waved them through without question.

City hours must be nice, James thought, looking at the workers crisscrossing the floor, leaning on desks, and exchanging weekend plans while running out the remainder of their day.

"Jesus, what were we thinking coming here late afternoon on a Friday?" James said, peering down hallways where employees were standing around, staring at the clocks ready to make their escape at any second.

"What do you mean?" said Deck who led the way toward a bulletin board with all of the rooms and their titles on display. "Best time to charm someone is when they're exhausted. No defense."

James watched Deck, thrown off by the interest in what he was doing. James could not remember Deck being this engaged outside of life-or-death scenarios and late-night bar visits.

"Okay, nice." Deck turned around and pointed at the board. "One floor up and at the other end of the building by the looks of it."

Deck led the way taking two stairs at a time, reaching their destination faster than James realized.

The office they entered was adorned with faded blue carpet and pre-Federation art hanging on the walls. A few scratched-up chairs with frayed turquoise cushions were positioned by the door. James was intrigued by the living history book they walked through, noting the lingering scent of mothballs in the air. An older woman in her early fifties sat behind a desk at the other end of the room with her HOLO displaying a game show.

She looked up at them briefly when they walked into the room and talked with her face to the counter when she spoke. "Yes?"

James and Deck glanced at each other before Deck took a deep breath and someone else emerged.

Deck's demeanor changed entirely. His back went rigid, and his neck cracked with a quick twist before relaxing. His shoulders sloped casually, giving him the stance of a friend approaching a familiar face. He sauntered up to the desk with a flirtatious grin gilding the corner of his mouth.

"Hi, I was wondering if you can help me find the City Records office?" said Deck in an almost mockingly earnest voice.

"You're here," the woman said. She took a second and looked at the two of them before focusing back on her HOLO. "What're you looking for?"

Deck inched up to the side of the desk and stood at a polite distance with his hands on his hips, his body relaxed while he spoke. "I was hoping to get some information on the city. Do you happen to have any of the blueprints or plans available for us to look over?"

James noticed the woman becoming frustrated already. They were messing up the remainder of her week.

"We have all of those, but what do you want? There are millions of records. We can't give you everything."

She finally paused her show with a huff poking the screen angrily, the blue light disappearing in an instant before looking at Deck who waited with a beaming smile. Her stubborn anger and Deck's casual flattery were a match made in heaven, James thought studying the exchange.

Deck chuckled in his throat before leaning a hand against the counter, the wood creaking beneath his weight. "No, of course not. We want to know about the records from the new stadiums, the harbor, the updated rail station, and the central market. If we could look at those or even get them sent to us in a HOLO file, it'd be great. Would that be possible? We've got a long weekend of putting together these plans for our class and want to make it easy on you. It is Friday after all." He held his palms upward, emphasizing his understanding.

She sighed and turned to a different HOLO popping up over the peeling wood with a simple tap of her finger. "What years?"

"Let's do the most recent records if you don't mind. Thank you! We owe you a favor," Deck said, pulling out his HOLO. He passed it to her, and she tapped the screen in front of him transferring all the necessary data with the swipe of a finger.

"Thank you!" Deck beamed, looking at the screen and scrolling through the data. "That is extremely helpful."

"Anything else?" the woman asked, slightly thrown off by the exuberant young man in front of her.

"Nope, this is perfect! Thank you so much." Deck slipped his HOLO emitter back into his pocket and reached across her desk. "I'm Deck, by the way. You are?"

"Ellen," she said, confused, shaking his hand.

"Nice to meet you, Ellen. And this is my good buddy, James. We'll be back soon, I'm sure." James waved awkwardly from the back of the room, still in a state of shock at the charm gymnastics Deck pulled.

"You, too…" said Ellen, questioning her response.

"See you around. Have a great weekend," said Deck cheerily as he walked away. James would not have been surprised if he blew her a kiss. When they were alone in the hall James glanced over at Deck who was whistling.

"What the fuck was that?" he said.

258

"That? Oh, nothing. Do you think we have time for a quick drink before we go home?"

Deck did not break stride when they reached the top of the stairs, leaving James to shake his head and grin.

CHAPTER 22

Wet shoes are the worst, thought James, liquid swishing around his toes. It was five days since they returned from City Hall, and it rained every day. The road overflowed with water, and streams ran across the sidewalks where the storm washed piles of dust into the sewers.

He stopped at a red light, moving his feet rhythmically, unwilling to let the wet clothes sticking to his body sap anymore energy.

The water line in the river was unnaturally high and James turned off the main road onto the path winding along the raging waters. He had to run. He had to think.

Since Jon finished uploading the city's blueprints, James focused solely on manipulating the data to get answers. The team spread throughout the city, using the model to influence their moves as they worked to determine: what made Midway special? From the stadiums to the sewer drains, nothing stood out. Their location was central, but there were bigger cities with high value targets miles away. Arms factories, centralized regional power grids, nuclear reactors, major interstate centers, and established military bases. Infrastructure and assets countries desperately need to protect in a war. The Federation was doing that. So, why was Brandt's command stationed here? Nothing added up. When he thought they found a solution, he was stonewalled with contrary evidence.

James stopped, putting his hands on his knees, and taking deep breaths in, one at a time. The water from the river mixed with the rain and the sweat dripping down his forehead left a salty, metallic taste on his lips.

The break had come the night before and he knew he needed to talk with Brandt.

If their lieutenant knew or even guessed the same conclusion James arrived at, then the Federation had no idea what was coming.

"Come on. Finish," James said, pulling in deep breaths and powering through the rest of the path.

He crossed the street at the end of the trail and made a beeline up the hill, letting his strides carry him. He waited for his energy to fail, but adrenaline proved in his favor.

The rain was almost non-existent by the time he reached Brandt's street. James walked with his hands clasped above his head while worms curled up on the sidewalk.

When he reached the house, he saw two cars in the driveway. Good sign, he thought, and knocked.

He heard a brief commotion inside with some indeterminate yelling before Riley pulled the door open with George glued to her leg, looking at James mischievously.

"James," she said, surprised. "I wasn't expecting you. Are you looking for Luke?"

"I was actually. He home?" James replied, wiping water from his face with the palm of his hand. "It will only take a second if you don't mind."

Riley opened the door, swinging her leg with George behind her as she did.

"Of course, come in! George, go on back. Tell them they can play the movie."

George ran off, careening around the corner before Riley turned back to face him shaking her head.

"Let me grab him for you."

"Thanks."

James waited in the foyer, careful not to get rainwater on the floor. The smell of salty, fresh popcorn floated through the air. James felt a pang of guilt for interrupting their family time.

The front room was filled with pictures of the family designed in a timeline of Riley and Luke's relationship. James studied the pictures of Brandt with a mustache and long hair, smoking a cigarette next to a pool with Riley sitting between his legs drinking a Corona, and smiling at the camera.

"Cabo nine years ago," Brandt said, pointing at the picture and walking through the doorway. "Fun place. Bad hangover."

James grinned. "I'll bet."

Brandt took a seat on the bench along the wall and crossed his legs, leaning back and spreading his arms across the backrest. They both looked around the room pretending to examine the rest of the pictures before Brandt asked, "So James, I can't imagine you ran here in the pouring rain because you wanted to say hi."

"No, sir," said James. "We did your reconnaissance." He let the sentence hang in the air as an invitation.

"Great!" Brand said enthusiastically. "You can send it all back to the HOLO address I sent you."

"I don't think so," James replied.

"Oh? Why's that?" Brandt asked good-naturedly. "Emitter a little wet from the storm?"

"I don't think we should be sending the model for how our enemy chooses its victim cities over an unsecured network. A lot of people would find it disturbing how the Federation plans to leave them high and dry. Especially considering they're almost perfect prototypes for the African countries they attacked."

Hearing nothing from his commander, James continued, "Once you told us to do reconnaissance, I was hoping we would be given more information. Be in the know on why you all showed up here in the first place. But nothing has ever been easy for us. So, we decided to get the answers for ourselves. We downloaded the

262

specs and built a full scale 3D diagram of Midway along with every layered view you can imagine.

"Turns out commercial enterprises don't need to post blueprints to web-based databases, but they do need to make publicly available copies ready for anyone with a reason to go in and ask about them. We were happy to learn students are included as acceptable, unquestioned recipients of such data, and Ellen in City Records didn't care anyway. After the blueprints were loaded into our model, we ran simulations. All the data you can imagine pouring through our HOLOs with traditional battle scenarios. We always came up empty. Why? What was so appealing about this city? What would you all be doing here?

"Without fail the result was a losing scenario for anyone attacking Midway. The BlankZone would technically win, but suffer mass casualties and for what? Nothing of importance, no massive power grid they can control, no military bases to take a chunk out of our forces—heck, there's not a factory around here within 112 miles they can use for anything more than gourmet dog food.

"What bugged me was why not just tear us apart? Scorched earth warfare like they did to Europe. But what's the point of that? All they'd accomplish was a random decimated city on the coast. What were we missing? I was stumped. We went back through all our analysis from Croyton's classes, reading the timeline from the battle forensic reports, trying to figure out the hidden elements."

James paused, turning around to look at Brandt whose eyes were focused on him with a steady intensity. James absorbed it, the energy from the last few days culminating in the moment.

"That's when I had a realization. It doesn't matter what *we* think about traditional military targets. It matters what *they* think about them. Do you know what we found? We're identical to all the initial cities the BlankZone attacked in Africa. No major military bases to provide easy backup. A service-based city industry. A large population without an easy method to leave and, most importantly, access from the sea. They'd decimate Midway and create a blank slate instilling fear and anger across the Federation, but for what? All that would do is motivate us to fight back. It still wasn't clear.

"So, we took it a step further and expanded our schematics including major cities up and down the coast. The places the Federation is so set on protecting at all costs. What would happen if those cities were attacked on both sides? How would they be able to defend themselves from a pincer attack? What we discovered is it would not go well. Over 93% of the time the cities fall—93% of the time, sir.

"Lieutenant Brandt, they're not looking to start an all-out war, at least right now. They're looking for the back door."

James sat on the stairs opposite the bench where Brandt continued to watch James.

"I guess the question is, what do we do now?"

Brandt's eyes dropped to the floor and the two of them sat in silence. Beneath the still air James heard the drips from his shirt hit the floor creating a puddle on the staircase.

"We won't be the only city," Brandt said finally. "I expect them to attack the other cities in the Federation matching the description you gave."

"Why don't we tell the Federation?" James asked.

"We did," Brandt said, standing and sighing. "We explained what you and your team found in detail to them, but they wouldn't listen and almost court-martialed me when I kept pushing it. Fact of the matter is military fights based on history and traditional sense would tell you to protect your major assets. Unfortunately, I don't think the folks in the BlankZone have the same idea as we do when it comes to what's valuable as a target."

"How so?" James asked.

"We look at a country we want to attack and the first plan is to go after their bases, factories, resource centers. We hit high value targets where they would rebuild. Makes sense, right? But where do you attack if you don't care about rebuilding? What if you just need a way in? The BlankZone wants those places intact because not only do they want to take us over, they expect to. The question becomes how do they get into a country with the least amount of critical infrastructure destruction while still inflicting serious damage?"

"They target population centers," James said.

"Bingo. They want this city—they want *these* cities— because they annihilate their opponents from the inside out. Smash and grab for one city and then methodically take control over the rest of the country. The Federation believes it needs to defend its assets. The BlankZone is hoping it will. It's why we volunteered to be here."

James nodded, still constructing the picture in his brain. The BlankZone was never going to leave the whole country in ruins. They would attack weak points the Federation wouldn't defend. Places with easy access to critical areas, allow them to amass troops on the ground. Locations where it was more convenient for them to leave piles of shattered cement and glass.

"James, we need to protect Midway. If we fall, we open the gap for the BlankZone to flood the North. They'll take half the Federation in a matter of months."

James's mouth was dry. This was why they were sent here. This was why Croyton made them the warriors they were. Front of the shield for an attack no one believed would happen. This was their purpose, James thought, the smoldering anger in his stomach cooling to solid stone.

"Well," James stepped onto the floor from the stairs. "Let's get ready for a war."

CHAPTER 23

The next few weeks were a buzz of activity. The team was in
constant motion swinging from one end of Midway to the other,
prepping hidden battle deposits, scouting areas for defensive
positions, or gathering information not readily available through
the city's records. During the process, James was pleased to see the
teams' skillsets emerging in force. Stacie choreographed their
actions from their new HQ, James's apartment, designing each step
of the operation. She possessed a unique ability to utilize
everyone's talents while catching potential issues early, a key to
their success.

Deck, Kyle, and James were the field team, delivering a
steady stream of information back to the group ensuring they were
up to speed on the latest intel. Construction sites, abandoned
buildings, permits bid on by contractors, commercial owners, even
the latest tenants in an abandoned building by the wharf—a small
family of raccoons James stumbled upon during his first visit to the
building's attic. Now, James refused to go into noticeably empty
buildings alone after being chased out onto the street by the mother
nipping at his heels with her brood hanging off her back.

Meanwhile, Bob, Jon, Kevin, and Clint designed dozens of
battle scenarios across Midway. Using the city plans coming into
the HQ at a steady clip, courtesy of Ellen, they managed to identify
key points of attack as well as operations and medical headquarters
for each defensive position scouted by their field team.

James stood on the balcony overlooking the skyline,
smoking a cigarette and drinking lukewarm coffee. His brain was
fried from the week, constantly chasing the next installment to a

never ending defense plan. A knock came at the door behind him. James peered around to find Clint waving. It was time to go.

James crushed his half-smoked cigarette into the wall, dropping the butt into an increasingly disgusting ash bucket, and walked back inside pouring the rest of the coffee out into the sink.

Back to it, James thought, half-slapping his cheeks and shaking his head side to side following Clint to the elevator.

They descended to the garage beneath the building and James hopped into the passenger seat of a black, mid-size SUV. Within minutes they pulled onto the main thoroughfare and James reached into the glovebox, removing a HOLO he unlocked with a retinal scan before swiping a finger along the 2D image of the city eliciting a 3D map display.

The aerial image of Midway was filled with color-coded sections. James scanned the areas trying to determine the best one to go with for the day.

The red indicated places still in need of work, yellow meant in progress, and green meant the battle plans were well-established with a fully supplied battle station. Blue were sites they needed to revisit based on new information or upgraded plans.

A lot of red, James thought, zooming in on a spot close to the water before he finally picked his target tapping on one of the zoned off red tinted districts. He focused his search on the new location and read the words "ARENA SECTOR".

He held it up for Clint to see who nodded and pulled off the highway into a side neighborhood. They were in an industrial part of town. The kind of area where hipster coffee shops, liquor distilleries, and breweries stood alongside homeless shelters and abandoned buildings.

They drove through an opened chain link fence into a gravel strewn lot, exiting the car together. They walked to the warehouse where Clint opened a door hidden in plain view from the street. Their feet echoed in the darkness when they stepped over the threshold. James was blind before Clint flipped on the lights.

Suspended halogen lights revealed assorted rows of military vehicles from Humvees to tanks stretched before them. The rest of the warehouse was still covered in darkness, and only the glint of glass and metal hinted at the depths of the building's size. The air was stagnant with a distinctive oil scent, and the ancient building emitted a nostalgic scent of rust and aging dirt giving James a feeling of comfort in the vast space.

"Beautiful, isn't it?" said Clint, admiring the vehicles lined up tire to tire from one side of the warehouse to the other.

"Sure is. What're you doing today?" asked James, walking to the nearest Humvee and jumping in the doorless driver's side.

"I've gotta service all the tanks in back. They're thirty years old and need a tune-up. Hell, half of them may need brand-new engines. The state some of this shit is in…" Clint let the rest of his sentence hang while he inspected the tools arranged neatly on the wall before placing his selections in a canvas tool bag or through the loops in his belt. "You can take a bike though. Finished 'em yesterday and the engines need to run."

"Roger that."

James jumped down from the Humvee and walked over to the neat row of dirt bikes. He pulled a faded red one with a dirty white outline from the lineup wheeling it to the clear space in front of the armory.

The bike was covered in dust and pockmarked by fingerprints around the engine. It reeked of dirt and evaporated gasoline, but the smell of fresh grease remained in the background. He turned the key in the ignition kicking the clutch and the engine turned over without a fuss. James checked the fuel level—full. Perfect, James thought, wheeling his ride to the doorway.

He was about to open the door when a shudder from the building halted him in his tracks. A dense cloud of dust descended from the ceiling. The wall before him let out a loud groan before moving upward producing a stream of ever-growing light through the opening.

James turned off the ignition and lay the bike against the wall waiting for the garage door to open fully. After what seemed like ten minutes, the door came to a halt above his head, the lights swinging ominously above the rows of cars now on full display in the sunlight.

That was close, James thought, glancing at the wall next to him still swaying slightly from the door's movement.

"What're you doing here?" a voice yelled out from the passenger side window of a beat-up sedan parked in the gravel drive. "We've got orders from LT. Gotta get all this shipshape."

The back door opened, and a woman emerged.

"Clint needs some help. About time you showed up," James said good-naturedly. He shook her hand as well as the hands of the other two women who had emerged from the car.

"He's probably breaking all our shit," one of the women said, peering into the mouth of the garage at Clint who walked out wiping his hands on a greasy rag.

"Screw you, Dolly. I'm the only reason half this crap is working, and you know it," Clint retorted.

Dolly, a tall, feminine figure clad in overalls with a pixie cut, rolled her eyes, and waved him away. "Yeah, yeah, yeah. Whatever you say"

Clint stood with his hands on his hips. "Mickey, Barb, good to have you all here. Taking care of those tanks in the back row."

"Those hunks of iron are a piece of work, huh?" Mickey said, her long fingernails brushing hair from her face. "Must be a few decades old. Don't know where the hell the lieutenant scrounged up half this shit."

"Beg, borrow, and steal. Gotta make it work. At least it's something," Barb said, tying her hair in a ponytail. "What are you doing here though? You're not motor pool," she said to James through the hair tie clenched in her teeth.

"Recon, arena sector," James said. "Gotta stay on top of this stuff."

"For sure, for sure. You talk to the LT lately?" Dolly asked while the rest of her crew made their way inside. "Turns out the Federation's doubling down on their plans. All naval personnel got redirected to leave us wide-open at sea. I thought LT was going to burn the whole city to the ground out of spite when he heard."

"What does that mean for us?" James asked.

"We're on our own when shit hits the fan. At least for the first few hours. Who knows? LT keeps on talking about the 'kill switch' and the Alamo. Acting like the psycho genius he is. Reminds me of when I first joined and his prep for trips to the BZ," Dolly said, casually tightening the toolbelt around her waist.

"Hold on, the BZ? Brandt's been behind the line?" Clint asked, stealing the words out of James's mouth.

"He never mentioned that," James said, processing the new information.

"You'll have to ask him about it. One thing I've learned about my commander over the past five years is he tells you shit when he's good and ready," Dolly said with a nod. "All right, buddy. Let's take care of these relics we've got to work with."

Dolly threw an arm around Clint and walked with him into the mouth of the garage, disappearing between the lines of vehicles already gathering a fresh layer of fallen soot in the glittering sunlight.

James followed, grabbing his bike while they disappeared between the cars and wheeled it to the edge of the lot.

He shouted back to Clint. "I'll be back in a few hours. Don't leave without me."

"You have your HOLO?" came the reply from Clint, his body hidden amongst the machinery.

270

"Yeah, man," said James, swinging a leg over the bike seat and starting the engine.

"Sounds good. See you in a little bit."

The door lurched back to life and he popped the clutch on his bike, peeling off, leaving behind a cloud of gravel before turning onto the abandoned industrial street.

After his discussion with Brandt, James had a new sense of purpose. He was serving the greater good while taking part in a plan bigger than himself. Bigger than any of them. Brandt's command took them under its wing, tuning them in on all their plans. The armory was the primary HQ for Brandt's folks, but they were spread out to the suburbs and back prepping major operations centers for the coming war.

Brandt introduced them to Dolly and her squad of mechanical engineers who were happy to get the expertise of someone like Clint. Personalities meshed well across the groups, and in three weeks James and the team were embedded with Brandt's crew. All aimed at the same distinct goal: protect Midway at all costs.

The wind whipped across his face while he rode on the highway, weaving in and out of cars. Federation school buses were dormant in parking lots during the day while playgrounds and parks were populated by young parents, nursery schools, and nannies with their charges.

James cruised through the arena sector noting landmarks, taking pictures with his HOLO, scanning structures they may be able to utilize, and taking notes detailing his inspection.

It was James's idea to prep the areas with any sort of communications or weapons prior to an attack. He pitched the idea to Brandt as above ground trenches. Use the city itself to mount their defense. Brandt loved the plan and they worked tirelessly since then to drive their vision to fruition. They erected sensors to detect enemy activity and assembled HOLO cameras along with

GPS locators to triangulate defensive positions for rapid response to any attack.

The first part of the plan required the field team to survey the area and feed real time data into a HOLO file for Jon to load into their model. Once that was done Kevin, Clint, and Bob would put together plans for how to best prep the area which Stacie operationalized in step-by-step guides on how to carry out their designs. Finally, the whole team would head to whichever sector needed finishing touches and they would set it up as discreetly as possible. James knew they needed to keep the situation as quiet as they could. The Federation and general public would be furious if they learned Midway was being prepped for the first major battle in an inevitable war, albeit for different reasons.

James stopped for a second, straddling his bike while scrolling through the data file he transmitted to Jon's servers, double-checking the area to make sure he sent everything he could. Satisfied he was done and encouraged by the fresh breeze blowing crisp air against his cheek, James pulled up the sector map again, hoping to rationalize a trip to the harbor. Please, tell me Deck didn't go yesterday, James thought, while the map popped up in front of his face.

The harbor was the first place they prepped and by far the biggest challenge given the constant activity along the waterfront. Less busy than during summer but still full of groups of students parading around behind their teachers and tour guides during the day. The groundwork was only able to get done at night. Sidestepping drunk people and a run-in with a particularly intimate couple who snuck onto a tour boat caused problems for them, but after two nights the whole area was ready to go.

Now, the sector's status was a steady blue and in need of a checkup. James took advantage of the opportunity by pressing the button next to the harbor sector's outline indicating he was on the way.

He parked by an old section of the harbor where interconnected grassy areas were designated as a public park. Birds and squirrels ran amok in the grass while tourists, office workers, and homeless people took over the benches with lunch from the surrounding food trucks.

James walked through them with a careful eye, smiling politely and moving swiftly. Making sure he was forgettable to the people milling about during their lunch break while inspecting the preparations hidden in the world around him.

His map was pulled up on his HOLO and he inspected the location, ensuring their hardware was in place. He continued around the harbor, pretending to admire the horizon while he checked the cameras embedded in the pylons or tying his shoes to test the pressure detectors they added.

He was on the last part of his circle when a notification popped up on his HOLO. A camera was awry. It was embedded in the front of a garbage can pointing at the entrance to the harbor's playground. He walked over and picked up a piece of discarded paper on the ground to cover his movements.

He threw the paper away and scanned the HOLO's serial number, syncing with its video feed.

He could not actually fix it now, but Jon would be able to troubleshoot once he uploaded the data. That or they would switch out the whole thing manually.

He sat on a bench and casually swiped up checking the footage.

After scrolling through, waiting for something to happen he realized the unit was not responding to any commands. Jon'll know what to do, he thought, slipping his HOLO back in the slot in his bag and standing up.

He walked back to his bike, hoping Clint would be ready to go upon his return. He could use a nap he realized yawning behind his fist when he heard someone call his name.

"James!"

He turned around and saw a small group waving at him from afar.

He picked out Riley from the crowd walking together with the kids across the harbor. James walked toward them greeted by a sprinting George who he managed to grab and pull into a swing. He giggled before James set him back in front of his mother.

Riley reached out and hugged him. "How are you? We haven't seen you all in a couple of weeks."

"We've been keeping busy," said James nonchalantly, unsure of how to answer.

"Ahh, I see," Riley said, tapping her nose and squinting her eyes. "Well, we're going to the playground."

"I'll walk with you."

The five of them made their way to the playground, playing a breakout game of tag on the way with James ending as the tagger trying to chase George until he made it to the safety of the sand which denoted the end of the game.

James admitted defeat, walked over to Riley, and sat next to her.

"They're a lot of fun," he said, smiling while he watched them sprint around the jungle gym

"They're exhausting is what they are," Riley replied, exaggerating her slouch into the bench. "These are the hardest times for them. I try to get them out as much as I can."

"Why now?" asked James.

"Luke's been busy, you know," Riley said dismissively. "Part of the job."

"Yeah, that's rough," said James. "At least you have these guys."

"Yeah, but they miss their dad. Hell, I miss their dad. This is what it is though. Duty calls and Luke would give anything in the world for us. We know he's devoted to us, and he knows we're devoted to him. No two ways about it. How it's been forever."

"Do you ever think it will change?" James asked.

"No. I don't think so. At least I don't want it to yet. I don't know what I'd do if he were home all the time. Probably drive me up a wall."

James laughed. "He has to have an agenda, huh?"

"You bet." Riley was silent and they both watched the kids. James imagined the carefree world in which they lived.

"But I do wonder how our lives would be if he were home more. Always in the back of my mind," Riley said, her voice far away. "Wishful thinking though." She smiled at James, who simply nodded.

James looked at his HOLO and realized his nap window was closing.

"I've gotta run. Tell them bye for me?" he asked.

"Of course. Any message for my husband?" asked Riley.

"Not yet. Hopefully not soon."

Riley smiled. "Good."

James walked away from the playground his hands in his pockets, his gait light and airy, refreshed.

James tried calling Clint on his HOLO. The ringing forwarded him to a mailbox twice before he saw Clint's handle pop up with a message:

Crashing on these tanks. Meet you back at the apartment tonight.

James responded with a thumbs-up and took one last breath of the fresh harbor air before putting the bike in gear and peeling off toward home.

He found the apartment empty.

That's a first, he thought, poking his head outside and all around, trying to find anyone else. James flopped on the couch and pulled up an old TV show with his HOLO. He settled back in the cushions, the floating screen before him getting blurry. Soon his chin was bouncing off his chest. He drifted in and out of consciousness, catching snippets of the show inching closer and closer to the rest he craved when the world around him shattered with a *BOOM.*

The violence of the moment was so intense it threw James across the room. He landed face-first on the ground, the world fading to black while chaotic sound drowned out even his own voice with a single thought running through his head.

It started.

CHAPTER 24

The ground was cold and hard when James came to. His eyes fluttered open, searching for anything familiar, but a gray blanket of dust hung in the air obscuring his vision. He coughed in his hand, nearly vomiting when he inhaled a grainy mixture of pulverized sheet rock and smoke. Standing shakily, he reached out grasping at air before pushing off the soot-covered ground, his knees jelly beneath him.

What the hell happened? James thought, blindly searching the area that used to be his apartment. Alarms wailed in the distance along with a dull echo James could not pin down but knew it must be tied to the carnage surrounding him.

The smoke dissipated and James ran a hand across his eyes, shifting the soot from his eyelids. When he opened them, he was dumbstruck by what he found.

The balcony to their apartment was gone, along with the wall where it was once attached. James stared at the sky before him, still confounded by their new picture window while he turned in a slow circle. Glancing upward, he formed a picture of how lucky he was to be alive. There was a gaping hole in the roof with wires and pipes dangling precariously. Bits of rebar poked through the cement slabs still intact.

The debris must have been flung somewhere else James realized as the space he occupied, though destroyed, was untouched by the absent ceiling.

Their war room was a jumbled set of shattered HOLO emitters and hard drives occasionally sputtering to life, blinking intermittent blue lights along with an alarm system Jon designed to warn them of attack.

Lotta good that did, James thought wryly while he picked up a HOLO emitter from the ground and hit the side, trying to stabilize its internal mechanisms.

As the screen's light pulsed, James heard an unmistakable explosion echo through the room. He ran to the opening where the balcony once stood, searching the surrounding skyline, spotting a skyscraper wavering. A chunk was missing from the top corner of the building, as if a ball whizzed by, clipping it, and leaving a hole of metal, cement, and glass. James watched, transfixed as it toppled into its neighboring structure. James was mesmerized by the balls of hyper-condensed light flying effortlessly through the sky, crashing haphazardly into the city in thirty-second intervals. He could almost hear the city scream as it was torn apart by the projectiles.

Finally, six such missiles finished their crushing rolls, gouging their own craters among the buildings before the activity stopped, allowing James the presence of mind to tear away from the scene.

Focusing on escape was his best path forward and he redoubled his efforts smacking the side of the emitter to get it to life.

"Come on, you stupid sonofabitch," he growled, willing the broken piece of machinery to revive when finally, its blue light sprang before him displaying a map of the city.

His fingers flitted about getting the settings tuned in for the view he needed. A live aerial image of Midway jumped to life giving James a holistic view of the assault.

The initial shelling he witnessed only told the beginning of the story. They were under a full-blown artillery attack. He could not see what was actively bombarding them, but whatever it was spread its fury throughout the city with zero plan or design in mind other than its result, mass death and destruction. The area was a blanket of smoke and fire. The craters and collapsed buildings melded together in a sea of devastation. People fled downtown in droves, picked up as a mass of shadow from his satellite image, only to be cut down by a falling building toppled by an incoming ballistic.

Terror gathered in James's mind. They were murdering them in cold blood. It was too much for James to wrap his thoughts around and all he could do was watch as the world burned.

"JAMES!"

James paused his viewing for a second, lifting his head.

"JAMES, RESPOND, GODDAMNIT!"

The voice came again pleading at him and James gathered air into his lungs yelling back, "I'M UP HERE!"

He waited a second before he heard a response. "DON'T MOVE. I'M COMING TO GET YOU!"

He made out Kyle's deep booming voice. Following his friend's directive, James sat on the only remaining couch cushion left on the sofa. His brain was still comprehending the battle raging around them, but his body's reaction was unmistakable.

The courses, the elimination, the jungle—it all came rushing to him, his body priming itself. He was fascinated at his response. His heart rate dropped to a steady thud. His hands and other extremities were poised and dexterous. His palms were dry. His stomach simmered with bounds of iron. He was in battle mode.

Moments later, Kyle burst into the room covered in soot from head to toe, his face layered with chalky dust.

Kyle brushed debris from his crew-cut hair, his voice calm as walked up to James and looked him over. "They're here. The city's under attack."

"I could tell," James said sarcastically; neither of them laughed.

He took a deep breath while the maze of neurons in his mind fired. Kyle finished his check-up and turned around, scanning the damage, his face hiding the shock James sensed was spinning through his mind.

"Help me up," James said, putting out a hand for Kyle to grab.

Kyle pulled him off the couch and motioned toward the door.

His skin was cool to the touch. They were human machines.

James followed his lead into the hallway, glancing one last time at their former home, now a mangled twist of metal.

They walked briskly down the hallway. The ceiling was ripped off, the early afternoon light casting shadows in front of them. Sounds of more explosions rippled throughout the city. To add to it, burning plastic was a constant aroma hovering in the background.

"How many ships?" James asked Kyle, bending under a sagging beam to walk through the doorway to the stairwell.

"Only one of the big ones, the other two are headed to the southern continent. We haven't heard anything from Central yet."

"Really? One ship?" James said.

"I know," Kyle replied, guiding James around a wall. "They're blanketing Midway in missiles. Brandt's directing the show, but comms are getting squirrely for some reason. Either way, he's prepping everyone according to the plan. Our goal is to stop them from gaining a defensive position on the ground and establishing the rubble as a base. Instructions are to get to the nearest HQ or if you can the armory and wait for his orders," Kyle said, practically jumping down sets of stairs.

"So, this was the closest one to you. Lucky you were late, huh?" James said, following, his body bouncing with increased adrenaline.

"I was heading to the armory when I saw the building get taken out. Clint reported your location and I sped over here."

"Thanks, man."

"No problem. You'd do the same."

They were quiet the rest of the way to the bottom floor, James contemplating how lucky he was. When they reached the ground smoke clung to the air like fog and they jogged to the beat-up pickup truck Kyle used for his recon missions.

Five survival packs were stowed in the bed, strapped in with frayed bungee cords.

Kyle designed the packs dropped at each base around the city. Lucky for us, he hadn't been able to finish his assignments for the day, James thought.

James hopped in the passenger seat while Kyle turned the ignition, flooring it past the hordes of people streaming toward them in panic. The streets were chaos with humans, cars, bikes, and buses running amok.

They drove as quickly as Kyle could, but crowds overtook the road. Kyle navigated his way around the abandoned vehicles and fleeing people, laying on his horn to avoid plowing into the mass of humans.

James looked at the people staring blankly while they drove. The first groups they passed were untouched by the attack, frantic while acting with purpose, but as they got closer to the city, James saw a marked difference in behavior and appearance.

Men, women, and children covered in soot and blood barely noticed the truck, forcing Kyle to simply drive around them. People acted more like the walking dead than humans fleeing disaster.

All the while, explosions rocked the city, shaking the ground, and sending fresh smoke wafting above them in billowing clouds. This is real, James thought, his eyes stuck on a man walking hand-in-hand with a little boy, unaware the child was crying while they stumbled along with the rest of Midway's shell-shocked population.

When they arrived at the armory, James and Kyle parked down the street, the lot packed with other vehicles from Brandt's command.

Kyle led the way. They weaved through the vehicles parked haphazardly on the road and walked into a scene of organized chaos.

The frenzy of activity was tangible. James tasted the anticipation of battle lingering in the air. The low hum of pre-battle adrenaline settled in across the dozens of seasoned warriors prepping themselves.

"Kyle! James!"

Kevin waved at them from the staircase leading to the catwalk that ran the length of the warehouse. "We're in the Nest. Come on!"

Kyle did not hesitate and made for the staircase with James in close pursuit. James followed him up the narrow entryway to the top of the warehouse.

They jogged the skinny walkway to the Nest, a secondary HQ Stacie set up for exactly this scenario. Thank God she's a planner, James thought, stepping into the tight circular room and glancing at the HOLOs showing a full view of the enemy at their gates.

One of the motherships from the BlankZone sat offshore. Its size alone was enough to cause concern from any angle, but it surprised him how calm he was looking at one of the largest warships ever created moored miles away from his current location.

"Jesus, man, how the hell did you survive?" James heard Clint say before he was embraced in his vicelike grip, the shorter mechanic's biceps constricting James's body until he thought he heard a crunch.

"Let him go. You're gonna strangle him," Stacie said, tapping Clint's arm.

"I shouldn't have let you go home," Clint said, letting him go and standing back, shaking his head.

"You didn't know what was gonna happen. Relax man. We've got a battle to plan." James said, putting a reassuring hand on Clint's shoulder.

"Jon, Stacie, I need updates. What's happening out there?" James asked, turning to face the floating screens forming one of the Nest's walls.

"Looks like they're taking a break. Haven't seen any other missiles coming into the city for a few minutes," Jon said from behind him while the images changed to various scenes of damage spread all over Midway.

There must be thousands dead, James thought.

"Do we know what they were using to bomb us?" James asked, zooming in on one of the blast sites and focusing on the melted metal pooling in superheated ponds.

"Nothing we've seen before, but none of this is. They've managed to decimate the city in an hour," Stacie said, her voice crisp, clear, and analytical. "In our best estimate this was, frankly, the worst-case scenario." James heard the break in her demeanor at the end of the sentence before he flipped his view to the ship off the coast.

Ten miles offshore, according to the HOLO's distance finder, a ship the size of a skyscraper hung in the air elevated just slightly off the water. He couldn't tell what part of the ship he was looking at, but his mind was stuck trying to piece together the mini nuclear station they would need to move the behemoth to the shore let alone across the ocean.

He took a breath, realizing they were up against an enemy no one understood before turning around to address the team when he heard a rumble from the HOLO emitters' speakers. The ship opened, its armor plate covering the top pulled back, revealing a row of cannons stretching the length of the ship.

The front armor retracted until it disappeared under the ship's bow. Meanwhile, the cannons lowered themselves, revealing another row of cannons behind them lining the length of the ship. The two rows of weaponry lowered themselves until they were parallel to the water.

What the hell is happening? James thought, hoping he was wrong about what was coming next.

He peered over the edge of the Nest railing to find the rest of Brandt's command watching the same activity on their HOLOs, huddled together, holding a collective breath in preemptive agony.

He scanned the faces below until he came across Brandt who stood with his arms folded, staring intensely at a set of HOLO screens, his jaw a ball of muscle.

The silence in the warehouse was eerie in its completeness and the first set of cannons exploded with a flash, followed moments later by a resounding boom.

A strand of light a mile long and growing wider flew toward Midway bathing it in a ghostly shadow before it crashed into the first set of buildings, crushing everything in its path.

Shortly after, the second round of charges slammed into the city's buildings tumbling through the structures ensuring destruction was total and complete.

They're razing the city, James thought numbly, as the concrete and steel crumbled to the ground while the massive balls of light tumbled through the pathways created by the initial attack.

The team was silent as the balls of light continued their roll, finishing off what the randomized attack set up for them in the first place. Utter obliteration. There was nothing left behind, only dust.

"Jesus..." Deck whispered under his breath. "What... I mean, how?"

No one else spoke. They did not have an answer.

Instead, their attention was drawn back to the ship. The guns were back in their original hiding places, but warehouse-like doors were opening along the water's edge releasing smaller boats.

"Troop transports," Stacie whispered.

James searched around, finding the old radio they rewired to hook up to their HOLO emitters. He plugged it in and flipped on the volume, tuning it to one of the local news stations. After messing with the dial for a moment or two, a staticky woman's came on over the speakers. Her normally confident newswoman voice was replaced by her emotions, rife with dread and fear.

"...buildings have been flattened. Millions of casualties along with deaths already in the hundreds of thousands. Military response gearing up along the east coast of the Federation from the southern continent and through the north. The first attack zone was a direct hit in the mid-Atlantic region. Secondary sightings of the ships have been seen off the coast in the south. We are still waiting for word from the President on plans of defense, mass evacuations are taking place with the assistance of local police forces.

"Bridges and tunnels are jam-packed with Delaware becoming the major causeway. Advice is to avoid interstate transit ways at all costs. People are reporting problems with HOLO technology, but please, stay tuned to get updates via AM radio. Advice from leadership is to stay..."

James turned down the volume until the voice cut off. That was enough, they needed to focus on their response. The BlankZone army was going to invade Midway and he was about to be on the front lines.

"We need to move," James said, searching for a part of the city still intact. His eyes flitted around the screens until he noticed a lack of smoke near the water.

"Jon, let's get an image of the harbor," James said, and Jon tapped his HOLO a few times before a live view of the harbor came up on the screens.

The buildings across the street from the concrete park bordering the waterline were destroyed, but the actual buildings and land surrounding the harbor's front were largely unscathed.

"That's where they're going to land," James said to the room. "Stacie, Jon, I need to know exactly what we have in the harbor after the attack. What's still working? What kind of gear is there? What other visuals can we set up? Is the HQ still operational? Can you pull all that information together for us?"

"We're on it," Stacie said, wrangling a HOLO displaying its images on the Nest's walls and flipping it to where she could start her work.

"Jon, figure out how long we have until the BZ troops make landfall," Stacie said, her eyes glued to the 3D images rotating above her.

"Yes, ma'am," Jon replied, working with the rest of the screens.

James addressed the rest of the group. "Clint, you should work with motor pool. Kevin and Bob, talk with your respective fields and see what they're doing. It's our first time here. Need to learn from the best and luckily, they're downstairs."

The three of them nodded, exiting the Nest in single file, their faces focused on the tasks ahead.

"Saving the best for last, I see," Deck said, leaning against the rail of the Nest.

"You got it. Let's go find Brandt. Stacie, Jon," James said, stopping at the exit to the catwalk, "keep us posted on any updates."

The two nodded, their eyes concentrated on their data feeds.

James made his way to the bottom floor where he landed in a beehive of military activity. Soldiers with furrowed brows and determined stares walked around the warehouse, prepping supplies. From MREs to tank reserves, they were gearing up for battle. Deck tapped James's shoulder, pointing to the set of

286

HOLOs where Brandt stood with his arms across his chest, reviewing the progress of the ships disembarking from their host.

So, this is what the beginning of war looks like, James thought after stopping for a group of medics pushing a shopping cart filled with triage units toward a line of trucks being packed by teams of soldiers.

James made it to Brandt and stood next to him, giving a salute as he spoke. "Lieutenant Brandt, Privates Coffey, Whelan, and Sam reporting for duty."

Brandt glanced back at him. "At ease, buddy. You don't even report to me."

James relaxed, clasping his hands behind his back, and staring with Brandt at the mass of ships combining to create an armada in front of the mothership.

"How many have you counted so far?" James asked.

"Right now, twenty-eight ships total. Looks like eight of them are gunships for protection while they disembark. Leaves us with twenty troop transports. No idea how many each can hold but wouldn't be surprised if it's 250 to 500 soldiers or more on each."

James did the math in his head. Best case scenario, there were 5,000 soldiers on those transports. There were only 300 of Brandt's men and the eight on James's team. They didn't stand a chance unless the Federation showed up.

"So, what's the plan?" James asked, pushing the numbers aside for the time being.

"Get to the harbor and set up a defense. We've got some surprises in store for them and hopefully can hold them back until the cavalry arrives. Doesn't look like they have any air attack planned, probably would interfere with their ground attack, but too early to tell. You all able to help out?" Brandt replied, his fingers moving around his HOLO, pulling a hundred images at once and flying through them, scanning various views of the harbor and the surrounding waters.

"Definitely. I've got Jon and Stacie determining our status. Any word from Central Command?" James said, hoping there was a time when help would arrive.

Brandt shook his head. "Nothing other than the standing orders we were given in the first place. Protect Midway at all costs."

James nodded, wondering when the top echelon of the Federation would act, but kept his mouth shut.

Dolly walked up with three packs, one with a remote hanging from a loop.

"Where do you want these, boss?" she asked, holding them up for him to see.

"Put them in the back of Barb's truck," replied Brandt, pointing toward the parking lot. "We need to get moving."

"You got it," she replied and walked out to the lot.

"Let's get to the harbor," Brandt said suddenly turning around to James. He motioned at Kyle and Deck for them to follow. "You all come with me."

James hopped in the front seat of his truck while Kyle and Deck piled into the pickup bed.

Brandt threw the car into gear backing it up. Kyle slid the back window open and pointed in the direction of his truck. "Let's grab those gear packs outta my bed. We're gonna need 'em."

Brandt nodded, spinning his wheel wordlessly and pulling up to the edge of the parking lot gate where he stopped to address six commandos with a portable power distributor.

"Finish prepping the rest of these vehicles then get a move on. I want the whole group mobilized. Meet us at the harbor."

A chorus of "yes sirs" greeted the end of his sentence.

Brandt stepped on the gas and pulled to the side of Kyle's pickup. Kyle jumped out and transferred the gear packs into the back of Brandt's truck. When he finished, he jumped into the bed with Deck and hit the car on the side.

"Good to go!" he shouted. Brandt burned out his tires, tearing down the street, and swerved wildly onto the still viable roadway headed to the harbor.

James held onto the roll bar.

"Fast driver," James said, grinning at Brandt, but Brandt's face was a mask.

"A lot at stake here," Brandt said through gritted teeth, uncharacteristically tense.

James realized he was probably concerned about his family, but they were so far outside of the city limits nothing but a direct hit would touch them. Not to mention James was sure Brandt and his command set up saferooms in their houses.

James looked at the smoke tunnels rising from the city trying not to imagine the number of dead bodies burning to ash. Instead, he eased the tension by talking plans.

"We have weapons cached all over the harbor. Stacie planned on the waterfront being the most likely landing spot for an enemy attack. We were ready," James said, looking out the window. "That's one spot I know is good to go. Hell, I was there today I saw…" James's stomach dropped. Oh, God, he thought, the idea so horrible he couldn't let it pass his lips.

"Hey, hey there, buddy, you crap your pants or something?" Deck said, clapping his shoulder and talking in his ear from the window to the pickup bed.

"Riley," James whispered, his voice inaudible over the roar of the engine and fire winds whipping across the city.

"What was that? Speak up. We can't hear you back here," Deck said, leaning through the open partition between. Brandt glanced over at James, concerned.

"James! Come on, what'd you say?" Deck said, slapping James's arm again. "Gotta talk, man."

James took a deep breath. "Riley. Riley and the kids. I was at the harbor, and I saw Riley and the kids today."

Brandt's eyebrows arched in surprise, replaced by a

smoldering gaze more intense than any James had seen before in his life.

"Oh, fuck," Deck said, leaning back.

"I'm sorry I didn't mention it until now. I completely forgot. I…" James was awash in agony. Why couldn't he have remembered sooner? Could they have survived the attack? Where were they now? All the thoughts and shame of failing the one man who supported him poured through James as the car's acceleration leapt forward.

"Where were they, James?" Brandt asked mechanically.

"The playground. On the south side of the harbor," James replied, as the world flew past with increasing speed.

The father sitting next to him pressed harder on the gas. They flew around obstacles, piles of embers, and charred corpses lying haphazardly in the street.

Blazing debris seeped into the air and the heat from the fire was palpable as they drove closer to downtown. Wave after wave of fire intensified and James watched through the sideview mirror as the remaining structures were engulfed in leaping flames.

He was numb to the world, kicking himself for not saying anything about Riley and the kids earlier. He was too wrapped up in his bullshit to think about anything else. He was barely human anymore.

They finally came to a point where the truck would not be able to move any further and the four of them yanked open their doors. James and Brandt sprinted to the harbor with Deck and Kyle stopping to get the gear in the pickup bed before following them.

As they approached the harbor, groups of people appeared huddled about or being helped by early arrival soldiers who were treating, carrying, or checking the hundreds of unmoving bodies.

This is war, James thought as he passed a cadre of soldiers pulling dead bodies into a line away from the water's edge.

James took a moment to glance at Brandt whose tight jawline and focused gaze said everything about his mindset. He

290

scanned the bodies on the ground when he ran. James prayed they weren't too late.

"Which way?" Brandt asked, not looking at James, his eyes searching the harbor, taking the scene in at once.

"Over here," James replied, peeling off toward the park where he worked on the camera earlier.

They sprinted over finding much of the space intact.

Brandt ran to the playground equipment, checking inside the slide and yelling the names of his family over and over again.

"Riley! Shannon! Danny! George! Riley! Shannon! Danny! George!" Brandt cupped his hands around his mouth, his throat growing raspy with each yell only worsened by the smokey air.

"RILEY!" Brandt screamed, letting out a guttural cry reserved for the truly desperate. He fell into a crouch, his head hanging, elbows perched on his knees, and he whispered his children's names into the woodchips.

James looked back at Deck and Kyle who stood awkwardly behind them, their faces matched James's anguish.

Unsure of what else to do, James put out a hand touching Brandt tenderly on the shoulder. "I'm sorry. Maybe they left. Maybe they got out," he said quietly.

"You know that's not what happened, James. We both know that's not what happened, don't we?" Brandt said, still talking to the ground. He stood up to his full height, pulling his shoulder back into a roll before cracking his neck and turning to look at James.

"This wasn't your fault. Understand?" he said, his voice at a level of command James did not know how to respond to other than with a nod.

"Good. Now let's go. We've got a fucking war to fight."

Brandt walked by him, relieving Kyle of one of the gear packs, slinging it over his shoulder, and removing the rifle.

The three of them stood and watched Brandt stride away, his shoulders square with one shoulder strap slung behind him, the rucksack swinging while he adjusted his grip on the rifle in his other hand.

James imagined the grief streaming through Brandt's thoughts. The family he would give anything to protect was no longer. He only knew them for a matter of months, but their emptiness affected James in a way he did not know it would. The father, husband, and warrior made his way toward the front line of the greatest war the world would ever see, motivated by a tortured pain James could not comprehend.

Just then a shudder moved the ground beneath him along with a spray of the ocean whipping into his face. What's happening out there? he wondered, placing his hand above his eyes and looking out at the water.

The mothership was leaving, her exit causing waves to crash into the sea wall, sending a salty mist whipping across the surface, but a distinct set of objects floated in the distance. A gray metal line glinted in the late afternoon sun.

"What is that?" Kyle said from behind him.

"It's the ships," James said, his voice steady, the familiar sense of adrenaline flooding his veins. "They're starting the invasion."

CHAPTER 25

The air in the harbor hummed with intense energy. It was a rapidly changing atmosphere with a hivemind preparing for the defense of their demolished city.

Soldiers flooded the area, dressed in a mixture of civilian clothes and military fatigues. Their mismatched attire may have suggested they were not ready for battle, but their faces told the real story. These were warriors.

James sidestepped lines carrying medical supplies, ammo, comms equipment, heavy machine guns, rocket launchers, sandbags, and ion shields designed to withstand blasts from cannon fire. Having witnessed the destruction wrought on Midway already, James was unsure how effective they would be against the weaponry the BlankZone army brought to the fight.

After losing Brandt in the hubbub James, Kyle, and Deck slipped through the continuously moving supply chain. They made their way to the north side of the harbor to meet with the rest of their team.

The waterfront was a sloping arc with nearly 900 yards of cement shoreline in a crescent shape, buffered up against the sea. Boutiques, museums, restaurants, and tourist outfits kept their brick-and-mortar locations in a series of stacked buildings 200 yards back from the water, elevated in a steppe design. The harbor was the only place deep enough for ships to attack. Its design made it perfect for defense, but the lack of fallback areas, limited their options if they were overrun.

Brandt's command set up the ion shields on the south side of the harbor in a trench formation with staggered rows of shields all the way to the shops at their rear. The transparent gray walls on the south side of the harbor were already deployed, their surfaces absorbed the late afternoon sun as James, Kyle, and Deck walked around them. The shields signaled a different stage in James's wartime experience.

James caught sight of Kevin at the water's edge and waved for Deck and Kyle to follow him. When they arrived, Kevin was shouting to a group of Brandt's soldiers deploying one of their heavy guns in front of the shield's reflection pods. "That's right. Put the big guns out front where we can attack from a distance," Kevin said, measuring the angle of the gun's nose. "Doesn't matter if those get hit. We'll stay protected back here. At least for a little while."

"How's it going?" James asked, sidling next to his friend, surveying the ongoing preparations.

"We've got it handled for now, I think," Kevin replied, not breaking his gaze away from the chaos. "Still a lot to do."

"Tell me where to jump in," James said, rolling up his sleeves.

"All good here. Stacie may need some help though." Kevin pointed at the tiki bar overlooking the water.

"When did she get here?" James asked, surprised at her speed.

"Don't know. Might want to run over there."

"Will do. Kyle, Deck." James turned to find they had already moved on with a group of Brandt's soldiers to set up more shields along the edge of the harbor.

Takes care of that, I guess, James thought before jogging to find Stacie.

Their HQ was a tiki bar placed awkwardly on top of a fancy seafood restaurant overlooking the water. Although the owner originally refused their request to pack comms equipment in her storage, Deck's charm prevailed, and she let them keep several preconfigured HOLO screens and other supplies in their unused basement space. It was an odd location for a battle station, but James was thankful the building was still standing.

When he walked through the bead-covered doorway, Jon wordlessly handed him a cord and pointed to an outlet strip sitting on the ground.

"I mean, how many monitors are we going to need? I think at least two per operational front, but that setup limits us to one watching from the drones. Do you think that's enough? I don't want to add more mid-battle, just want to stay in front of the firing line." Stacie spoke with her hands on her hips, searching the bar's equipment for an answer to her problem.

"Let's start with two. Not hard to change," Jon said, kneeling to plug wires together. "Besides, we can send the drones higher to get a better angle on what's happening at sea," he added, tapping the HOLO emitter strapped to his wrist. A 3D image of the front line sprang to life on the screens above him.

Stacie bobbed her head in agreement and started setting up the rest of the command center, carefully arranging her series of HOLOs to control the battlefield.

"Any word from the higher-ups, Stace?" James asked.

She looked at him blankly, still registering his question before shaking her head. "Negative, still waiting. We're having trouble with the communications equipment too. Direct connections won't work. Our signal's jammed, but Jon's going to get to it."

"After I finish doing everything else," Jon quipped, wheeling a fridge outside, and tipping it over the edge of the balcony.

"Oh, pipe down. You know you're the only one of us who can hack them back," Stacie said, waving him off.

"Yeah, yeah, yeah," Jon grumbled, eyeing the bar for more items he could discard to create space in their tight quarters.

"Let me know when you hear back," James said, leaving them to finish getting ready. He stopped at the railing to get a sense of where the rest of the command was headquartered. He scanned the horizon, avoiding the line of ships approaching from the sea. He spotted a group of trucks outside a hotel lobby, receiving instructions from a man out front before they chugged off in the direction of the line.

Brandt will be there, I bet, James thought, running down the steps toward the command center.

When he entered the hotel lobby, he was surprised by the level of preparedness they accomplished in such little time. He spied Brandt standing with one of the packs Dolly had been carrying strapped to his back, the remote control dangling behind him and his rifle slung over the other shoulder. James wondered what the pack was for.

Jesus, man. Who gives a shit? Get up there and help. James mentally chastised himself for getting distracted while he made his way over to the set of HOLOs Brandt was examining.

"How far away are they?" asked Brandt quietly.

"Six miles offshore, sir," replied the techie manipulating a cloud of drones to watch their enemy's movement. "Looks like they've stopped moving."

"We need our shields up now. James, how's your team doing?"

"Preparations are moving along, sir. Looks like we're running into a comms interference issue though. Jon and Stacie are working on it."

"We're having the same problem. Glad they're working on it." Brandt spoke to his people. "I want this all tied up in a bow within the next ten minutes. Let's go, people."

Shouted "yes sirs" followed Brandt as he brusquely exited the room through the front doors. James jogged to catch up when a rumble sounded and a group of twenty mismatched tanks turned the corner. One of the hatches opened and Dolly emerged. Her face was smudged with grease and her short hair was pulled back with a headband. She leaned against the edge of the hole at the top of the tank.

"Twenty tanks, sir," she said. "All primed and ready to blow shit up." She slapped the side of the hulking machine.

Brandt nodded. "Good work. Let's get these to the waterfront. Keep 'em spread out, especially the ones in front of the shields." He jumped on top of the steel giant and leaned casually against the turret. "Move her out, Dolly!" Brandt yelled, slapping the armored plating.

"Yes sir," she replied and they pulled away from the front of the building.

The colossal machines thundered their way to the front line, but the last one stopped in front of him. The hatch popped open, and Clint's head appeared. He squeezed his shoulders through the opening before looking at James.

"Here we go, huh?" Clint said with a wink.

"Guess so. See anyone else on your way in?" James asked.

"Bob's finalizing the medical tents in back before going to check supplies in the triage areas. Told him I would swing back if he needed a ride. You want a lift to the line?" Clint asked, motioning down to the hole.

"I'll ride on top," James said, getting a sudden wave of claustrophobia thinking of the tank's narrow quarters.

"Hop on up!"

James stepped onto the metal tread, grasping Clint's hand to pull him on top. He sat next to the hatch opening, his hands bracing for the ride.

"Comfy up there?" Clint asked, eliciting a thumbs-up from James before he yelled into the opening. "Hit it, folks!"

With a jolt smoother than James anticipated, they were off, flattening even the concrete in front of them.

From this vantage point James had a better view of the enemy. They lined up in long rows with massive gunships in a diamond formation protecting the more vulnerable transporters.

James was astounded by the size of the force the BlankZone sent to attack the city. He was even more taken aback when he realized this probably did not even comprise 1% of the fighting force they anticipated the BlankZone had at its disposal. His stomach lurched at the thought, sending him into a wind tunnel of anxiety.

Clint whistled under his breath. "What a view…"

James didn't respond, his eyes fixed on the gunship in the middle of the BlankZone's attack formation. The ship was getting taller, a single column rising against the sky.

A siren wailed and a scratchy voice blared over the speakers. "TAKE COVER! I REPEAT, TAKE COVER!"

"Here we go…" James said, jumping off the tank as Clint plunged into his chamber.

James sprinted toward the front line, diving behind a semi-constructed sandbag wall.

A lot of good these will do, James thought, looking around for a better option.

He spied Kevin and Kyle working furiously behind a stack of sandbags to align a complex series of wires to power the north flank's ion shields. He checked his surroundings before abandoning his position and sprinting the fifty yards to where his team hurried to complete the initial hookup to the self-charging generators.

Not wanting to disturb the two of them, he glanced at the snack bar, unsurprised to see shields already running in front of their shelter, the blue light HOLO lights pouring through the gaps in the walls.

Suddenly the low purr of the generators began in full swing and the telltale signs of the shields' standby signal glowed orange.

"Ready to engage," Kevin yelled, his hand primed over his HOLO screen.

"Copy, powering on." Kyle stepped back, swiping up on his HOLO and the shields sprang to life turning the sea before them into a shade of a gunmetal gray. Sporadic power currents rippled through the otherwise glassy surface.

"Nice work, gents," said Deck, materializing with five duffel bags in his arms and one slung across his back. "We'll need these I think. Full gear setup in each bag." James unzipped one of the bags and inspected the contents. Tactical suit, assault rifle, sidearm, a few explosives, hand grenades, knife, earpiece, the works.

"Just like the good ol' days, huh?" said Deck, pulling out a tactical suit and examining it in the sunlight, watching the colors alter to match its surroundings.

"Didn't think it'd be as stressful for some reason," said James, pulling his t-shirt over his head. "Now we're in it."

"Heads up!"

A random shout made their eyes snap to the horizon where the eight gunships held their position surrounding the transporters. The forward ship elongated its central tower into a mammoth column structure surrounded by cords of tracks looping along the bottom of the pillar. A ball of light grew at the top of the column and other similar balls flowed into the tracks. The sides of the structure filled with iridescent white light.

James exhaled in a deep, calming sigh.

"Get these suits on," he said, pulling off his sneakers and unbuttoning his jeans, "Whatever comes, we're gonna want to be ready."

While James undressed, the column on top of the central gunship slid the balls of light into a triangular formation where they sat in a compartment at the top of the structure. He zipped up the front of his suit as the tower leaned back dipping so far only a glow of light hovered behind the ship. James finished dressing, placing his dead earpiece in place before clipping his rifle to the front of his body armor. In a single motion, almost too quick for

299

the human eye, the balls flew out, catapulting through the air like they were thrown from a giant jai alai basket.

"What the..." Deck said under his breath. They tilted their faces skyward watching the trio of projectiles arch in the air. When they reached their apex, the projectiles hung for a second before jettisoning toward the city.

"Get down!" yelled James. He dove behind the ion shields, his hands over his head, and braced for impact. He heard the first crash behind him and waited for the wall of fire to crush him.

He counted his heartbeats, his skin vibrated, and he focused on the moment at hand while his body was still intact. After a few seconds when he was still conscious, he lifted his head hesitantly and looked around him. They were all fine.

Others looked up from behind their ion shields and people pointed back at the city skyline. One of the orbs tore a hole through the rubble, replacing loose chunks of concrete with dust.

"What happened?" asked Kyle.

James caught sight of Stacie and Jon moving with furious speed inside their tiny office-like bomb shelter.

"I've got a pretty good guess," he said, pointing at Stacie and Jon. He looked at the oncoming ships, deciding to take the risk. "I'm going to check on them." James didn't wait for a response and sprinted across the harbor, flying up the steps to the luau-themed bar.

"What'd you do?" he asked Stacie and Jon, still caught in a frenzy of activity.

"Used the heavy guns as a defense mechanism. Worked well this time but be prepped for more any second. James, we can't count on air support. We need Brandt's guys to get up and running. We can keep the guns for defense for now, but eventually..." Her voice trailed off and she looked him in the eye.

James understood returning her gaze, they would have the transports to focus on soon enough. They needed to get on offense.

"We've got a lot to do," she added, politely telling him to go away.

"Well, thanks," he said, before running back to the rest of the team. He heard a robotic "you're welcome" behind him.

"Get in defensive positions. Stacie and Jon can take care of the heavy weapons for now. We need to get Bob and Clint—" James was cut off by the loudspeaker.

"More orbs on the way! Back to defensive positions!"

James turned to the skyline. Two dozen orbs were above them, hovering in the air, ready to wreak havoc.

He sprinted to the shields as the orbs streaked to the ground. The cannons reacted, firing at the targets speeding toward the harbor, while others crashed into the destroyed city behind them.

Missiles intercepting the balls of white light, collided in midair before imploding. The result created a sensation of solar wind and vibrating pulses in the air.

"We've got movement out there," Kevin said, pulling an image up on his HOLO.

James watched the catapult structures fold back into their carriers, he felt another drop in his stomach. The ships maneuvered until parallel walls of gunships formed a V formation. They flattened themselves lowering their position in the water and pulled back their armored plating, much like their mothership, revealing a series of cannons arranged in an attack position. While all this was happening the transport ships organized themselves behind the line and started progressing toward land in groups of five.

"PREPARE FOR ATTACK!" the loudspeaker boomed.

James picked up his rifle, chambering a round and clipping extra ammo magazines on his vest. He stood behind the shields and pulled out his HOLO, displaying the formation of the approaching ships. They raced toward shore, cannons ready to fortify their assault. His stomach hardened into a resolute stone, his heart pounded with adrenaline and fear. James took in the mayhem

301

through the haze of the ion shield, feeling the tremors through the concrete as the heavy guns fired in front of him.

This was it, the moment they trained for.

A transport ship hit the harbor's edge. The BlankZone made landfall.

The first wave hit with a fury James was not prepared for. His hands were numb in minutes from the rifle's recoil.

Troops disembarked on self-releasing platforms. Soldiers with white face masks poured from them, firing as they moved in coordinated patterns at the ion shields.

Once the soldiers were on land, the platform folded back inside, and a new platform emerged with a fresh set of soldiers. James watched in dread. How many more would come from those ships?

Brandt's stationary guns performed their jobs admirably. The pile of bodies at the landing site spilled into the sea. Still, James continued to unload his rifle at a ridiculous clip. He was running through his duffle full of reserves, replacing the empty magazines in his suit's ammo compartments repeatedly.

Another group of soldiers released from the ships. It was James's first glimpse of the enemy. Their masks were contoured to mold onto the wearer's face and over the top of the head making each soldier identical. They wore dark gray suits, similar in style to James's, but without the camouflage technology.

Once on land, they were automatons. They stayed in formation, following unheard orders, and moved with inhuman efficiency. When a soldier was gunned down, another stepped in to take the fallen one's place without hesitation. It was unsettling for James to watch their battlefield discipline, people walking into a line of bullets without a second thought.

The groups from each platform moved with their unit, half of them dead when their feet hit land, the other half finding refuge from the onslaught of bullets and explosives. While James's team and Brandt's soldiers were making it difficult for them to amass troops on land, their numbers were steadily building.

The defenses closest to the waterfront were almost overwhelmed. Eventually, they would have enough troops to push the line, James thought as another ship unloaded its cargo.

A shield covering Brandt's soldiers was blown into the air from a well-placed missile and bodies tumbled after it like ragdolls.

A misfire from a gunship crashed into a group of soldiers disembarking from a BlankZone transport taking out another score of Brandt's troops holding the line along with it.

"Goddammit," James hissed through his teeth, hoping it wasn't as bad as it looked. Suddenly, two missiles rocketed overhead, shocking James with their noise, flying toward the two farthest gunships at the back of the formation eliciting direct hits and massive explosions.

Nice shot, Stacie and Jon, he thought. The explosions were larger than he expected, and James realized the firepower packed under their decks created ship size bombs primed to take out anything in their vicinity.

The next moment five more transports, working to unload another group of soldiers, were hit by the tanks with a barrage of fire. The plumes of smoke were so dense James could only tell the ships were still there because of the explosions rocking the area.

"Fuck, yeah!" Kyle stood behind him, cheering with his gun held above his head.

The smoke cleared and James was unsurprised to see four transports sinking while the remaining one tried to unload its passengers who were quickly dispatched by gunfire from Brandt's team.

"Well, that's one way of doing it," Deck said, impressed. "Done for the day?"

But already another set of ships glided across the water into the harbor.

"So much for that…" Deck said, reloading his rifle and clipping extra rounds to his vest.

James was about to do the same when he heard static out of his earpiece, "James… James… JAMES!"

"What?" he replied, surprised. "Wait, when did these start working?"

"After we hit those gunships. Jon figured out they were jamming a signal somehow, but that's beside the point. Also, only working between our team for now so keep that in mind. Does Brandt know his family's here?" Stacie asked.

James's heart skipped. "What? Are they with you?"

"They came out before the first wave. Didn't have time to tell you. Does Brandt know?" James heard a child crying in the background.

"No, we thought they were gone! Do you know where he is?" James shouted back, hitting Deck on the shoulder mouthing the words, "They're alive."

"Somewhere in the middle of the line by the harbor. Let me get you a location."

James waited, his relief matched the expression on both Deck and Kyle's faces.

"Sending it to you now."

"Copy. And thanks. Tell Riley I'm going to find Brandt," James said, sprinting off, following the route Stacie provided.

He still couldn't believe they were alive when he slid next to Brandt behind one of the cannons holding the line.

"James, what the…? What are you doing here? We need you on the north side of the harbor. Get your—" Brandt was getting angry, but James cut him off.

"Sir, hold on a second," he said, touching a finger to his earpiece. "Stacie, can you put her on?"

Brandt looked at him inquisitively but said nothing.

James handed the device to Brandt who put it up to his ear.

"Hello?" he said, annoyed.

In the next second, Brandt transformed from a broken man to one elated beyond all measure.

James turned away letting them talk in private. He concentrated on the enemy, the rest of their fleet was headed to shore. Six gunships and ten transports, all converging on them at once. Terror gripped him while he watched their progression when he felt a hand on his shoulder.

"You have a good team there, James," Brandt said, brushing a hand under his eyes.

"They'll keep them safe," James said, planning his course back to his team.

"I know they will. Keep your head on a swivel and listen for orders. We're going to get these comms back up and running. Then we'll finish this."

James nodded and raced back to his team.

When he arrived, Clint and Bob stood before him, zipping the fronts of their suits. James patted Clint on the chest. "Glad you two made it. Nice work on those transport ships."

"One got away," Clint said, shrugging. "Happy to be in on the action. Figured you could use me back here."

"Definitely."

"Incoming!" Kevin shouted. Another group of orbs soared above them. A new set of transport ships landed.

"Hold them back!" James shouted, kneeling near the edge of the ion shield. He alternated positions with Deck to reload while they peppered the soldiers disembarking but were losing ground fast. The enemy's numbers were stunning.

Stacie wouldn't be able to use the missiles again. Not yet anyway, the remaining vessels were too close to Brandt's men and the explosions would decimate the harbor walls instantly killing any troops in the vicinity.

"Keep firing!" James shouted before touching Deck on the shoulder getting his attention. "We have to cover their retreat. Set up a defensive position farther back."

305

Deck nodded and moved to relay the message to Kyle, alternating positions with Kevin while Clint and Bob held their position on the far side of the shield.

James glanced at his team. They were all in position, holding their spots, waiting for James to make the first move. James flashed back to their courses, Croyton's wrath over mistakes or miscalculations all coming together for them now. Without another thought, James signaled to Kevin and began their move.

Unspoken communication was second instinct as bodies shifted interchangeably retreating from the front line. They used the rows of shields behind them to cover their movement, firing at the faceless soldiers pouring off the enemy ships, inching closer every moment.

He had no idea how many of the enemy he hit, but he was down to two reserve magazines and was running low on the one in use. He felt the tap on his shoulder to move back. He ran in a crouch to the next set of ion shields, unleashing the rest of his clip when he got there. He ducked back to reload.

We need more firepower, he thought. James leaned around the barrier and took out a few of the enemy who made it to shields forty yards away.

The gunships were busy in defense mode. Stacie and Jon's heavy guns laid into the transports, joined by the tanks and Brandt's command team firing everything they had left.

The tanks rolled to the front of the line under fire from troops and ships alike. They broke into three different groups and, with a final salvo unleashed hell on the southern flank of gunships. Brandt's ground troops fled springing toward James's team's position on the line. James watched as the tanks erupted one by one until finally the central gunship exploded violently eliminating its counterparts in the process but taking out the remaining tanks with a mushrooming inferno.

Three more of those to go, James thought. The troops were already far enough from the line to avoid friendly casualties. Now the only problem was the gunships would destroy their own defenses and take out all the shields and guns at the harbor's edge. James gritted his teeth and kept firing, covering the retreat.

While Stacie and Jon hammered the transports, James and the team focused on the troops disembarking from the ships with steady and demoralizing speed.

Deck popped up next to James. "We've got to keep moving back! There's too many of them!" he shouted. He unloaded on a group who moved within twenty-five yards of their position. "Where the hell is Central?! We need air support!"

"I don't know," James yelled, "but we have to assume it's not coming. Keep moving back. Tell the rest of Brandt's men to follow our lead."

James kept his rifle steady and covered Deck as he ran to the next set of shields relaying the message. James called over his mic to Stacie. "Have we heard anything else? Where the hell is our air support?!"

"Nothing yet," Stacie replied. "Brandt's coming up front now."

James bit his cheek in frustration and whipped his rifle around the shield, taking out more soldiers getting closer to his position.

Dropping behind the shield to reload, James was bowled over by an explosion. A team of Brandt's soldiers flew through the air followed by chunks of concrete. The gunships were starting to focus farther back on the line. They'd be able to take out Stacie and Jon soon. They needed to act. He shouted into his mic making an executive decision. "Stacie, blow those fuckers out of the water."

"Roger," she said, and let loose a barrage of missiles taking out the last three gunships. The heavy steel plates sunk in a swirl of smoke and flame, their final explosions knocking out power to the shields along the front line. When the smoke cleared

James saw the stationary guns were torched from the ensuing explosion.

Without Brandt's guns providing firepower the transport ships unloaded at will. A horde of enemy soldiers pushed ashore, destroying what remained of the defensive guns and moving swiftly in his direction.

There was a pat on James's back. Brandt crouched next to him with Dolly and two other soldiers. Dolly held her arm, a crimson stain of blood spreading from her shoulder to her chest.

"We've got this for now. Drop back and get situated. You need to cover the retreat. Help Dolly."

James nodded. "Yes sir."

"Go! Now!" Brandt shouted, standing with the rest of his men to fire into the crowd of enemy troops rushing their position.

Dolly grunted as James wrapped an arm around her waist, and the two of them moved as fast as their legs would allow. Bullets whizzed by their heads, and they somersaulted over a concrete highway barrier. They landed hard on the asphalt. An animalistic scream of agony erupted from Dolly, and James pulled her over to one of the last ion shields still intact while she clutched her arm.

"I'm gonna cover them," James shouted to her, the noise around them deafening. Dolly tried to respond but was delirious from pain. James rested her head on the ground before swinging his rifle over the barrier to cover Brandt's retreat. But Brandt had other plans and James watched the scene unfold.

Brandt and the soldiers around him separated from one another. The two soldiers accompanying Brandt sprinted into the enemy falling at various steps in a rain of flying metal. Brandt was crouched behind an ion barrier, watching the army advance.

"What the hell are you doing?" James muttered, confused.

When the line of soldiers was within five yards of Brandt, he turned around and leaned his back against the shield. He gripped the remote control and tilted his face to the sky. James swore Brandt smiled before he removed the power to the shield.

With a sudden flash, James threw his body over Dolly. The force of the blast lifted them off the ground, and James lost track of her tumbling through the air. He landed, numb, as the world was consumed and spit out by light.

CHAPTER 26

Hi James,

I'm sorry I missed you this last weekend! I wanted to reach out to say how much I miss you already and how glad I am you're alive. It's still strange reading about you on the news or hearing your name during random conversations, but I guess that comes with the territory of being a rock star who saved the Northern Federation, you stud you.

As you probably heard, I got accepted into the military's MedCorps and am training on the southeast coast! Not sure what my specialization is yet, but I guess you learn that during training. I know, I know. I'm getting ahead of myself, but I'm excited to get involved, especially after what we saw happen a few weeks ago. What you and the rest of your team did—it was inspiring. Anyway, James, I guess what I'm trying to say is I miss you. But I get the feeling you can't be with someone, and I understand that. Maybe we'll meet somewhere during a deployment in the future. I'd be lucky to have you there for more than one reason ;). I hope you know I am and will always be a friend. See you down the line.

Love,
Kaylie

James tapped his screen archiving the message in a saved folder marked "Important" before disembarking the plane.

"Welcome sir." A man in his late twenties saluted and took his bags as James stepped from the gangplank to the tarmac of their training base.

"Thank you. And your name is?" James said, pulling the second strap of his backpack over his shoulder.

"Private Darren, sir. Also, I can take that for you." Darren pointed at James's pack.

"I've got it. No worries," James replied. "I can take those, too."

"Nonsense," Darren replied. "It's my honor. It's a pleasure to meet you. We're all excited to have you on the base."

"Excited to be back," James said, looking at the other two planes circling above him.

"How was home?" the man grunted as he threw the bags in the back of the small vehicle.

"It was nice," James replied amiably, hoping he could ride in quiet the rest of the way.

"Great to hear, sir! Did you get to see all your friends and family?"

"Yes, thank you." Get the hint, buddy, James thought, settling into the passenger seat and leaning back into the hard cushion.

"Good, good. Well, we're excited you're here, sir."

"Thanks again."

James sat in silence the rest of the drive and was dropped off enthusiastically by Darren five minutes later outside his old training quarters. Darren insisted on bringing the bags into the room and probably would have helped him unpack if he asked him to, but James wanted to be alone.

He sat on the edge of his bed and looked around the room. The other bunks were already occupied with his team's belongings. He lit a cigarette and walked to the window looking out over the base. So much had changed since his first stay.

The new activity threw him off from the previous setup when it was his team training relentlessly under Croyton's tutelage. The base, at one time their private refuge and personal hell, was transformed into a multi-functional command center with ongoing

311

construction spread throughout the complex intended to house thousands of soldiers.

His life was forever different. After he convalesced in the hospital for a few weeks, the Federation released him to recover at home with his family. It was a relief at first, healing his wounds, and seeing people in a trickle. He would occasionally turn on the news to get an update on the infiltration in the Southern Federation but would turn it off if Braxton or the battle came up.

He got to see his friends from high school. They visited in small groups, each one entering hesitantly. But life shifted quickly back to normal. He fit in well until he left the house for the first time.

A simple trip to his favorite deli turned into a nightmare. He arrived unnoticed, but within minutes of being recognized, he was mobbed by groups of people saying thank you and telling him how happy they were to see him. James waved politely, shaking hands, accepting hugs, walking through the crowd shyly.

Soon a camp of publicists, photographers, and journalists hounded his parents' home. The Federation eventually placed guards at both ends of his street. He hated it. The attention, the uncomfortable words of gratitude. It was a ceaseless parade of people who all meant well but were interrupting his life. He felt more trapped than free.

Even his highly anticipated reunion with Kaylie was thrown off when her mother answered his HOLO call and, after another uncomfortable thank you from the entire family, informed him she had joined the Medic Corps in the Federation's military. He thanked her and hung up, ready to leave.

By the time his four weeks were up, he was ready to get back to his team.

James heard a bleep from his bed and picked the HOLO up from the pillow, reading a summons from the camp to meet in the hangar in the next five minutes.

He stubbed out his cigarette before changing his shirt and throwing on some deodorant. He walked outside where he caught sight of his team walking together. The relief and sense of belonging were instant, and he jogged to catch up with them.

"Well, home was different," he heard Deck say when he got close enough to hear them. "All over the place, it's fucking people coming up to you."

"So popular!" said James, sarcastically from the back.

"Well, look who it is."

"James!"

"How you feelin', man?"

The words and sentiments streamed in. This was the first time since he left the hospital he felt comfortable around people.

James sat next to Jon explaining his nightmare getting home and back from the south. "It was horrible. They had a parade. A fucking parade! I mean, I was honored, but it was too much."

James nodded, but their conversation was cut short by a throng of dark suited men who walked into the room suddenly.

The hangar became eerily silent as the President was ushered in behind his armed guards and James watched warily as Braxton took center stage.

"Before I begin, let me express my sincere thanks and apologies for not meeting with all of you earlier." Silence echoed off the steel walls before he continued. "We are officially at war and expect the situation to get worse before it gets better. Each and every one of you is a hero and I commend your bravery, courage, and fortitude in the face of overwhelming odds."

Braxton held his arms out in a sweeping motion to show his sense of inclusiveness. A very political stance, James thought, but kept his face devoid of emotion. "We lost a lot of great men and women in the fight, but the war is far from over. I expect heroes like you will play a major role in the future.

"Before we get into orders, General Croyton is here to debrief all of you. Once he's done, we can talk about the next steps." He turned to the side and from behind the group of suited guards walked Croyton.

James thought he looked different, calmer, and more measured. His face was thinner, weathered, and tired.

"Soldiers, you did a commendable job on the battlefield," began Croyton, but James stopped listening. He was watching Braxton who returned to the side and moved behind his armed guards while he scrolled through a HOLO. Braxton bugged James, but he couldn't figure out what it was. The sincerity of his thank you, the politicking to a group of soldiers, the strange way in which Braxton simply appeared out of nowhere and then hid behind his guards. It bugged him. Also, why did Croyton need to debrief them now? Why not have someone else do that? It was, after all, nearly three months since the battle. It was time to focus on the future.

"...well done," Croyton finished and turned on his heel, walking out the door without another word.

Braxton didn't even look up from his HOLO until the door banged shut behind Croyton.

"Well," Braxton said composing himself, "your orders will arrive on your HOLOs soon. Best of luck, lady and gentlemen."

They waited in stiff-backed silence until Braxton and his men were gone and the sound of the motors drifted away in the distance.

"Anyone else want a drink?" asked Clint.

"Hell, yes," said Stacie, leading the way out of the hangar.

The next few hours were spent drinking beers outside in the cold fall air catching up with one another. James realized he hadn't even thought to give Deck a call when he was home. He felt better after Deck told him he left pretty quick, reasoning, in his own words, "It's tough to live the life I want when everyone's watching."

314

He heard about the receptions each one received when they returned home, from the fireworks display Clint's brothers put on for him to Stacie connecting with her extended family for the first time. James smiled the entire time. He missed this.

"Anyone else hungry?" asked Kevin, standing and steadying his large frame against the side of their bunker.

"Yes, let's do something about that!" yelled Bob, who stood with gusto and stumbled his way toward the mess hall.

They all followed, laughing, and playfully shoving one another. James got up and realized he had to pee. "I'll catch up to you guys!" he yelled to no one in particular and walked inside to the bathroom.

He was still smiling while he wiped his hands on his pants. The folks in the mess hall were about to be very entertained, he thought. He spotted a manila envelope on his bed.

There were no others in the room and the front of the envelope was blank. James opened it curiously. The words "OPERATION DROP ZONE" were stamped in bolded letters across the page.

There was a handwritten note in the top right corner:

You've got a good head on your shoulders. Make the decision you think is best, but whatever you do, know you make it for your whole team. They are in your charge. Burn this when you're done.

PS, they'll follow you anywhere.

James's confusion was taken over by breathless anger as he read the first paragraph of the memo.

Envoys are enroute from the East. We have enough firepower on the coast to take out the initial advance but need the war movement on our side. We must convince the country we are truly at risk to gain full support. The only way to convince them is

through a battle. Divert resources North, to ensure we limit
potential fallout.

James kept reading, his fingers grew white as he held the
document tighter and tighter. They believed Brandt. They meant
for this to happen. They ignored the communications. They
designed the massive loss of life. They destroyed Midway. They
started the fall of the Southern Federation. Braxton ordered it.

James turned the page, his brain struggling to function.
There was a final note on the last page of the folder along with an
old, printed photograph. In it stood Brandt with his arm slung
around his wife's shoulders. On the other side was a grinning but
stiff-looking Croyton gazing at the camera.

James picked up the picture his head spinning, the room
melting around him. He turned it over and found another
handwritten note:

Memorial is tomorrow. I've got transport figured out for
you. Plane leaves at 0430. She wants you there, don't disappoint.

James clipped the picture back into the folder and brought
it outside with one of the metal trash basins in the room. He lit a
cigarette and held the edge of the folder to the lighter, glaring at
the flames as he dropped the burning evidence in the trash. His
mind was a searing coal of pain and anger.

The next morning, James woke up and snuck out to the
tarmac unnoticed. A prop plane was waiting for him. The pilot
didn't say a word when James entered and sat in the back, staring
out the window. His mind was concentrated on the contents of the
folder. He was hungover, even after excusing himself early. He
tried to fall asleep but awoke in fitful starts, the white light from
Brandt's last stand playing on a loop, torturing his dreams.

They landed at a small airport about an hour later. At the bottom of the gangplank, James saw a white sedan and was greeted by a driver who gave James a bag when he entered the car.

"The man said to give you this," the driver said. He threw the car into drive and took off.

James looked inside the bag where he found a gray suit jacket, khakis, a button-up, and a tie. He changed in the back, throwing his civilian clothes in the bag along with his HOLO.

They pulled up to a white chapel in the middle of the countryside. A graveyard lay on one side and a playground stood on the other.

He went to take his bag but was stopped by the driver.

"I'm staying here. Don't worry."

James nodded and looked at the open doors of the church. It was dark inside, though welcoming, and James smelled aged wood as he approached. He made his way up the staircase and entered a quiet but full church. James took one of the programs from an usher and sat in a pew in the back.

He looked at the pamphlet reading Brandt's name scrawled inside a Gaelic cross, the dates of his life printed across the bottom of the folded paper.

Conversations stopped, the doors closed, and an old organ began to play "Amazing Grace." James's chest tightened as the procession made its way up the center aisle. He stood quietly, watching them as if observing from a great distance, his brain had trouble reasoning where he was.

Riley was the last in line surrounded by her children, clinging to her dress. James could not imagine her pain. At the front of the church, Croyton guided them with a gentle touch on the shoulder into the pew beside him. His behavior and actions were far different from any past experiences James had with his former commanding officer.

The pastor started the ceremony by mentioning why they were there and handed the pulpit off to a long line of people listed in the program.

James listened to people rattle off old stories. Memories and occasions highlighting Brandt's life including the true story of the birth of his first child when he caught four flights back-to-back in military cargo holds from a posting at the bottom of the Southern Federation to arrive in Louisiana in time for Shannon to be placed in his arms. James laughed and teared up more than once, his reactions dictated by memories of a man he watched sacrifice himself to save James and countless others.

When the last person stepped down from the pulpit the room filled with a heavy silence. The eaves in the roof seemed to sag as Riley stood from her pew. Brandt's picture displayed on the altar looked alive as she walked, bowing her head slightly before ascending the carpeted steps. She bent and whispered to Brandt's picture before she put her hand to her mouth, kissed her fingertips, and laid them gently on Brandt's lips in the picture.

"Goodbye, Luke," she said with a longing sadness that took James's breath away.

The pastor took a moment, letting her farewell hang in the still church atmosphere. He told the funeral attendees a reception would be held outside, and Brandt's brother informed them all the keg was tapped and no one was leaving until it was gone.

James made his way outside and lit a cigarette by the graveyard. He felt a hand on his shoulder and turned to find Dolly smiling at him.

"You got another one of those?" she asked. "I've got a buck."

James grinned. "Save it." He held out his open pack and she took a cigarette between her fingers, taking a drag while James lit it for her.

They stood there, quietly smoking. James didn't know what to say, but part of him was relieved by the silence. He was too keyed up to make any sense but knew he could not remain quiet.

"I'm sorry." The words tumbled out like an awkward two-year-old trying to talk.

Dolly nodded and looked out in the distance. James turned away, wishing he'd stayed quiet.

"How's your arm?" he asked, surprised at the lack of a sling.

"Doing fine. Healing nicely. Just glad Luke was there to pull me out." She paused, looking at the graveyard distantly before she added, "He's her dad, you know. Croyton."

James was surprised and for the first time in a while didn't care if it showed on his face.

"Loved the LT like a son. When he was home, he would take all of the LT's time, dragging him around and pulling strings in the military to make sure they ended up together. Bothered the crap outta Riley at how well they got on sometimes. Disappearing for days on hunting trips that were secretly missions." Dolly laughed as she took a drag. "She knew the general would never let anything happen to the Lieutenant. He was protective, especially with people he liked. But the Federation caught on and separated them. They were worried about the implications any preferential treatment might have on the general's ability to lead. So, when he got you all, he pushed you away as much as possible. And when he found out where you were going and what was happening, he made sure the one man he trusted the most was in charge of you."

James's eyebrows lifted.

"Don't be so surprised. I know all at this point, buddy. I was with Brandt for five years, but before that the general was my captain. Funny little world we live in. I know he can be a tough person to get along with, but you were a special group. Needed you to get up to speed fast. Couldn't have them pulling you away. He's never been one to do things half-assed. As you proved when you confronted him." She winked at James.

James remembered the steel in Croyton's eyes the last time they spoke face to face and for the first time, realized how much he was being protected.

"I—" he started.

"He gets it. Don't worry," Dolly interrupted offhandedly. "Anyway, I wanted you to know the lieutenant saw something different in you. Your leadership, your intelligence, but most of all your instincts. You have amazing intuition, James."

James didn't know what to say and nodded stupidly while he ground out his cigarette in the crabgrass next to the church.

Without warning, Dolly's arms wrapped around him, and her cheek brushed against his, wet with tears.

"Good luck, James. Follow your gut. They believe in it more than you know." She turned around and walked through the church's side door flicking her cigarette to the side.

James made his way back to the cab, his mind peeling back the layers of what transpired. It was Croyton who woke him up. It was Croyton who obtained the leaks from the military. It was all Croyton. The good and the bad. Back to the tests in grade school, Croyton.

When he made it back in the air, he was ready. It was time to make a change.

He found the rest of the group lying against the barracks smoking cigarettes and sipping beers, but a little less enthusiastically than the day before.

He was greeted by Kevin first. "Where the hell you been, man?"

"Yeah, we thought you got lost," said Bob, looking at him with hazy red eyes.

James explained to them what happened. He relayed all the information from the folder, his revelation of Croyton's relationship to Riley, and the puzzling future he was left to solve.

"Fuck. That's quite the tale," said Deck, taking a long swig from his beer before finishing his thought. "What's the move now, man?"

James surveyed his group. All of them looked at him with a sense of trust he knew he would dedicate the rest of his life to earning.

"We leave."

The silence was only momentary before a murmur rippled across the group. They agreed.

"Where to?" asked Stacie.

"South. We need to move fast. The BlankZone is probably already spreading."

"I vote yes," said Deck, standing up. "I like the heat and hate this winter."

"But summers would suck, man," said Clint. "I've liked it here."

"Yeah, but in the south, you only have to deal with a hurricane every once in a while."

"And snakes."

"True. Good call. Maybe we should think this through more... James?"

James shook his head grinning and walked inside, pulling the door behind him.

A half hour later, James tucked his father's letter into the front of his pack and exited their barracks for the last time going outside to join his team.

They walked shoulder to shoulder away from their bunks. A timed charger was set to ignite a fire in the next three hours. By then, they would be long gone. They'd steal one of the armored cargo planes, find another way to travel, and disappear.

Jon rigged a virus to erase any initial tracking data connected to the plane, and in a show of final commitment, they all threw their HOLO emitters onto the incinerating charge to guarantee they were destroyed in the flames.

The weight of their decision was on his shoulders. They were at war, and they would be direly needed. But he wasn't alone. James glanced at the lean, hardened warriors in charge of their destiny. He held a sense of duty to the men and woman who trusted him. And James, even with all the uncertainty, was prepared for what lay ahead.

ACKNOWLEDGEMENTS

This book started a decade ago sitting in a coffee shop in DC. I began very much on my own but have to thank so many people who got me on the path to writing and finally publishing my story after all these years.

For my college writing class that suggested I get inside James's head more, your feedback set me on the right track. To my friend Zach for driving me to and from campus, waiting for me while I wrote in the library, thanks for all the rides and arguments. It was more beneficial than you may know.

To my Peace Corps friends, you were the first people I told out loud that I wanted to be a writer, thanks for making me admit it. To my friends from college, home and DC. Some of you may find yourselves mentioned in these pages directly but all your qualities combined to generate these characters, thank you for providing a lifetime of creative inspiration. To two friends in particular, Mike and Chris, thank you for reading my first pages, your feedback was truly helpful and it meant a lot to have someone spend time reading a very poorly written draft.

To my editor Hanna, your work gave me the confidence to keep pushing forward with this project and brought my writing to a level I did not know existed. To my graphic designer Daniel, thank you for showing me a visual representation of my work, it sets the tone for the series and made the book real.

To my in-laws and extended family, thank you so much for your feedback on the book design. In particular to my sister-in-law, Dana, thank you so much for being the final set of eyes to read the book prior to publication. Your input was immensely valuable.

To my sisters, growing up with you gave me the exact sense of family I wanted to emulate with all my characters. To my parents, thank you for a lifetime of support and allowing my imagination to spiral the way it did, my upbringing provided the confidence to pursue this endeavor in the first place. To my mother in particular, I cannot thank you enough for spending your time editing the final parts of the book. To my Nonnie who read out loud to me as a kid and kickstarted my love of books. To Mar, the only adult who listened when I was growing up. To my dogs, walking you helped keep me in check when I couldn't get through a certain idea.

Now to the two most important people in my life, my wife and daughter.

Alexa, you are the reason this book is written. Without your encouragement, support, love and understanding of a self-critical (verging on hating) writer I'd still be struggling to get through part two. You have no clue how much you inspire me to work hard every single day.

And to my daughter. I finished this book sitting and thinking while I fed you at night. Without those quiet moments I would still be stuck. So thank you for being an amazing kid already, I can't wait until you're old enough to read this one day.

Finally, I want to thank anyone who read this book. I was always told you shouldn't write to make other people happy, but screw that advice. I hope you loved this book and can't wait to read the rest of the series because I wrote it with you in mind the entire time. So, thank you for giving me your time, energy, and the precious space in your brain to think about James and the team. It was an honor to be chosen.